MANY-COLOURED FLEECE

MANY-COLOURED FLEECE

edited by

Sister Mariella Gable, O.S.B.

SHEED & WARD - LONDON
1951

FIRST PUBLISHED 1951
BY SHEED AND WARD, LTD.
110/111 FLEET STREET,
LONDON, E.C.4

MADE AND PRINTED IN GREAT BRITAIN
BY PHOTOTYPE, LIMITED, LONDON

ACKNOWLEDGMENTS

THE DEVIL IN THE DESERT, by Paul Horgan; reprinted with the permission of the author and Messrs. Hughes Massie and Co. Ltd.

SANTA LUCIA, by Joseph Petracca; reprinted with the permission of the author and the William Morris Agency Inc.

SONG WITHOUT WORDS, by Frank O'Connor; reprinted from *Crab Apple Jelly Stories and Tales* with the permission of the author and Messrs. A. D. Peters.

THE MIRACLE OF TEPAYAC, by John Steinbeck; reprinted with the permission of the author and Messrs. Curtis Brown, Ltd.

BAA-BAA, BLACK SHEEP, by Stephen B. Earley; reprinted with the permission of the author.

THE KNIFE, by Brendan Gill; originally published in *The New Yorker*. Reprinted with permission of· the author. Copyright 1940 Brendan Gill.

THE ROAD TO THE SHORE, by Michael McLaverty; reprinted from *The Game Cock and Other Stories* with the permission of the author and Messrs. Jonathan Cape, Ltd.

THE RELUCTANT HANGMAN, by Hugh Dickinson; reprinted with permission of the author and *The Commonweal*.

SATURDAY NOCTURNE, by Richard Sullivan; reprinted with the permission of the author and Messrs. A. M. Heath and Company, Ltd.

HOME, by Langston Hughes; reprinted from *The Ways of White Folk* with the permission of the author and Messrs. George Allen and Unwin, Ltd.

TROUBLE WITH THE UNION, by Dennis Harrington; reprinted with permission of the author.

BARRING THE WEIGHT, by W. B. Ready; reprinted with permission of the author and Messrs. A. M. Heath and Company, Ltd.

v

GINGERBREAD, by Betty Wahl; reprinted with permission of the author and Messrs. A. M. Heath and Company, Ltd.

PREFECT OF DISCIPLINE, by Joseph Carroll; reprinted with permission of the author. Copyright Joseph Carroll.

PROTHALAMION, by Edward Sheehy; reprinted with permission of the author.

MISSIS FLINDERS, by Tess Slesinger; reprinted from *The Unpossessed* with the permission of the author and Messrs. Simon and Schuster, publishers.

I TOOK THEE CONSTANCE, by Ted Le Berthon; reprinted with permission of the author and The Story Press.

THE LITTLE GIRLS, by Lucile Hasley; reprinted with the permission of the author.

A TABLE BEFORE ME, by Jill O'Nan; reprinted with permission of the author.

YUNG MARI LI, by Bryan MacMahon; reprinted from *The Lion Tamer* with the permission of the author and Messrs. MacMillan and Co. Ltd.

UNHOLY LIVING AND HALF DYING, by Sean O'Faolain; reprinted from *Teresa and Other Stories* with the permission of the author and Messrs. Jonathan Cape, Ltd.

THE JILTING OF GRANNY WEATHERALL, by Katherine Anne Porter; reprinted from *Flowering Judas and Other Stories* with the permisson of the author and Messrs. Jonathan Cape, Ltd.

BROTHER BONIFACE, by Mary Lavin; reprinted from *At Sallygap and Other Stories* with the permission of the author.

THE HINT OF AN EXPLANATION, by Graham Greene; reprinted from *Nineteen Stories* with the permission of the author and Messrs. Pearn, Pollinger and Higham, Ltd.

CONTENTS

vii

INTRODUCTION

This book is the third in a series of anthologies in which I have collected short stories which ought, for one reason or another, to be of special interest to Catholics. For the sake of convenience they will be referred to hereafter as Catholic fiction.

Because art speaks a universal language the appeal of these stories is, however, not limited to Catholics. This fact is attested by their publication in secular magazines, ranging all the way from *Horizon,* the *Atlantic,* and *The New Yorker* to *The Woman's Home Companion,* and in books, not one of which was brought out by a Catholic publisher. Only two of the stories in this volume made a first appearance in Catholic magazines.

The role of an anthologist is two-fold: He is a salvager and a critic.

He is first and foremost one who salvages for countless readers what would otherwise be lost to them. Since our best Catholic fiction continues to appear in secular magazines, widely divergent in type and locale, most of it would be lost to the general reader unless it were collected and made easily accessible. And since the Catholic writers who have published single volumes of fine short stories often include many secular stories, there is need for selecting their Catholic stories and collecting them, along with the best from magazines, in a volume such as this.

Moreover, by the very act of selecting the best that has been written, and making it generally known, the anthologist brings strong influence to bear upon taste and upon the direction of new developments.

The second function of the anthologist is to be a critic, particularly a constructive one. Where the fiction writer hypnotizes, it is "the function of criticism to supply the sharp sound that awakens us." The critic sees beyond the achievement of the present, which in Catholic fiction is only a vigorous beginning, to the vast undeveloped potentialities of the future. He indicates what are the unsolved problems of Catholic fiction, and examines the literary temper of the present as well as the social milieu in order to see whether or not we have an appropriate climate in which to solve our problems.

To begin with the last. Never since the popular development of prose fiction, about two centuries ago, have we had a climate so favorable as we have now for the development of Catholic fiction. The western world has tried to live without God. The result is such chaos, bitterness, and despair that the world, both Catholic and Protestant, is experiencing a profound spiritual revival. Humanity stands terrified and starving, arms out begging, as it were, for a great fiction of spiritual affirmation.

It asks and asks for the power of such an art. I use the word "power" advisedly. For this word calls our attention at once to the peculiar role of fiction as compared to non-fiction. DeQuincey in his essay *The Literature of Knowledge and the Literature of Power*, named the distinction between the two: Non-fiction is like the rudder on a boat; without knowledge of truth one cannot steer straight. But fiction is like the sail or the engine; without it there is not power to move. Our spiritual revival has produced a magnificent body of non-fiction, ranging all the way from the profound philosophical contributions of Jacques Maritain to Thomas Merton's popular odyssey of a soul. That is as it should be; nobody wants a boat without a rudder. But a rudder is not enough. If we had a comparable Catholic fiction the power and might of a great spiritual wind would move the world to stunned astonishment.

Not only are people psychologically ready for a fiction of spiritual affirmation, but they are also due to be helped by the very

science which has so long deceived them into thinking that tech-
nology could make them happy. Science and religion could never,
of course, really be in conflict with each other, for truth is one,
and if science goes far enough, it must support and confirm religion. We are, at the moment, on the threshold of such a development, as has been pointed out by the eminent scientist, Dr. Charles
Steinmetz, in his forecast for the science of the next fifty years.
Says Dr. Steinmetz:

> I think the greatest discoveries will be made along spiritual
> lines. Some day people will learn that material things will
> not bring happiness and are of little use in making men and
> women creative and powerful. Then the scientists of the
> world will turn their laboratories over to the study of God
> and prayer and the spiritual forces which, as yet, have been
> hardly scratched. When that day comes the world will see
> more advancement in one generation than it has seen in the
> last four.

We have, of course, already turned our laboratories over to such
study, though the drift of psychiatry has scarcely been recognized
as yet for what it is: a powerful movement of science toward religion. For as soon as you begin to ask what makes men tick, what
makes them happy, what makes life tolerable or intolerable to
human beings, you are bound to end up with God. Regrettable
as was the pan-sexualism of Freud, he was still asking the right
questions. Psychiatry has steadily gone forward in its correction
of his wrong answers. Science will ultimately reveal that the only
sound psychology in the world must be built up on the rock-bottom
truth expressed by St. Augustine: "Thou hast made our hearts
for Thee, O God, and they are restless (psychotic, neurotic) until
they rest in Thee." Science is moving faster than we realize toward
a new synthesis with religion.

At the same time the development of secular fiction has arrived at the point where either it will die or become profoundly spiritual. The great Spanish philosopher, Ortega y Gasset, has stated this point by defining modern fiction as "mature." Avenues of experiment on the natural level have all been explored. For the future there can be only the cultivation of techniques accompanied by diminishing vitality.

The need for freshness in fiction has been a progressive movement downward toward an ever lower, sub-human, animal interpretation of man, culminating in naturalism. The smart young men who were its purveyors "thought they were being sophisticated when they were only unbuttoned." Mere exhibitionism won by shock what art earns by blood and tears.

But nastiness and perversion are not infinite in variety. In spite of contemporary interest in psychiatry, minute analyses of degenerates, homosexuals, introverts, pathological personalities, sadists, masochists, cretins, and idiots have become intolerably boring. Naturalism is dead.

But freshness is a necessity of art. Jean Cocteau, in writing to Jacques Maritain, gave us a profound statement concerning it:

> The need of change in art is nothing other than the need of finding a fresh place on the pillow. Put your head on the fresh spot, it soon ceases to be so; newness is freshness. The need for novelty is the need for freshness. God is the only freshness that never grows warm.

God is not only the only freshness that never grows warm; He is the only unexplored freshness left to the writer of fiction. Fiction has gone as far away from God as it can go. There is no unexplored nastiness, perversion, or animality. Either fiction will bring God in, or perish in stagnation.

Nor is this alternative like the others: today mysticism; yesterday romanticism, realism, humanism and all the rest. We are not here dealing with just another cool spot on the pillow—a new area of experience, a new angle of vision. We are here concerned with a new dimension.

And this brings us to the heart of the distinction between secular and Catholic fiction. Even Catholics have wrongly supposed that Catholic fiction is limited, narrower in its subject-matter, curbed and curtailed in what it may do. The fact is: Secular fiction is limited. Catholic fiction is unlimited; it embraces all reality. Secular fiction is one-dimensional; Catholic fiction is three-dimensional.

Let me explain. Fiction is about people. Take any drawing-room full of people. The first reality with which we are confronted is the individuality of all present. God never repeats himself. He manifests something of the mystery of His fecundity as a Creator in the infinite variety of human beings—no two on the face of the earth precisely alike. In our drawing-room are the witty, the depressed, the insecure, the amicable, the lonely, the garrulous, the silent. But one witty man differs from another witty man, one silent man from another inarticulate one as color differs from color. Yet they are all bound by the bond of coloredness—the mystery of the one and the many. Moreover a psychological and social chemistry takes place whereby color fades into color or clashes with it. Traditional fiction has been sociological. It has dealt with man in relation to man. It has interpreted the many-coloredness of man in society—whether transcending his environment or a victim of it. It has dealt with the reality of a material world, and in doing so has projected a fiction of one dimension.

But there is another reality in that drawing-room. Every person present is either in a state of grace or of damnation. In other words, hell and heaven are present in the room. A fiction which extends its boundaries to include this reality is eschatological, besides being sociological. It is three-dimensional. Three-dimensional fiction embraces all planes of reality. It extends boundaries.

It is Graham Greene's distinction that he has done more than any other contemporary writer of fiction in English (the French have, of course, gone farther) to extend these boundaries. *The Heart of the Matter* is eschatological. People cared tremendously whether Scobie was damned or saved. His plight was argued by the literary elite and callow youth—at cocktail parties, in bars, in monastery parlors, and over Cokes in drugstores. Greene has only faintly indicated, however, the amazing complexity of human psychology in three-dimensional fiction. In further exploration of this psychology lies the one clear avenue for development of fiction.

The title of this collection of stories symbolizes the complexity of three-dimensional fiction. It suggests the many-colored individuality of human beings as they manifest themselves to each other; but it is many-colored *fleece*. Fleece, for we are all God's sheep, in reality either black sheep or white sheep, no matter what brilliant hues of red, or blue, or gold we exhibit to the world. If the title seems to put the emphasis on the color rather than on the fleece, it is because our Catholic fiction is still largely in the mode of a one-dimensional art. Yet there is the clear indication of a strong development in the apprehension of spiritual values—as the stories in this volume indicate.

In the Middle Ages when man's thinking was popularly and predominantly eschatological, fiction assumed the form of allegory. The spiritual reality was more important than human individuality. In medieval allegory the characters were only symbols —often dehumanized.

The question arises as to whether or not we can expect at the present time a return to allegory. Really, it raises a larger question which must be answered first: a question which involves the whole relationship of substance and form. We have witnessed, during the past three decades, the emergence of the New Critics, such men as Yvor Winters, I. A. Richards, William Empson, Robert Penn Warren, Kenneth Burke and others. One of their sound contributions to literary criticism, and one on which they are fairly unanimous, though they differ in so many other respects, is their conviction that substance and form are integral. Form is not something added. It is not a style, not a decorative metaphor, not a glove on the hand. Form and substance are one.

Furthermore they have been preoccupied with an analysis of contemporary literature as communicating man's loss of faith, his loss of God. Its form is chaotic, disturbed, often unintelligible, reflecting in its mode of expression the thing it expresses.

The way, therefore, not to be a great Catholic writer is to sit at the feet of contemporary artists and study their form. The craft of the God-less cannot be the craft of the God filled. The substance expressed will always determine the form of expression.

Nor is it a matter of indifference, in so far as artistic excellence is concerned, what the substance is. T. S. Eliot has expressed this truth with memorable accuracy. It ought to be burned into the consciousness of every Catholic critic, for *mirabile dictu,* we still have many of them who maintain that the whatness of the thing communicated is unimportant if the howness is artistically correct. Here is T. S Eliot's statement:

> The greatness of literature cannot be determined *solely* by literary standards; though we must remember that whether it is literature or not can be determined only by literary standards.

I should like to go farther and state the same in positive terms: The greatness of literature can be determined by the degree to which a three-dimensional substance is integrated with perfect artistic expression. But the artistic expression of three-dimensional content can never be in the same mode of expression as one-dimensional content, for substance and form are one. A three-dimensional fiction lays greater demands on the artist *qua artist* than does one-dimensional fiction. The Catholic writer must be a greater artist than his secular confrere. And by the standards of pure art three-dimensional fiction must be a greater fiction.

Will it, then, return to allegory as an appropriate form? It has already done so. The new interest in allegory ranges all the way from the heretical existentialism of Jean Paul Sartre to the mildly inadequate excursion into the symbolism of Purgatory by Anthony West. But perhaps most illuminating for our purposes is the allegory of Franz Kafka (1883-1924). Kafka was a God-smitten man. Strongly influenced by Kierkegaard's minute study of the "razor-edge decision" of human free will which determines man's personal relation to God, he has written allegories which explore the complex psychology of faith. A strong Kafka cult among the literary elite testifies to the contemporary hunger of man for God. Though Kafka never arrived at an orthodox theology, his preoccupation with God and with man's absolute need for submission to God found appropriate expression only in the form of allegory. Esoteric to a degree, his allegory seems scarcely fourth-cousin to the simple, and easily equatable medieval allegory.

But this is as it should be, for cycles of literary trends never repeat exactly. Yet there are cycles. According to Sorokin there are three: First, an ideational art, highly spiritual in content, which normally expresses itself in allegory; second, an idealistic art which unites the best of the spiritual with a full and faithful portrayal of man in all his fascinating individuality; and third, a sensist art which gradually eliminates all spiritual values until it exhausts itself in decadence. We have just lived through the third; the first is again due.

But the first, allegory, is not three-dimensional. The third is not three-dimensional. Only the second is three-dimensional—and it is, by all odds, the greatest and the most to be desired. And by some strange accident of acceleration in our own day we seem to have moved very swiftly past allegory into the second. To return to *The Heart of the Matter*: Scobie is an individual, not an allegorical abstraction.

But perhaps in a very specific sense, we as Catholics have served a longer apprenticeship in allegory than we realize. The countless number of undistinguished, but "edifying" stories in the popular Catholic magazines are essentially allegories, for they sacrifice the truth of human nature to the purposes of pious teaching. Of course, allegory is a type which can be either good or bad, great or poor. Yet, on the whole, it is small praise of God to ignore our first-dimensional world in which the infinite variety and immeasurable complexity of human nature testify to His creative fecundity.

Dante is our greatest Catholic writer and one of the few great poets in the world. His art, for all its intricate symbolism, is three-dimensional. He knew exactly how to unite an eschatological and a sociological emphasis. He knew how to communicate the Hell of sin and the Heaven of grace without ever sacrificing the human individuality of his characters.

He placed his beloved teacher, Brunetto Latini, in Hell for being a homosexual. But how does he depict Brunetto as he walks and talks with him under the rain of burning flakes? As cultivated, charming, intelligent, affectionately devoted to his most gifted student, noble, lovable and indescribably individual. He does more. When Brunetto explains that most of the homosexuals are highly cultivated, professional people he has pin-pointed a nexus between individuality, the profession it chooses, and the moral failure stemming from that peculiar combination. Modern writers of three-dimensional fiction could well sit at Dante's feet. We need to see how the three dimensions touch and affect each other.

We not only need to see how the three dimensions interlock, but also, and this is perhaps our greatest unsolved problem, we need to interpret the dimension of goodness with artistic integrity.

The psychology of goodness is very rarely explored with anything like the artistic success that commonly distinguishes the analysis of evil or of spiritual failure. Here the techniques are, for the most part, still undiscovered. Here lies the challenge to the artist of the future.

Consider the dichotomy as it now exists: Most of the people we know are orientated toward goodness; most of the people in fiction are orientated toward evil. St. Augustine remarked in the *City of God*, Book XI, Chapter 9, "Evil has no positive nature; but the loss of good has received the name evil." In the art of literature it would seem to be the other way round.

We know how difficult it is to write of goodness convincingly. The intention to present the side of the angels is never enough. Milton meant to argue God's cause, but his devils are magnificent, while God the Father and God the Son talk like two smug Presbyterian ministers sipping tea before a fire-place. Artistically they are a failure; artistically the evil in his poem comes off with stunning success.

In other words, as soon as a man begins to write fiction, his soul has joined a nudist colony and strange revelations are made. Kenneth Burke puts it this way:

> A writer may *profess* allegiance to a certain cause, for instance, but you find on going over his work that the *enemies* of his cause are portrayed with greater vividness than its advocates. Here is the truth about his profession of belief.

It is simply a fact that if we want our good characters to be as artistically successful as our villains, we must have holy writers. This fact is not news to the critics. Usually it is stated something like this: An artist cannot write what he thinks he ought to say but only what is dictated to him by his deepest subconscious and conscious natural allegiance.

If, then, we are to have a successful fiction which gives us an acceptable psychology of goodness—an art which moves the reader to accept the good as lovable—then we must have writers who have made some progress in the spiritual life.

Such a fiction will certainly not be dull. It will, in fact, be most exciting, for the sharpest conflict in the world begins to take place the moment a soul sets out to seek God in earnest. Self immediately kicks and screams for the center of attention. And if somewhat flouted in the struggle, self-seeking can disguise itself in a million ways to look like God-seeking. The fiction of the future which will present a sound psychological analysis of the struggle will be a new kind of who-done-it, a mystery thriller with all the suspense of an Erle Stanley Gardner, plus a substance and reality, which will make most contemporary fiction seem intolerably shallow and dull—which it is.

I had hoped, in this volume, to illustrate the kind of fiction about which I am writing by including the brilliant story *Brother Ass* by the well-known South American writer Eduardo Barrios. Its length (it is a short novel) and some other considerations made it impossible to do so. But the reader is strongly encouraged to investigate this story, which may be found in a volume called *Fiesta in November,* edited by Flores and Poore, and published by Houghton Mifflin, 1942. In the first place, its method is exactly right. The center of interest is the soul of Brother Lazaro—what takes place between himself and God. The entire story is in the form of a diary, which Lazaro addressed to God. But Lazaro is, like so many of us, a romantic egoist, and he fools himself into thinking he is seeking God when he is seeking himself. Since this is the great, universal mistake made by those who fail in the spiritual struggle, and often made for many years by those who succeed, and since this story is artistically of the first order, it is unquestionably a classic which will become well-known as time goes on. Already accepted by the Latin Americans, they have taken it to their hearts as one of the great stories of the world.

It points up, moreover, a distinction that needs to be made, the distinction between stories which deal with spiritual problems as different from ethical problems. In life there are many areas of experience. The most neglected area of experience in fiction is that which deals directly with man's search for God—the good man trying to unite himself with God here and now by knowing and loving Him in contemplation and in doing His will. What happens between the soul and God? Everyone wants to know. But the task of fiction is not only to give the information, but to impart on the level of pure art the vicarious experience.

It is true, of course, that spiritual experience is bound up closely with ethical problems. But the barrenness of much of fiction in the past stems from the fact that ethical experiences are examined only on the natural level—are seen in terms of only the first dimension.

But in much bad Catholic fiction a different fault has predominated. Good characters are presented as being in a state of simon-pure goodness. A holy character is never even tempted to pride, envy, anger, sloth, avarice, gluttony, or lust. In other words, this Catholic fiction assumes that a certain amount of goodness transfers the character from the state of original sin to some Eden-like perfection never seen on land or sea. The presupposition is heretical. What we need in the new psychology of goodness is plain honesty—the kind of truthfulness which makes *The Devil in the Desert* a fine story. Here Father Louis is a hero, but we see that pride, anger, and wilfulness are the defects of his virtue.

Artists might long ago have taken a hint from the Liturgy and from Scripture—especially from the Psalms. There we see man rising and falling alternately. At one moment he is full of trust in God, at another he is despairing; at one moment he adores, in the next he has sinned and strikes his breast. The soul of man

day after day makes contact with both the second and the third
dimension. But how man ticks when he moves toward goodness,
what his spiritual problems are as he makes three steps forward
and two back, this is the area of experience in which lies the
development of future fiction. But if it is written for edification at
the expense of truth, or if the writing springs from the desire to
create what ought to be written rather than from deep compul-
sion, then it has already failed.

Though we look forward to a new fiction in which spiritual
success will be communicated as effectively as failure, we must
realize that negative fiction often carries a tremendously positive
impact. In fact, the story of failure is often like the hole in the
wall, without which we could not *see* the thickness, strength, and
solidity of the masonry. For instance, the great story on birth
control, "Missis Flinders." In it a husband and wife have freed
themselves from the troubles, expense, and responsibility of
parenthood by an abortion. Apparently unhampered by any
religious scruples, they suffer frightfully in their subtle contempt
of each other. They have broken a natural law, and nature pun-
ishes them. Since many Catholics feel that Mother Church is
hard on them in holding immovably to her legislation against
birth control, it is well to see from what horrors, even on the
natural level, the apparently rigorous ruling saves her children.
The strength and thickness of the protecting wall could scarcely
have been seen unless a hole in it had been exposed by what we
call negative fiction.

Let no one suppose, however, that I hold a personal preference for negative fiction. In making the selections for this book,
as well as for the two preceding anthologies, I have always chosen
the positive story, where the quality of writing has permitted such
an alternative. Sometimes an anthologist is blamed for not including stories which have not as yet been written. But perhaps he
can cause them to be written by collecting the best which have

appeared up to the present moment and appreciating their achievement, thus forming a strong beach-head for further conquest of unsolved problems.

Along with learning to portray the psychology of goodness on a spiritual level successfully, the Catholic fiction of the future must move its center of focus from nuns, monks, and priests to the layman. If one judges by extant fiction one must arrive at the conclusion that religion is the nearly exclusive possession of the clergy. Here there is an almost incredible lag between reality and art. For the most important aspect of the great Catholic revival, in the midst of which we are living, is the discovery of the Catholic layman.

For the first time in history all the techniques of the spiritual life which were formerly regarded as proper only to monks and nuns have been taken over generally by average people in the world. Spiritual reading, for instance. Our age will be remembered for its spate of brilliant and readable spiritual books which are read eagerly by laymen. Laymen are understanding and participating in the Liturgy. Forty years ago one could not have bought a Missal if one had wanted to. Now the layman commonly assists at Mass by following the service. Laymen meditate; they understand that contemplation is the normal fruit of Christian life, not an esoteric delicacy reserved for Trappists and Carmelites. Laymen savor in a new way the whole meaning of the Christian life and the Sacraments.

They are becoming increasingly aware of the terrifying incompatibility between the pagan society in which they live and their Christian responsibility. Many of them are developing a union with God, a charity, a spirit of abnegation which would put many a religious to shame. All around us we see beautiful Christian families where the deepest type of spiritual growth is manifest, where there has been a complete shedding of the whole deplorable shuck of externalism so common for generations.

Cardinal Suhard begged for "great daring, originality, and novelty" in making the treasures of the faith accessible to all men. Catholic laymen have manifested their charity in a stunning diversity of apostolates: Friendship House, The Catholic Worker, the cell movement, the editing of *Commonweal, Integrity, Today,* the apostolate for the Negro, the poor, the neglected wherever they are. Laymen have responded wholeheartedly to clerical leadership in such movements as Cana conferences and the Christophers.

But for the most part, this new Christian vitality in family life has been left unexplored by the writers of Catholic fiction. A notable exception is Jill O'Nan, whose story "A Table Before Me," with its thoughtful consideration of the problems involved in rearing a Christian family within a worldly environment, stands alone in the present collection, as representative of a fresh development capable of a great yield in fiction about the layman.

Meanwhile there is an alarming gap between reality and art. Father Reinhold complained recently that America is the most clerical of Catholic countries. I do not know whether America is actually more clerical than Ireland, but the fact remains that in English writing the Catholic story is almost inevitably a story of the clergy. When the *Cosmopolitan* recently advertised on its cover that it was serializing "The first great novel of Catholic life" it was a foregone conclusion that the story would be about the hierarchy. One student recently asked, "*Must* Catholic fiction be about priests or nuns?"

It might well be that *They Are People* did something to crystallize that impression. The publication of that anthology of short stories about nuns, monks, and priests in 1942 was the fruit of long searching for stories of quality which gave a fairly accurate portrayal of religious life. Now such stories can be had for a dime a dozen. In making this book it would have been a simple matter to collect a volume of them and turn them over to the public under the title *More People*.

But such editing would have added impetus to a tendency which ought to be stemmed. In 1942 there was every reason to rejoice at the kind of story which appeared in *They Are People*. The stories in that book marked a great advance in Catholic fiction. In the past, fiction had depicted convents as cemeteries for broken hearts. If a monk so much as saw a maiden, he fell in love. It was a matter of significant progress that we began to get a realistic interpretation of conventual life, in spite of the fact that the stories dealt for the most part with surface appearances rather than with the depth of spiritual problems. I wrote in the Introduction to these stories: "The things of the spirit are for the most part revealed only obliquely. The story of the future will present them directly."

The story of the future will present man's affairs with God directly, not only in so far as monks, nuns, and priests are concerned, but more especially in so far as the layman is concerned. The layman himself will have to break the bad tradition he himself has created. The very strange thing about all these stories of nuns, monks, and priests is that they are written by laymen. We cannot accuse the clergy of lifting a single pen point to keep themselves in the limelight, except in the recent *Vessel of Clay* by Father Trese. The persistent preoccupation of laymen with the clergy as the only subject for religious art may well testify to strong clerical influence in social consciousness.

Since one of the basic laws of art is that the writer must create out of his personal experience, it would seem axiomatic that laymen would write of their own spiritual problems. Of course, there is this to be said: human nature remains the same no matter how thickly covered by cassock, cowl, or habit. Out of the firm conviction that he could not go astray if he remembered that churchmen are men, Anthony Trollope created the memorable portraits of

Anglican bishops and minor clergymen which have made the Barchester novels cherished classics. Yet they are only one-dimensional. Since the layman is fast achieving a spiritual adulthood and learning first-hand what are the conflicts, problems, costs and rewards of the spiritual life, and since these are the same in "religion" or out of it, he can, of course, give us a more profound art—if he wishes to continue his interest in the clergy.

But the layman ought to write of himself. Here is the unexplored area of experience. He ought to bridge the gap between his spiritual struggles and Catholic art. There are countless beautiful Christian families where matrimony is lived as a sacrament every day, all day. Where large families are accepted in a Christian spirit in spite of nearly insurmountable economic handicaps. Where in the bosom of the family an intelligent and loving spirituality is being developed through family worship, through a complete participation in the Liturgical life of the Church, but most of all through a vital discovery of the Beatitudes. No longer do these people ask: what do I get out of this? They ask: what can I give? They practice an astonishing charity. Could those among them to whom God has given the gift to write be persuaded to communicate their experience? To close their eyes firmly upon the bad tradition in Catholic art which has not dared to explore the psychology of goodness realistically? To share on the level of artistic creation the violent conflicts they suffer in learning to build Christian homes in a pagan society?

Recently an average white-collar worker, the father of four children, wrote, after reading von Hildebrand's *Transformation in Christ*: "I actually wept over my own barren state. To be even a mediocre Christian this day and age calls for a superhuman effort of the will and intellect. Most Catholics, including myself, labor and live in a world completely given over to materialism, peopled with creatures whose only god is self . . . To live in this kind of world and associate with its people and at the same time *to try* to live a life in Christ calls for heroic fortitude."

Where are the Catholic writers who will communicate to us in a worthy art this heroic fortitude? All around us it exists. All around us are lay apostles embracing voluntary poverty. All around us lies the reality out of which a great and noble fiction might be made. Yet the layman will not look within himself; he prefers to perpetuate the dress-parade of nuns, monks, and priests.

Perhaps we will have to wait for the next generation. Out of our new Christian homes must come a great Catholic fiction. By the very law of averages some of the children will be born with the gift to write. The depth and strength of their own spiritual life will be such that in merely expressing what they need to say, they will communicate the highest reality we know, man's contemplative experience of God. The as-yet-unthought-of form will be born as part of the bright and burning splendor of the art which makes articulate this transcendent experience. Until that generation comes with its great Catholic art (and I firmly believe it is coming) those who have not the gift to write, create the fiction of the future by creating the homes from which it must come.

In the meantime there will be many books, each one moving a little closer to the goal. Among them is this anthology, *Many-Colored Fleece*. Whenever literary quality made it possible I gave preference to the stories of laymen over stories about nuns, monks, and priests. Yet the clergy are in the majority. This clerical preponderance, however, interferes in no way with the entertainment value of these stories. Perhaps enjoyment is even increased, for there is the perennial curiosity of the layman to peer behind the serge curtain and discover the secrets of parsonage and cloister.

Looking at this book from the viewpoint of contemporary

secular standards, it seems to me that it exhibits a general high level of literary proficiency, a much higher than usual level of entertainment, and a humor so dominant that one is forced to consider the place of humor in Catholic fiction.

Is humor an element that must of necessity be part of Catholic art? Perhaps yes. The incongruous incites to laughter. In spite of man's high dedication as a child of God, he still remains weak and human and full of vagaries. He is like a king in royal robes who seven times a day slips on the banana peel of his weak human nature. Viewed from one angle his failure is uproariously funny. From another it is immeasurably serious and gives a resonance and spiritual significance to one's concept of man's nature. Only a noble view of human nature can be humorous. There is nothing funny about an art which depicts man as falling off the floor.

Particularly representative of the humor which ranges from gay to wry and ironic are the stories "Song Without Words," "Santa Lucia," "Unholy Living and Half Dying," "The Road to the Shore," "Trouble With the Union," and "Prefect of Discipline." Yet perhaps even more significant is the flavor of humor which pervades a solemn study of conscience like "The Reluctant Hangman," or the pure poetry of "Brother Boniface," or the fantasticalities of "Yung Mari Li."

Looking over the contents of this book from a different point of view (or is it the same?) one cannot but be struck by the predominance of Irish authors. Irish writers seem to find the form of the short story much more congenial than do authors of other nations. To begin with, there are the big five: Frank O'Connor, Sean O'Faolain, Michael McLaverty, Brian Mac-Mahon, and Mary Lavin. Though Mary Lavin was born in America, she returned with her parents at the age of ten to Ireland where she has lived since, and to all intents and purposes is regarded along with the other Irish-born authors, who have published, not just occasional fiction in magazines, but volumes of distinguished short stories.

In America only two Catholic authors have published comparable volumes and both of them are Irish: J. F. Powers, well known for *Prince of Darkness,* traces his lineage directly back to the auld sod, while W. B. Ready, whose volume of short stories, *Barring the Weight,* will be published in 1951, is a Cardiff Irishman.

In England both Graham Greene and Evelyn Waugh have published books of short stories, but there are two things to be noted of their volumes: both men are primarily novelists whose shorter fiction is secondary; Waugh's short stories are completely innocent of Catholic substance, while the Catholic interest in Greene's short stories is very infrequent. As Catholic short story writers they scarcely rank with the Irish.

To turn from the Irish writers, who have published volumes of short stories, to those who publish occasionally in magazines, we find that here again the Irish practically have a corner on short fiction with a special Catholic interest. To mention just a few: Paul Horgan, Richard Sullivan, Dennis Harrington, Joseph W. Carroll, Brendan Gill—and one can make a safe bet that if it's a new Catholic writer of promise, the odds are five to one that he is Irish.

Finally, there is the basic question: Are the stories in this volume three-dimensional? The degree to which a second and third dimension can be made manifest in fiction varies greatly. Elsewhere I have defined the categories of Catholic fiction by means of a symbol, that of a target, showing that Catholic fiction ranges all the way from peripheral, giving only the externals of Catholic local color, to that which is God-centered and hits the bull's eye. The critical essays in which I have described these categories have been published by Sheed and Ward under the title *This Is Catholic Fiction.* There seems no valid reason for redefining them here.

It does seem necessary, however, to repeat the fact that a story which is rich in the local color of Catholic life without any further spiritual significance is only one-dimensional, or at best suggests by indirection the existence of a second and third dimension. Some of the stories in this book, such as "The Road to the Shore," "Prefect of Discipline," and "Barring the Weight," utterly charming in their human insights, are of this peripheral variety. I think it important, however, to cherish this fiction which depends for its appeal on the local color of Catholic life, giving us on the natural level the precise flavor and atmosphere of daily life in the bosom of Mother Church. Catholic artists are only beginning to mine this heretofore unexplored rich vein of experience. The more we have of it in literature the sooner we will outgrow our feeling of inferiority and begin to feel at home in the cultural mores with which the Church surrounds the life of a Catholic.

But it is also important that we do not overestimate this one-dimensional fiction and place it in the same category with fiction of spiritual depth. *Many-Colored Fleece* opens and closes with two strong stories which come to grips directly with the basic problem of good and evil. "The Devil in the Desert" and "The Hint of an Explanation" are as different as two stories can be, yet both say something significant about the same problem which drew into being *Paradise Lost* and *Prometheus Unbound*. Between these two stories the whole range of human individuality as it is wedded to various ethical and spiritual experiences is fairly well covered. Yet there is no story which hits the bull's eye directly as would have "Brother Ass," if that story might have been included. The fiction which communicates man's experience in his serious effort to keep the first commandment has not as yet been written—except, in its highest ranges, by Bernanos in his novels.

But much that comes close to hitting the precise spiritual center has been written, and in order to assist the reader in discovering to what degree the second and third dimensions have been touched, critical notes have been prepared to stand at the head of each story. For those who resent preliminary critical judgment, there is the simple expedient of skipping.

Not all the stories lent themselves to groupings. But some of them did. For instance, there are the stories which interpret the commonest Christian experience: turning to God in prayer of petition under the pressure of suffering or acute need. Does God suspend the natural laws of the universe and answer such prayers by working a miracle? Four stories in this volume approach this same problem from different angles. They are "Santa Lucia," "The Miracle of Tepayac," "Baa-Baa, Black Sheep," and "The Knife." "The Miracle of Tepayac" is John Steinbeck's flawless retelling of the apparition of Our Lady of Guadalupe, based carefully on fact. Here the heavens open and, without any petition from poor Juan, the miraculous surrounds him as dazzlingly as it did the three apostles on the Mount of the Transfiguration. Fittingly, it stands as an indisputable affirmation in this group of stories, which are concerned entirely with characters who have a profound faith in God's miraculous intervention in their affairs. What happens to them presents appropriate variety: one miraculous answer to prayer, one chilling negation, and two doubtful cases. But because the stories are artistically right they open depth upon depth of insight transcending any abstract statement of the spiritual problems they explore.

To turn to a different group, there are five stories which throw some light on marriage: "Prothalamion," "Missis Flinders," "I Took Thee, Constance," "The Little Girls," and "A Table Before Me." "Missis Flinders," a remarkably strong story on the problem of birth control, and "I Took Thee, Constance," which underlines with striking originality the strength of the bonds of the sacrament of matrimony, are flanked on either side by

"Prothalamion" and "The Little Girls" for reasons which the reader is invited to discover for himself.

Then there is the race problem. In this country it concentrates itself largely around the Negro, simply because Jim Crowism has taught us to suppose that pigmentation prevents a man from being a human being like his white brothers. Exactly like. No less, no more. Two stories throw light upon this problem: "Saturday Nocturne" and "Home." In the first of these we see the problem as it is apprehended in the parsonage, where two priests find themselves in disagreement as to methods for ameliorating racial prejudice. In spite of the young priest's zeal for action, one cannot but feel that the full horror and criminal injustice suffered by his black brothers in Christ is only dimly realized. "Home," a stark story of lynching, shocks the reader into full awareness. It is the hope of the editor that no one will ask why a story like "Home" finds a place among Catholic stories. Both it and "Missis Flinders" communicate the reality of a natural law upon which the Church has built legislation.

A brief look-in on the personnel functioning in Catholic educational institutions is provided by "Barring the Weight," "Gingerbread," and "Prefect of Discipline."

"Trouble With the Union" is the only story which embodies the Christian attitude on labor problems, and "Yung Mari Li" the only one which deals with the problem of bringing a stray sheep back into the fold. Any zealous priest looking for practical pastoral hints will, however, have to look elsewhere for guidance —for only once in a globe-time would such fantastic methods for winning the back-slider be invented or attempted by a pastor. Also among the single stories is "The Reluctant Hangman," a classic statement concerning the primacy of conscience.

Finally, a cluster of three stories stand as a climax to this anthology, stories which probe the experiences of old age and death. Age and death are two of the least attractive words in the

English language and might well frighten away the reader who is looking for entertainment. The fact of the matter is, however, that the fullness of life on its most meaningful level as well as on its most human and entertaining, has been distilled in these stories. There is the broad humor of "Unholy Living and Half Dying," the zest and vitality of "The Jilting of Granny Weatherall," and the pure poetry of "Brother Boniface." But over and above all that makes these stories lovable as interpretations of the natural world, there is the clear vision of a second and third dimension giving to life as well as to death appropriate significance.

The making of this book has been a communal project. Interested readers of *They Are People* and *Our Father's House* have sent short stories from England, Ireland, Australia, Canada and the United States. For all of these stories, both those which were not suitable for inclusion and those which were, I am deeply grateful. Out of an alert and constructive spirit of cooperation must come a climate in which a three-dimension art will flourish. I thank the authors and publishers who have given their kind permission to reprint the stories in this volume, and the generous people who have assisted the editor with typing, proof-reading, and critical advice.

Before conquest there is always the laborious building of the beach-head. In literature I believe this initial establishing of a foot-hold is accomplished by appreciation for what has been accomplished, along with the firm refusal to regard a beach-head as a continent. In this spirit *Many-Colored Fleece* has been assembled. In this spirit may it be received.

Sister Mariella Gable, O.S.B.

February 10, 1950
Feast of St. Scholastica
College of St. Benedict
St. Joseph, Minnesota

MANY-COLOURED FLEECE

The greatness of literature cannot be determined solely by literary standards; though we must remember that whether it is literature or not can be determined only by literary standards.

T. S. ELIOT

If a writer is so cautious that he never writes anything that cannot be criticized he will never write anything that can be read. If you want to help other people you have got to make up your mind to write things that some men will condemn.

THOMAS MERTON

THE DEVIL IN THE DESERT

PAUL HORGAN

Well known for his fiction which distills with miraculously evoked mood the spirit of the Southwest, Paul Horgan takes us in this story to the Rio Grande country. More important, however, than the heat-bitten desert is the unforgettably courageous devotion to his people of Father Louis. And yet so perfectly integrated is the story that the priest seems as much a part of the landscape as the thorny mesquite. He is one of the few heroic figures in Catholic fiction whose goodness is artistically convincing—very likely because the author has been at pains to let us see the complex manner in which anger, pride, and wilfulness are the concomitants of his heroism. In the fantasy near the end the story rises to magnificent symbolism. In the conversation between the priest and the snake the mystery of good and evil is projected with startling clarity and stunning insight. Here we have significance of subject matter wedded to beauty of form— something not often achieved in fiction by Catholic writers.

Paul Horgan is an established novelist, an historian of the Southwest, and a short-story writer. His Harper prize-winning novel The Fault of the Angels *brought him recognition in 1933. Since then he has published three novels,* The Common Heart, *1942, being of special interest to Catholics. Particularly well known are his short stories, "The Surgeon and the Nun" and "To the Mountains."*

One summer morning almost a hundred years ago in the town of Brownsville, near the mouth of the Rio Grande on the Gulf of Mexico, Father Pierre awoke before dawn in great distress.

"Yesterday," he said to himself bitterly; "I should have told him yesterday."

He listened in the dark of his room, whose little window was just showing the first pearly ghost of day over the gulf. Yes, he could hear what he dreaded to hear. Deep in the house were sounds of footsteps moving about. Father Pierre could tell where those steps went, and what their maker was doing. Now he was in the study taking up certain printed blanks for baptisms, marriages and First Communions which could be filled in as occasion required. The footsteps receded toward the refectory, and there a battered leather knapsack soon was being filled with a cheese, two loaves of bread, a little sack of dried meal, a flask of red wine and a jug of water. Presently a distant door opened and closed, and the foosteps went across the paved garden to the side door of the sacristy in the church, where another leather case would be stocked with sacred vessels, holy oils, communion wafers and a set of vestments made in France of thin silk from Lyons.

The sacristy door sounded again, and Father Pierre knew that the next stage of all these preparations for a journey would move out beyond the rectory and the church to the ragged field where, in a corral, the two priests of the parish kept their horses. There, he knew, Pancho, the eight-year-old gelding that was the color of rusty weeds along the river, was going to be captured after an absurd moment of delicacy and apprehension, saddled and brought back to the courtyard, where the saddlebags and knapsacks were waiting. By then it would be light enough outdoors to see where you were going. It would be time to go.

From the sounds which he could hear and the activities which he could imagine, Father Pierre knew all over again something of the formidable man who was getting ready to depart. If those footsteps sounded like those of an old man, trotting and tentative, yet there was in them a stubborn force. There was plain contempt for human comfort in the noise he made before dawn when others might be sleeping; but he seemed to say that if one man could get up to make all that noise in the name of God, then any other should be glad to awaken to it.

Father Pierre knew there was grim joy in the world that morning for his friend and colleague, Father Louis Bellefontaine. He knew also that Father Louis tried to control a capacity for anger which could flare as quickly and as madly as a cat's. In the new stone rectory the two men lived together harmoniously, for the most part. It took much government of their natural temperaments to make this possible, for over everything lay the difficulty that Father Pierre, who was many years the younger, was the pastor; while Father Louis, who had come from France a generation before Father Pierre, was the assistant, and so, subject to the orders of his junior. But they made jokes about this, as they did about Father Pierre's polished education. Father Louis knew only his God, his duties and what he had learned from hard contests with nature. He knew it was proper for a fine gentleman like Father Pierre to be his superior; and he would wrinkle his old face with shrewd estimate and relish of silken details when Father Pierre was busy with narratives about life at home—which meant France, where one day without doubt the younger priest would be consecrated a bishop. But Father Louis never envied his superior anything, for he knew that in his own work he was a great master—a master of the distance, the heat, the fatigue; the menace of brush desert and the murderous Indian, whose soul was within him, but not yet formed; the fears, hopes and needs of the Christian families who lived so widely separated along the inland course of the Rio Grande. For thirty years Father Louis had ridden, mostly alone, and twice a year, on his journeys up the river.

He always undertook them with a sense not only of duty but of escape. Nowhere else did he feel so close to God as alone in the hard brush country riding to bring comfort, news and the Sacraments to some family in a jacal hidden by solitude and open to the hot sky. The older he grew, the more Father Louis longed for his escapes from town and parish. The more infirm he became with the years, the stronger was his sense of mission. Father Pierre would see a glow of youth come back over that sunstung, seamed old face as time drew near for Father Louis to make his plans to go on his ride into the upriver country, which would take him from two to three months. If his eyes were dim with age, not so the vision in his mind, which showed him so much of what people wanted of him, and of what he could bring to them. If his hand now trembled so that he could hardly write down the names and the dates on one of his sacramental certificates, he could always joke about it, and assure his families that the deed was recorded in heaven, anyway. If sometimes his heart fluttered like a dusty bird in the cage of his ribs, and made him wonder what was ready to take flight, he could lie down for a few minutes and feel the thing calm down; and however unworldly he may have been, he always clamped his jaws together with sardonic satisfaction that his time had not yet quite come. He had things to do, and would do them.

Much of this was known to Father Pierre by intuition, and he recalled it as he arose this morning. He hastened, for if he was going to catch Father Louis and say to him what should have been said yesterday, and even long before that, he would have to hurry. *Do you suppose it could be,* thought Father Pierre, *that I am afraid of him? Or am I afraid for my dignity? What if he simply will not listen to me? He has pretended before this to be deaf like an old man when he has preferred not to hear me. Or do I not want to see a look of pain in his small old blue eyes? Actually, is there not a possibility that what I must tell him will shock him so that it might make him ill?*

Father Pierre shrugged angrily at his doubts and tried to answer them reasonably:

Nonsense. After all, a letter from the bishop has approved my decision and given me authority to do what is wise. Why must I heed for a second the individual feelings of anyone, myself included, when a duty is to be done? If I have been a coward for days, in spite of all my prayers for strength and enlightenment as to how best to do what needs doing, must I not be doubly strong today?

And yet as he went downstairs and out to the courtyard, where a rosy daylight seemed to emerge from the ocher limestone of the church wall and glow in the very air, Father Pierre was as never before conscious of the difference in years between him and the old man who was at this moment hauling at straps and buckles, with one knee raïsed against Pancho's belly to brace himself.

It was a picture, as Father Pierre could not help pausing to notice. The horse was laden, ready and patient. His summer coat was nicely brushed. His bridle was of woven horsehair. His saddle was bulky and tall, with some of the leather worn away so that the wooden forms of horn and cantle showed through. That saddle was chair and pillow, living room and cradle and crutch to Father Louis. To it he had attached many ingenious and cranky accessories, among which there was nowhere any provision for carrying a weapon. Father Louis went unarmed.

The old priest was dressed in a long homespun coat and heavy trousers. On his head was a woven-cane hat with a wide brim, under which his face peered around at Father Pierre like a crab apple underneath a shelf. His boots were high, the color of dried clay. Now, in the presence of the younger man, he redoubled his efforts at finishing his preparations. He made extra movements, to show how difficult the job was, and he completed them with a little flourish, to show how easily he overcame all. His breath went fast, making his voice dry and thin when he spoke.

"Well, Pierre, I am just about off. I hoped I'd see you before I went."

Father Pierre laughed. His heart beat. He said to himself, *Now, now, I must tell him now.* But he heard himself reply only, "How did you think anybody could sleep with all your racket?"

"Ha." It was a dry, indifferent comment. And then Father Louis looked sharply into his superior's eyes. What he saw there made him hurry. "Well, I have everything. I'll send word back to you if I meet anybody coming this way."

"Yes, do. But before you go—"

Father Louis began to slap at his breast pockets with sudden dismay.

"Oh, Pierre, think of it. I nearly forgot my sunglasses, the new ones, you know the pair, which my niece sent to me from Vitry-le-Francois?"

"I have seen them, yes. They have green glass and metal rims, I believe?"

"The ones! Would you be a good angel and just get them for me? They must be in my room."

"You'll wait for me?"

"But of course."

"I'll be right back."

How could it be, and yet it was. Father Pierre, at the very point of discharging his sorry duty, was sent off on an errand by his victim. He shook his head. What did he fear so? The mere rage of Father Louis? The years of unspoken submission of the older man to the younger? The human aches which can invade the hearts even of those promised to God? He didn't know. All he could believe was that the unshaven, knobbled old man waiting down there by his packed horse, with his hands which trembled on a regular slow beat and his old blue eyes, was stronger than he. Father Pierre was tall and slender and chiseled in man's noble likeness. His soutane was always clean. His white face and dark eyes could blaze with the Holy Ghost. He had proper respect for authority, but could not now use his own.

Lifting piles of papers, and putting aside apples which had dried up and mineral specimens blanched by dust, he searched Father Louis' room for the green sunglasses with their oval lenses and tin rims. He smiled at the condition of the room. He did not find the glasses. He returned to the courtyard.

Father Louis was already in the saddle. In his hand he held the sunglasses. "I found them," he said. "I am sorry you had to go for them. Good-by, Pierre. Give me your blessing. I must be getting along now."

Through his thin old voice and his clouded eyes there spoke a boy who was off to a picnic. Father Pierre's heart sank as he looked at him. He knew now that he was not going to tell what it was his duty to tell. Chagrined at his own weakness, he lifted his hand and made the blessing of the cross, to which Father Louis bent his body.

After all these years he had a map in his head. The river came on a long diagonal, so. An old Indian trail went off northwestward at another angle, so. The farther inland, the farther apart they were from each other. There was one kind of country here by the sea-coast. Presently it changed to something else. Finally, in the distance of weeks, where the map would have only faltering scratches of the pen, based on rumor and legend, lay the farthest wilderness of Father Louis' journeys. The natural limits of his endurance were determined by water. His private map had an X for the end of each stage of travel—a settlement, a farm, a creek, a spring, a water hole—and pray it was not dry.

For the first several days, on these journeys, he hardly seemed to have left home. The earth was still low and sandy, and he could read in it how epochs ago the sea itself was here, hauling and grinding the stuff of ocean bottoms where now he rode. The air was moist, and little clouds came to be and to vanish almost before his gaze. He could not closely follow the river, for it wandered and turned, in places doubling back upon itself. And so he followed the Indian trail, leaving it only to go to the isolated river farms in turn.

At such a one he might spend the night, or longer, depending upon what he found. Sometimes death approached in the family, and he gave the last Sacraments. Sometimes there were infants to baptize. In the morning under a tree on rough-hewn planks set across a pair of hogsheads he would say Mass and give Communion. He listened to the local news from Mexico across the Rio Grande—there was talk of another war between ranchers of Coahuila and the Mexican troops; it had not rained for a hundred and seventy days; robbers came over the river lately and killed four men here in Texas and stole some cattle and horses and went back across the river; a child was born in the Bolson de Mapimi who spoke, quite clearly, at three days old, of a flood that would come, but who, when further questioned, seemed to have lost the power of speech; and so on.

Father Louis, in his turn, told how things were at Brownsville, and farther up the coast at Corpus Christi and Galveston, and across the sea in France, where, under the new emperor, business was booming, and trade with Mexico was growing, as you could tell by the many ships which came from Marseille and Le Havre into the Gulf of Mexico. And then, after receiving gifts of food from such a family, the rider left the river and returned to the trail, going northwestward once more.

Days later, though the sky did not cool during the daytimes, the quality of the heat changed, and was dry, as the old seacoast plain gave way to a wilderness of rolling country thickly covered with thorny brush. When he encountered it as it wandered, the river bed was rocky, and rock showed through the hard prickly ground. Everywhere he looked he saw only that endless roll of empty land. Here, near to him, it was speckled with the colors of the olive, both green and ripe, but not with any of the grace he remembered from long ago in Southern France, where the olive trees gave a silver sweetness to the landscape. Farther away in the distance, the land rolls swam in glassy heat. Way off at the horizon there was a stripe of hazy blue where the hot white sky met the earth. Nowhere could he see a mountain, either in Mexico or in Texas.

As he rode, the country tried to hold him back. The thorns of the mesquite dragged at his boots and tore his clothes. Pancho was clever at avoiding most of the hazards, but in places they were so thick that all they could do, man and horse, was go slowly and stoutly through them. But this was nothing new. Father Louis had persisted before against the thorns and had prevailed.

As for water, there was always too much or too little. Too little when, after years of drought, certain springs he looked forward to would, as he came upon them, reveal only dried white stones. Too much when, in hot spells so violent that they could be ended only with violence, there would be a cloudburst and the heavens would fall almost solid and bring the first water, which, as it struck the baked earth, actually hissed and made cracking sounds until the desert was slaked enough to receive the water in its fissures and let it run.

When it ran in such quantity, every fingerlike draw became a torrent in which a man and a horse could easily be drowned. If he crossed one in safety, another was waiting to engulf him beyond the next roll. There was no place for shelter. When the rain stopped, the sun came back and dried everything the same day except the running arroyos, which went dry the next day. All too soon there was bitter dust that sparkled in the light and rose with the hot wind. Against it Father Louis tied across his face his great bandana, which came from New Orleans.

And they went on, making a small shadow of horse and man moving slowly yet certainly across that huge empty map where days apart, each from the other, little clusters of human life and need clung to being and shone in Father Louis' mind and purpose like lanterns in the darkness—which usually was the first image he saw of his destination, when, by his reckoning, he knew it was time to reach another of his families.

Was this a hard journey? Very well, then, it was a hard journey. But so was the life hard which he found at the end of each stage of his travels. He had seen men grow old and die in his visits here, and their sons with their wives bring new souls to this wilderness in turn. They learned severe lessons in isolation, heat and the hostility of the animal and vegetable world. Every-one—the child, the grandfather, the husband, the wife, the youth, the horse, the maiden—worked unceasingly against dust, thorn, ignorance and scarcity from dawn to dark. The great world was but a rumor here, and, by the time it came to brush deserts, mostly wrong. But a world without limits of dimension dwelt behind the eyes of all those parched brown people obedient to the natural terms of their lives. It was the world of the human soul, in which could live promises so beautiful and satisfactions so full of ease that the hardships and the betrayals of impersonal Nature could be survived, if only someone came from time to time with the greatest news in all life.

For Father Louis knew in a simple flatness of fact—fact as hard as a rock, as mysterious as water, as dazzling as light—that without God the richest life in the world was more arid than the desert; and with Him the poorest life was, after all, complete in a harmony which composed all things. To be the agent of such a composition put upon him a duty in the light of which all peril on his journeys became at worst mere inconvenience. Everyone he toiled overland to see needed and deserved that which he, at the moment, under existing circumstances, alone could bring.

In a very practical way he was still awed by the mystery of his office. And as a human being he could never deny himself the joy it gave him to see in their faces what his coming meant to his people in the harsh wilderness. They knew what he had come through. They were proud to be thought worth such labor and danger. They loved him.

His mind was active in the solitude through which he crawled day after day, mounted on Pancho. One of his favorite fancies was this: that a great triangle existed between God in heaven, and any little ranch toward which he rode through the days, and himself. It was an always-changing triangle, for one of its points was not fixed: his own. As he came nearer and nearer to his goal of the moment, the great hypotenuse between himself and God grew shorter and shorter, until at the last, when he arrived, there was a straight line with all in achieved communion. He smiled over this idea, but he respected it, too; and sometimes he would take a piece of charcoal from a fire and draw a series of pictures of what he meant, explaining it to the people he was visiting, and they would murmur and nod, and consult one another, and enjoy the notion with him, marveling.

One day at noon on the present journey, he knew he should soon see what would look like a long thin blade of cloud shadow far ahead on the earth that slowly quivered with wafts of light like those in wavering mirrors. But it was not a cloud shadow, as he had found out nearly thirty years ago. It was the distant gash of a long canyon whose yellow rock walls were stained with great stripes of slate blue. It came from the north, and far away to the south opened into the rocky trough of the Rio Grande. In its bottom were all the signs of a river but running water. Here and there were shallow pools fed by the underground flow which needed storm water to call it continuously to the surface. Father Louis always paused at such a pool for a bath. There were sores on his body from the catch of thorns through which he rode. Sometimes a needle of the brush would break off in his flesh and burrow its way under his skin. For the most part he was unaware of such an affliction, but by its comfort the warm alkaline water of the pool reminded him of the misery he had forgotten to notice.

It was usually midafternoon by the time he reached the canyon after first seeing it. Shadow was already rising up the cayon wall as the sun went lower. The place was like a palace to him, open to the brassy sky. Wrens and hawks came to look at him in their wary turns. To be below the surface of the rolling plain in the canyon was to have for a little while the luxury of privacy, some-

how. He bathed, and dozed as he dried, and sat in the shade reading his breviary. He knew when it was just time to gather himself
together and resume his ride in order to come by nightfall to the
house and the spring of Encarnadino Guerra, where he could
spend the night.

This friend was a boy of ten when Father Louis first met him.
He was now the father of six children, the husband of a silent,
smiling woman named Cipriana, the son of a widowed mother
called Doña Luz, who, on his last visit, told Father Louis she
would not live to enjoy the next one. He remembered how she sat
blinking in the brilliant shade of the desert, bowing to him over
and over, while a triumph of patience went over her face, eroded
by time and trouble and work and pain, as she said, "At night,
when everything is quiet, and I am awake and alone—for I cannot sleep much any more—something speaks to me, and tells me
to be ready, and not to make any other plans."

She looked at him with hardly any light in her small eyes, and
he knew she was right. When he said Mass for them that time, he
thought he saw in her face some powerful, direct understanding
of the Holy Sacrifice which during all her pious life had slum-
bered within her, but at last came clear in her whole, small,
withered being.

He wondered whether through any dry, desertlike tenacity she
might still be living.

But when he rode up in the arching twilight to the dwelling
of the Guerras, almost the first thing they told him after their
excited greeting was that Doña Luz had died early in the summer
while sitting in the shade on her bench, holding her stick of
ocotillo cactus which her hands had shined so smooth.

In the light of the candle lantern the family looked at him and
then at one another. They were shocked by how he had changed
since last year. He was stooped and he slowly trembled all the
time. He had to peer at them to see them, even though he pre-

served a smile to make nothing of this. Burned by the wind and the sun, his face looked smaller. He breathed shallowly, with his mouth a little open. He seemed to them a very old man, all of a sudden. It was like a secret they must keep from him.

After their first start, they got busy to make his supper. The younger children lost their shyness and came from behind chairs and the edges of tables to see him, and at last climb upon him. He smelled dry and dusty to them, like the earth.

After supper he held lessons in catechism for the younger children, who tomorrow would receive their First Communions. The parents and the two older sons listened also.

After that, there was a little time left for gossip. The family's news was all of the seasons. The priest's was boiled down out of letters and newspapers from France. The Guerras already knew that the earthly love of his life was his native country, which he had not seen for over thirty years, but which still spoke in his darting eyes, his cleverness at description and in the accent with which he spoke Spanish. They listened respectfully while he made picture after picture in his talk of what he loved and missed, but they could not really see with him either the cool green fields, the ancient stone farmhouses, the lanes of poplar trees, the clear rivers; or the proud old towns, or the glorious towering cathedrals, or the silvery web of his dear city of Paris sparkling delicately in daytime, glowing in the long dusk with golden lamps and violet distances.

But they were honored simply to have him here, and stared before his marvels, and held their breath for tomorrow, when he would give them the Sacraments.

In the morning he visited the grave of Doña Luz. Everybody went with him. She was buried a little way off from the adobe house. When he saw how little earth she displaced, he nodded and smiled, as though meeting all over again her modest character which he knew so well. Guerra brought some water in an earthen vessel—not much, but enough. Father Louis took the jug and held it in both hands a moment, and gazed into it. They were all reminded of how precious water was on the earth, how it determined by its presence the very presence of life. Then he blessed it, and they all knew what this meant in terms of their daily struggle. Then, reciting prayers for the dead, he walked around the small mound of the grandmother and sprinkled the holy water upon it, and they knew he was keeping once again a promise made between heaven and earth a long time ago.

After that they returned to the house and he took them one by one and heard them confess their sins, of which, as they were contrite, he relieved them. Then, at an altar improvised against the wall where the old woman used to sit for so many hours, he said Mass, wearing his embroidered French silks and using the pewter chalice that came out of his saddelbag.

The family knelt on the ground in a straight line facing the altar. The famous triangle of Father Louis was brought into a straight line also. God and mankind were made one. As he recited the words during the offertory, "O God, who hast established the nature of man in wondrous dignity, and even more wondrously hast renewed it—" Father Louis felt behind him the bodily presences of that isolated family, and an almost bitter sense of the dearness of each of their souls humbled him at his altar.

When Mass was over they returned within the house, where, at the raw table polished by countless unnoticed contacts of all the family, Father Louis sat down to fill in certificates of First Communion for the younger children. He had a flask of huisache ink and a German steel pen. Sitting as far back from the documents as he could, the better to read, he began to write. A look of disgust came on to his face as his trembling hand gave him trouble. Exclaiming impatiently, he put his left hand on his right wrist to add strength and steadiness where they were needed, but this did not help much, and when he was done, he pushed the papers toward the head of the family, saying, "Nobody ever can read my writing except God."

They all took him seriously, prouder than before of their papers.

"But that is enough, isn't it?" he demanded fiercely.

They had a merry breakfast, when everyone talked as though they would not soon again have a chance to talk, which was true; everyone except Guerra, who was going to speak of something as soon as he had built up enough silence. Finally he was ready.

"Father," he said, leaning back a trifle in his chair and half closing his eyes to disguise deep feelings, "you won't be going on anywhere else, after us, will you?"

"Oh, yes."

"Where will you go, Father?"

"Why, I plan to ride from here over toward the river. I have a couple of families over there, and I may go as far as the town of San Ygnacio, to see if the priests from Mier are making visits there, as they ought to. Why?"

Guerra put his head on one side and shrugged. He did not want to say that the old man was exhausted and ought not to go so far in the pitiless country under the searing sun. It would not be polite to say the old man was older than his years, and he must be seventy anyway. He might be misunderstood if he said that everybody reached a time, after a life of hard work, when he must pause and rest and let stronger people do what needed doing. It would hardly do to show outright that he thought Father Louis should give up, and stay here, and rest a few weeks, and then perhaps Encarnadino Guerra might leave everything here in the hands of his two strong, quiet boys, and just ride with Father Louis until he saw him safely back in Brownsville.

Father Louis peered close to his younger friend and saw enough of these thoughts to stir him up.

"Eh?" he said, rapping hard with his knuckles on Guerra's skull. "What goes on in there?" He was sharp and angry. What were they all thinking? That he was a feeble old man? He knew all there was to know about that, but if anything was to be said about it, he, not they or anyone else, was the one to say it. "Mind your manners, you, boy," he said to Guerra, screwing up his small eyes until all that showed of them were two sharp blue points of light. "Eh? You have opinions, have you? Who told you to think anything! Eh? When I want you to think anything about anybody, I'll tell you. Eh? I got here, didn't I? How many times have I managed to come? And what for? Does anybody tell me to come? Or where to go? Or when? Or why? Then you keep your place, and thank God for your blessings, and for your friends, and understand that it is just as bad to hold an impolite thought as it is to say an impolite thing. Eh?" His whole body shook with passion which he tried to control. "Bad. You'd just better be careful, that's all I have to say, do you hear?"

The family was appalled at his burst of feeling. They sat with downcast eyes, fearing that it would be disrespectful to look upon Father Louis in his rage. But they had little glimpses of his unshaven face whitened with anger, and they could hear how pulse-shaken his voice was. Guerra was more Indian than anything else, and his countenance became fixed. He leaned back and took his dressing down without response. He was not even hurt by it. He knew why it came to him. He knew how much it proved him right in his concern. He admired the flare of spirit in the old man. He was at peace with himself for trying what he had tried.

The youngest child, not understanding what had taken place, now, belatedly, felt the emotion among all the older ones, and turning up her little clay-doll face she burst into wails of misery and fear, bringing her tiny creature paws to her howling mouth until she resembled the small sculptured masks of earth buried with the dead centuries ago deep in Mexico.

Father Louis roughly took her upon his lap. He bent his bristly face close to hers, cactus and blossom together, and in barely audible murmurs quieted the child and himself, which took about five minutes.

This act reclaimed them all for one another. Once again the visitor was kind and smiling, and the family without fear.

"And so, good-by for this time," said Father Louis, putting the child down and standing up. "If you will get my horse for me?"

Guerra spoke to one of the boys, who went to fetch Pancho. They all met him outside. Cipriana brought some tortillas for the saddlebag. Everyone knelt down to be blessed. The hot sunlight smote them. They had lingered long over their breakfast. It was late. Father Louis, mounted and ready, blessed them three times, and then turned and rode off to the south. After a while he looked back. They were still kneeling. The next time he looked back it was hard to see them, for at even a little distance they made the same shadow as the scrubby bushes which grew on the caked earth, and seemed just as eternally rooted there.

He had a bad morning. The sun seemed hotter to him than before. The savage brush seemed animated with spite as it clawed at his legs going by. Pancho, after all these years and a lifetime in the brush country, took it into his head to be terrified of familiar things, and from time to time without warning executed a rapid dance step to one side while throwing his head back and rolling his eyes at his rider.

"Hush, you fool!" Father Louis exclaimed at such times. "You fool!"

But he addressed himself as much as he did the horse. For the first few hours of that day's ride, he reviewed many times the loss of his temper at Guerra, and developed a masterly case, closely reasoned, lucid as only a French argument can be, compassionate with largeness of heart, yet as logical as music in its progression, as to why it had been not only natural but actually necessary to reprove Guerra for having presumed to hold views about him. Reprove? Perhaps actually more of a scolding. Scolding? Thinking it over, possibly even a tongue-lashing. And the knuckles? The furious raps on the head? Still, how else could he be made to understand? But understand what?

It was no good. As he always did, in the end, he lost the argument with himself. He knew that after hours of exhausting search for conclusions which would excuse him for what he had done, he would at last come to the truth, which was that he had offended God and man through his lifelong besetting sins of pride, self-esteem and attempted condonement of his own shortcomings; and that there would be nothing left to do but go down upon his knees and admit how wrong he had been, and pray to be forgiven and to be granted strength once more to conquer himself.

He began his penance with a resolve not to eat or drink until nightfall.

By midafternoon, the brush grew thicker. Only occasionally did he come to a little clearing between the mesquite bushes, which rose higher than himself mounted on Pancho. In spite of his green sunglasses, the ground sparkled and glared enough to hurt his eyes. He watched for but he could not see the long pale blur which would tell him that another canyon lay ahead which he would follow until it took him, after several days, to the Rio Grande. He kept the sun on his right, for it was declining to the west in the white sky and he was going south. The day was still.

But how was this? He thought he heard a singing wind, but when he tried to notice whether he could feel the air stirring or see dust rising ahead of him, there was no sign of wind. He halted Pancho. What did he hear, then? He turned his head. Yes, he could hear something, now far ahead, now here in his very ear. He searched the undulating horizon, but he saw nothing except the wavering image of glassy heat where the white sky met the dusty earth.

As he rode on, the singing in the air became louder. It sounded like the voice of the desert heat. He shook his head, resentful of natural conditions which hid behind mystery. And then suddenly he knew, and scornfully rebuked himself for taking so long about it.

He was riding into a swarm of cicadas, and now he could see the first ones, clinging to the mesquite as they raised their shrieking song of the heat. The farther he rode, the louder they became. He bent his head under their stinging assault upon his hearing. There were thousands and millions of them. Blindly they fulfilled their natures in their collective scream of response to the sun and the desert. The very atmosphere seemed to be in flames, and the sound of the stridulating insects added to the illusion.

Father Louis had touched the desert often enough. He had smelled it. He had tasted it when its dust rose on the wind. He had seen it in every state. But never before in so real a sense had he heard it.

He was suddenly exhausted. In a clearing, a little lake of baked dust a few yards in diameter, he halted and dismounted, tying Pancho to a stout mesquite branch. Disturbed, a cloud of cicadas rose on crackling threads of flight and found another bush. The ringing song rose all about him. He could not even hear the sound of Pancho stamping his foot to shake off flies. He clapped his hands, but made barely a sound against the strident song in the air. He felt removed from himself. All desert natures combined to render him impersonal. Here, humbled not only from within but from without, he could find real contrition. He knelt down to pray.

The sunlight was brilliant in the center of the clearing, a little open room hidden by time, distance and mesquite clumps. At the west side of it there was lacy shade, cast by tall bushes. But Father Louis rejected it and knelt in the plain sunlight. He bent his head under the beat of his spirit and of the insect scream which seemed to invoke the zenith. He prayed to be forgiven for his miserable anger. He always prayed in French, the language through which he had first met God.

He was not long now at his contritions, for he knew that prayer was not so often a matter of length as of depth. Much sobered, even saddened, by his intense self-discovery, he arose wearily from his knees and went over to the shade to lie down. He went as deeply into the under boughs of the thorny mesquite as he could. He closed his eyes. At once he felt cooler, just to have the hot light shaded from his sight. Ah, this was delicious, just to lie for a few moments and gather strength to go on for the remaining hours of daylight. He felt how his limbs all went heavy on the earth as he let himself drift off to sleep.

Little coins of light fell over him through the intricate branches. Where he lay, he made solid shadow himself under the mesquite tree. He was as quiet and substantial as a rock. And if he used Nature, it in turn used him without his knowing, for he was asleep.

He did not see, or smell, or feel what came in slow inquiry along the trackless ground, striving forward in orderly, powerful progress, flowing in a dry glitter and advancing through always-new and always-repeated thrust of form from side to side and yet ahead. It was a diamondback rattlesnake in search of shade and the cool. It came from deep in the scattered brush, and it found the heavy-sleeping man under the bushy tree. With what seemed almost conscious caution against awakening the sleeper, the snake drew closer and closer in infinite delicacy, until it lay heavily at rest in the shade of Father Louis' right shoulder, its length doubled back and forth in inert splendor.

The sleeper did not stir for a while and then Father Louis grew tense in dream, his mouth fell open and, awakening with a jerk, he sat up, lost in forgetfulness of where he was or how he came there. He stared at the white sky.

The thick snake, at the first quiver of motion beside it, drew instantly into its coil and shook its dozen rattles. Their song could not be heard over the general din of the cicadas.

"Ah, yes," sighed Father Louis, as he discovered where he was,.

and why, and whither he was going. He put his hand to his brow and sank roughly back to the earth to take a few more minutes of rest. The snake struck him in the shoulder, and struck him again. Its coils turned dust into liquid light as they lashed. The strikes came like blows made by the thick, powerful arm of a young man.

"What then?" said Father Louis at the sudden stabbing pain, and the blows that shook him. He first thought of mesquite thorns on a springy branch; they were long and, as he had often said, sharp as fangs, and they could fester if not treated. It occurred to him that this would be troublesome now, as he could hardly reach his own shoulder to wash, cut open the skin and dig out the thorns if they had broken to stay in the flesh.

But he turned to see the branch which had attacked him, and saw the snake instead. The snake was retreating. He could see its eye with its glaring drop of light. His heart began to beat hard. He had a surge of rage. He wanted to kill the snake, and actually rose to one knee and scraped the ground with his hands for something to attack with—a rock, a club of dead wood, anything —but he could find nothing. He sank down again, and out of habit in any crisis brought his hands flat together with crossed thumbs in the attitude of prayer.

"No, no; no anger," he beseeched of himself with his eyes shut. He had just endured and come through the storm of his own pride, and he must not now create another. He opened his eyes and looked after the snake, and saw it where it paused half in, half out of the dappled shade of the next bush.

"Go," he said to it.

What he meant by this came to be more and more clear through calm and struggle in the next hour or so. The snake, as though it heard him, resumed in infinite slowness the gliding flow of its retreat until it was lost to sight among the hot thickets where the insects still sang and sang.

"Yes, go," he repeated bitterly; and was ashamed to discover that he was weeping. It was the humanity in him which wept because death was coming. He fell over upon his face and put his cracked and dusty hands over his eyes. His mouth was open and took into itself the loose acid earth with his breath. His tears ran down his fingers. His heart was pounding rapidly upon the ground. It seemed to shake the earth. It told Father Louis that he was afraid.

Afraid? Of what? he thought. Afraid of death? But I have dealt with it all my life and I have robbed it of its terrors for those who knew how to die. Is death the only victory of life? Or do we have to defeat life in its own terms? That depends. It depends upon whether sin is ever outside oneself or always within. Yes, this is a very interesting matter.

He made himself lie quietly without thought for a moment. If perhaps he conserved his energy he might by natural vitality, by pure goodness, defeat the murder which had been dealt him by the desert. He forced himself to relax, and promised that in a little while his head would be clearer, his heart would calm itself, and moving with infinite caution he would arise, mount his horse and go slowly, steadily, cleverly, toward the long evening, and come to the canyon where there must be a familiar trickle of water. A cool night with much prayer, a stout will, and tomorrow he would go forward and by the end of the day come to friends who would know how to make poultices and feed him and recover him to the use and enjoyment of many more years of duty, work and acquired merit.

But the poison worked rapidly, and he felt it charging his mind with throbbing pain which confused him. Shining blades went across his vision behind his eyes like spokes of a great wheel. He was dazzled by their power. When he raised his head they took it with them, rolling and rolling until he fell down again upon the ground with his cheek cut by little pebbles of gypsum. He tried to speak and to say, "Let me not live for vanity, though, Lord."

Questions now became academic, for he went blind in his inner vision, and lay trembling involuntarily as the terrible message which had been stricken into him traveled the course of his blood and reached him everywhere within.

Tied to his mesquite tree, Pancho stamped and waited. Presently Father Louis believed that he awoke.

His mind was working sharply and with, it seemed to him, exquisite new ease and clarity. He saw all his thoughts in crystal depths of cold fresh water. He knew he was in the mesquite thicket, and what had happened to him, and he possessed this knowledge with a beauty of feeling which all his life he had known in the state of grace, after receiving or administering the Sacraments. It was more than mere physical well-being. It was a sense of delivery from the ordinary guilt of his own clay, and the exasperating weight of communion with all that lay beyond himself. In such a state, truth needed no seeking and no definition. It was here, within, and it was there, without. It was everywhere. When all was known, there could be no astonishment.

He was therefore not astonished now when right before him, lying at ease in the light of the sun, was the snake, gazing at him with piercing sweetness.

He spoke to it. "I do not hate you. It is enough that I recognize you."

The snake replied, "That is my damnation."

"Yes," said Father Louis, "for when evil is recognized, all other powers move together to defeat it."

"And yet they never do defeat it, do they? How do you explain that?"

"Ah. You and I do not see it in quite the same way. You conceive of the possible death of evil as being one final end, after which only goodness will survive."

"I do."

"That is your vanity. For the fact is that evil must be done to death over and over again, with every act of life. One might even say that this repeated act is a very condition for the survival of life itself. For only by acts of growth can more life be made, and if all evil, all acts of death, were ended once and for all, there would be nothing left for the soul to triumph over in repeated acts of growth."

The snake sighed despondently and said, "Do you not permit me a comparable purpose and privilege? That is, of triumphing repeatedly over all acts of good—that is, of life—until only I remain?"

"I permit you your established role, but I do not admit the possibility of your triumphing repeatedly over all acts of life. I must point out that, historically, your premise is untenable."

"And yet I have played a part in every human life."

"Oh, admittedly. We are not discussing the fact that your powers exist; only the fact that they have their limits."

The snake smiled. "This? From you?" it asked with ironic politeness.

"What do you mean, sir?"

"If my powers have their limits, then how is it that I have killed you? What greater power is there than that?"

Father Louis passed his hand across his face to hide his amusement. "You have betrayed the weakness of your whole position," he replied. "For it appears to be impossible for you to know that the death of matter is of no importance, except to other matter. The materialist can see only destruction as the logical end of his powers. I, and my brothers, and my children, know that beyond matter lies spirit, and that it is there where answers are found, and truths become commonplace, and such efforts as yours, so restless, so ingenious, so full of torturing vanity, are seen for what they really are."

The snake frowned for a moment, but then shook off its irritation and said, again with politeness, even with charm and appeal, which Father Louis was the first to admit, "Everyone must do that which his nature dictates."

"There again," said Father Louis with assumed gravity, "there is much behind the formation of that nature which you do not take into account."

"Oh, come. After all, I am a snake, I came from snakes, I do a snake's work. How could I behave like anything but a snake?"

"The outer form is hardly the point. You can assume any form you choose, I believe?"

The snake hesitated before answering. A gleam of admiration went through its expression, and it marveled frankly for a moment at the astuteness of Father Louis.

"I must say, even if we are enemies, you force me to admire and like you," it said.

"Thank you," said Father Louis. "Viewed abstractly, you have great and beautiful qualities of your own."

"Do you really think so?"

"Oh, yes, I do. But I must add that they seem to me less important, in the end, than they do to you."

"You can also be very rude, you know."

"I do not think of it that way," said Father Louis mildly. "Finally, it doesn't matter how things are said or done, it is what things are said or done. For example, I really believe you can do things far more expertly than I can. But when we come to what things, there I have you."

The snake looked far from pleased.

Father Louis resumed, "I can't assume any form, for example, as you can. I remain always what I am, a man, an old man, a dirty old man when water is scarce or I am busy, an old man full of pride and sin and vanity and all the rest of it; but nobody is ever in doubt as to what I mean or as to what I think life means, and with all my mistakes in style and good form, the garden I scratch keeps growing."

"And I?"

"And you, sometimes you are a snake, and sometimes a whisper, and again, a daydream, a lump in the blood, a sweet face, an ambition, a scheme for making money, a task for an army. Sometimes you can even be a man and disarm everyone entirely who cannot see your heart. But someone there is who always sees. Goodness is often performed without the slightest knowledge of its doing. But evil is always known."

"Yes, I think more people know me than the other thing."

"But don't congratulate yourself upon that," said Father Louis, "for it means always one of your uncountable defeats when you are known."

Father Louis saw that the snake would have to grow angry unless the subject was changed. The snake changed it. "I wonder," it mused, "why I ever came to you today."

Father Louis shrugged. "Sooner or later, we would have come together," he said.

"Did you expect me?"

"I've been expecting you all my life; though not exactly in this particular guise. You came to me in my sleep, like an evil dream."

"All I wanted was a little comfort. It was so hot. So dry."

Father Louis smiled in delight. "You see? For comfort, even you have to appeal to the powers of goodness."

"Why did you let me go?"

"I had no weapon."

"You could have stamped upon me."

"I do not believe in killing."

"Yet I am your enemy."

"Yes, you are. But I believe there are greater ways to dispose of you than in revenge."

"You do not have much time left, you know. Just think of all the time you would have left if I had not come to you. If you had seen me and killed me first."

"Yes, I have thought of that. But you speak as though time were my property. It is not. How can I count it? Or know how much of it is my share?"

The snake scowled and looked from side to side evasively. Unwillingly, against its own comfort, it asked, "Who else can decide your share? Where do you get it? What do you refer to?"

The snake began uneasily to bring its coils together. There was anguish in its movement, slow as it was. It seemed to be obeying desire which was hurtful and yet impossible to deny.

"You do not really want to hear," said Father Louis tenderly.

"Oh, yes, I do; tell me," said the snake with broken breath, already suffering under the answer which it demanded.

Father Louis bent over the snake with compassion. There was torture in the creature, as with glittering sweet power it besought Father Louis to answer.

"Very well, my poor sinner," said Father Louis gravely. "I, and all creatures, draw our share of time in this life from God, our Father in heaven."

At these words the snake, with the speed of lightning, knew convulsion in its dread coils, and with mouth wide open and fangs exposed, struck again and again at the earth, where the dust rose like particles of gold and silver. Father Louis regarded it with pity as its paroxysm of hatred and chagrin spent itself.

At last, gasping softly and stretched out in exhaustion, the snake said sorrowfully, "And so it is not by my will that you die now?"

"No."

"I was only the means?"

"Only the means."

"Your hour was designated elsewhere?"

Father Louis looked upward. His face was radiant. "My hour was fixed by our Heavenly Father."

The snake closed its eyes and shuddered reminiscently. Then it said, "And my hour?"

"You will die in your bodily form by His will."

"I do not want to die."

"But you will live in your quality of evil by His will."

"You're sure?"

"Yes. But you will live only on earth, no matter what form you assume."

The snake grew pale. "Oh, no."

"Yes," said Father Louis as his argument drew to its close, "for there can be no evil in heaven."

The snake lay with its mouth open, its tongue like a little tongue of fire, flickering in despair, its eyes staring without sight. It was vanquished, destroyed, made trivial. Father Louis shook his head over it and wished it might not have suffered. Then he felt his brow, where the diamondlike lucidity of the past quarter of an hour seemed to be clouding over. His skull was cracking under blows that beat and beat there. How could he feel so bad after feeling so well?

"And now you must excuse me," he said uncertainly to the snake. "I have things to do, and, actually, I do not feel too well. Thank you, if you will just go now," and he looked to see if the snake was leaving, but the snake was already gone.

The battering pains in his head brought Father Louis from vision to consciousness.

"Oh, my God, my God," he said devoutly and with much effort, even with modesty, representing his trouble to Him whose suffering he had dwelt upon so deeply in a lifetime.

He looked around. The air seemed entirely silent. This was because there was a ringing in his head so bewildering that he

could no longer hear the myriad insects at their screaming celebration of the heat.

He saw Pancho tied to the tree. "No, you must not stay with
me," he said, and tried to stand up. He could hardly stand, for
his legs were weak as paralysis crept into them. And so he
crawled across the open place among the thickets until he could
hold to his stirrup, haul himself up and lean with his head on the
saddle for a moment.

"You need not die here, tied to a tree," he said. "Let me get
my things, and you may go."

He fumbled with the buckles and straps until he was able to
haul the saddle off the horse. It fell to the ground. He worked at
the bridle until he had freed it enough to pull it off over Pancho's
head. The horsehair bridle hung from the thorny tree and trailed
in the dust.

"Huya! Huya!" cried Father Louis, waving his hand at
Pancho to make him trot away, as so often he had done after un-
saddling the horse at the corral at Brownsville. But Pancho
simply stood and regarded him.

"Very well, very well; in your own time, then," he said, and
went down to his hands and knees, fondling a pouch on the
saddle. Out of it into his hands came the objects he wished to
hold once more. Holding them to his breast, he crawled back to
his fatal shade across the clearing. The sun was almost down.

"My soul doth magnify the Lord," he murmured in Latin
while pains like blades pierced him through and through. Even
the heavy washing waves of death could not erase entirely from
his foundering mind the terrible privilege of knowing in a final
hour what saints might have endured. "And my spirit has rejoiced
in God my savior," he said, without knowing he spoke. But he
brought a lifetime of prayer with him to death's door, and in a
little while it entered there with him.

Pancho late the next evening finished finding his way through the brush back to the house of Encarnadino Guerra. The family saw that he was without his saddle and bridle. Guerra and his big sons went searching, and, though they persevered for days, found nothing in that wilderness of repeated clump and glaring shadow and lost sameness. They had to give up. Later that year, when surveyors from an expedition of the United States Army came by his place on their way to Brownsville, Guerra told them the news, and asked them to see that it reached the proper authorities, along with the horse Pancho which he hoped they would take with them.

And then one day eight years afterward, Guerra was on his way to San Ygnacio on the Rio Grande to see his new grandson, born to the household of his oldest boy, who now lived there. Coming into a small clearing in the brush, he found quite by accident what he had looked for long ago. There was not much left, for the desert earth and sky were voracious. Coyotes and blowing sand, vultures and beating sunlight and wind had worked with the years on flesh and leather, French silk, parchment and homespun. Reverently Guerra took up the few bones that had not been scattered, and the few hard things that still stayed by them: the pewter chalice, a rosary of small sea shells, three American silver dollars, the pair of green sunglasses, and, from a mesquite tree where it hung now off the ground, the horsehair bridle.

When he could, he made the journey to Brownsville, bringing the relics of his old friend with him. He found his way to Father Pierre Arnoud.

"How these things speak to us!" said Father Pierre, after hearing the end of the story that had begun eight years before. He looked at Guerra and saw that this was a man who had lost a dear friend, who would understand anything said to him in the name of Father Louis. He added, "I am leaving soon for France. Do you know where that is?"

"Yes. He used to tell us much about it."

Father Pierre was making ready to obey a summons to return home to receive the dignity of bishop of a French diocese.

"I am going there to assume new work," he said. "These things, this sacrifice," he said, indicating what Guerra had brought, "will help me to do it better."

Guerra nodded.

"We will bury him here in the churchyard," continued Father Pierre, "and you must be present. As you were his friend, and have served him so well, now I would like to ask your permission to keep this."

He held up the little string of seashells.

"Yes," said Guerra, accepting with simplicity the power to dispose.

"I wonder how he died," murmured Father Pierre. "Indians? A heart attack?"

"Not Indians."

"Why not?"

"They would not have let the horse go."

"True. What then?"

Guerra made a gesture with his mouth, putting his lips forward as though he would point to a place far from there and long ago. He saw the clearing in the thorny brush again, and he knew its nature, all of it.

"I think I know."

"How could you possibly?"

"He did not die suddenly."

"No?"

"No. He had time to free his horse."

"True."

"If he thought he could have saved himself, he would have come with the horse."

"Undoubtedly."

"But he did not come. He stayed. That means he knew there wasn't any use."

"Yes?"

"Where I found him was just like the place where it would happen."

"What would happen?"

With his hand Guerra made in the air a slow, sinuous motion from side to side in an unmistakable imitation.

"No!" said Father Pierre. "A snake?"

Guerra nodded. "I think so," he said.

Father Pierre shuddered at the nature of that fate, and then presently he kindled at the memory of an old weakness and an old strength.

"Do you know? I will tell you something," he said. "Our dear friend was an old man, tired and ill, when he went on that last journey. For days before he left, I was supposed to tell him that he could not go. I tried and I tried. But I could not tell him. Even on the last morning I could not give the order." Father Pierre put his hands together in emotion. "What could I have saved him from? From dying at his work? That is how we—all of us—want to die when our time comes."

He looked earnestly at Guerra, but if he thought he would find the abstract pardon of life there, he was mistaken. Guerra simply looked back at him with the impersonal judgment of the world.

"No, I could not give the order," resumed Father Pierre. "And do you know? I am sure he knew what I had to say. He would not let me say it. He gave the orders. Just to prove it, he even sent me upstairs to find his green sunglasses. I went, and I did not find them. When I came down again, there they were; he had them all the time."

Guerra laughed out loud at the crankiness this recalled, and what it meant. He bent over, took up the pair of green glass spectacles with their rusted tin rims and, with a gleam of meaning, handed them to Father Pierre.

"Then keep these also," he said.

"Thank you," said the bishop-elect soberly.

SANTA LUCIA

JOSEPH PETRACCA

Mama has the passionate faith of the Italian immigrant class. Papa is a roaring atheist. Pitting herself against her husband in a moment of crisis, the whole swarming, screaming, superstitious neighborhood in the background, mama comes out the victor. The gusto, robust humor, bursting-at-the-seams vitality of this story earned its acceptance as an Atlantic "First." Joseph Petracca is a salesman in Los Angeles by day, a writer at night. He has written plays as well as short stories.

I didn't get to see my first miracle until I was nearly ten years old. Anyway, that's what Mama always calls it whenever she talks about it. Any little favor from Upstairs or any little wish that's granted, in whole or in part, right off becomes a miracle to Mama; but in all fairness to her, this one really was.

It was one of those hot August days, and I was playing shinneger stick with Dominick Bianchi, a kid my age who lived underneath us. I had just belted the tapered wooden cat two sewers when Mama stuck her head out of the window and started screaming. Dominick and I began to run, figuring she was yelling at us for sawing off the broomstick handle, when all of a sudden she started to moan, one of those crying moans, like when Natale, my kid brother, was born. Halfway up the street we stopped and looked up. Mama was bent double over the window ledge, wailing and pulling her hair and entreating all the saints in heaven to help her. She cried so loud that pretty soon all the women in the neighborhood came running out of their houses and gathered under the window.

"What'sa matter?" asked Mrs. Simonelli, the iceman's wife. Mama didn't answer, just kept on wailing and the women downstairs began to buzz-buzz among themselves, all of them trying to guess what could have happened. Mrs. Bianchi, Dominick's mother, appeared in the window and put her arm around Mama to console her.

"What'sa matter?" Mrs. Simonelli asked again.

"He had a stroke," said Mrs. Bianchi.

"Who?" asked Mrs. Quattrocchi, the barber's wife.

"Nonno," said Mrs. Bianchi, meaning my grandfather.

"Oooooh!" Mama screeched, rocking back and forth on the window ledge as if she were going to throw herself off.

"*Poverella*," said Mrs. Petito, the street cleaner's wife, shaking her head from side to side and clucking sympathetically.

"He'sa blind—blind!" Mama shouted to the tops of the roofs across the street, and all the women in the street crossed themselves and kissed their thumbnails.

"*Poverello*," said Mrs. Petito, biting her knuckle. "Do you want me to get LaZingara?" asked Mrs. Ferrante, whose husband was out of work and playing Brische in the Cafe. Mrs. Ferrante and Mama never called in a doctor when anybody got sick; they always called LaZingara, a bent-over old woman who mixed herbs and leaves, and mumbled dark Sicilian prayers over you. No matter what you had, her treatment was always the same.

"*Si, si*—right away!" Mama said, looking down at Mrs. Ferrante and wringing her hands at her. Mrs. Ferrante elbowed her way through the crowd of women, and Mama looked after her pleadingly, speeding her on her merciful journey. Then Mama began to cry again, distractedly. I couldn't stand it.

"Mama—" I said.

"Joey," Mama said, looking down at me.

"Can I do something?"

"Call Papa."

"Sure."

"Tell him to come home."

"Which dock is he working?"

"I no know. Look, look."

"Sure, Mama."

As Dominick and I left to find Papa, Mrs. Bianchi was leading Mama into the front room.

Papa was stevedoring at the Wallabout Basin, a big tub of dirty water with a lot of cat-sized rats in it. Every time a breeze blew in from Manhattan or a scow pulled out from the scummy piles, a sour stink blanketed the entire neighborhood. There was nothing to do about it except, perhaps, to move to Manhattan, but Papa wanted to be near his job, and so we stayed in Williamsburg.

Dominick and I tried a couple of docks before we found Papa, but by then it was nearly time for the twelve o'clock whistle to blow, so we sat on a crate and watched him work. And Papa was something to watch. If the other longshoremen carried one sack of sugar, Papa carried two; if it took two of them to carry down a box, Papa carried it down by himself. It was the same way with everything he did; he always had to give it that extra something. Even when he played Brische at the Cafe, he had to rap his knuckles on the card table harder than the others. It didn't make any difference to Papa if it was a deuce or a four, or some other unimportant card, he'd bang the table just the same as if it were a trey or an ace.

Now Papa was using the gaff, the longshoreman's hook, and dancing a heavy crate, like a tarantella partner, to the loading platform. Papa loved that hook. Every morning when he left the house to shape up for the day's work, he stuck it in his shirt pocket, wearing it like a badge, which announced to all the neighbors that this man was no *zappatore*, common laborer, or ditchdigger. No sir! See that hook? This man is a longshoreman!

When the noon whistle blew, Papa walked to the far end of the pier, wiping his face and neck with a polka-dot bandanna. Before he sat down, he blew his nose into the ground, a nostril at a time, and then put his bandanna away and began to eat.

"Papa," I said, walking toward him.

Papa looked up from his sandwich, startled, his cheeks bulging with salami and *provolone*. The only time any of us went down to call him was when there was trouble, or when he forgot to take his lunch. He was eating his lunch, so it must be trouble. He jumped to his feet and began to shake me. "What'sa matter? Who it is? Concetta? Amelia? Natale?"

"No," I managed through all his shaking.

"Mama?" he demanded. "Talk! Talk!"

Dominick came to my rescue. "It's Nonno," he said.

"Nonno," Papa said, dismissing me and the news contemptuously. Nonno was the economic albatross around Papa's neck, a quiet old man who just sat around the house, smoking his pipe and looking out of the window.

"What'sa matter f' him?" Papa asked, like a man asks about his father-in-law.

"Mama says he's blind," I said.

"He'sa fake," Papa said.

"No, Papa. He had a stroke," I said.

"Stroga!" Papa scoffed. "He'sa fake! Now go home. *Vatine!*"

"But Mama told me to tell you to come home."

"You tell you mothe' I go home when I fineesh the job. *Capisci?*" he said, twisting my ear.

"But—"

"No but. Go home."

"But Mama said—"

"But, but!" Papa said. "Go home, *se* no I take offa my strap!" And Papa started to undo the buckle on his belt, but Dominick and I were already streaking it up the pier.

2

When I got upstairs, LaZingara was in the kitchen mixing her herbs and leaves in the big macaroni pot, the same as she did for me the year I had the measles. Seeing her, I was glad Papa didn't come home. The year I had the measles, she wrapped a hot herb poultice around my head, like a turban. Then, fingering a string of amulets like a rosary, she beseeched the ceiling with some ancient Sicilian sorcery, while Mama knelt on the other side of the bed, babbling like a terrified Greek chorus.

'When Papa came home and saw me sitting up in bed with the spinach bandage, as he called it, around my head, and LaZingara with her hands clasped to heaven, he grabbed his hook and made a head-long dive for her. La Zingara screeched bloody murder and ran around and around the bed. Papa cursing her and menacing her with his hook, and Mama pummeling Papa on the back with her little fists, imploring him to stop or the whole family would come down with the Evil Eye. But Papa kept right after LaZingara, Evil Eye or no Evil Eye, and chased her clear out of the house, down the stairs, and up the street, swinging his hook and calling her a gypsy and a witch at the top of his lungs. When he got back upstairs, Mama was praying before a picture of St. Joseph she had borrowed from Sister Carmela that afternoon. Papa snarled an atheist snarl at Mama, and came over to me and asked, "What'sa matter?"

"I got measles," I said, and began to cry.

"Shutupa," he said, and went out to get Dr. Capolongo.

Well, here was LaZingara again, mixing the herbs for Nonno and bent over the macaroni pot, stirring and sniffing, mumbling something to the brew. She was such a skinny old woman, and so well-intentioned, that even though I was sure she could turn me to stone if she wanted to, I still felt a little sorry for her. She was a poor woman and nobody ever gave her money for her services, everybody figuring she got her herbs, leaves, and roots for nothing in Fort Greene Park. Once in a while Mama gave her a hard piece of *mozzarella* that was left over from the *lasagna,* or now and then a saucer of wine with a piece of stale bread to dip into it, but never any money.

Nobody knew how she lived because nobody was brave enough to step inside her house to find out. Whenever Mrs. Ferrante or Mama went to call her, they knocked on her door with a crucifix clutched in their hands and then stepped back quickly, making the sign of the cross and kissing the crucifix. When she came out, you could be sure she would be wearing the same peasant clothes she wore all year round, a lot of long flouncy skirts and a dark woolen shawl, which she wrapped around her head in the winter and dropped to her shoulder in the summer.

She was really a pathetic figure, and I was thinking to myself it's a good thing Papa didn't come home, when, at that moment, I heard his voice in the hallway, downstairs. He was talking to Mrs. Bianchi. "What'sa matter f' the old man?" he said.

"He's blind," Mrs. Bianchi said with that cluck in her voice.

"Ah, he'sa fake," Papa said, starting to clump up the stairs. With Papa coming up the stairs, I felt more sorry for LaZingara than ever, because I knew that if he got his hands on her this time, he would surely kill her. I walked over to her and tapped her lightly on the shoulder. "Papa's coming," I said. "He musta finished early."

"Oh!"

And with that she threw all her uncooked herbs into the macaroni pot and started to run around the kitchen, opening closet doors and bedroom doors, looking for the quickest exit. The back-yard window was open, and before I could warn her about Mama's trays of tomato conserve that were blocking the fire escape, her skirts were swishing through the air and she was rolling out of the room. A fiendish shriek greeted Papa as he opened the door, and it wasn't hard to guess why: LaZingara had landed smack into the sticky tomatoes.

Papa rushed to the open window, but LaZingara was already scampering down the fire escape, cursing Papa from one end of Italy to the other and inviting all the demons of hell to visit him that very night. But Papa cursed her right back and shook his hook at her. By this time the neighbors were all at their windows, and when they saw LaZingara running across the yard, her backside a dripping red mass and Papa wildly waving his hook, they nodded their heads with grim understanding: "So he finally got her."

Papa looked at the neighbors and then began to laugh, a slow swelling laugh. He was still laughing when Mama came rushing out of Nonno's room, her dark eyes sparking and the muscles in her jaw quivering. She walked right up to Papa and demanded, "Where's LaZingara?"

"Who?" Papa said, still laughing.

"LaZingara, LaZingara," Mama said impatiently.

"She'sa here? I no see here," Papa said, laughing at his little technicality.

"She'sa was here," Mama said, clenching her little fists on her hips. Even though Papa was a squat mound of muscle, with hands like big *caciocavalli*, and Mama was built like a spaghetti, he was afraid of her when she got mad. He turned his back to her and twirled the hook around his finger.

"I no know what you talk."

"Joey," Mama said, bringing me into it, "where's LaZingara?"

"She went down the fire escape," I said, looking at Papa and wondering if I was a snitcher.

"You chase her out," Mama said to Papa.

"I'ma?" Papa said.

"Yes you," Mama said.

Papa smiled like when he makes a good shot in Boccie. "Joey, I'ma chase LaZingara? Go 'head, tell you mothe'."

"No, Mama," I said, glad to get back on Papa's side.

"There," Papa said, "what I tell you?"

"Then she'sa hear you come and run away."

"What you wanna f' me? I canna come my own house?"

"But Patsy," Mama said, "LaZingara gonna cure Nonno."

"Pah!" Papa said.

"No pah, is true," Mama said. "When Mingucci gotta the stroga, he no walk. Then in one weeks LaZingara make walk. No?"

"No," Papa said.

"Yes," Mama said.

"Was Nature," Papa said.

"No Nature," Mama said.

"You know what is Nature?" Papa said.

"Patsy, I no wanna hear," Mama said, pressing her hands tight against her ears while Papa expounded his borrowed philosophy of Nature. To Mama, Nature was synonymous with Bruno Cardinale, the self-styled atheist who owned the *capozelleria* and *pizzeria* where Papa went every Saturday night to eat a snack and play Three Sevens. Once or twice a year Papa took me along. I enjoyed eating the *pizza,* it's rubbery cheese stretching to arm's length and then snapping, but the *capozella,* lamb's head, was something else. I couldn't even look at the halved head in the plate, let alone eat it. I used to watch with a sickening fascination as Papa ate the whole thing—meat, brains, and eyes —right down to the dry bone, sucking with such gusto and relish that it turned my stomach.

After two servings of *capozella* and a large *pizza,* washed down with a soda bottle filled with wine, Papa and Bruno settled down to their card game. Between hands, while Papa shuffled, Bruno indoctrinated him with his eclectic and mixed-up interpretations of Roberto Ingersolle, Carlo Marze, and Nature. Bruno had two children and he used to boast to everyone who came into the store that they were not baptized. One afternoon I heard Mrs. Cardinale tell Mama that she had had them secretly baptized, and that if Bruno ever found out, he would kill her, or what was much worse, divorce her. Mrs. Cardinale sympathized with Mama; she had lived with "Nature" for fifteen years.

"Nature, Nature, Nature!" Papa was saying, winding up his case.

Mama turned with her hands still pressed tight against her ears, and ran into Nonno's bedroom. Papa followed her, yelling, "Nature, Nature, Nature!"

When I got to Nonno's room, Nonno was lying in bed with his eyes open, staring vacantly ahead, while Papa passed his hand back and forth before his eyes. Nonno didn't flinch or bat an eyelash.

"Nonno," Mama said, "you want something?"

"Where'sa my pipe?" Nonno said.

"On the rocka chair," Mamma said. "Joey, get."

I got. When I returned with the pipe and tobacco, Papa took them from me and began to pack the bowl with the dry, crumbled shreds of Italian cigars.

"I'ma hear blind men no like smoke," Papa said.

"*E possibile,*" Nonno said.

Papa put the pipe stem into Nonno's mouth and struck a match to the tobacco, which crackled like burning twigs and smelled like burning garbage. Papa watched the expression on Nonno's face with a curious interest. "Well," he said, after Nonno was settled back and puffing away contentedly.

"*Grazie,*" Nonno said.

"You like?" Papa said.

"*Si,*" Nonno said, and blew a cloud of smoke to the ceiling.

"Doctors," Papa said, strengthening his argument, "say blind men no like smoke."

"I like," said Nonno.

"If you canna see the smoke, what's the use to smoke?"

"I like," Nonno said.

"If you blind," Papa said, bending down close to him, "why you no call Dr. Capolongo?"

Nonno shrugged his shoulders and puffed his pipe.

Papa turned on Mama. "*If* he'sa blind, why you no call Dr. Capolongo?"

"Oh, Patsy," Mama said. She regarded Dr. Capolongo as another irreverent tinkerer who, like Bruno Cardinale, was sure to wind up Downstairs.

"No, oh Patsy!" Papa yelled. "Why you no call Dr. Capolongo?"

Mama walked to the other side of the bed and adjusted the dusty yellow palms that were arranged in bows around the crucifix. Papa pursued her, the question still burning in his eyes, "Why?"

Mama turned to face Papa, defiantly. "Because is a waste money, that's why!"

"Waste money!" Papa shrieked, throwing his hands wildly in the air. "To go movapitch two times a week, you no waste money! To put a quarter the collecsh every Sunday, you no waste money! To lighta the candles f' you mothe' who'sa dead twenty years and canna even see the candles burn—that's no waste money!"

"Patsy, no talk about my mothe'," Mama said, crossing herself quickly.

"Candles! She no could see if the whole church wasa burn!"

Mama crossed herself twice.

"Well, I'ma go get Dr. Capolongo," Papa said, and stormed out of the room, sneering on the way out at Nonno, who just lay there smoking, and maybe wishing he was deaf besides.

3

After supper we all waited in the kitchen for Dr. Capolongo
to come, except Mama, who was inside with Nonno. Papa was
in his undershirt, sitting at the table and drinking wine, scowling
after every glass in the direction of the bedroom. Concetta and
Amelia were arguing about whose night it was to dry the dishes,
and Natale and I were playing marbles with the wooden beads,
Mama's homework from Mr. Greenberg's dress house on Myrtle
Avenue. Mama was supposed to crochet covers for the wooden
beads, and was to be paid so much a dozen, but there were so
many interruptions, so many meals to cook, so many clothes to
wash, so many neighbors to visit, and so many movies to see,
that Mama never got past the first dozen. It was the same thing
with the sewing machine Papa bought for her; the only thing
that ever came out of it was a pair of bloomers for Amelia, but
it was a godsend to Mrs. Bianchi, who made shirts, dresses, and
even suits for her family.

It was nearly eight o'clock when Dr. Capolongo knocked on
the door. Papa jumped up from his chair, pulled his pants over
his belly, and opened the door. He greeted the doctor effusively.

"Ah! Dr. Capolongo! Come in, come in! Give me you hat."

"My wife tells me you called this afternoon," Dr. Capolongo
said, looking around the room.

"Who is it this time?"

"Nonno," Papa said.

"What seems to be the matter?"

"Ah! You see."

Papa was hanging the doctor's hat on the closet door when
Mama came in, wearing her black Sunday dress and carrying the
picture of St. Joseph rolled up under her arm.

"How are you, Mrs. Esposito?" Dr. Capolongo said, smiling
at Mama.

"Good, thanga you," Mama said without looking at him. To Papa she said, "I'ma take the pitch San Giuseppe back to Sister Carmela," and went out, stomping angrily down the stairs.

"What's the matter with her?" Dr. Capolongo asked, looking after her with a puzzled expression on his face.

"*Niente, niente,*" Papa said, and led Dr. Capolongo into Nonno's bedroom.

Natale and I resumed our game with the wooden marbles, while Concetta and Amelia sat at the table, cutting out pictures of their favorite stars. About fifteen minutes later, when I was knuckling down to a tough shot behind the drain pipe of the washtub, Papa and Dr. Capolongo came in again.

"It's a very unusual case. The stroke seems to have impaired the optic nerve only—"

Papa couldn't understand any of this, and asked impatiently, "But he'sa blind?"

"Oh, yes," said Dr. Capolongo.

"You sure?" said Papa.

"Well, of course."

"How long is gonna be?"

"It's hard to say. It may be a week, a month, a year. But he must have absolute rest. Keep him propped up so that the pressure on the brain is drawn away, and"—Dr. Capolongo hung up his sentence while he wrote on his pad—"give him this before each meal." Papa took the prescription, looked at it as though he knew what he was reading, and then gave the doctor three dollars.

"Call me in a couple of days and let me know how he's doing," Dr. Capolongo said.

"Dr. Capolongo," Papa said, with the tone of a man who is still bothered by something. "Blind men smoke?"

"What makes you ask?" Dr. Capolongo asked.

"Blind men smoke?" Papa repeated, trying to look wise and mysterious.

"Well, offhand I'm not familiar with the statistics," Dr. Capolongo began.

"You no know," Papa interrupted.

"No, I don't," Dr. Capolongo said.

"I know." Papa looked at the doctor levelly.

"Well, that's fine," said Dr. Capolongo, putting on his hat.

"I tell you, Dr. Capolongo," Papa said.

"Some other time. I've got a very urgent call to make. Well, good night, Mr. Esposito," he said, and he waved his black bag into the room and went out. Papa closed the door after him and muttered, "Fake! Everybody's fake!"

4

It was nearly ten o'clock when Mama got back. She had a big package under her arm, and without saying a word to Papa, she went right into Nonno's bedroom. Papa, who was sitting on the window ledge, fanning himself with a copy of the *Progresso,* announced angrily, "Everybody go to bed!"

"Aw gee," Natale whined, but Papa cut him off with a quick motion for his strap.

There was no light in our room, but the moon was bright, so Natale and I wrestled until he got so tired from being pinned down that he went to sleep. I tried to sleep, but it was too hot. I tossed and turned and finally gave it up and folded my hands under my head and looked up at the ceiling. It was so hot that even the water pipe was sweating.

I was beginning to get hungry, and had just about decided to look in the icebox for some *capocollo* or *prosciutto,* when I heard Mama get up and go to Nonno's room. I jumped out of bed and stood in the open doorway, looking down the dark corridor.

"Joey," Mama called in a whisper.

I went towards Nonno's room, where Mama's voice came from, and when I got closer I saw her standing outside the door, waiting to go in.

"Joey," Mama said, "me and you pray f' Nonno."

Mama felt that since I was an altar boy, and that since next month I would receive *la cresima* Confirmation, my prayers might carry some extra weight. It was sound reasoning, but I was hungry.

"Can't I get something to eat first?"

"After," Mama said, and opened the door.

When we stepped inside, the first thing I saw was a two-foot statue on the table next to the bed with a two-foot candle burning on each side of it. It was a statue of a woman saint, the eyes closed and looking down at a plate she held in her hand. In the center of the plate were two eyeballs. The eyes in the plate reminded me of Papa eating *capozella,* and I began to get sick.

"That's the statue of Santa Lucia," Mama explained in Italian. "She's the patron saint of the eyes. Sister Carmela gave it to me."

"That's Saint Lucy?" I asked horror-stricken, pointing at the statue.

"No point!" Mama said, slapping down my finger. "You give us bad luck."

Nonno groaned and turned over, pulling the bed sheet over his shoulder, so that we could only see the back of his head. Mama shushed me and knelt down quietly in front of the statue. I knelt down beside her. It was hot enough as it was, but with two candles burning right next to us it was intolerable. I fidgeted and sweated and tugged at my union suit, which clung to me intimately and wetly.

"*Commenze,*" Mama said, clasping her hands and closing her eyes. I did the same thing, only every so often I peeked up at Mama, whose lips were moving in prayer. I don't know what prayers she used, but I alternated an "Our Father" with a "Hail Mary." They might not have been the most appropriate prayers, having nothing to do with blindness, but they were the only prayers I knew, except for the Act of Contrition, which was out of the question.

Along about the tenth or twentieth "Our Father," Nonno suddenly groaned again. Mama opened her eyes. She looked at Nonno first, and then at the statue. Then she froze, her eyes staring fixedly ahead. I followed her eyes, turning my head slowly and fearfully. Then I froze. *There on Saint Lucy's cheek was a big tear.* Open-mouthed, Mama and I watched as the tear started to roll slowly down past her lips, past her chin, stopped there for a second, and then fell, making a tiny splash in the plate containing the two eyes.

"Joey," Mama said in an awed whisper, as though she had just seen God. I wanted to say something but the words stuck in my throat. I started to get up, but Mama forced me down. "We pray some more. *Commenze.*"

Just then Nonno sat up in bed. "Whatch you two do?"

"Oh, Nonno!" Mama said.

"I wanna sleep," Nonno said, slumping back into bed.

"Santa Lucia!" Mama screamed.

Nonno jumped in the bed and Mama seized him by his nightshirt. "Nonno, how you know is two of us?"

"Because I'ma see two, that'sa how."

"You see, Nonno?" Mama cried.

"I joosta say," Nonno said. "What Joey's do in undwear?"

"A miracle! A miracle!" Mama shouted, running into the hall, through the house, pounding on every door and waking everybody up. I could hear Papa grumbling and cursing, and the children following Mama with questioning, terrified squeals. When Mama came back she was followed by Papa, barefooted and pulling his strap around his pants, and by Concetta, Amelia, and Natale, who stood in the doorway, rubbing their eyes.

"What the hell'sa matter?" Papa said.

"A miracle! A miracle!" Mama kept shouting, hugging and kissing first Saint Lucy and then Nonno, who was trying to go back to sleep. This was Mama's victory celebration, her answer to the Cardinales and Capolongos, the supremacy of faith over fact, the triumph of the prayer over the pill.

"You craze?" Papa said, shaking her by the shoulders.

"Patsy, Nonno can see!"

"What?"

"Nonno can see! He's no blind!"

"Ah!" Papa shouted, like the time he sneaked up on me and caught me smoking. "So Nonno can see! I told you he'sa fake!"

"No fake," Mama said. "It's Santa Lucia."

"Santa Lucia!" Papa scoffed. "He'sa fake all along."

"Patsy, me and Joey pray—"

"Pray, no pray! What'sa *differenza*?" Papa said, walking around Nonno. "So you wanna stay the bed?" Papa said to Nonno, who was already beginning to snore. "You wanna waiter f' you hands and foots? But you canna fool Patsy, eh Nonno?"

"Patsy, you craze," Mama said.

"Sure, I'ma craze," Papa said.

"Even Dr. Capolongo," Mama said, quoting the devil, "say he'sa blind. Patsy, you craze."

"You even foola the doctor, eh Nonno?" Papa said.

Nonno answered Papa with a loud snore.

"Fake!" Papa said. "You no foola me! Now you wanna fake you sleep," he scoffed, shaking Nonno violently. Nonno woke up for an instant, shook Papa's hands off, and went back to sleep.

"Sleep, sleep!" Papa said, hitching up his strap. "You no foola me."

"Patsy, was a miracle! I swear my dead mothe'!" Mama said, making a spit cross on her neck.

"Shutupa miracle," Papa said, raising the back of his hand. "Everything is miracle with you!"

"Was a miracle!" Mama shouted. "Me and Joey pray, and joosta when the tear came outta Santa Lucia and fall ona the plate, Nonno open' his eyes—and no more blind."

Papa just looked at her, that sorry look he reserves for raving lunatics.

"Ask Joey," Mama said.

"Mama's right, Papa. It was a miracle," I said.

From the way he looked at me, you'd think I had told him that the earth was flat. From then on, Papa gave up any hope that I would be a doctor like he wanted me to be; I was too much like Mama.

"*Farfallone*—Snotnose!" he called me. "Go to sleep, everybody. Go on, go on," he said, shooing us all out of the room.

"*Farfallone!*" he shouted after me.

After pushing Natale to his side of the bed, I got in and pulled the cover over my head, afraid that if I looked at anything, another miracle would happen, that the natural laws would be suspended, and that I would go flying off into space. Under the sheet, sweating and panic-stricken, I recited my entire repertoire of prayers to ward off the impending disaster. The Act of Contrition seemed the most appropriate this time, so I said it over and over again. "O my God, I am heartily sorry. . . ."

It was getting hotter and hotter under the sheet, but I counted twenty-five Acts of Contrition before I finally kicked the cover off. I breathed deeply a few times and looked up at the ceiling. The water pipe was still sweating.

Far away I could hear Mama and Papa still arguing, and the last thing I remember, before dozing off, was Mama shouting to Papa, "A miracle! A miracle!" and Papa shouting to Mama, "Fake! Fake!"

But Mama was right, because I saw it myself.

SONG WITHOUT WORDS

FRANK O'CONNOR

*Unlike many of the contemporary stories of monastic life which are
content to skim the surface of reality, this story comes to grips with the
central problem of religious life: the temptation of the monk who, after
he has heroically given up "his chance of a wife and kids, his home and
family, his friends and a job," attaches himself to some trifle. "One little
thing to remind us of what we gave up," says Brother Michael bitterly;
". . . I suppose we all have our little hiding hole, if the truth was known,
but as small as it is, the whole world is in it."*

*This is, however, neither a bitter nor a solemn story. It is the way of
Frank O'Connor to adjust his palette at the angle of humor and to lay on
the colors with gusty, earthy laughter. "Song Without Words" is a very
funny story, besides being deeply significant. Frank O'Connor is one of
the best short story writers at the present time, very frequently making
use of various aspects of Irish Catholic life. He was born in Cork, 1903.
His name is Michael O'Donovan, but under the pseudonym of Frank
O'Connor he has published several novels, verse, a study of Michael Collins
and the Irish Revolution, and several volumes of short stories, the best of
which are* Crab Apple Jelly *and* The Common Chord.

Even if there were only two men left in the world and both of
them to be saints, they wouldn't be happy even then. One of them
would be bound to try and improve the other. That is the nature
of things.

There were two men one time in the big monastery near our
place called Brother Arnold and Brother Michael. In private life
Brother Arnold was a postman, but as he had a great name as a
cattle doctor they put him in charge of the monastery cows. He
had the sort of face you'd expect to see advertising somebody's
tobacco; a big, innocent, good-humoured face with a pair of blue
eyes that always had a twinkle in them. Of course, by the rule

51

he was supposed to look sedate and go round in a composed and measured way, but wherever Brother Arnold went his eyes went along with him, to see what devilment would he see on the way, and the eyes would give a twinkle and the hands would slip out of the long white sleeves and he'd be beckoning and doing sign talk on his fingers till further orders.

Now, one day it happened that he was looking for a bottle of castor oil and he suddenly remembered that he'd lent it to Brother Michael in the stables. Brother Michael was a fellow he didn't get on too well with at all; a dour, silent sort of man that kept himself to himself. He was a man of no great appearance, with a mournful, wizened little face and a pair of weak, red-rimmed eyes—for all the world the sort of man that, if you shaved off his beard, clapped a bowler hat on his head and a fag in his mouth, wouldn't need any other reference to get a job in a stable.

There wasn't any sign of him around the stable yard, but that was only natural because he wouldn't be wanted till the other monks came back from the fields, so Brother Arnold banged in the stable door and went to look for the bottle himself. He didn't see the bottle but he saw something else he'd rather not have seen, and that was Brother Michael, hiding in one of the horse-boxes. He was standing against the partition, hoping he wouldn't be noticed, with something hidden behind his back and the look of a little boy that's just been caught at the jam. Something told Brother Arnold he was the most unwelcome man in the world at that minute. He got red and waved his hand by way of showing that he hadn't seen anything and that if he had it was none of his business, and away with him out and back to his own quarters.

It came as a bit of a shock to him. You could see plain enough that the other man was up to something nasty and you could hardly help wondering what it was. It was funny; he always noticed the same thing when he was in the world; it was the quiet, sneaky fellows that were always up to mischief. In chapel he looked at Brother Michael and he got the impression that Brother Michael was also looking at him; a sneaky sort of look to make sure he wouldn't be spotted. Next day again when they met in the yard he caught Brother Michael looking at him, and he gave him back a cold look and nod as much as to say he had him taped.

The day after Brother Michael beckoned him to come over to the stable for a minute, as if there was one of the horses sick. Brother Arnold knew well it wasn't one of the horses, but he went all the same. He was curious to know what explanation he would be offered. Brother Michael closed the door carefully after him and then leaned back against the jamb of the door with his legs crossed and his hands behind his back, a real foxy look. Then he nodded in the direction of the horse-box as much as to say "Remember the day you saw me in there?" Brother Arnold nodded. He wasn't likely to forget it. So then Brother Michael put his hand up his sleeve and held out a folded newspaper. Brother Arnold grinned as much as to say "Are you letting on now that that was all you were up to, reading a paper?" but the other man pressed it into his hands. He opened it without any great curiosity, thinking it might be some local paper the man got for the news from home. He glanced at the name of it, and then a light broke on him. His whole face lit up as if you'd switched an electric torch on behind, and at last he burst out laughing. He couldn't help himself. Brother Michael didn't laugh, but he gave a dry little cackle which was as near as he ever got to a laugh. The name of the paper was *The Irish Racing News*. Brother Michael pointed to a heading about the Curragh and then pointed at himself. Brother Arnold shook his head and gave him another look as if he was waiting for another good laugh out of him. Brother Michael scratched his head for something to show what he meant. He was never much good at the sign language. Then he picked up the sweeping brush and straddled it. He pulled up his skirts; he

stretched his left hand out, holding the handle of the brush and
began flogging the air behind him, with a grim look on his
leathery little puss. And then Brother Arnold nodded and nodded
and put up his thumbs to show he understood. He saw now that
the reason Brother Michael behaved so queerly was because
he read racing papers on the sly, and he read racing papers
on the sly because in private life he was a jockey on the Curragh.

He was still laughing away like mad with his blue eyes dancing,
and then he remembered all the things he thought about Brother
Michael and bowed his head and beat his breast by way of asking
pardon. After that he took another look at the paper. A mis-
chievous twinkle came into his eyes and he pointed the paper at
himself. Brother Michael pointed back at him, a bit puzzled.
Brother Arnold chuckled and nodded and stuffed the paper up
his own sleeve. Then Brother Michael winked and gave the
thumbs-up sign, and in that slow cautious way of his he went
down the stable and reached up to the top of the wall where the
stable roof sloped down. That was his hiding hole. He took down
several more and gave them to Brother Arnold.

For the rest of the day Brother Arnold was in the best of
humour. He winked and smiled at everyone round the farm till
they were all wondering what the joke was. All that evening and
long after he went to his cubicle, he rubbed his hands and giggled
with delight every time he thought of it; it gave him a warm,
mellow feeling as if his heart had expanded to embrace all
humanity.

It wasn't till next morning that he had a chance of looking at
the papers himself. He took them out and spread them on a rough
desk under a feeble electric light bulb high up in the roof. It was
four years since last he'd seen a paper of any sort, and then it was
only a bit of a local newspaper that one of the carters had
wrapped about a bit of bread and butter. Brother Arnold had

palmed it as neatly as any conjurer; hidden it away in his desk
and studied it as if it was a bit of a lost Greek play. There was
nothing on it but a bit of a County Council wrangle about the
appointment of seven warble-fly inspectors, but by the time he
was finished with it he knew it by heart. So he didn't just glance
at the papers the way a man would in the train to pass the time.
He nearly ate them. Blessed bits of words like fragments of tunes
coming to him out of a past life; paddocks and point-to-points
and two-year-olds; and there he was in the middle of a race-
course crowd on a spring day, with silver streamers of light floating down the sky like heavenly bunting. He was a handsome fellow in those days. He had only to close his eyes and he could see
the refreshment tent again, with the golden light leaking like
spilt honey through the rents in the canvas, and there was the
little girl he used to be sparking, sitting on an upturned lemonade
box. "Ah, Paddy," she said, "sure there's bound to be racing in
Heaven!" She was fast; too fast for Brother Arnold, who was a
quiet-going sort of fellow, and he never got over the shock when
he found out that she was running another fellow all the time.
But now, all he could remember of her was her smile, and afterwards, whenever his eyes met Brother Michael's he longed to give
him a hearty slap on the back and say "Michael, there's bound to
be racing in Heaven," and then a grin spread over his big sunny
face, and Brother Michael, without once losing that casual,
melancholy air, replied with a wall-faced flicker of the horny eye-
lid; a tick-tack man's signal; a real expressionless, horsy look of
complete understanding.

One day Brother Michael came in and took out a couple of
papers. On one of them he pointed to the horses he'd marked;
on the other to the horses that came up. He didn't show any sign
of jubilation. He just winked, a leathery sort of a wink, and
Brother Arnold gaped as he saw the list of winners. It filled him
with wonder to think that where so many clever people lost, a

simple little monk, living hundreds of miles away, could foresee it all. The more he thought of it, the more excited he got. He went to the door, reached up his long arm and took down a loose stone from the wall above it. Brother Michael nodded slowly three or four times, as much as to say "Well, you're a caution!" Brother Arnold grinned broadly. He might have been saying "That's nothing." Then he took down a bottle and handed it to Brother Michael. The jockey gave him one look; his face didn't change, but he took out the cork and sniffed. Still his face never changed. Then all at once he went to the door, gave a quick glance up and a quick glance down and raised the bottle to his mouth. The beer was strong; it made him redden and cough. He cleaned the neck of the bottle with his sleeve before he gave it back. A shudder went through him and his little eyes watered as he watched Brother Arnold's throttle moving on well-oiled hinges. The big man put the bottle back in its hiding-place and beckoned to Brother Michael that he could go there himself whenever he liked. Brother Michael shook his head but Brother Arnold nodded earnestly. His fingers moved like lightning while he explained how a farmer whose cow he had cured left a bottle in the yard for him every week.

Now, Brother Michael's success made Brother Arnold want to try his hand, and whenever Brother Michael gave him a copy of a racing paper with his own selections marked, Brother Arnold gave it back with his, and then they contented themselves as well as they could till the results turned up, three or four days late. It was a new lease of life to the little jockey, for what comfort is it to a man even if he has all the winners when there isn't a soul in the whole world he can tell? He felt now if only he could have a bob each way on a horse, he'd never ask any more of life. Unfortunately, he hadn't a bob. That put Brother Arnold thinking. He was a resourceful chap, and it was he who invented the dockets, valued for so many Hail Marys. The man who lost had to pay up in prayers for the other man's intention. It was an ingenious scheme and it worked admirably.

At first Brother Arnold had a run of luck. But it wasn't for nothing that the other man had been a jockey. He was too hardy to make a fool of himself, even over a few Hail Marys, and everything he did was carefully planned. Brother Arnold began carefully enough, but the moment he struck it lucky, he began to gamble wildly. Brother Michael had often seen it happen on the Curragh, and he remembered the fate of the men it happened to. Fellows he'd known with big houses and cars were now cadging drinks on the streets of Dublin. "Aha, my lad," he said to himself, thinking of his companion, "God was very good to you the day he called you in here where you couldn't do harm to yourself or those belonged to you."

Which, by the way, was quite uncalled for, because in the world Brother Arnold's only weakness was for a drop of stout, and it never did him any harm, but Brother Michael was rather given to a distrust of human nature; the sort of man who goes looking for a moral in everything, even when there's no moral in it. He tried to make Brother Arnold take a proper interest in the scientific side of betting, but the man seemed to take it all as a great joke, a flighty sort of fellow. He bet more and more wildly, with that foolish good-natured grin on his face, and after a while Brother Michael found himself being owed the deuce of a lot of prayers. He didn't like that either. It gave him scruples of conscience and finally turned him against betting in any shape or form. He tried to get Brother Arnold to drop it, but Brother Arnold only looked hurt and a little indignant, like a child you've told to stop his game. Brother Michael had that weakness on his conscience too. It suggested that he was getting too attached to Brother Arnold, as in fact he was. He had to admit it. There was something warm and friendly about the man that you couldn't help liking.

Then one day he went in to Brother Arnold and found him
with a pack of cards in his hand. They were a very old pack that
had more than served their time in some farmer's house. They
gave Brother Michael a turn, just to look at them. Brother Arnold
made the gesture of dealing them out and Brother Michael
shook his head. Brother Arnold blushed and bit his lip, but he
persisted. All the doubts Brother Michael had been having for
weeks turned to conviction. This was the primrose path with a
vengeance; one thing leading to another. Brother Arnold grinned
and shuffled the deck; Brother Michael, biding his time, cut for
deal and Brother Arnold won. He dealt two hands of five and
showed the five of hearts as trump. Just because he was still waiting for a sign, Brother Michael examined his own hand. His face
got grimmer. It wasn't the sort of sign he had been expecting, but
it was a sign all the same: four hearts all in a bunch; the ace, the
jack, two other trumps and the three of spades. All he had to do
was surrender the spade and pick up the five of trumps, and there
he was with an unbeatable hand. Was that luck? Was that coin-
cidence, or was it the Old Boy himself, taking a hand and trying
to draw him deeper down into the mud? He liked to find the
moral in things, and the moral in this was as plain as a pikestaff
though it went to his heart to admit it. He was a lonesome, melancholy little man and the horses had meant a lot to him in his bad
spells. At times it seemed as if they were the only thing that kept
him from going clean dotty. How he going to face maybe twenty
or thirty years more of life, never knowing what horses were running or what jocks were up—Derby Day, Punchestown, Leopards-
town and the Curragh, all going by and he knowing no more of
them than if he was dead?

"O Lord," he thought bitterly, "a fellow gives up the whole
world for You, his chance of a wife and kids, his home and his
family, his friends and his job, and goes off to a bare mountain
where he can't even tell his troubles to the man alongside him;

and still he keeps something back. One little thing to remind him of what he gave up. With me 'twas the horses and with this man 'twas the sup of beer, and I daresay there's fellows inside that have a bit of girl's hair hidden somewhere they can go and look at it now and again. I suppose we all have our little hiding hole, if the truth was known, but as small as it is, the whole world is in it, and bit by bit it grows on us again till the day You find us out."

Brother Arnold was waiting for him to play. He gave a great sigh and put his hand on the deck. Brother Arnold looked at it and then looked at him. Brother Michael idly took away the spade and added the heart, and still Brother Arnold couldn't see. Then Brother Michael shook his head and pointed down through the floor. Brother Arnold bit his lip again as though he were on the point of crying, threw down his own hand and walked away to the other end of the cow-house. Brother Michael left him so for a few moments. He could see the struggle that was going on in the man; he could almost hear the Old Boy whispering in his ear that he, Brother Michael, was only an old woman (Brother Michael had heard that before); that life was long and that a man might as well be dead and buried as not have some little thing to give him an innocent bit of amusement—the sort of plausible whisper that put many a man on the gridiron. He knew that however hard it was now, Brother Arnold would be thankful to him in the next world. "Brother Michael," he'd say, "I don't know what I'd ever have done without the example you gave me."

Then Brother Michael went up and touched him gently on the shoulder. He pointed to the bottle, the racing paper and the cards in turn. Brother Arnold heaved a terrible sigh but he nodded. They gathered them up between them, the cards and the bottle and the papers, hid them under their habits to avoid all occasion of scandal and went off to confess their crimes to the Prior.

THE MIRACLE OF TEPAYAC

JOHN STEINBECK

Told with a beautiful simplicity by one of America's top-ranking novelists, is this story of the manifestation of our Lady of Guadalupe. Steinbeck's writing has been consistently marked by compassion for the poor and the underprivileged. Most congenial to his natural sympathies, therefore, were Juan Diego's status as a poor man and Our Lady's words to him, "I have seen the suffering of your people and I have come to them through you." With not a touch of the sentimentalism which is characteristic of his better-known novels, and none of the naturalism which has marred them, he has here woven the facts of the miracle of Tepayac into a perfect story.

John Steinbeck won the Pulitzer prize in 1940 for the Grapes of Wrath. *Among his better known books are* Tortilla Flat *and* Of Mice and Men. The Pearl *can be recommended without reservations.*

The Spaniards came to Mexico with war and pestilence and ruin but they brought also the faith of Jesus Christ and His Mother Mary. Many of the Indian people were baptized, and among the first of them Juan Diego and his wife Maria Lucia. They were humble people and they lived in the little town of Cuautitlan, to the north of Mexico City.

For many years they had lived together in felicity. They had no children, so that their dependence on each other was very great. Their dwelling was a one-room hut of mud bricks, and they tended a garden and they were happy. Then one dawn Maria Lucia was feverish and at mid-morning her eyes were swollen and her breath labored. At noon she died.

They had lived in love, and Juan Diego was lost in his sorrow. He had no relatives but the uncle named Juan Bernardino who had cared for him in his youth. Now that his wife was dead, Juan

Diego took to wandering over the hills, spending his strength the way a grieving man does. In the night he was wakeful and restless.

It is told that one December day he arose before the dawn and walked through the frost of the harsh stony land until he came to the hill of Tepayac. Just as the day was breaking he climbed the hill and there came to him, first softly, and then louder, the sound of many birds' songs.

The songs grew to an earthly music so that he stopped and wondered, for the music seemed to come from everywhere. He looked up the hill and the dawn light was brighter than any he had ever seen; the music swelled and echoed about him.

Juan Diego went quickly toward the light that shone from the hilltop and a voice from the music said, "Juan Diego, come here."

In a moment his grief was gone and the fullness of beauty was in him. The path up the hill was lined with mesquite and cactus and sharp with stones. He came half running to the brow. The music swelled and retired. And he saw the Queen of Heaven standing in the rocky path with the light around her, so that the stones gathered it and glittered like jewels. And the dark mesquite was bright.

For a moment Juan Diego gazed at Her, and then he backed away in shyness and in fear.

The vision said, "Juan Diego, my son, where do you walk?"

And he answered, "My Lady, I was walking in sorrow to find peace for my heart, but now I am not sad."

The Lady said, "Do you know who I am?"

And he answered, "I think—I know."

She spoke quietly in the light, "I am Mary, the Mother of Jesus. And I wish that here on this bleak hill a temple may be built in witness of my love for your people. I have seen the suffering of your people and I have come to them through you."

M C F

D

Juan Diego tried to speak, but she silenced him:

"You must go to the bishop in Mexico and tell him that here by the hill of Tepayac my temple must be built, from which my love may go out to all of your people."

Juan Diego bowed. "I will go, My Lady," he said, and as he spoke, the light faded into ordinary day and the stones were stones and the mesquite black. The Lady was gone.

Juan Diego went slowly down the path, and the world was pale after his vision. He took the north way through the marshes where the tall reeds grew and his road was the stone causeway, for the Valley of Mexico was a broad lake, and the city stood in the midst of it.

Juan Diego was filled with terror now. He had never traveled to the city in all of his life. After his mud village the growing buildings and the new churches were things of wonder to him. He asked his directions many times before he came to the palace of the bishop, a lordly building, magnificent, new. Humbly Juan Diego asked to see the bishop.

The bishop of Mexico was a scholarly man. From the first he had defended the Indians against the brutal soldiers and the nobles of Spain and it was his custom to hear anyone who came to him. When Juan Diego was led to his chamber, the bishop expected a complaint or a petition. Many tragedies passed before him every day.

Juan Diego looked at the splendor of the room. He who had never seen anything but coarse cactus-fiber cloth, saw crimson velvet. It was a room of carved wood and colored plaster, instead of the mud walls of his experience.

The bishop looked up as the silence continued. "Yes, my son?" he said impatiently.

Suddenly the words poured out of Juan Diego. "The Queen of Heaven!" he cried. "I saw Her in a pool of light on the hill of

Tepayac. She told me you must build a temple to Her by the hill."

The bishop smiled wearily, "Why there?"

"To be a sign to our people," Juan Diego cried in triumph. "She is ours—our own Mother."

Now the bishop frowned. "You are excited, my son," he said. "Go reflect and come back when you are calm. Go with God!"

His heart heavy with failure, Juan Diego went blindly in the evening to the hill of Tepayac, for his vision was fading and he was afraid the bishop had spoken the truth, and that his grieving had turned his mind to dreams. As he came to the hilltop the night was falling. The light sprang up and the Lady was before him again.

Juan Diego fell to his knees in joy, for he knew now that he was right. But he felt weakness, and he cried, "Holy Mother, send someone of importance. Send some lord, or better, shed your light on the bishop himself."

Her voice was imperious. "Juan Diego, I have chosen you for a reason to be understood only gradually, but it will be stronger, because everyone will find the reason for himself. I have many messengers, but I have chosen you. Juan Diego, my son, go as my messenger and order the bishop to do as I have said. Say to him that Holy Mary Ever Virgin, Mother of God, has sent you. That you and no other are the messenger."

The light about Her flared and the whole valley glowed and sparkled, and then it was dark, and Juan Diego was alone on the desert hill of Tepayac. He went down the path to his mud house and he washed himself and ate a little and lay down on his mat, but sleep would not come to him, for when he closed his eyes he saw the light and the beauty again. . . .

Before dawn he went again over the marshes and over the

north causeway. As he approached the city he heard the church bells ringing, for it was Sunday.

The bishop had many duties on a Sunday, and Juan Diego squatted in a corner waiting. Again and again he demanded entrance, but the servants refused him. Now Juan Diego's message burned in him and he shouted his demands. Tears were in his eyes and the fury of frustration in his heart. The bishop heard him shouting and quietly gave word to let him in.

Juan Diego fell to the floor before the throne. "Our Lady says you must build the temple!" he cried. "She says it is Her wish. Do you hear? She orders the temple to be built in the valley by Tepayac."

The bishop said sternly, "You are ill. You are unbalanced." Juan Diego shouted, "Our Lady orders you!"

The bishop sat quietly thinking, and then he said with calculation, "I will tell you . . . words are empty, and men sometimes see things that are untrue. Ask for a sign beyond words. Then we will know beyond doubt. Now go."

"What sign?" Juan Diego demanded.

The bishop smiled and signaled, and his servants held Juan Diego's elbows and led him away.

When he was gone the bishop called two men and said, "Follow Juan Diego. See where he goes. And see that he does not hurt himself nor any others."

The men followed Juan Diego and at last they came to a ravine before the valley below Tepayac, and a rare mist covered Juan Diego from their sight.

They could not find him anywhere. At last they returned to the city and told their story. The bishop sat alone and he was troubled, and Juan Diego remained in his thoughts.

The cloud moved along with Juan Diego and it grew luminous, and in the midst of it the Lady appeared. In his weariness Juan

Diego bowed and he said, "The bishop wants a sign. He will not believe words. But he would not say what sign."

The Lady's voice was sweet to the weary man. "Go to your rest," she said, "and in the morning come again and I will give you a sign."

Then Juan Diego went toward his house. But on the way a neighbor came to him saying, "Your uncle is dying of the fever called cocolxtle, the same that destroyed your wife."

Juan Diego went toward his uncle's house and found breath. His uncle whispered to him, "Go to Father de Grado. He knows curing herbs. And if they fail he will give me the rites of the church."

Juan Diego went to find help for his uncle. His promise to the Holy Mother worried him, but it seemed good to him to have a humble duty to do, for Her mission had frightened him. The emotion of it had wearied him, for one must bring something to great beauty, and it is a burden on a man to be a great man. He thought: I will not take the short cut over the hill of Tepayac. I will go the longer way around the hill and then the Holy Mother will not see me, and I can put aside the duty. He said to himself: *She could not blame me for trying to help uncle.*

He took the longer path and he felt the mesquite bushes pulling at his cloak. His feet stumbled on the rocks in the dark way.

And suddenly the light broke around him and the Lady stood before him. In grief and shame Juan Diego knelt before Her.

"I was coming to the hill as soon as I could get help for my uncle," he said.

She replied with compassion, "You cannot go around, my son. You cannot ever go around. Particularly you. Forget your uncle. He is well now. I have made him well. Go now to the right path over the hill of Tepayac and gather what you find there."

Then Juan Diego went back to the hill path and in that deso-late place he saw roses of Castile fresh and lovely growing in a place where roses could not grow and blooming in a frosty month when roses do not bloom. In the dawn he gathered the flowers and then the Virgin was beside him, and she took the blooms from him and laid them in his cloak. "This is my sign," she said. "Go now to the bishop."

Juan Diego came to the palace and he entered carrying the roses wrapped in his cloak. The servants in the hall jeered at him, and they struck him and pulled at him to put him out of the hall. But Juan Diego guarded his cloak. "It is the sign!" he cried. "I have brought the sign from the Holy Mother!"

As they pushed him a corner of his cloak came free and they saw the roses and they were silent. One man put his hand to the flowers and he could not touch them. And then he went quietly to the door of the bishop's chamber and opened it, and Juan Diego entered.

The bishop looked at the Indian with annoyance, but Juan Diego was not afraid. "Here is the sign," he said, and released the corners of his cloak, and the roses uncrushed and unwilted fell to the floor.

And then the bishop saw the cloak of Juan Diego and he got to his knees. On the rough cactus-fiber cloak of the Indian Juan Diego was the image of the Mother of God.

At Tepayac they raised a simple hermitage on the place where She had appeared, to serve until the temple could be fashioned. And Juan Diego built a new mud house near by and planted a garden. He swept out the chapel and cared for it until he died. He was very happy. And it is possible he did not know that through his heart Our Lady of Guadalupe had become the Holy Mother of his people.

BAA-BAA, BLACK SHEEP

STEPHEN B. EARLEY

This is a story of faith. And of love. And a miracle. Its romanticism may very likely contribute more pleasure to the reader than the realism of grimmer tales. Under the pseudonym Stephen Beaupland, Reverend Stephen B. Earley, S.J., who is now with the Jesuit Missions, published this story in the Woman's Home Companion!

I've been in this navy hospital a little over four months now. War, they say, makes strange bed-fellows; and for the last four months and eight days, mine was a crazy chaplain. If somebody had told me five months ago I'd be beating out my brains to help cure a padre—I'd have laughed at him.

Doc Wilson, the house doctor, asked me to write up the affair for his records, just in case he'd ever have to go through the thing again. At first I tried to do it in formal language, official red-tape navy communications language; I had all the facts but they didn't make sense. So I'm just going to write it out in pencil as I remember it; and if someone wants to correct the mistakes later, let him do it. I know it's true, the Holy Joe knows it's true; and so does Doc Wilson. I was going to call it The Case of the Crazy Chaplain but maybe this is a better name.

I got mine at Tarawa in a TBF bomber. We went down with two five-hundred-pound bombs to wipe out a well-emplaced Jap mortar outfit; and got so close to them the radioman swore he saw gold fillings in a Jap's mouth. But we pulled out of the dive too suddenly, came out with the blood pouring out of our noses, our insides plastered up against our ribs and our heads singing like high-tension wires in a whirlwind. I got it worst. Something happened to my vocal-cords; they snapped or congealed or something; and though I could make all the motions of talking—nothing came out but a dull beastlike sound.

For a while I hoped; but after three months shuttling back and forth between doctors, electro-therapy, massages, gargles . . . after three months of that and more, I gave up. You see, I'm twenty-five. According to my identification card, I'm six-foot-one, weigh one hundred and eighty-three pounds, have brown hair and brown eyes. I'm also a lawyer, even though I never tried a case. I was engaged too. I wish you might have seen Ann Marie; she's a pert little thing, and people used to call us Mutt and Jeff. She lives in Scarsdale, in a little brown house set off from the road, with acacia trees on the sides of the path going in—at least I guess she still lives there. I haven't written to her since this happened and I didn't let anyone know where I was. A lot of good a lawyer is without a voice.

She wrote me a letter that I got in the South Pacific. I'll bet I've read it a million times. "No matter what happens to you,"—I know this line by heart—"we're going to be married. No matter what happens, Bob, I love you with all my heart." I almost wrote once from the base hospital, another time in Honolulu when somebody draped a lei around my shoulders, and once or twice from here when the dull monotony of the Pacific waves and Holy Joe's half-witted tenderness got me down—but I didn't. I couldn't seem to force myself to do it.

I came down here by bus from San Francisco. It was raining and as I walked into the foyer of the hotel which the navy has taken over for a hospital, I was lower than I had been in all my life.

"Ensign Robert Baker," I wrote on a slip and gave it to the orderly.

"What's the matter with you?" he asked incuriously, with scarcely more than a glance up.

I pointed to my throat and made my animal noises.

"Oh, a dummy," he said and I just glared at him. Well, after all, wasn't he right? "We're all filled up," he said. "How many rooms do they think we have down here?"

Of course I couldn't say any of the things I was thinking so I glared some more.

"You aren't going to be the best company in the world," he said reflectively, "and some of these lads need company. A dummy would drive them nuts. But . . . there's a lieutenant here we can't put in with anybody. He's shell-shocked, harmless but batty. Do you want to go in with him for a while till we can get a room for you?"

"Put me any place," I wrote on the card. All I wanted to do was get away—we'd make a good pair. A dummy and a nut. What difference did it make?

"The only thing is," he said, "this guy's a Holy Joe."

That did make a difference. The Holy Joes are all right and for some lads they are down-right essential. But I'm one of those people who can take religion or let it alone. And the only vision I ever had thirty thousand feet up was Ann Marie. I had my own ideas about convalescing, and the Pacific, and what happens if I should shuffle off this mortal coil. They weren't pretty ideas but after you've flown twenty or thirty missions, you sell life fairly cheap. What difference did a few days make? Maybe a batty Holy Joe would be better than a sane one.

There was no question about the fact that the navy does right by its convalescents. My room was long and low, with big French windows opening on the Pacific. The beds were walnut, box springs, and inviting. The Holy Joe's corner was piled shipshape and with one exception everything looked normal. His bed was near the door and up against the wall close to the window was a small statue of a nun. In front of it were a low candle and three roses in a drinking glass. I pointed to the statue and raised my eyes to the orderly.

"He calls it his sister, the Little Flower I think it is. But take a word of advice and don't kid him about it."

I nodded briefly. Voice or no voice, I don't need advice from an orderly. Of course as I unpacked I kept wondering what the Holy Joe would be like. And I must admit I was shocked when I saw him. He was bigger than I, and I'm not small. Black Irish, I thought. Coal-black hair and deep blue eyes, with a swell smile. Not good-looking, but honest-looking—intelligent-looking too. I figured he was between thirty-five and thirty-eight, and he must have weighed close to one hundred and ninety.

"I dropped a penny in the wishing well," he said informally; "you can have the wish, if you want." He dropped down on his bed. I didn't say anything . . . I keep writing that I didn't say anything. I couldn't say anything.

"But if you really want the wish," he said, "you can have it."

I took a piece of paper and wrote on it, "I lost my voice in a plane accident."

"I'm very glad to meet you," he said.

I suppose he was a kind of sorry sight, big fellow as he was and all; but right then I wasn't having any sympathy for anyone but myself. I buried my head in a letter I was writing, which I never expected to send.

"My name is Joe," he said coming over and sitting on my bed. "It really isn't Joe, it's Father Tom. But everyone down here calls me Joe. What's your name?"

I flipped my identification card over to him. It's easier that way. He studied it very seriously. Finally I looked at him again and saw he was reading it upside down. I turned it around and he read it aloud.

"That certainly is a nice name," he said. "I hope you're a Catholic."

I just shook my head.

"Too bad, but I'm sure my Little Sister won't mind. Of course if she minds, you'll have to go. This is really her room, her chapel, you know." And with that he got up and started a low conversation with the statue of the nun. I never did get used to those conversations, though Lord knows they happened often enough. Finally he turned back toward me.

"It's all right. She says it's all right," he said. "And I'll pray that she will drop a rose petal from heaven for your voice. If she sends you a rose petal, you will be cured no matter what is wrong with you. Did you see the Song of Bernadette?"

Just then they rang mess and I was certainly tickled to death to get out of the room.

It was at mess two days later that I got another slant at Holy Joe. Of course there's always a certain amount of shoving in the food lines, though usually in officers' mess it's quite gentle. But here and there you find a boor; this one wore the Great Lakes campaign ribbon, meaning of course he'd never been out of the States.

Generally the Holy Joe was so interested in telling someone about his Little Sister that he'd hold up the chow line and you'd just have to shove him gently along. Only the boor from Great Lakes didn't see it that way. He made a couple of remarks, and really shoved Joe. I can't tell you exactly about the eyes of men who have served in the Asiatic theater; but there's something about them that gives you the creeps. I saw a lieutenant who had served in that theater turn around quickly. There was silence in the line almost immediately and though his voice was low, its distinctness carried right through the room.

"I wouldn't do that again, chum," he said, "I wouldn't do that." And there was that funny look in his eyes that made the Great Lakes hero back water. Two others put Joe back in line, served him and led him to a table. And the Great Lakes lad beat a quick exit out of there.

I sat down with a couple of fliers I know slightly. Generally I eat by myself but my curiosity was aroused. "How come?" I wrote on my pad and passed it to one of the fliers.

"He was on a cruiser that spearheaded one of the early Canal attacks. They got hit hard and lost a lot of men. A lot more lay wounded on the deck. The ship was damaged and they couldn't get out and had to lay to with all the lights doused through the night.

"Well, the way I hear the story, he worked all through the day and then kept going right through the black. He was sorting out bodies all night and helping them die, carting the injured ones below. He was all set to retire when a hit exploded right on top of him and blew him fifty feet. When he regained consciousness he was like this."

I shook my head in sympathy. "That's tough," I wrote on the card.

"Some of the doctors want to put him away," he said, "but Doc Wilson has fixed it up so that as long as he remains harmless he can stay here. He's the only nut we have. Every time he moves off the property, somebody trails him to see he doesn't get into trouble. Last time his cruiser made San Francisco they hired a couple of buses to come down to see him. And it would be awful unhealthy to get him in trouble; they're a tough outfit."

I didn't say anything. I didn't have anything against Joe—I had troubles of my own. The way I figured it, one more examination; and if they still gave me the brush-off, well, there was a lot of deep Pacific out there where a fellow could lose himself.

After mess the following morning I'd come back to my room to write another letter to Ann Marie that I'd never send. I have quite a collection of them.

The Holy Joe was kneeling in front of his statue and reading a black book. He used to read it all the time without turning the pages. Suddenly he shut the book and rose to his feet.

"Of course," he said, "of course I'll do it. I should have thought of it myself. We'll do it together."

I guess I told you that the only difficult part of living with Joe was the conversations he had with the nun. Generally he paid no attention to me, and I certainly paid none to him. But he turned round and came over to where I was sitting. "We're going to teach you to talk."

I raised my eyebrows a little and waited.

"I guess I should have thought of it before; but I don't think of things. So this morning my sister told me I should teach you, and if she says we should teach you, you are sure to learn. Isn't that wonderful?"

Teach me to talk. I'd been through that routine; I'd made my noises in some of the best navy clinics on the coast. And nothing doing. So he was going to teach me to talk! "Sorry," I wrote.

"Oh, but you must," he said, "my sister said so."

"Look, Padre," I wrote, "all I want is to be let alone. I can't talk and never will. See?"

He just smiled and I felt like a five-year-old caught in the cooky jar.

"Definitely, NO!" I wrote in big letters and got up to walk out. But he looked so crestfallen and disappointed, I didn't want to leave him that way. I grabbed my pad again. "I'm going swimming," I wrote.

"I don't know how to swim," he said when he read it, "nobody ever taught me. You teach us to swim and we'll teach you—"

I didn't hear any more because I slammed the door and strode out of there. So I suppose I was pigheaded. Sometime you go through three months of clinics and draw a complete blank; and then have some nut—priest or no priest—tell you he's going to teach you to talk in one easy lesson, trade you swimming lessons for talking lessons!

I walked down the boardwalk, past the various concessions and out across the bridge and up to the bluffs. For an hour I watched the Pacific smashing up against the rocks, watched the savage attack of the waves and the imperturbable way the rocks resisted. But you could see the way the rocks were worn down.

I got to wondering how long I'd last if I jumped in then and there. Suicide is a rather horrible-sounding word. But in a way it's like olives—you get accustomed to the taste of it and after a while your mind doesn't pucker at all. When I first started thinking about it, I thought it was something big. I was just about set to leap when a bass fisherman came up with a cheery greeting and spoiled it; so I started back.

I went down to the office to see about getting a new room. Doc Wilson was at his desk making out charts. He wore horn-rimmed glasses and looked slightly like an owl.

"Bob," he said, "I'd like to tell you something about the padre. There isn't a thing physically wrong with him—that is, there's nothing physically wrong with his head."

I raised my eyebrows and looked at him.

"We put his type of difficulty under the general class we call NP's. Neuropsychosis. There are a lot of different kinds but it means that battle shock set something wrong inside of him, something there's no medicine to cure. But you could do something we couldn't do. There's a chance, a slim one, that if he got interested in teaching you to talk, he might snap out of it."

I just smiled and shook my head. I was no Florence Nightingale, nor was I meant to be. Physician, cure thyself, I thought. Maybe that is why his next remark threw me off stride.

"There's even a chance it might work both ways," Wilson said, "he might cure you, or you might cure him."

Or I might go nuts, I thought, and he might go dumb. I got up and walked to the door.

"Well, look," he said, "stick it out a couple more days until I can get a decent room for you. Meantime give it a try."

The Holy Joe was doing push-ups when I opened the door of our room. He kept going up and down till the back of his fatigue blouse grew dark with sweat. Finally he stopped and rolled over on his back.

"When do we start?" he asked.

I was licked. "Tomorrow," I motioned with my lips.

"Today," he said, "now. We'll learn the way babies do. A baby couldn't say Massachusetts. So we'll start with baby words. I'll say them first and you watch me. All right now, we'll start with ma-ma. *Maa-maa. Maaa-maa!*"

We worked on "ma-ma" for two days; and then started on "da-da." I don't know why I did it. When I finally got on to ma-ma, it sounded like Vodor in need of oil. But there was something about Joe. There's something about a big man like that reduced to a hulk; and being a priest seemed to make it even worse. It got all of us, so I'm not ashamed to say it got me. After about a week we were working most of the morning at the lessons. But you could see it was useless. I think the only reason I kept at it was to please him. One day I'd gone on "guard-duty," following him around to see he got in no trouble.

Guard duty wasn't the easiest thing in the world. He got up at six, and dressed in his khakis. He always shaved meticulously, brushed his hair and his uniform until both of them shone. Sleepy-eyed, I left the hotel after him and shivered in the early morning fog. I was sort of eager to find out where he headed each morning.

He headed straight for the mission. It's a lovely thing, rebuilt some years ago. Joe marched stolidly through the streets, up to the mission door, and rang the bell.

"Good morning, Monsignor," Joe said.

"Good morning, Father. A beautiful day it'll be."

"This morning, Monsignor?" he asked.

"Now, son," the pastor said, "I told you that the day Almighty God will give you your Mass, I'll be shouting it from the house-tops."

And with never another word Joe turned and sat down on the step. If I ever saw a dejected look on a man's face, it was the look on his.

The pastor is a tremendous giant of a man, with red face, and booming bass voice, but gentle as a mother. He reached down and brought Joe to his feet. "Come on, lad," he said, "I've a pot of coffee on the stove waiting for you. And you come in too, boy," he said looking at me.

We sat in a cheery breakfast room and drank our coffee.

"Sure he misses his Mass," said the Monsignor as he buttered a piece of toast and handed it to Joe. "It's a shame, a fine lad like him. He comes here every morning at exactly this time. And every morning I have to tell him the same thing."

I think that was the reason I kept to the lessons; I'd seen big planes too broken up to fly again. They'd kept them in the hangars to reclaim the parts as other ships needed them. No flier likes to look at the hangar queens; the outside shell is the last thing to go and you get the feeling that they almost know how useless they are. Joe was like one of those hangar queens. The outside of him was so full and vital. There wasn't anything empty in his smile; it was a real smile and his blue eyes had a good clean hard soul in back of them. One thing, taking those lessons to please him made me half forget my own misery. My grand-mother used to say that the best cure for your own misery is to help somebody else.

Well, after we got through "da-da" we went on to "baa-baa, black sheep." Just that, over and over again, with him sitting on the floor, face intense, his eyes looking straight up at me, saying over and over again: "Baa-baa, black sheep," me sitting in the easy chair, my face dripping sweat from the effort to force my vocal cords to pronounce. I never got much better. And he never got discouraged.

Finally we reached "yes" and "no." They weren't much use to me, because those were two signals I could always make with my head. I do have to admit, though, it was a thrill the first time I said, "Yes." It sounded more like the Japanese "Yiss," but there were general congratulations and someone even opened a bottle to celebrate the occasion.

Joe beamed brighter than any father with his child's first sentence; he spent about an hour praying to his statue of the Little Flower—thanking her, he told me. He kept flowers in the drinking glass and after a while I even got to collecting a couple myself when he forgot for a day or two.

The next day was probably one of the most hectic days I've ever spent. We were hard at work in the room about ten o'clock in the morning trying to master the intricate sound of "Please," when the door opened and three navy doctors walked in. Two of them were strangers, and the older one had four stripes.

"I tell you, Dr. Seward, he's utterly harmless," our own medico said earnestly. "And he does something for our morale here."

The four-striper brushed it aside. "It's against regulations, Doctor. I can't imagine how he got here in the first place. Come over here, Lieutenant," he said to Joe.

It certainly looked bad. Joe was sitting on the floor where he usually sat, his long legs spread out before him. He'd bought a kid's book and had it open in front of him. He didn't move.

"Lieutenant . . . Joe . . . stand up, please," Dr. Wilson said. Joe stood up still holding the book.

Even the four-striper was impressed by his size and by the

rugged look of his face. "What are his symptoms, Doctor?" he asked.

"They are on his chart, Doctor," Wilson said. "Usual battle-shock. No responsibility. No reaction to time limits. The men take turns walking with him when he goes out of sick bay."

"Ever unmanageable?" Seward asked.

"No, sir, never."

"Drink?"

"No, sir."

Joe smiled happily. "Have you ever met my sister?" he asked the two doctors. "Soeur Thérèse, these are navy men. We must pray for them. We must ask for a rose petal for them." Then, completely disregarding the doctors, he went over and knelt in front of the statue. I could have shot him, and pink-faced statue too.

"He has a great devotion to the Little Flower," Wilson said apologetically. We thought it was all right for him to have the statue in his room."

Captain Seward raised his eyes and looked at his junior. Junior shook his head negatively. The stinker, I thought, he's out to get some extra stripes the easy way.

"Dr. Wilson, it is against all regulations for this man to be here. There are other convalescent homes where he will get adequate treatment."

"Sir," Wilson said seriously, "if you take him away from here it will do him tremendous harm. And not only him but everyone else."

"Supposing he were to break loose," Seward said, "and injure someone. Who'd be to blame? The navy, Doctor, and you and I."

"The men here will assume the responsibility."

"No."

"Please—" The word came out of my lips before I knew it was

coming. Other words crowded my throat, but they wouldn't come out. I got to coughing and blushed like a schoolgirl.

"What is it, Ensign?" The four-striper looked at me coldly.

"You've just heard one of the three words the ensign can pronounce," Wilson said. "The padre spends four to five hours a day teaching him to talk. What he wants to say is that he will watch Joe like a hawk."

I grinned a little and gestured with my hands.

The four-striper looked at me searchingly, then at Joe kneeling before his statue. Slowly and with an effort he shook his head.

At heart he seemed like a pretty nice guy.

"It's too risky," he said finally.

Wilson made one more effort. And I stood there on the side-lines cheering for him.

"Doctor," he said, "the chaplain hasn't one mark against him in eight months. For all that time he's been ballast here, making the lads forget their own troubles to feel sorry for him. Won't you let him stay here, doing his job, saying his little prayers? I suppose I shouldn't feel as intensely as I do. But he gets you."

I knew what he meant. Right then I'd have given an arm to be able to say something. Seward looked at me and I tried to say things with my eyes. It seemed like minutes he looked at me before he said anything. I think I upset him.

"I'll give you my final word tomorrow," he said. He looked at me again, and at Joe, then turned smartly and left the room.

That was ten o'clock Wednesday, and by the time Seward, Wilson and Junior had left the room I was sweating all over. At twelve-thirty the bus arrived. We had just come out from mess and Joe was up in his room. A couple of us were out on the lawn when this navy bus pulled up. As soon as they started to pile out, I knew they were no convalescents; about half of them made direct for Eddie's just across the street from the hospital. They made more noise than a legion convention.

"It's the bunch from the cruiser," a navy gunner beside me said.

"Joe, Joe, we want Joe. Joe, Joe, we want Joe," they started to chant. Then they made a serpent chain and started to march on the front door. Not all of them wore campaign ribbons, but those who did sure had collected some plain and fancy colors.

At that moment Joe stuck his head out the window. "Hi, gang," he yelled.

A minute later he was down on the lawn and they crowded all around him. Funniest thing you ever saw: they all had presents. One of them brought a grass skirt and Joe put it on. And another had a Japanese officer's sword that must have cost him plenty.

"How's the Little Sister?" one of them asked.

"Great, great," he said. "I tell her about you all the time."

"Well, what are we waiting for?" a big husky yelled. "Let's go swimming!"

As they passed us on the lawn, Joe stuck out his hand and grabbed me by the arm. And so pell-mell we pushed across the little street. They took over the beach. There's a little stage there on the sand where they hold shows, and five or six of them pushed back the chairs. From the bus somebody had brought boxing gloves and two of them were donning them.

"Joe's going to referee," a blond kid said to me. "He loves it. Used to do it all the time on board, and he's good. Wait till you see the guys try to pull some rough stuff, and watch him."

He was good, all right. He must have refereed a lot of CYO bouts before he stood for his hitch in the navy. And when the two youngsters started to pull some rough stuff, he slapped them both on the back with an awful wallop. You could hear it over the drone of the merry-go-round and the shouts of the sailors.

The next thing was softball. He pitched. There was no wild

swinging when he threw one; I played second base and a couple
came down to me that even the sand couldn't stop.

Then they went swimming and Joe and I lay in the sand and
watched them. I got the idea that even the Pacific was tired
when they were in there for ten minutes. These lads beat anything I'd ever seen.

A lanky towhead from the middle west came up and sat where
he could see Joe. "Greatest guy I ever met," he said to me. "You
figure it out . . . he loses a knob that's really worth something
and we don't even get a scratch."

Five o'clock came very quickly and they took mess with the
enlisted men and Joe. About eight o'clock they finally got off
with more wild shouting.

Joe made a kind of nice sight as the bus pulled out. There he
was standing big and square on the corner of the lawn, with the
sun bouncing off the waves and putting a glow all round him.
But he was tired; you could see that.

I took a little walk out on the pier to watch the smelt fishers,
and it was about quarter to nine when I got back to the room.

"Baa-baa, black sheep," I said as I came in the door. That was
a password between us and indicated that everything was under
control. It's queer how you can make words do things they never
were intended to do. We used it to say good morning, good night
and a hundred other things.

There was no answer. Joe wasn't there.

I figure now that maybe if I'd started to look for him right
then, there would have been no trouble. I thought, though, that
maybe he'd rather be alone. I guess I should have known he
didn't have enough sense left to him to want that—but it was
always hard to think of him as subnormal; and you just couldn't
think of him as insane.

At ten o'clock I got worried and started looking around. Nobody remembered seeing him, and as far as we could think, no-body had been assigned to follow him; he never left the place at night. By ten-thirty everybody in the place knew he was out. We kept it away from Wilson and the doctors, but even they knew something was wrong.

Of course we finally had to tell Wilson, so we could get per-mission to go out and hunt for him. But he played it close and the four-striper, Seward, didn't hear a thing about it. We split up the town—it's really not a very big town—and started out search-ing. Nobody had seen him. We looked all over the beaches and up along the Cliff Drive as far as the lighthouse. We drew blank all round.

It was eleven-thirty when we got back to the hospital, com-pletely dejected.

"What happened last time that bunch came down?" I wrote on a pad and gave it to an old-timer there.

"If I remember rightly," the old-timer said, "he had the dumps for a couple of days. I kind of got the idea he knew his buttons were short."

"That's right," someone else remembered, "he stayed in his room the whole next day, praying to his statue."

Then I got it. I knew where he was. But I had to get rid of the mob before we brought him in. "Scram, guys," I wrote. "I think I know where he is."

I turned to another ensign, whose name was Foley, and wrote just two words.

I was right. There he was huddled up on the steps of the mis-sion fast asleep. He had his jacket around his shoulders, his cap was off and his hair was wet with fog.

And then it happened. Of course the excitement was too much for the lads convalescing and their noise had brought Captain Seward out of his office. He was standing in the lobby when we entered. Wilson came hurrying up, but Seward just gave us one look and turned and walked back into his office. He didn't have to put a ticket on it. It was written all over his face.

Foley and Wilson helped me undress Joe. He had a pair of yellow and red mandarin pajamas that one of his visitors had brought him. We decided to put him into them. Finally we got him into bed and he was asleep before we drew up the covers.

"I'll get in a beautiful jam over this," Wilson said.

Foley looked over the bed. "I'll give three to one he'll trade those pajamas for a strait jacket before next month."

I picked up my pad again. "You did your best. We all did our best. Sometimes you don't get the breaks."

"This is going to be tough on you," Wilson said.

"Baa-baa, black sheep," I said.

The three of us shrugged our shoulders all at once and they left.

I couldn't get to sleep, so I went over and looked out the big French windows to the Pacific. The moon had come up and was shining wetly through the fog.

They take him away, I thought darkly, and, Mr. Moon, you're going to shine on a pretty navy corpse. There's not much consolation in a moon and it just kept grinning wetly down at me.

Suddenly I began to swear. I'm not a swearing man and I've laid off almost entirely since I've been living with Joe. But I began to swear and even if no sounds came out of my throat, I was doing a good job of it. The more I swore, the madder I got; and the madder I got the more I swore. Well, you can't go on too long that way and I finally got to a point where either I didn't know any more swear words or I couldn't get any madder. Just as I turned my head back into the room, the glow of the candle lit up the face of the statue.

The pink face glowed sweetly, smugly—sardonically, I thought.

I'd got so mad there were tears in my eyes and I just hauled off one shoe and let it fly. It didn't hit her, but I felt better. The shoe landed on the edge of the table, tottered uncertainly a few seconds, then fell to the floor.

It was the shoe that did it. The shoe and the moon and the peaceful rhythmic lapping of the waves out front.

I kept looking at the flickering light in front of the statue for a few minutes. Then I went over and got down on both my knees and started to pray.

I tried to think of some prayers I knew as a youngster and could only recall, "Now I lay me down to sleep." We once learned a psalm, I think it was the Twenty-third. I used to like it. A phrase of it came back to me: "Surely goodness and mercy shall follow me all the days of my life."

I got thinking about the psalm, but mixed up with it were all sorts of pictures: of Ann Marie, of screaming in on the beach at Tarawa, of Joe standing out there in the sunlight and of what that navy kid from the midwest said.

Then I guess I went to sleep. I know I must have, because when I woke up I was stiff from the fog breaking in through the French windows. I don't know how long I slept, but I had a dream, or a vision, or whatever you want to call it.

Funny thing, generally in dreams you go off to some distant spot; but I stayed right where I was. I could see myself on my knees, only the statue was different. It was bigger, or I was smaller. I know I wasn't surprised when it started to speak. I kind of had a feeling that the Mad Hatter was somewhere around and that pretty soon we'd see the Queen.

"*Bon soir*," she said.

I nodded politely.

"You can speak without your voice," she said, "and I can hear you very well."

There was an accent to her voice, I thought, but it may have been my imagination.

"It'll kill him if they take him away," I said.

"*Mon petit frère?*" she said. "No, it will not kill him. The shell did not kill him."

"Look," I said, "I know you people know everything. But why Joe? Why not some of the blockheads of this world? Why ruin a swell person like him?"

"Why did you go down on your knees tonight?" she said.

I didn't know what to say to that. "Well," I said slowly. "I've seen Joe praying for everybody in the hospital. Maybe I figured somebody ought to pray for him."

"He has prayed for you."

"I know," I said.

"And I have listened to both prayers. From Our Father I have permission to give His help to one of you." She looked right straight at me and her little face grew very serious. "I do not know which one it should be."

"No difficulty about that," I said. "It's Joe." I wasn't a hero. That's the way I felt about him, the way everybody felt. I certainly didn't feel like any hero.

"Is your prayer, then, better than his?" she asked.

"You know I don't mean that," I said.

"I think, perhaps, we should wake *mon frère*."

"Why do that?" I blurted. "I won't take your favors. I didn't ask for them anyway."

Then she laughed and my lack of manners made me blush.

"I have the idea," she said lightly. "I will cure you, my friend, and you will help my brother."

"Wait a minute!" I said rudely.

"Even in heaven, we have heard how clever are Americans," she said and smiled again.

I started to get up, but cramped my leg and rolled over on the floor. That's where I was when I woke up.

Rolling over on my back, I stared for several minutes at the little dancing glow on the ceiling. The statue didn't look smug any longer but it didn't look much like the Sister of my dream either. I could hear the wash of the waves on the shore and Joe's deep breathing.

"Now is the time," I said softly and aloud, "for every good man to come to the aid of the party. . . . The quick brown fox jumped over the lazy dog . . ."

"Roger!" I said even more softly and my voice sounded harsh and unaccustomed. Somehow I felt no elation. I'd thought of this minute often, but now it brought none of the joy I'd anticipated. I lay stretched out there on the floor. Dream or no dream, I could talk again.

I looked over at the statue again. "Thanks, little lady," I said, "I pay my debts. I'll pay this one too."

It took me a couple of minutes to find my shoe in the dark. I got it back on and slowly moved down the stairs to Wilson's room. When I opened the door, he was in bed, boning a medical book.

"You once said maybe Joe'd help me," I said. "Well, you were right. Listen to this."

"Let's go see Seward," he said when he heard the story.

"He's asleep by this time," I said.

"We'll wake him, then," Wilson said, "and let me do the talking. Seward's a good egg if he's handled right. You better say another prayer as we go."

"We both better," I said.

Doc Wilson gave me both thumbs up. "Baa-baa, black sheep!" he said.

It took me most of the night to finish this, but I wanted to have it done. I get the seven-o'clock bus out of here this morning for a thirty-day leave before I return to active duty. Thirty days isn't much but it'll give me plenty of time to get to Scarsdale and to that weathered brown house with the acacia trees on the front lawn. A few minutes ago I looked out the window. Joe, in his meticulously polished khakis, was walking along Ocean Avenue on his way to the mission; he'll be attached here for the duration and as long after as he wants to stay. About fifteen feet in back of him a sleepy-eyed ensign yawned and followed after. I watched them until the fog closed in and hid them from my sight. A wisp of the fog blew in through the French window and somehow caught in my eye.

THE KNIFE

BRENDAN GILL

Published a little over a decade ago this brilliant little story has deservedly achieved the status of a minor classic. It lays wide open the problems which confront the Christian who pins his faith to prayers of petition. Yet it is not a problem story at all, but a moving human document.

In the Introduction to Our Father's House *I have interpreted it as a satire on the fiction writers in the Catholic pulps, who, in grinding out indiscriminate miraculous answers to prayers of petition, think of themselves as having more pity than God. Like the father in this story, such writers, as well as the editors who purvey their fiction to Catholic readers, will have to make, on some far day of reckoning, some dreadful explanations to the readers they have fooled.*

Yet this story need not be interpreted as such a satire. Like all art it can be viewed from many angles, and from any one of them is seen to be good, true, and beautiful. Brendan Gill, who is known to his friends as "the black Irishman," is a frequent contributor of fiction to The New Yorker, *the* Saturday Evening Post *and other magazines. He is married, has a family, and lives at Norfolk, Connecticut.*

Michael threw himself down, locked his hands over one of his father's knees, and began, in a loud whisper, " 'Our Father, who art in heaven, hallowed be thy name, kingdom come, will be done, earth as it is in heaven, give us this day—' "

Carroll folded his newspaper. Michael should have been in bed an hour ago. "Take it easy, kid," he said. "Let's try it again, slow."

Michael repeated distinctly, " 'Our Father, who art in heaven, hallowed . . .' " The boy's pajamas, Carroll saw, were dirty at the cuffs; probably he had not brushed his teeth. " '. . . as we forgive them, who trespass against us'—what does 'trespass' mean, Dad?"

"Why, hurting anybody."

"Do I trespass anybody?"

"Not much, I guess. Finish it up."

Michael drew a breath. " 'And lead us not into temptation, but deliver us from evil. Amen.' "

"Now," his father said, brushing back Michael's tangled hair, "what about a good 'Hail, Mary'?"

"All right," Michael said. " 'Hail, Mary, full of grace, the Lord is with thee, blessed art thou among women, and blessed is the fruit of thy womb, Jesus.' " Michael lifted his head to ask if a womb got fruit like a tree, but thought better of it. His father never answered questions seriously, the way his mother used to. Michael decided to wait and ask Mrs. Nolan. "Is Mrs. Nolan coming tomorrow?" he asked.

"She'll be here, all right," Carroll said. "I give you ten seconds to finish the prayer."

Michael grinned at the ultimatum. "I thought you wanted me to go slow. 'Holy Mary, Mother of God, pray for us sinners, now and at the hour of our death. Amen.' " He unlocked his fingers. "Will she?"

"Will she what?"

"Will she now and at the hour of our death. A-men?"

The words of Michael's prayer caught in Carroll's mind and stayed there, a long way beyond his smiling face. "Yes," he said, and set his pipe in the broken dish on the table beside him. He had not emptied the dish of ashes in two days. Mrs. Nolan would give him a piece of her mind tomorrow morning, as she did each week when she came in to give the apartment a general cleaning and to do the laundry.

"What good can she do?" Michael asked.

"Climb into bed, young ragamuffin," Carroll said sternly. "It's past nine."

"What *good* can she do?"

"She'll help you get anything you want. I suppose she'll help you climb up into heaven when the time comes. You know all about heaven, don't you?"

Michael felt himself on the defensive. "Of course."

"Well, then, get along with you."

But Michael had something difficult to say. "You mean she'll ask God for anything I want and He'll give it to her for me?"

"She's His mother."

Michael stood up and kissed his father carefully on the cheek. Then he walked from the room, and Carroll could hear his bare feet crossing the hall. The bed creaked as Michael lay down on it. Carroll opened the newspaper, read a paragraph, then dropped it in a white heap on the rug. He felt tired; perhaps tonight he might be able to get some sleep. He got up, slipped his suspenders from his shoulders, unknotted his tie, kicked off his shoes. He had learned to undress quickly in the last six months, since his wife had died.

His pajamas were hanging inside out in the bathroom, where he had left them that morning. When he had undressed he felt Michael's toothbrush with his thumb; it was dry. He should have explained to the child what happened to a person's teeth when he forgot to clean them every night and morning.

Carroll stared at his face in the mirror above the basin. He tried smiling. No one could honestly tell what a man was thinking by the way he smiled. Even Michael, who was like a puppy about sensing moods, could not tell. He entered the bedroom on tiptoe. Feeling the sheets bunched at the foot of the mattress, he remembered that he had made the beds in a hurry. The sheets felt fresh and cool only on Saturdays, when Mrs. Nolan changed them.

Michael was not asleep. "Dad?" he whispered.

"Go to sleep."

"I been asking Hail Mary for something."

"Tomorrow."

"No, I been asking her right now."

Carroll lay on his back with his hands over his eyes. "What've you been asking her for, Mickey?"

Michael hesitated. "I thought I'd better make it something easy first. To see what happened." He sat up in bed. "A jack-knife."

A few blocks away the clock of the Metropolitan Life tower was striking ten. Michael was deep in the noisy middle of a dream. Carroll listened to his breathing. He tried matching his own breath to Michael's, to make sleep come, but it was no use. Every night Carroll pretended to himself he was just at the brink of falling off to sleep, but his eyes always widened with wakefulness in the dark. Now, as the clock stopped striking, Carroll got up and walked into the bathroom and dressed. Then he went into the living room, unlocked the outside door of the apartment, and then locked it again before he walked down the two flights of stairs to the sidewalk. Shops reached out of sight down both sides of Lexington Avenue. Carroll walked uptown as he always did. He stopped in front of each bright shop window, studying its contents for the fifth or sixth time. He knew by now the day on which each window was changed and by whom. Certain plaster models, certain fringed crepe papers were old friends.

At the top of a long slope Carroll waited for the lights to change. On his left was a bar; on his right, across the street, a drugstore. Carroll waited a moment outside the bar. Between the slats of its cheap orange Venetian blinds he could see the gleaming mahogany counter, the stacked glasses, the barman slicing foam from a mug of beer. A man and a girl were sitting at a table by the window, a foot under Carroll's eyes. They did not seem to be speaking. The man's hand lay halfway across the table and the girl's black dress made her throat look soft and white. Carroll turned away and crossed the street to the drug-store. The owner, Sam Ramatsky, stood sniffing the night air under the painted sign bearing his name.

"Well, Mr. Carroll, nice night for March."

"Yes." Carroll wanted only to hear a voice. "How's business?" he asked.

"Can't complain." Sam grinned, shaking his head. "I take that back. It's *lousy*. I got to break myself of this old 'Can't complain.' I got to remember how serious it is. Business is lousy."

Carroll leaned back against Sam's window, which was crammed with hotwater bottles, perfumes, toys, and two cardboard girls in shorts and sandals. The girls had been there for two months. There was dust on their teeth and on their smooth brown legs. "You ought to brush their teeth, Sam," Carroll said, "and run your hand down their legs now and then."

"You walk a lot," Sam said. "I figure on you, ten or eleven, every night."

"I guess I do," Carroll said.

Sam patted his hard belly. "Nothing like exercise keep a man in shape."

Carroll nodded impatiently. It was not Sam's voice he wanted to hear, after all. "Give me a milk shake, Sam."

They walked into the store. Carroll sat down on one of the round stools at the fountain and watched Sam pouring milk into the shaker. "Nothing like milk," Sam said, "keep a man's system clean." Carroll watched the hands of the electric clock above the door. Ten-forty-five. He could not go to bed before twelve. He glanced at the packed counters behind him. "Sell any jackknives, Sam?"

"Sure, I sell everything. That's what keeps me broke. Nothing like keeping a thing in stock to kill demand." Sam lifted a tray of jackknives from a counter, brought it over, and set it down on the fountain. "Beauties," Sam said. "Fifty cents up."

Carroll looked at several of them and finally picked up the biggest and shiniest one. "I'll take this one," he said.

"Such expensive taste! One buck."

Carroll paid for the milk shake and the knife, said "Good night, Sam," and walked out into the street. In another hour and a half he should have walked six miles. By that time his body would be tired enough so that he could sleep. By that time, he hoped, no voice could rouse him.

It was morning when Carroll awoke. He lay with his face on his hands, listening to the sound of the March rain against the windows. He remembered suddenly the absurd song that everyone used to sing: "Though April showers may come your way, they bring the flowers that bloom in May." March rains brought you nothing. March rains only shut you in your room without any hope of escape.

Michael and Mrs. Nolan were talking together in the kitchen. Michael's voice was high with excitement. "Look at it, Mrs. Nolan, look at it! Isn't it beautiful?"

"It is that," Mrs. Nolan said in her deep voice. Carroll sat up in bed. It was too late to give Mrs. Nolan warning.

"Do you ask for things when you say your prayers, Mrs. Nolan?" Michael demanded.

"I do." A pan clattered to the floor. "I've seen many a nice clean sty I'd swap for this dirty kitchen," Mrs. Nolan said. "You live like a couple of savages from week to week. God love you."

"Do you always get what you ask for?" Michael said.

"It all depends. I sort of try to guess what the good Lord wants to give me, and I ask for that."

"That's how I got this knife," Michael said. "It's got a big blade and a little blade and a screwdriver and a thing to punch holes in leather with and a file."

"You must have said yourself a fine prayer," Mrs. Nolan said. There was no hint of surprise in her voice.

"It was only a 'Hail, Mary,'" Michael said, "but I did it very slow, the way Dad told me to." Michael was silent for a moment.

"But I'm asking for the real thing tonight. The knife was just to see. Someone's going to be here when you come next week."

Mrs. Nolan made a clucking sound in her mouth. "Someone instead of me?"

"She was here with Dad and me before you came," Michael said, his voice thin with its burden, "and she's coming back."

"Michael!" Carroll shouted.

Michael ran to the doorway. The knife gleamed in his fist. "Look what I got," he said. "I was showing Mrs. Nolan."

"Come here," Carroll said. When Michael reached the edge of the bed Carroll bent over and fastened his arms behind the child's back. There was only one thing to say, and one way to say it, and that was fast. "I'm glad you like it," he said. "I bought it for you at Ramatsky's last night. The biggest and shiniest one he had."

THE ROAD TO THE SHORE

MICHAEL McLAVERTY

*Michael McLaverty is a gifted writer. Unquestionably among the
artists who have made the short story a thing of sensitive beauty, he shares
with the reader, in this mildly humorous story, the one day of the year
when the Sisters are permitted to leave the convent for a trip to the seashore. As in all of Mr. McLaverty's stories we see here a cameralike
accuracy of observation wedded to poetry of phrase.*

*Michael McLaverty was born in Monaghan and was educated at St.
Malachy's College and Queen's University, Belfast. He has published several novels and* The Game Cock, *a volume of distinguished short stories.*

" 'Tis going to be a lovely day, thanks be to God," sighed Sister
Paul to herself, as she rubbed her wrinkled hands together and
looked out at the thrushes hopping across the lawn. "And it was
a lovely day last year and the year before," she mused, and in
her mind saw the fresh face of the sea where, in an hour or two,
she and the rest of the community would be enjoying their annual
trip to the shore. "And God knows it may be my last trip," she
said resignedly, and gazed abstractedly at a butterfly that was
purring its wings against the sunny pane. She opened the window
and watched the butterfly swing out into the sweet air, zig-zag-
ging down to a cushion of flowers that bordered the lawn. "Isn't
it well Sister Clare isn't here," she said to herself, "for she'd be
pestering the very soul out of me with questions about butterflies and birds and flowers and the fall of dew." She gave her
girdle of beads a slight rattle. Wasn't it lovely to think of the
pleasure that little butterfly would have when it found the free
air under its wings again and its little feet pressing on the soft
petals of the flowers and not on the hard pane. She always main-

95

tained it was better to enjoy Nature without searching and prob-
ing and chattering about the what and the where and the where-
fore. But Sister Clare!—what she got out of it all, goodness only
knew, for she'd give nobody a minute's peace—not a moment's
peace would she give to a saint, living or dead. "How long would
that butterfly live in the air of a class-room," she'd be asking;
"do you think it would use up much of the active part of the air
—the oxygen part, I mean. . . . What family would that butterfly belong to. . . . You know it's wrong to say that a butterfly
lives only a day. . . . When I am teaching my little pupils I
always try to be accurate. I don't believe in stuffing their heads
with fantastical nonsense however pleasurable it may be . . ."
Sister Paul turned round as if someone had suddenly walked into
the room, and she was relieved when she saw nothing only the
quiet vacancy of the room, the varnished desks with the sun on
them and their reflections on the parquet floor.

She hoped she wouldn't be sitting beside Clare in the car
today! She'd have no peace with her—not a bit of peace to look
out at the countryside and see what changes had taken place inside twelve months. But Reverend Mother, she knew, would
arrange all that—and if it'd be her misfortune to be parked beside Clare she'd have to accept it with resignation; yes, with resignation, and in that case her journey to the sea would be like
a pilgrimage.

At that moment a large limousine drove up the gravel path,
and as it swung round to the convent door she saw the flowers
flow across its polished sides in a blur of colour. She hurried out
of the room and down the stairs. In the hall Sister Clare and
Sister Benignus were standing beside two baskets and Reverend
Mother was staring at the stairs. "Where were you, Sister Paul?"
she said with mild reproof. "We searched the whole building for
you. . . . We're all ready this ages. . . . And Sister Francis
has gone to put out the cat. Do you remember last year it had

been in all the time we were at the shore and it ate the bacon?"
As she spoke a door closed at the end of the corridor and Sister
Francis came along, polishing her specs with the corner of her
veil. Reverend Mother glanced away from her, that continual
polishing of the spectacles irritated her; and then that empty expression on Sister Francis' face when the spectacles were off—
vacuous that's what it was!

"All ready now," Reverend Mother tried to say without any
trace of perturbation. Sister Clare and Sister Benignus lifted two
baskets at their feet, Reverend Mother opened the halldoor, and
they all glided out into the flat sunlight.

The doors of the car were wide open, the engine purring
gently, and a perfume of new leather fingering the air. The chauffeur, a young man, touched his cap and stood deferentially to the
side. Reverend Mother surveyed him quickly, noting his clean-
bright face and white collar. "I think there'll be room for us all
in the back," she said.

"There's a seat in the front, Sister," the young man said, touch-
ing his cap again.

"Just put the baskets on it, if you please," said Reverend
Mother. And Sister Clare who, at that moment, was smiling at
her own grotesque reflection in the back of the car came forward
with her basket, Sister Benignus following. Sister Paul sighed
audibly and fingered her girdle of beads.

"Now, Sister Paul, you take one of the corner seats, Sister
Clare you sit beside her, and Sister Benignus and Sister Francis
on the spring-up seats facing them—they were just made for you,
the tiny tots!" And they all laughed, a brittle laugh that empha-
sized the loveliness of the day.

When they were all seated, Reverend Mother made sure that
the halldoor was locked, glanced at the fastened windows, and
then stood for a minute watching the gardener who was pushing
his lawn-mower with unusual vigour and concentration. He

stopped abruptly when her shadow fell across his path. "And, Jack," she said, as if continuing a conversation that had been interrupted, "you'll have that lawn finished today?"

"Yes, Mother," and he took off his hat and held it in front of his breast. "To be sure I'll have it finished today. Sure what'd prevent me to finish it, and this the grandest day God sent this many a long month—a wholesome day!"

"And, Jack, I noticed some pebbles on the lawn yesterday— white ones."

"I remarked them myself, Mother. A strange terrier disporting himself in the garden done it."

"Did it!"

"Yes, Mother, he did it with his two front paws, scratching at the edge of the lawn like it was a rabbit burrow. He done it yesterday, and when I clodded him off the grounds he'd the impertinence to go out a different way than he came in. But I've now his entrances and exits all blocked and barricaded and I'm afraid he'll have to find some other constituency to disport himself. Dogs is a holy terror for bad habits."

"Be sure and finish it all today," she said with some impatience. She turned to go away, hesitated, and turned back. "By the way, Jack, if there are any drips of oil made by the car on the gravel you'll scuffle fresh pebbles over them."

"I'll do that. But you need have no fear of oil from her engine," and he glanced over at the limousine, "she'll be as clean as a Swiss clock. 'Tis them grocery vans that leak—top, tail and middle."

Crossing to the car, she heard with a feeling of pleasure the surge of the lawn-mower over the grass. Presently the car swung out of the gate on to a tree-lined road at the edge of the town. The nuns relaxed, settled themselves more comfortably in their seats and chatted about the groups on bicycles that were all heading for the shore.

"We will go to the same quiet strip as last year," said Reverend Mother, and then as she glanced out of the window a villa on top of a hill drew her attention. "There's a house that has been built since last year," she said.

"No, no," said Sister Francis. "It's more than a year old for I remember seeing it last year," and she peered at it through her spectacles.

Reverend Mother spoke through the speaking-tube to the driver: "Is that villa on the hill newly built?" she asked.

He stopped the car. "A doctor by the name of McGrath built it two years ago," he said. "He's married to a daughter of Solicitor O'Kane."

"Oh, thank you," said Reverend Mother; and the car proceeded slowly up the long hill above the town.

Sister Francis took off her spectacles, blew her breath on them, and rubbed them with her handkerchief. She took another look at the villa and said with obvious pride: "A fine site, indeed. I remember last year that they had that little gadget over the door."

"The architrave," said Sister Clare importantly.

"Aye," said Sister Paul, and she looked out at the trees and below them the black river with its strings of froth moving through the valley. How lovely it would be, she thought, to sit on the edge of that river, dabble her parched feet in it and send bubbles out into the race of the current. She had often done that when she was a child, and now that river and its trees, which she only saw once in a year, brought her childhood back to her. She sighed and opened the window so as to hear the mumble of the river far below them. The breeze whorled in, and as it lifted their veils they all smiled, invigorated by the fresh loveliness of the air. A bumble bee flew in and crawled up the pane at Reverend Mother's side of the car. She opened the window and assisted the bee towards the opening with the tip of her fountain-pen, but the bee clung to the pen and as she tried to shake it free the wind carried it in again. "Like everything else it hates to leave you," said Sister Benignus. Reverend Mother smiled and the bee flew up to the roof of the car and then alighted on the window beside Sister Paul. Sister Paul swept the bee to safety with the back of her hand.

"You weren't one bit afraid of it," said Sister Clare. "And if it had stung you, you would in a way have been responsible for its death. If it had been a Queen bee—though Queens wouldn't be flying at this time of the year—you would have been responsible for the deaths of potential thousands. A Queen bumble bee lays over two thousand eggs in one season!"

" 'Tis a great pity we haven't a hen like that," put in Sister Francis, and they all laughed except Sister Clare. Sister Francis laughed till her eyes watered and, once more, she took off her spectacles. Reverend Mother fidgeted slightly and, in order to control her annoyance, she fixed her gaze on Sister Clare and asked her to continue her interesting account of the life of bumble bees. Sister Paul put her hands in her sleeves and sought distraction in the combings of cloud that streaked the sky.

Reverend Mother pressed her toe on the floor of the car and, instead of listening to Sister Clare, she was glaring unconsciously at Sister Francis who was tapping her spectacles on the palm of her hand and giving an odd laugh.

"Your spectacles are giving you much trouble today," she broke in, unable any longer to restrain herself. "Perhaps you would like to sit in the middle. It may provide your poor eyes with some rest."

"No, thank you," said Sister Francis, "I like watching the crowds of cyclists passing on the road. But sometimes the sun glints on their handlebars and blinds me for a moment and makes me feel that a tiny thread or two has congregated on my lenses. It's my imagination of course."

"Maybe you would care to have a look at *St. Anthony's Annals*," and Reverend Mother handed her the magazine.

"Thank you, Mother. I'll keep it until we reach the shore, for the doctor told me not to read in moving vehicles."

The car rolled on slowly and when it reached the top of a hill, where there was a long descent of five miles to the sea, a strange silence came over the nuns, and each became absorbed in her own premeditation on the advancing day. "Go slowly down the hill," Reverend Mother ordered the driver.

Boys sailed past them on bicycles; when some did so with their hands off the handlebars a little cry of amazement would break from Sister Francis and she would discuss with Sister Clare the reckless irresponsibility of boys and the worry they must bring to their parents.

Suddenly at a bend on the hill they all looked at Sister Paul for she was excitedly drawing their attention to a line of young poplars. "Look, look!" she was saying, "look at the way their leaves are dancing and not a flicker out of the other trees. And to think I never noticed them before!"

"I think they are aspens," said Sister Clare, "and anyway they are not indigenous to this country."

"We had four poplars in our garden when I was growing up —black poplars, my father called them," said Sister Paul, lost in her own memory.

"What family did they belong to? There's *angustifolia, laurifolia,* and *balsamifera* and others among the poplar family."

"I don't know what family they belonged to," Sister Paul went on quietly. "I only know they were beautiful—beautiful in very early spring when every tree and twig around them would still be bleak—and there they were bursting into leaf, a brilliant yellow leaf like a flake of sunshine. My father, God be good to his kindly soul, planted four of them when I was young, for there were four in our family, all girls, and one of the trees my father called Kathleen, another Teresa, another Eileen, and last my own, Maura. And I remember how he used to stand at the dining-room window gazing out at the young poplars with the frost white and hard around them. 'I see a leaf or two coming on Maura,' he used to say, and we would all rush to the window and gaze into the garden, each of us fastening her eye on her own tree and then measuring its growth of leaf with the others. And to the one whose tree was first in leaf he used to give a book or a pair of rosary beads. . . . Poor Father," she sighed, and fumbled in her sleeve for her handkerchief.

"Can you not think of what special name those trees had?" pressed Clare. "Did their leaves tremble furiously—*tremula, tremuloides.*"

"They didn't quiver very much," said Sister Paul, her head bowed. "My father didn't plant aspens, I remember. He told us it was from an aspen that Our Saviour's rood was made, and because their leaves remember the Crucifixion they are always trembling. . . . But our poplars had a lovely warm perfume when they were leafing and that perfume always reminded my father of autumn. Wasn't that strange?" she addressed the whole car, "a tree coming into leaf and it reminding my poor father of autumn."

"I know its family now," said Clare, clapping her hands together. "*Balsamifera*—that's the family it belonged to—it's a native of Northern Italy."

"And I remember," said Paul, folding and unfolding her handkerchief on her lap, "how my poor father had no gum once to wrap up a newspaper that he was posting. It was in winter and he went to the poplars and dabbed his finger here and there on the sticky buds and smeared it on the edge of the wrapping paper."

"That was enough to kill the buds," said Clare. "The gum, as you call it, is their only protective against frost."

"It was himself he killed," said Paul. "He had gone out from a warm fire in his slippers, out into the bleak air and got his death."

"And what happened to the poplars?" said Clare. But Sister Paul had turned her head to the window again and was trying to stifle the tears that were rising to her eyes.

"What other trees grew in your neighborhood?" continued Clare. Sister Paul didn't seem to hear her, but when the question was repeated she turned and said slowly: "I'm sorry that I don't know their names. But my father, Lord have mercy on him, used to say that a bird could leap from branch to branch for ten miles around without using its wings."

Sister Clare smiled and Reverend Mother nudged her with her elbow, signing to her to keep quiet; and when she, herself, glanced at Paul she saw the sun shining through the fabric of her veil and a handkerchief held furtively to her eyes.

There was silence now in the sun-filled car while outside cyclists continued to pass them, free-wheeling down the long hill. Presently there was a rustle of paper in the car as Sister Francis drew forth from her deep pocket a bag of soft peppermints, stuck together by the heat. Carefully she peeled the bits of paper off the sweets, and as she held out the bag to Reverend Mother she said: "Excuse my fingers." But Reverend Mother shook her head, and Clare and Benignus seeing that she had refused, felt it would be improper for them to accept. Francis shook the bag towards Paul but since she had her eyes closed, as if in prayer, she neither saw nor heard what was being offered to her. *"In somno pacis,"* said Francis, popping two peppermints into her own mouth and hiding the bag in her wide sleeve. "A peppermint is soothing and cool on a hot day like this," she added with apologetic good-nature.

A hot smell of peppermint drifted around the car. Reverend Mother lowered her window to its full length, and though the air rushed in in soft folds around her face it was unable to quench the flaming odour. Somehow, for Reverend Mother, the day, that had hardly begun yet, was spoiled by an old nun with foolish habits and by a young nun unwise enough not to know when to stop questioning. Everything was going wrong, and it would not surprise her that before evening clouds of rain would blow in from the sea and blot out completely the soft loveliness of the sunny day. Once more she looked at Paul, and, seeing her head bowed in thought, she knew that there was some aspect of the countryside, some shape in cloud or bush, that brought back to Paul a sweet but sombre childhood. For herself she had no such memories—there was nothing in her own life, she thought, only a mechanical ordering, a following of routine, that may have brought some pleasure into other people's lives but none to her own. However, she'd do her best to make the day pleasant for them; after all, it was only one day in the year and if the eating of peppermints gave Sister Francis some satisfaction it was not right to thwart her.

She smiled sweetly then at Francis, and as Francis offered the sweets once more, and she was stretching forward to take one there was a sudden dunt to the back of the car and a crash of something falling on the road. The car stopped and the nuns looked at one another, their heads bobbing in consternation. They saw the driver raise himself slowly from his seat, walk back the road, and return with a touch of his cap at the window.

"A slight accident, Sister," he said, addressing Reverend Mother. "A cyclist crashed into our back wheel. But it's nothing serious, I think."

Reverend Mother went out leaving the door open, and through it there came the free sunlight, the cool air, and the hum of people talking. She was back again in a few minutes with her handkerchief dabbed with blood, and collected other handkerchiefs from the nuns, who followed her out on to the road. Sister Paul stood back and saw amongst the bunch of people a young man reclining on the bank of the road, a hand to his head. "I can't stand the sight of blood," she said to herself, her fingers clutching her rosary beads. She beckoned to a lad who was resting on his bicycle: "Is he badly hurt, lad? He'll not die, will he?"

"Not a bit of him, Sister. He had his coat folded over the handlebars and the sleeve of it caught in the wheel and flung him against the car."

"Go up, like a decent boy, and have a good look at him again."

But before the lad had reached the group the chauffeur had assisted the injured man to his feet and was leading him to the car. The handkerchiefs were tied like a turban about his head, his trousers were torn at the knee, and a holy medal was pinned to his braces.

"Put his coat on or he'll catch cold," Reverend Mother was saying.

"Och, Sister, don't worry about me," the man was saying. "Sure it was my own fault. Ye weren't to blame at all. I'll go back again on my own bicycle—I'm fit enough."

Reverend Mother consulted the chauffeur and whatever advice he gave her the injured man was put into the back of the car. Sister Francis was ordered into the vacant seat beside the driver, the baskets were handed to Paul and Clare, and when the man's bicycle was tied to the crate they drove off for the hospital in the town.

The young man, sitting between Reverend Mother and Sister Paul, shut his eyes in embarrassment, and when the blood oozed through the pile of handkerchiefs Reverend Mother took the serviettes from the baskets and tied them round his head and under his chin, and all the time the man kept repeating: "I'm a sore trouble to you, indeed. And sure it was my own fault." She told him to button his coat or he would catch cold, and when he had done so she noticed a Total Abstinence badge in the lapel.

"A good clean-living man," she thought, and to think that he was the one to meet with an injury while many an old drunkard could travel the roads of Ireland on a bicycle and arrive home without pain or scratch or cough.

" 'Tis a blessing of God you weren't killed," she said, with a rush of protectiveness, and she reached for the thermos flask from the basket and handed the man a cup of tea.

Now and again Sister Paul would steal a glance at him but the sight of his pale face and the cup trembling in his hand and rattling on the saucer made her turn to the window where she tried to lose herself in contemplation. But all her previous mood was now scattered from her mind, and she could think of nothing only the greatness of Reverend Mother and the cool way she took command of an incident that would have left the rest of them weak and confused.

"How are you feeling now?" she could hear Reverend Mother asking. "Would you like another sandwich?"

"No, thank you, Sister, sure I had my good breakfast in me before I left the house. I'm a labouring man and since I'm out of work this past three months my wife told me to go off on the bike and have a swim with myself. I was going to take one of the youngsters on the bar of the bike but my wife wouldn't let me."

"She had God's grace about her," said Reverend Mother. "That should be a lesson to you," and as she refilled his cup from the thermos flask she thought that if the young man had been killed they, in a way, would have had to provide his widow and children with some help. "And we were only traveling slowly," she found herself saying aloud.

"Sure, Sister, no one knows that better than myself. You were keeping well in to your own side of the road and when I was ready to sail past you on the hill my coat caught in the front wheel and my head hit the back of your car."

"S-s-s," and the nuns drew in their breath with shrinking solicitude.

The car drove up to the hospital, and after Reverend Mother had consulted the doctor and was told that the wound was only a slight abrasion and contusion she returned light-heartedly to the car. Sister Clare made no remark when she heard the news but as the wheels of the car rose and fell on the road they seemed to echo what was in her mind: *abrasion and contusion, abrasion and contusion.* "Abrasion and contusion of what?" she asked herself. "Surely the doctor wouldn't say 'head'—abrasion and contusion of the head?" No, there must be some medical term that Reverend Mother had withheld from them, and as she was about to probe Reverend Mother for the answer the car swung unexpectedly into the convent avenue. "Oh," she said with disappointment, and when alighting from the car and seeing Sister Francis give the remains of her sweets to the chauffeur she knew that for her, too, the day was at an end.

They all passed inside except Reverend Mother who stood on the steps at the door noting the quiet silence of the grounds and the heat-shadows flickering above the flower-beds. With a mocking smile she saw the lawn-mower at rest on the uncut lawn, and found herself mimicking the gardener: "I'll have it all finished today, Sister, I'll have it all finished today." She put a hand to her throbbing head and crossed the gravel path to look for him, and there in the clump of laurel bushes she found him fast asleep, his hat over his face to keep off the flies, and three empty porter bottles beside him. She tiptoed away from him. "He has had a better day than we have had," she said to herself, "so let him sleep it out, for it's the last he'll have at my expense. . . . Oh, drink is a curse"; and she thought of the injury that had befallen the young man with the Abstinence Badge and he as sober as any judge. Then she drew up suddenly as something quick and urgent came to her mind: "Of course;—he would take the job as gardener, and he unemployed this past three months!" With head erect she sped quickly across the grass and into the convent. Sister Paul was still in the corridor when she saw Reverend Mother lift the phone and ring up the hospital: "Is he still there . . . He's all right . . . that's good . . . Would you tell him to call to see me sometime this afternoon." There was a transfigured look on her face as she put down the receiver and strode across to Sister Paul. "Sister Paul," she said, "you may tell the other Sisters that tomorrow we will set out again for the shore." Sister Paul smiled and whisked away down the corridor: "Isn't Reverend Mother great the way she can handle things," she said to herself, "and to think that on tomorrow I'll be able to see the poplars again."

THE RELUCTANT HANGMAN

HUGH DICKINSON

Conscience doth make cowards of us all. But of Patrick Garritty it made a corpse. It was all right for gentle, tenderhearted Patrick to be sheriff of a backwoods county in Northern Pennsylvania when all he had to do was "post notices, hold sheriff's sales, haul in drunks and bust up an occasional Saturday night brawl," but when his official duty required him to hang a murderer and his conscience was all against it, that was another matter. The story speaks eloquently of the primacy of conscience. Humor and dry wit, a masculine pace, a richness of detail, a robust savoring of pioneer life integrate this moving human story. The author comes from Ithaca, New York.

Early in the Eighties, when my great-uncle Patrick Garritty was sheriff of a backwoods county in Northern Pennsylvania, an aging widow bashed in the heads of her paramour and her hired girl. She was hanged for the crime. But the odd thing about her execution—aside from being the first in the history of the county, and the last—was that it caused the death of my great-uncle who acted, most reluctantly, as her hangman. It was a case of conscience, something queer and puzzling to his contemporaries in the rough lumbering camps of the day.

I heard my elders retell the story often in my childhood, and liked best to hear it from my great-aunts, formidable fates who sat in judgment on all the events of their time. Their account was always the fullest. For they were marvelous reporters. They repeated verbatim the private conversations of others. They knew what had been said of the case in barber shops and taprooms where they would not dream of setting foot. They seemed, indeed, to know the very secrets of the confessional. In my presence they spoke elliptically of the relationships involved in the double murder, and they hurried over the sordid details on quick intakes of breath, the tissue paper in their basques rustling with their effort. But this only made it more interesting for me.

Uncle Pat fared ill at the hands of this Greek chorus. All my great-aunts deplored his pathetic end as a needless thing. To them it sprang from a weakness no man should be troubled with. And they referred to him always as "poor Uncle Pat" in a way that implied he was next door to daft.

He had been elected to the office of sheriff in 1881, three years before the murder and just after the new court house and jail had been built in Rockywood, the county seat. Pat was a big, silver-haired lumberjack—innately pious, capable and strong enough not to have to take any man's guff, but actually mild-mannered and peace-loving.

Stag County was a remarkably peaceful neck of the woods, all things considered, and Pat had little to do but post notices, hold sheriff's sales, haul in drunks and bust up an occasional Saturday night brawl between the lumbermen and the tanners. His wife, Amy, managed the jail for him. During his campaign she had proudly pictured herself occupying in dignity and leisure their special quarters in the new "bastille." But Pat meant to save enough money in office to retire, since the law of the commonwealth made a second term impossible. So Amy had to cook and wash for a stream of raffish, roaring county boarders. Hers was by far the harder job, and she told him so—often. But Pat, despite his wife's complaints, was well pleased with his prospects for the next four years and with the thought of retirement.

Then came the damnable affair of the Widow Jelm. She had a farm in Rockywood Township and enough money left her by her late husband to hire a country girl, Annie Summers, to do the work of the place while she drank and dallied with a shiftless rustic named Nat Wallengreen.

Until he met Sarah Jelm, Nat had barely got along by fishing,

hunting and sometimes hiring out for farm work. When he found
her so accommodating, he gave up his other pursuits, moved to
her farm and devoted himself to the making of moonshine. But
he couldn't keep his hands to himself, and one day the Widow
Jelm spied him making up to Annie by the barn, where the girl
went to get firewood. Sarah was a violent woman, fierce, possessive
and jealous. Keeping her discovery to herself, she went back to
the kitchen, brewed some tea, and made her plans. They proved
to be extremely primitive.

That night she waited until Nat went to bed, then knocked out
his brains with a hatchet she had hidden under her pillow. She
left his body where it lay, took the hatchet to the kitchen to wash
it, and sat up all night drinking tea until Annie Summers came
to work the next morning. She said nothing to Annie about the
scene in the barn. Apparently it did not even occur to her to try
to find out whether the girl had encouraged or fought off Nat's
advances. Willing or unwilling, Annie had become her rival: she
had betrayed her by stealing Nat's easy affections. So she had
to die.

Sarah sipped and watched until Annie's back was turned, then
finished her off with the hatchet that had bludgeoned Nat. After
that, she got very drunk on Nat's moonshine and sat at the table,
with the jug at her elbow, weeping and cursing Annie's body,
which sprawled where it had fallen. This went on until Annie's
father came to the Jelm farm about midnight to look for her. He
discovered the widow in the kitchen, out cold in a chair beside
his dead daughter. Then he found Nat's body.

That was the situation when Sheriff Garritty, thunderstruck,
entered the farmhouse. When he questioned her, Sarah Jelm
made no effort to hide her enormities; she simply would not talk
about them. There was nothing for it but to arrest her for the
murders and lead her off to jail. Not until she went on trial for
her life did she say a word about the crime.

With the atrocities at the Jelm farm, a change came over Uncle Pat. When he realized the part which, by law, he would have to play in the proceedings, his mild, peace-loving nature suffered actual shock. He ceased to be jovial and easygoing: he withdrew into himself: he became almost as silent as his notorious prisoner. He detested any mention of the murders, forbade his wife to discuss them, and, of course, met with talk of nothing else wherever he went in the county. With their sure instinct for the lurid, people began to look at him oddly. He was no longer plain Sheriff Garritty—he was the man who would hang Widow Jelm. There could be no doubt of her guilt, and Pat lived both night and day with the problem it posed.

Good gracious, said my great-aunts, the talk there was! The male gossips in Rockywood gathered daily at Harry Simon's barber shop to discuss the latest news of the case. Here was a crime of passion, with blood enough to paint a house! It threw them into a tizzy. Every man became a Pinkerton, a lawyer, a judge. Customers had to push through gesticulating groups to reach the chairs, and the barbers had scarcely room to work. As the trial drew near, the spitting and arguing increased. Harry Simons said that never had the brass spittoons been so full of butts at the day's end, nor the boys so careless of their aim.

Strained and nervous from secret worry, Sheriff Garritty found that his hands had begun to tremble and that he could no longer safely shave himself. He became a daily visitor at Simon's place where, at his entrance, an eager hush fell. Then would come a sprinkle of questions, as the men tried to pick out of him news of Sarah Jelm. At first Garritty said little, but the questions would go on. To pay him for his silence, the men would turn to discussing the unpleasant job awaiting Pat. At the start they were prying but respectful. When this got them nowhere, they began to goad him into speaking.

"I sure don't envy Pat the job he'll have to do." . . . "I'll say!

Are you keeping your nerve, Pat?" . . . "Sarah Jelm's a tough old witch. You'll need a strong rope to make that old Jezebel swing." . . . "How's she taking it? Does she like the idea?" . . . "Say, have you started to build the gallows yet, Sheriff? Who's got the contract for the work?" (This was good for a hearty laugh.) "Kind of different from posting notices and jailing drunks, ain't it, Garritty? Whoever said bein' sheriff of this county was a cinch?" (Another laugh, with a mean edge to it, for this was hitting Pat where it hurt.) "Why not let his wife do it? She does most of the work around the jail, anyway."

Harry Simons would say mildly: "Now, boys, you'll have to go easy on Pat Garritty. He's got bigger problems than the rest of us nowadays."

One day the sheriff had endured as much as he could. With a curse, he flung himself out of the barber chair and left, one jowl still white with lather. Thereafter, Pat's wife shaved him. It was one more labor added to her daily woes. Word of it got around, and the men had another laugh at Pat's expense.

His torment drove Uncle Pat to confession late one Saturday night, a few days before the trial began. Father Austin, the gruff old parish priest who knew the voice of every penitent behind the grill and the handkerchief, recognized him when he began to recite the Confiteor and interrupted him.

"Pat, are there many more out there? I'm fair jumpy for a smoke."

"I'm the last, Father."

The priest heard his confession, then heaved himself out of his stall. At the church door he lighted a cigar, hitched up his cassock and jammed his hands into his rear pockets. Uncle Pat, coughing diffidently, joined him there after saying his penance. "Father, there . . . there was something I was wanting to ask you."

Father Austin rolled his cigar to the other side of his mouth and shot a glance at him.

"What is it?"

"About this Jelm woman . . ."

"God save us! A filthy business. You'll have your troubles with that one."

"It's sure to be murder in the first degree," said Pat, sweating in the cool night. "And if she hangs for it, I'll be the one to hang her."

"Eh. A bad, bad business."

"Tell me, Father . . . I know it's the law, and all. But will I be doin' the right thing?"

"And why wouldn't you be? Seeing, as you say, it's the law. . . ."

"I don't know," said Pat, shaking his head. "I'll have it on my conscience," he added doggedly. "I will that."

"You'll have no such thing," said the priest brusquely. "You're sworn to uphold the law, ain't ye?"

"Yes, Father."

"Where's your courage, then? It's a bad business, I know. But if the law finds her guilty after a fair trial, and says she must die . . . that's that. Get home now," he urged, trying to soften his manner. "Take a drink and forget it."

"Yes, Father. Thank you."

"Take one for me, too."

Uncle Pat did as he was told, but the dilemma still hung in his mind, refusing to be banished. Through the wakeful nights he put the question to himself endlessly: did he . . . did anyone . . . have the right to take a human life?

In his distress he tried at last to share his problem with Amy, hoping that she might understand. If Amy upheld him, he might have the courage, not to do it, but to refuse to do it.

"You're daft!" she flung at him, when he had unburdened himself. "Plain daft! And scrupulous, that's what you are. Honest people have a right to the protection of the law from such as her. An eye for an eye, I say. Sarah Jelm should be hung twice over to settle the score . . . even if Nat Wallengreen was no good, a fornicator and a drunkard."

Amy rattled the pans and whipped about the kitchen venting the scorn and righteousness pent up until now because Pat had forbidden her to speak of the case.

"Tell me now! Am I married to a man or a scrupulous ninny? Tell me that, Patrick Garritty. Have you no guts in ye?"

She fixed him with a malicious glare.

"D'ye want *me* to spring the trap that'll hang Sarah Jelm? If so, I'll do it . . . and take joy in the doing. I might as well; I do all the work around here, as it is." She shook a wet, work-reddened finger at him. "If you don't hang that woman, there'll be no words for what I think of you, Sheriff Garritty. And I'll not relish being the wife of a coward and the laughing-stock of the county. That I'll not!

"Now," she finished darkly, "you may act accordingly."

The trial began, and during the two short days it lasted, my great-uncle searched desperately for a way out. Father Austin had said: "If she gets a fair trial . . . " Well, Pat meant to see that she did.

He concentrated feverishly on the conduct of the case. He scrutinized the drawing of a jury more closely than Sarah's lawyer. When he was called to testify, his statements were scrupulously exact. When old Summers took the stand, Pat cross-examined him in his mind more carefully than the defense attorney. He passed private judgment on each character witness and clung hopefully to every objection the defense could raise.

It was useless. For, when Sarah Jelm took the stand against her attorney's wishes, she confessed everything. She seemed weary;

neither proud nor fearful, merely indifferent. She had her fair trial, and the jury went through the motions of deliberating on the evidence. Two hours later the jurors returned with a verdict of guilty in the first degree. The judge set the date of execution two months hence.

My great-aunts contended that the verdict affected Sarah less than it did Pat. He treated the condemned woman kindly, and his manner was so tentative and circumspect that Sarah guessed he wished to ask her something. He did so one day, when the jail had been emptied of its other inmates.

She knew, didn't she, that he would have to act as her hangman? Yes, she knew; what the hell difference did it make . . . to him or to her? Well, did *she* think he'd be doing the right thing? Did she think that he . . . or anyone else . . . had a right to take a human life?

"My God! Are *you* asking *me?*"

Sarah dropped back on her cot and stared at him.

Then she roared with laughter. She choked and coughed, while Pat winced but waited with dogged patience for her answer. She sat up suddenly, then, all laughter gone from her raddled face.

"You big fool, you! You big, Irish fool! What're you trying to do? make fun of me?" she demanded. But she knew he wasn't. "God! You're plumb crazy. I'm the one to worry about the rights and wrongs of this, if anybody is. Forget it."

"But . . ."

"Forget it, I said!" She grew fierce: the grotesque comedy tired her. "Just forget it. The best thing you can do for me is to get me a big drink of 'shine."

Although it was against the law, Pat went and got it for her.

A few days before the hanging, a carpenter began to build a scaffold in the courtyard, and people strolled there in the evenings to note his progress. When it was done, the sheriff, shud-

dering plainly, tested the trap again and again. He felt as if one
more sin blackened his soul each time he sprang the trap. But it
had to work, not only because they were all watching him—snig-
gering, saying he was a drone and a coward—but also because,
for Sarah Jelm's sake, it must be done quickly; she must not
suffer when she died by his hand.

Early on the morning of the execution, Mrs. Garritty changed
to her best clothes and elbowed her way through the buzzing
crowd to a place beside the platform. The barber shop lawyers
were there. Indeed, said my great-aunts, who viewed the hanging
from a discreet distance, so jammed was the court house square,
you wondered who had stayed behind to do the work of the
world. Farmers had come from the farthest backwoods of the
county, and beyond, to see the hanging of Sarah Jelm. The pol-
iticians had obtained seats of vantage for their families and
friends in the windows of the court house that faced the gallows.
The crowd spread out to the streets that gave upon the square.
People straddled gables and boys climbed trees to see the novel
sight. Even Father Austin stood in the crowd, fingering his black-
thorn and thinking his own thoughts.

Whatever the onlookers hoped to see, Sarah Jelm cheated them
of all but the sight of her body dangling at the end of a slippery
noose. She stood erect and silent. When Uncle Pat fumbled the
blindfold she was to wear, she took it roughly from his trembling
hands and herself secured it over her eyes.

Amy, never taking her eyes off Pat throughout the ritual, feared
and wondered and waited. But at last he did it: he thrust out
one still shaking hand and sprang the trap.

It was over. The coroner declared Sarah Jelm officially dead
and motioned to the undertaker. The silent crowd stirred and
shifted. Mrs. Garritty ran up the steps of the scaffold and led her
husband from the platform. Pulling him by the hand, she fought

her way through the throng. No sooner had she got him safely inside the jail than he fainted.

She put him to bed, and he never got up again. He lay there, refusing food and wasting away before her very eyes. He became old and shrunken, a feeble creature who could not sleep and would not say a word, except to cry out in his nightmares.

Just before the end, he sent for Father Austin. He made his last confession, and in it he accused himself of having taken a human life against the dictates of his conscience, out of fear and human respect. Then he died.

SATURDAY NOCTURNE

RICHARD SULLIVAN

The tension between the older and the younger generation is not barred from parsonages. Yet when one knows that Richard Sullivan is the writer, it is a foregone conclusion that the strain between pastor and assistant will be handled with gentle charity. Sullivan's distinction as an author is his ability to write of ordinary good people with pure artistic excellence. "Saturday Nocturne" combines the human interest of priests adjusting to each other with the theme of racial prejudice, its depth and complexity being quietly and effectively suggested.

Richard Sullivan's short stories have appeared in many of America's best magazines and have been singled out for honors by the late Edward O'Brien. He teaches in the department of English at Notre Dame, writes book reviews for the New York Times *and the* Chicago Tribune, *and has published four novels:* Summer After Summer, The Dark Continent, The World of Idella May, *and* The First Citizen.

After the angelus rang that Saturday evening, Father Shay heard the confessions of the two people still in line. He waited a few minutes then, as he always did, in case there were others coming; he always had the feeling that there might be just one more, and it would have worried him to leave that one unheard. But tonight when no one else came he left the confessional willingly. He had been in it since three-thirty that afternoon, and his homely young face was red and damp over his wilted collar. Outside, hurrying across the yard from church to rectory, he pulled the hot cassock away from his chest and took deep breaths of the cool twilight air. He was a large young man with a wide mouth and a twisted, flattened nose; he moved with long steps and swinging shoulders.

When he came in the back door, Mrs. Bell, the housekeeper,

was in the kitchen, and he heard Father Lordy in the dining room.

"Has he started eating?"

"Well," said Mrs. Bell; she looked at the alarm clock on the window sill, "it's a quarter after six."

"Tell him I'll be there as soon as I wash."

When he got to the table, Father Lordy was at his pie and coffee, and was reading the evening paper. Shuler's Bake Shop, Father Shay thought, peering at the pie; why doesn't she ever bake it herself? He said grace and sat down. Mrs. Bell had put the platter of cold cuts and the other dishes over close to his place, and he started helping himself.

"Lots of excitement in town this afternoon," Father Lordy said, without looking up from his paper.

"Oh?"

"Riot out at the ball park." Head down, he glanced up between white eyebrows and silver-rimmed glasses; his voice was gruff; hesitating, he seemed to speculate on how the young priest would take serious news. "Negroes," he said.

"What started it?" cried Father Shay sharply. His fork made a brittle clatter on his plate; he stared across the table.

"Ah, it's one of those things," said Father Lordy. "You can't tell *how* it started." He sat back and shoved the newspaper out on the table. Father Shay hastily reached for it. "No, no, it's not in the paper. I heard it on the radio just now. Somebody pushed somebody else when they were all standing up for the seventh-inning stretch—"

"The lucky seventh!" cried Father Shay.

"And four people were hurt—"

"All Negroes?" Father Shay's face was dark and accusing.

"Three, I think."

"Yes, you see! Three out of four!"

"There was nobody seriously hurt," said Father Lordy. "They

got it under control so fast I don't suppose you could really call it a riot."

"But the same thing's happening all over the country!" cried Father Shay. "It's not just that nobody was hurt—it's the *idea* of the thing!"

"Anyhow, it wasn't like some of those big riots in the cities. It was all over in twenty minutes."

"But these things *grow!*" Father Shay was terribly upset, as if he had been offended personally.

"It's a nasty thing," said Father Lordy, shaking his head. "It's the first time anything like that has happened in this town in all the time I've been here." He stood up and made the sign of the cross. Then for a moment he hesitated as if he had something more to say about the trouble at the ball park; but when Father Shay looked at him expectantly he only frowned and shook his head again.

"It's enough to make a man sick!" burst out Father Shay. "It's shameful! Why, there are people who think Negroes have no souls! No wonder there are riots!"

"I know, I know," said Father Lordy. "I'll be in on the couch," he said. "Call me when you go over."

Father Shay ate his supper broodingly. He had been ordained just two months, and this was his first parish. In the few weeks he had been here, he had frequently felt inexperienced, so that he had been ashamed of his own youth and foolishness; but now his sense of inexperience made him resentful. He didn't know anything about Negroes, he was ready to admit it; he didn't even know any Negroes. But he did know injustice when he saw it, and in this town he had seen it from the first. It was not a very large town, and there were not a great many Negroes here, proportionately, but those who were here, he thought, were being pushed around: they were paying exorbitant rents for foul housing; some of the factories refused them work entirely; others took them on but carefully kept them down; and there was a feeling in the air, a vague, unphrased but strong feeling, that this was the way things were supposed to be; at least no one said that this was *not* the right way to have things.

He had been shocked by the news Father Lordy had given him. But now, brooding, he felt more deeply shocked by what seemed to him the casualness, the indifference of the old priest. Oh, it was probably true that the extraordinary surge of people to town to work in the factories had made disturbances like this of the ball park more likely; they were effects of the times. Yet underneath them, there was a kind of permanent and horrible evil. Father Lordy seemed to have no sense of it, no sense of what was happening. He'd been pastor here for nineteen years now; he was probably so used to the town that he couldn't see it freshly any more. But he ought to see it freshly; that was his obligation. The acceptance of injustice seemed to Father Shay almost worse than injustice itself. Bolting his supper, he felt a passion of bitterness and urgency. "No pie, Mrs. Bell," he told her when she started to clear away dishes.

"Coffee, Father?" Mrs. Bell slanted her eyebrows in hurt indifference about the pie.

"What time is it?" He started fumbling for his watch.

"You have twenty minutes."

"All right. Coffee."

When he went in to call Father Lordy five minutes later, he was still bitter and urgent. "That rioting at the ball park," he said. "You know we ought to do something about it!"

Father Lordy sat up on the old leather couch; he was in his shirt sleeves; he combed his white hair with his fingers and fastened his collar, then reached for his cassock. "It's a nasty thing," he said.

"I'd like to preach about it tomorrow."

"What would you say?"

"Well . . . it's unchristian . . . it's beastly!"

"Look, young Father Gene," said the old priest, buttoning his cassock buttons with big deliberate fingers. "I know how you feel. I've been thinking, too. But it's not enough just to say it's bad. That's fine, to say it, of course . . . but what are you going to do about it?" He paused and sniffed, almost in embarrassment. "You see, I know as well as you do that it's unchristian. It's evil, that's what it is, evil, and there are generations of evil behind it. That makes it hard" . . . he shook his head . . . "generations of evil. I'm troubled by it, I admit. It bursts out this way all of a sudden." He paused. "I don't know just what to do about it," he said.

The two of them had walked together through the kitchen, past Mrs. Bell clattering at the sink; now they were going across the backyard in the dusk to the church. The clock in the steeple started striking seven as they walked. Father Shay was silent. He doesn't know what to do, he thought, so he won't do anything: the slow, passive defeat. He felt himself drifting into a deep black melancholy. But he was going to do something. Maybe he didn't know just what to do either, but he was going to do something.

At the side door of the church Father Lordy cleared his throat gruffly. "Maybe it's just that I'm an old man," he said. "I won't say you shouldn't mention it tomorrow. Only be careful. It's too important to be careless and emotional about. Think it over and we'll talk about it later tonight. I'd like to talk about it with you." He opened the door. "If I knew what to say I might mention it tomorrow myself," he said gloomily.

Father Shay bounded up the stone steps with the sudden conviction that he had won the old man over, that he had made a conversion. He shook his big clenched fists tightly at his sides. If Father Lordy had been another kind of man, he would have thumped him on the shoulder at that moment. As it was he grinned happily, his white teeth bright in the dusk against his rough red face. "Thank you, Father," he said.

Hurrying up the south aisle to his confessional, he heard the old priest's heavy footsteps clumping on the rubber matting of the north aisle, like echoes of his own; there was a kind of companionship, a kind of sympathy, in the mingling sounds. As he stooped to get into his confessional Father Shay felt exhilarated and eager. Tomorrow, he thought. He tried to recall just what he'd said to Father Lordy, but it didn't really matter; it was probably the way you said a thing as much as the thing itself, anyhow. If people could be made to *see* that a thing was wrong, if it was made *clear* to them, they would change; they *had* to change. At the seminary a priest had once told Father Shay that he had a too great confidence in the perfectibility of human nature. He did have; he knew it now, sitting in the confessional; he felt a quick exuberance; he was glad of his own great confidence. Tomorrow he'd make them *see*. But now people coming to confession got in the way of his plans. He had to concentrate on them; he took all his obligations very seriously.

In a little while he thought of combining penances with his own intentions. "For your holy penance say three Hail Mary's for the spread of Christian charity among all men," he whispered to one person through the white screened grill. To the next, "For your holy penance say five Our Father's and five Hail Mary's for the spread of justice and charity in our town. Now make a good act of contrition." To one woman he gave a decade of the rosary to be said for all oppressed people; to what sounded like a young man, the litany of the saints for grace to love and respect his fellow men. It gave him a deep satisfaction to tie these penances in with his own urgent concern. It seemed to him an effectual thing to get prayers said; he wondered if perhaps it was not more effectual than his preaching tomorrow would be. Reflecting on that, he decided that what he was really doing was making a fine practical combination of prayer and good works.

An old man whose false teeth smacked and clopped was in the box, but Father Shay's attention wandered a little. He thought of the rioting at the ball park that day, and imagined himself there, in the shouting and fury, quelling the mob. With his head bent sideways towards the grill he listened to the old man's mumbling, but at the same time he was surrounded by rioting Negroes who did not understand that he was not their enemy; they were cursing and shrieking, a ring of dark men and women; they were grabbing at his outstretched arms, expecting him to fight back, but he would not; they beat at him; his breath in the confessional quickened. He listened to the old man, but at the same time he was making a heroic sacrifice of himself. "It's all right!" he was crying in his imagination to the mob. "Go ahead! You're right, you're right! You've stood enough—take it out on me! I'm white—take it out on me!"

Beyond the screen, the false teeth smacked once finally, and the voice was silent. Father Shay shook his head sharply. Remotely, with a sudden drop of emotion, he pulled himself from the heroic vision and concentrated on what the old man had said. He murmured for a moment; then, "For your holy penance say three Our Father's for the sake of the oppressed people of our town." He heard the grunting and scraping, then the soft, woody thump of the confessional door—usually it didn't slam, the one going out holding it open for the one coming in. He waited; no one came; in the darkness his watch glowed green: 8:40. He stuck his head out of his own little door and saw that the church was empty, and Father Lordy was gone, his confessional door wide open.

Presumption, he thought, returning to his dream of the rioting. It had been so real, so exciting, that now in memory it was like an actual experience. But a person would really have no right to offer himself to a mob that way. All the same they deserved a

victim. But it would really be inciting them to sin, to offer yourself to a mob. A doubt hung in his mind, though; he went into
the vestibule to switch off lights. It wouldn't have to be sinful; it
would depend on the way you did it; he wondered how martyrs
felt ahead of their martyrdom. If you did something like that in
complete honesty, out of justice . . . but then they'd probably
not attack you at all; they'd understand and be changed. He saw
himself in the centre of a dark converted throng, the voices dying,
the fists unclenched, the once angry faces awe-struck; and standing in the vestibule he swallowed once, hard.

The front door rattled open; he turned; it was the janitor come
to lock up.

"All through, Father?"

"Looks like it, Joe."

The janitor slid a bolt on the door. "See the Sox took the second one in the double-header," he said.

"They *did?*" Father Shay suddenly remembered that he had
forgotten to tune in on the baseball scores at supper time. "What
was . . .?"

"Eight to two," Joe said.

"Ah, they start at the end of the season," said Father Shay.
"They never get going until the end!"

He went out one of the side doors, lighted a cigarette, and
started across the school yard towards the rectory. Gravel
crunched beneath his shoes; the sky overhead was massed with
moonlit clouds, a bright exciting sky. Again he saw the imaginary
mob about him, and again he offered himself to it. "You've stood
enough! Take it out on me!" As he walked across the crunching
gravel he stretched his arms out and threw his head back, whispering the words.

He couldn't find Father Lordy in the house. He finally went
down the back hall and tapped on Mrs. Bell's door. She opened
it so quickly that she surprised him.

"Well, he made some phone calls, Father, and then he went out at eight o'clock. He told me to be sure and tell you he'd be back a little after nine."

"Oh," said Father Shay. "All right, Mrs. Bell."

He went up the back stairs to his own room. For a moment he stood in front of the dresser, frowning absently at the still un-framed photograph of his class at the seminary. Then he slowly took off his cassock and collar, opened the bottom dresser drawer and took out an old blue sweater. He pulled it over his head; then, smoothing his hair with his hands, he glanced at himself in the mirror. In the heavy crew-necked sweater, with the fuzzy twisting ends of yarn at the shoulder where he had ripped it that time two years ago playing touch football, he looked curiously tough and burly. He peered at his big raw face, his twisted nose. Enough to scare a dog, he thought. He turned and went out, down the back stairs.

"Mrs. Bell," he called, "will you please tell Father Lordy I'll be back in twenty minutes?"

She opened the door again before he was ready for her. He saw the way she looked at the sweater. "That is, if he gets back before I do," he said.

"I'll tell him," she said, and her eyebrows slanted ever so slightly as she closed the door.

In the front hall he switched off the light, then waited at the door for a moment to see if anybody was going by outside. When he had first come here, a few weeks ago, he had put on this old sweater one afternoon, intending to run a couple of miles as a workout; but Father Lordy had stopped him at this very door. "You're not going outside in the broad daylight in that rig," he told him. "Have you no dignity?" Father Shay had explained meekly that he honestly needed the exercise; without it he put on weight quickly and got sluggish; he had always led a strenuous life. It was arranged then that he take his workouts at night, when no one was likely to see him in his disreputable sweater. "There are ways to do a thing," Father Lordy said, "and there are ways *not* to do a thing." He had been standing right here in this hall when he had said it, and it had been impossible to tell what he was thinking. Going out the doorway now, Father Shay wondered whether the old priest considered these nightly workouts ridiculous or whether he really approved of them. It was a little hard to be sure of Father Lordy. He jogged down the sidewalk wondering.

He had by now established a regular course for his nightly run: six blocks down to a little park, a block square; three times around this block and the six blocks home made two miles, as he figured. But the park was so small that he wondered sometimes if his figuring wasn't a little generous.

Tonight he went the first few blocks slowly, loosening up. He held his head down when he passed street lights or people, because, of course, he agreed with what Father Lordy had said about dignity. Still, he wasn't going to stop running just because people might find it amusing and talk. He had always had a dread of being afraid, of being shamed into a kind of dishonorable prudence.

He was running at a good moderate clip when he came to the park. A couple of little boys whom he recognized as belonging to the parish were playing around a water bubbler at the corner. As he ran at them out of the darkness they dodged into the street, startled. He kept his face turned away, and tried to imagine how he looked to them. Behind him he heard them run across the street out of the park.

He slowed down a little, staring at the black trees and the spottily moonlit grass. Often when he came here at night, there were people scattered about on the benches in the park, but now the place seemed deserted. He wondered suddenly if the trouble at the ball park could be responsible, people not wanting to come out tonight after a thing like that. But the idea seemed far-fetched. His feet made quick regular patting noises on the cement sidewalk, and as he began the second round his breath was coming deep and easy and he pushed his stride.

Then ahead of him, in the dark tunnelled stretch at one edge of the park, where small thorn trees grew for about twenty feet close on each side of the walk, he saw a man standing. It startled him, to see this unexpected figure dark in the darkness, moonlight behind him—he hadn't been there before, unless he'd been hiding, and it was such a very small park that he couldn't have come in without being seen. Father Shay kept running, and the man suddenly laughed, a clear but intimate laugh, as if someone had just told a joke; at the same instant a girl stood up from a bench where she had been sitting—a bench in a kind of nook among the thorn trees; Father Shay hadn't seen it before—and she laughed too, rather raucously, with the man.

The priest was now about ten paces from them; he swerved onto the narrow strip of grass, giving them the sidewalk. He felt at once that they were laughing at him. They had been watching him here, they had recognized him, and now they were laughing. Resentful, angry, embarrassed, he kept his head down and ran; there were roots twisting up out of the grass; he tripped on one, and grunting furiously plunged forward almost at the feet of the two on the sidewalk.

"O-oh-h!" the girl cried. "Sa-a-ay!" said the man. For an instant they both stood back, almost as if they were afraid of him. Then—"Help him up, Sonny! See if he's hurt!" the girl said. The man hesitated an instant, then stooped.

Looking up, still angrier, breathing hard, Father Shay saw first the man's white shirt looming above him, then the dark apprehensive face, then the girl's face: they were Negroes. With a kind of dazed clarity he understood at once their air of caution, their hesitancy; they were worried by what had happened this afternoon; he saw how he must have looked to them a moment before, big, unknown, lumbering up out of the darkness; he even knew how threatening his face must look right now, and he struggled to smile, to seem friendly. Getting up, the man's hand under his arm, he remembered his proud dream of the riot, himself against the mob; and he was humiliated by the irony of this moment. These people were not attacking him; they were helping him. He felt foolish and ashamed. Lurching onto his feet, he clutched the man's arm gratefully. Close up he saw the girl's face, staring, saw her eyebrows shoot up and her mouth open. "Sonny!" she cried to the man. "Watch out!" Father Shay knew then what was coming; he wanted to stop it; with a fierce, desperate gesture he thrust out his hand towards the girl. "No, no!" he cried. But the man had already broken from his grasp, the girl was already running; the man darted after her. "Wait!" shouted Father Shay. "Wait!" Frantic, he started after them. "Please, wait!"

But they were yards ahead, running wildly, the man looking back. Father Shay stopped, stood there on the sidewalk; his homely face twisted grotesquely, and he beat one fist into the palm of the other hand. "O God," he said, "O dear God!" Things reeled through his mind: the hopeless enormity of their feeling, and its unexpectedness, the generations, the generations, too important to be careless about, and Father Lordy shaking his head, saying, "Only I don't know what to do," and the incredible enormity of injustice, the impossible strength of evil.

He watched the Negroes to the far corner of the park; when they crossed the street he turned and started walking towards home. His mind worked in dull slow whirls, over and over. With awful clarity he realized that he was a fool. Going to straighten things out, zip, like that, with a neat little sermon in the morning. A serene fool, full of good will, of course, and full of pride and of easy heroics of the imagination. In the darkness his lips drew tight and trembled like a boy's under strong shame. He was walking too slowly—he made himself take brisker steps. He felt his mind thump heavily over, and a question which had been murky and unphrased now came into focus: What was he going to say to Father Lordy when he got back? "I'd like to talk it over with you," Father Lordy had said. After all, he thought, feeling himself wince—after all, preaching in this parish isn't much use anyway. He knew that he was excusing himself, but he was so flattened and empty that he didn't care, for just that moment. Still, he thought wearily, something still has to be done. This hadn't changed the necessity; it was more urgent than ever now, really, to do something—and harder than ever. Thinking of the difficulty, he felt powerless, as in a nightmare.

When he came very quietly in the front door he saw Father Lordy on the old leather couch in the front room. He was sitting up straight, in street clothes, reading his breviary. Father Shay tiptoed down the dark hall.

"That you, Father?" The old priest's voice was sharp and impatient.

Father Shay turned and came back. When he looked into the room he said nothing.

"Come in! Come in! I've been waiting for you!" Father Lordy didn't seem to notice the sweater; he pointed with his breviary at a chair. "Sit down. I'll be through with this in a minute."

Father Shay sat down. He watched the light glint dully on the crinkled toes of his shoes, side by side on the thin brown carpet; then he looked up at the old priest's face. Frowning intently, Father Lordy was whispering the words of his office; his lips made little loose quick movements, and his eyelids fluttered behind his glasses. He was sitting up very straight, the book in both hands before him; he seemed eager to be finished, as if he had something important to attend to then, yet determined not to hurry or not to turn to the next thing until his present one was done. Watching him, Father Shay felt a queer and unexpected reassurance—the old man looked so busy, so purposive, sitting there praying. Father Shay began to pray in his own mind, rather unsteadily, for strength and for guidance. Just then Father Lordy snapped his breviary shut. "Now!" he said. He laid the book on the couch beside him.

Father Shay cleared his throat. "I—I have something to tell you, Father. Something that happened—" He broke off; he didn't know exactly how to tell it.

"Well, I have something to tell you first," Father Lordy said. He looked very pleased yet very severe, as if he were holding himself in with difficulty. "What you said after supper got me to thinking, you know. It really got me to thinking. You see, we've never had trouble like this in town before." He paused reminiscently; but almost at once he leaned forward, hands on his knees. "Well!" he said. "Anyhow, I left church early tonight, and I've been around seeing a few people—just little hurry-up calls, you know, but people who'll work with us on this thing. It's nothing revolutionary, you understand, nothing sensational right now—I'll tell you all about it—but it'll grow. We have to start things like this carefully if we don't want to make mistakes. There's a way to do things and a way not to do them. Now I'll tell you." Leaning forward he pointed one finger at Father Shay, and his voice grew almost conspiratorial—"We're *both* going to preach tomorrow, and afterward—"

But Father Shay couldn't follow the plans clearly just then. It was as it had been in the church earlier tonight, their footsteps sounding together: a sense of companionship, of being *with* someone. He felt the firm reserved strength of the old priest; and if he couldn't make out the words clearly, the voice itself was enough just then, it was what he most needed. In his relief, or beyond it, over it, a faint happiness stirred him; because in a way he was himself responsible, in a way he had started all this. As he sat there, staring at Father Lordy, he felt what seemed an ancient and far-away excitement rising warm and green within him for tomorrow.

HOME

LANGSTON HUGHES

The stark-naked sinfulness, horror, ugliness, and stupidity of the white man's refusal to accept his pigmented brother in Christ are powerfully projected in this simple story.

Langston Hughes is an American Negro poet whose work is marked by bitter clowning and the rhythms of Negro folk music. Many of his poems have been translated into German, French, Russian, Yiddish, Czech. Besides several volumes of poetry, he has published plays, a novel, an autobiography, and a volume of short stories, The Ways of White Folks.

When the boy came back, there were bright stickers and tags in strange languages the home folks couldn't read all over his bags, and on his violin case. They were the marks of customs stations at far-away borders, big hotels in European cities, and steamers that crossed the ocean a long way from Hopkinsville. They made the leather-colored bags and black violin case look very gay and circus-like. They made white people on the train wonder about the brown-skinned young man to whom the baggage belonged. And when he got off at a village station in Missouri, the loafers gathered around in a crowd, staring.

Roy Williams had come home from abroad to visit his folks, his mother and sister and brothers who still remained in the old home town. Roy had been away seven or eight years, wandering the world. He came back very well dressed, but awfully thin. He wasn't well.

It was this illness that had made Roy come home, really. He had a feeling that he was going to die, and he wanted to see his mother again. This feeling about death had been coming over him gradually for two or three years now. It seemed to him that it must have started in Vienna, that gay but dying city in Central Europe where so many people were hungry, and yet some still had money to buy champagne and caviar and women in the night-clubs where Roy's orchestra played.

But the glittering curtains of Roy's jazz were lined with death. It made him sick to see people fainting in the streets of Vienna from hunger, while others stuffed themselves with wine and food. And it made him sad to refuse the young white women trailing behind him when he came home from work late at night, offering their bodies for a little money to buy something to eat.

In Vienna Roy had a room to himself because he wanted to study and keep up his music. He studied under one of the best violin teachers. But it was hard to keep beautiful and hungry women out of his place, who wanted to give themselves to a man who had a job because in turn the man might let them sleep in his room, or toss them a few bills to take home to their starving parents.

"Folks catch hell in Europe," Roy thought. "I never saw people as hungry as this, not even Negroes at home."

But it was even worse when the orchestra moved back to Berlin. Behind the apparent solidity of that great city, behind doors where tourists never passed, hunger and pain were beyond understanding. And the police were beating people who protested, or stole, or begged. Yet in the cabaret where Roy played, crowds of folks still spent good gold. They laughed and danced every night and didn't give a damn about the children sleeping in the doorways outside, or the men who built houses of packing boxes, or the women who walked the streets to pick up trade.

It was in Berlin that the sadness weighed most heavily on Roy. And it was there that he began to cough. One night in Prague, he had a hemorrhage. When he got to Paris, his girl friend took care of him, and he got better. But he had all the time, from then on, that feeling that he was going to die. The cough stayed, and the sadness. So he came home to see his mother.

He landed in New York on the day that Hoover drove the veterans out of Washington. He stayed a couple of days in Harlem. Most of his old friends there, musicians and actors, were hungry and out of work. When they saw Roy dressed so well, they asked him for money. And at night women whispered in the streets, "Come here, baby! I want to see you, darlin'."

"Rotten everywhere," Roy thought. "I want to go home."

That last night in Harlem, he couldn't sleep. He thought of his mother. In the morning he sent her a telegram that he was on his way.

II

"An uppty nigger," said the white loafers when they saw him standing, slim and elegant, on the station platform in the September sunlight, surrounded by his bags with the bright stickers. Roy had got off a Pullman—something unusual for a Negro in those parts.

"God damn!" said the white loafers.

Suddenly a nasal voice broke out, "Well, I'll be dogged if it ain't Roy Williams!"

Roy recognized an old playmate, Charlie Mumford, from across the alley—a tall red-necked white boy in overalls. He took off his glove and held out his hand. The white man took it, but he didn't shake it long. Roy had forgotten he wasn't in Europe, wearing gloves and shaking hands glibly with a white man! Damn!

"Where you been, boy?" the white fellow asked.

"Paris," said Roy.

"What'd yuh come back for?" a half-southern voice drawled from the edge of a baggage truck.

"I wanted to come home," said Roy, "to see my mother."

"I hope she's gladder to see yuh than we are," another white voice drawled.

Roy picked up his bags, since there were no porters, and carried them toward a rusty old Ford that seemed to be a taxi. He felt dizzy and weak. The smoke and dust of travel had made him cough a lot. The eyes of the white men about the station were not kind. He heard some one mutter, "Nigger." His skin burned. For the first time in half a dozen years he felt his color. He was home.

III

Sing a song of Dixie, cotton bursting in the sun, shade of china-berry trees, persimmons after frost has fallen. Hounds treeing possums October nights. O, sweet potatoes, hot, with butter in their yellow hearts.

"Son, I'm glad you's done come home. What can Ma cook for you? I know you's hungry for some real food. Corn bread and greens and salt pork. Lawd! . . . You's got some mighty nice clothes, honey, but you looks right thin. . . . Chile, I hope you's gona stay home awhile. . . . These colored girls here'll go crazy about you. They fightin' over you already. . . . Honey, when you plays that violin o' your'n it makes me right weak, it's so purty. . . . Play yo' violin, boy! God's done give you a gift! Yes, indeedy! . . . It's funny how all these Hopkinsville white folks is heard about you already. De woman where yo' sister works say she read someplace 'bout that orchestry you was playin' with in Paris. She says fo' Sister to bring you up to de house to play fo' her sometime. I told Sister, no indeedy, you don't go around playin' at nobody's house. Told her to tell that white woman de Deacon's Board's arrangin' a concert at de church fo' you where everybody can come and pay twenty-five cents to de glory of God and hear you play. Ain't that right, son? You gwine play fo' de Lawd here in Hopkinsville. You been playin' fo' de devil every

night all over Europy. . . . Jesus have mercy! Lemme go and
get ma washin' out! And whiles you's practicin', I'm gonna make
you a pumpkin pie this afternoon. I can see yo' mouth a-waterin'
now. . . . Honey, Ma's sho glad you's done come home. . . .
Play yo' violin, son!"

IV

CAPRICE VIENNOIS

AIR FOR G STRING

SONATA IN A

AVE MARIA

THE GYPSY DANCES

What little house anywhere was ever big enough to hold
Brahms and Beethoven, Bach, and César Franck? Certainly not
Sister Sarah Williams's house in Hopkinsville. When Roy played,
ill as he was, the notes went bursting out the windows and the
colored folks and white folks in the street heard them. The classic
Mr. Brahms coming out of a nigger's house in the southern end of
Missouri. O, my God! Play yo' violin, Roy! Tonight's your
concert.

The Deacons and the Ladies' Aid sold a lot of tickets to the
white folks they worked for. Roy's home-coming concert at Shiloh
Church was a financial success. The front rows were fifty cents
and filled with white folks. The rest of the seats were a quarter
and filled with Negroes. Methodist and Baptist both came, forgetting churchly rivalry. And there were lots of colored girls with
powdered bon-bon faces—sweet black and brown and yellow girls
with red mouths pointed at Roy. There was lots of bustle and
perfume and smothered giggling and whispered talk as the drab
little church filled. New shoes screeched up and down the aisles.
People applauded because it was past the hour, but the concert

started colored folks' time anyhow—late. The church was crowded.

V

Hello, Mr. Brahms on a violin from Vienna at a colored church in Hopkinsville, Missouri. The slender brown-skin hands of a sick young man making you sing for an audience of poor white folks and even poorer Negroes. Good-evenin', Mr. Brahms, a long ways from home, travellin' in answer to your dream, singin' across the world. I had a dream, too, Mr. Brahms, a big dream that can't come true, now. Dream of a great stage in a huge hall, like Carnegie Hall or the Salle Gaveau. And you, Mr. Brahms, singin' out into the darkness, singin' so strong and true that a thousand people look up at me like they do at Roland Hayes singing the Crucifixion. Jesus, I dreamed like that once before I got sick and had to come home.

And here I am giving my first concert in America for my mother and the Deacons of Shiloh Church and the quarters and fifty cent pieces they've collected from Brahms and me for the glory of God. This ain't Carnegie Hall. I've only just come home. . . . But they're looking at me. They're all looking at me. The white folks in the front rows and the Negroes in the back. Like one pair of eyes looking at me.

This, my friends, . . . I should say, *Ladies and Gentlemen*. (There are white folks in the audience who are not my friends.) . . . This is the *Meditation from Thaïs* by Massenet. . . . This is the broken heart of a dream come true not true. This is music, and me, sitting on the doorstep of the world needing you. . . . O, body of life and love with black hands and brown limbs and white breasts and a golden face with lips like a violin bowed for singing. . . . Steady, Roy! It's hot in this crowded church, and you're sick as hell. . . . This, the dream and the dreamer, wandering in the desert from Hopkinsville to Vienna in love with a street-walker named Music. . . . Listen, you bitch, I want you to be beautiful as the moon in the night on the edge of the Missouri hills. I'll make you beautiful. . . . *The Meditation from Thaïs.* . . . You remember, Ma (even to hear me play, you've got your seat in the amen corner tonight like on Sunday mornings when you come to talk to God), you remember that Kreisler record we had on the phonograph with the big horn when I was a kid? Nobody liked it but me, but you didn't care how many times I played it, over and over. . . . Where'd you get my violin? Half the time you didn't have the money to pay old man Miller for my lesson every week. . . . God rest his unpaid soul, as the Catholics say. . . . Why did you cry, Ma, when I went away with the minstrel show, playing coon songs through the South instead of hymns? What did you cry for, Ma, when I wrote you I had a job with a night-club jazz band on State Street in Chicago? . . . Why did you pray all night when I told you we had a contract to go to Berlin and work in a cabaret there? I tried to explain to you that the best violin teachers in the world were in Berlin and that I'd come back playing like that Kreisler record on the old victrola. . . . And didn't I send you money home? . . . Spray like sand in the eyes. . . . O, dream on the door-step of the world! Thaïs! Thaïs! . . . You sure don't look like Thaïs, you scrawny white woman in a cheap coat and red hat staring up at me from the first row. You don't look a bit like Thaïs. What is it you want the music to give you? What do you want from me? . . . This is Hopkinsville, Missouri. . . . Look at all those brown girls back there in the crowd of Negroes, leaning toward me and the music. First time most of them ever saw a man in evening clothes, black or white. First time most of them ever heard the *Meditation from Thaïs.* First time they ever had one of their own race come home from abroad playing a violin. See them looking proud at me and music over the heads of the white folks in the first rows, over the head of the white woman in

the cheap coat and red hat who knows what music's all about.
. . . Who are you, lady?

When the concert was over, even some of the white folks shook
Roy's hand and said it was wonderful. The colored folks said,
"Boy, you sure can play!" Roy was shaking a little and his eyes
burned and he wanted terribly to cough. Pain shot across his
shoulders. But he smiled his concert-jazz-band smile that the gold
spending ladies of the European night clubs had liked so much.
And he held out a feverish hand to everybody. The white woman
in the red hat waited at the edge of the crowd.

When the people thinned out a little from the pulpit, she came
to Roy and shook his hand. She spoke of symphony concerts in
St. Louis, of the fact that she was a teacher of music, of piano
and violin, but that she had no pupils like Roy, that never in the
town of Hopkinsville had anyone else played so beautifully. Roy
looked into her thin, freckled face and was glad she knew what it
was all about. He was glad she liked music.

"That's Miss Reese," his mother told him after she had gone.
"An old maid musicianer at the white high school."

"Yes'm," said Roy. "She understands music."

VI

The next time he saw Miss Reese was at the white high school
shortly after it opened the fall session. One morning a note had
come asking him if he would play for her Senior class in music
appreciation some day. She would accompany him if he would
bring his music. It seems that one of Miss Reese's duties was the
raising of musical standards in Hopkinsville; she had been telling her students about Bach and Mozart, and she would so appreciate it if Roy would visit the school and play those two great
masters for her young people. She wrote him a nice note on clean
white paper.

Roy went. His mother thought it was a great honor for the

white high school to send for her colored son to play for them.
"That Miss Reese's a right nice woman," Sister Williams said to
her boy. "Sendin' for you to play up there at de school. First
time I ever knowed 'em to have a Negro in there for anything but
cleanin' up, and I been in Hopkinsville a long time. Go and play
for 'em, son, to de glory of God!"

Roy played. But it was one of those days when his throat was
hot and dry, and his eyes burned. He had been coughing all
morning and, as he played, his breath left him and he stood
covered with a damp sweat. He played badly.

But Miss Reese was more than kind to him. She accompanied
him at the piano. And when he had finished, she turned to the
assembled class of white kids sprawled in their seats and said,
"This is art, my dear young people, this is true art!"

The students went home that afternoon and told their parents
that a dressed-up nigger had come to school with a violin and
played a lot of funny pieces nobody but Miss Reese liked. They
went on to say that Miss Reese had grinned all over herself and
cried, "Wonderful!" And had even bowed to the nigger when
he went out!

Roy went home to bed. He was up and down these days,
thinner and thinner all the time, weaker and weaker. Sometimes
not practicing any more. Often not eating the food his mother
cooked for him, or that his sister brought from where she worked.
Sometimes being restless and hot in the night and getting up and
dressing, even to spats and yellow gloves, and walking the streets
of the little town at ten and eleven o'clock after nearly every one
else had gone to bed. Midnight was late in Hopkinsville. But for
years Roy had worked at night. It was hard for him to sleep before
morning now.

But one night he walked out of the house for the last time. The
moon had risen and Roy scarcely needed to light the oil lamp to
dress by when he got up. The moon shone into his little room,

across the white counterpane of his bed, down onto the bags with the bright stickers piled against the wall. It glistened on the array of medicine bottles on the side table. But Roy lighted the light, the better to see himself in the warped mirror of the dresser. Ashy pale his face was, that had once been brown. His cheeks were sunken. Trembling, he put on his suit and spats and his yellow gloves and soft felt hat. He got into an overcoat. He took a cane that he carried lately from weakness rather than from style. And he went out into the autumn moonlight.

Tiptoeing through the parlor, he heard his mother snoring on the couch there. (She had given up her room to him.) The front door was still unlocked. His brothers, Roy thought, were out with their girl friends. His sister had gone to bed.

In the streets it was very quiet. Misty with moonlight, the trees stood half clad in autumn leaves. Roy walked under the dry falling leaves toward the center of the town, breathing in the moonlight air and swinging his cane. Night and the streets always made him feel better. He remembered the boulevards of Paris and the Unter den Linden. He remembered Tauber singing *Wien, Du Stadt Meiner Traume*. His mind went back to the lights and the music of the cities of Europe. How like a dream that he had ever been in Europe at all, he thought. Ma never had any money. Her kids had barely managed to get through grade school. There was no higher school for Negroes in Hopkinsville. For him there had been only a minstrel show to run away with for further education. Then that chance with a jazz band going to Berlin. And his violin for a mistress all the time—with the best teachers his earnings could pay for abroad. Jazz at night and the classics in the morning. Hard work and hard practice, until his violin sang like nobody's business. Music, real music! Then he began to cough in Berlin.

Roy was passing lots of people now in the brightness of the main street, but he saw none of them. He saw only dreams and memories, and heard music. Some of the people stopped to stare and grin at the flare of the European coat on his slender brown body. Spats and a cane on a young nigger in Hopkinsville, Missouri! What's the big idea, heh? A little white boy or two cat-called, "Hey, coon!" But everything might have been all right, folks might only have laughed or commented and cussed, had not a rather faded woman in a cheap coat and a red hat, a white woman, stepping out of the drug store just as Roy passed, bowed pleasantly to him, "Good evening."

Roy started, bowed, nodded, "Good evening, Miss Reese," and was glad to see her. Forgetting he wasn't in Europe, he took off his hat and his gloves, and held out his hand to this lady who understood music. They smiled at each other, the sick young colored man and the aging music teacher in the light of the main street. Then she asked him if he was still working on the Sarasate.

"Yes," Roy said. "It's lovely."

"And have you heard that marvellous Heifetz record of it?" Miss Reese inquired.

Roy opened his mouth to reply when he saw the woman's face suddenly grow pale with horror. Before he could turn around to learn what her eyes had seen, he felt a fist like a ton of bricks strike his jaw. There was a flash of lightning in his brain as his head hit the edge of the plate glass window of the drug store. Miss Reese screamed. The sidewalk filled with white young ruffians with red-necks, open sweaters, and fists doubled up to strike. The movies had just let out and the crowd, passing by and seeing, ob-jected to a Negro talking to a white woman—insulting a White Woman—attacking a WHITE woman—RAPING A WHITE WOMAN. They saw Roy remove his gloves and bow. When Miss Reese screamed after Roy had been struck, they were sure he had been making love to her. And before the story got beyond the rim of the crowd, Roy had been trying to rape her, right there on the main street in front of the brightly-lighted windows of the drug store. Yes, he did, too! Yes, sir!

So they knocked Roy down. They trampled on his hat and cane and gloves as a dozen men tried to get to him to pick him up —so some one else could have the pleasure of knocking him down again. They struggled over the privilege of knocking him down.

Roy looked up from the sidewalk at the white mob around him. His mouth was full of blood and his eyes burned. His clothes were dirty. He wondered why Miss Reese had stopped to ask him about Sarasate. He knew he would never get home to his mother now.

Some one jerked him to his feet. Some one spat in his face. (It looked like his old playmate, Charlie Mumford.) Somebody cussed him for being a nigger, and another kicked him from behind. And all the men and boys in the lighted street began to yell and scream like mad people, and to snarl like dogs, and to pull at the little Negro in spats they were dragging through the town towards the woods.

The little Negro whose name was Roy Williams began to choke on the blood in his mouth. And the roar of their voices and the scuff of their feet were split by the moonlight into a thousand notes like a Beethoven sonata. And when the white folks left his brown body, stark naked, strung from a tree at the edge of town, it hung there all night, like a violin for the wind to play.

TROUBLE WITH THE UNION

DENNIS HARRINGTON

*Take a Franciscan brother, who loves to work for the joy of it, and let
him tangle with the union, where anything above the day's neat quota is
scab labor, and you have the setting for this rollicking yarn by an Irishman
about Irishmen—and one commie whose name really was not Stalinovsky
at all. In spite of being stream-lined and light-hearted, this story has
something important to say about the right spirit of work.*

A full moon shone on Brooklyn, but only a cynic would say it
shed its light indifferently on rich and poor and good and bad
alike. Over the lovers in Prospect Park it diffused a deceitful
radiance that turned warts into dimples; it camouflaged the
scrawny yard back of the tenement where Mrs. Donahue lived
and tipped a neighborly wink at the old lady herself as she sat
by her kitchen window soaking her tired feet in a pan of hot
water; but into the courtyard of St. Damian's High School for
Boys it poured the full power of its harsh beam and, like a spot-
light at a police line-up, pointed its questioning finger at a man
who was creeping stealthily across the garden toward the tangle
of steel framework and scaffolds of the newly begun school building.

The baleful figure pursuing this silent way was Brother
Aloysius, and on him the moonlight didn't look good. It masked
him with black eye sockets, pulled his rough-hewn nose down an
inch or two, pointed up corners of a craggy brow into a pair of
horns and gave him an evil companion in a shadow that magni-
fied his cunning by copying each crafty step with exaggerated
mimicry. Now, by all the rules under which he lived, this was
truly a strange performance for Aloysius to be giving at this hour.

Were he a priest of the community stealing off to a secluded
corner to ponder his next Sunday's sermon or a lay brother savoring the small pleasure of a late pipeful after a long day of chores
in the kitchen, he might have reason to be abroad in the moonlight, but Aloysius, as a teaching brother of the Order of St.
Francis, should have been in his tiny cell, fast asleep on his hard
pallet an hour ago; morning prayers at four o'clock scarcely encourage night prowling.

Yet here he was, like some conspirator from the very medieval
history that he taught five days a week, working his sandaled feet
cautiously over the rubble that littered the ground around the
new building and carrying, so as to avoid any noise, an assort-
ment of tools that might possibly be of use to a dynamiter, but
were certainly not the usual accessories of a high-school teacher.
In one hand Aloysius had a bricklayer's trowel and a spirit level,
in the other a garden hoe, and tucked in the cord that clinched
his long brown habit at the waist was a double-bitted adz. Occasionally the handle of the adz would tangle with the rosary that
hung from the same cord and set the heavy crucifix and beads to
rattling. Aloysius would stop, quiet the noise and peer around for
any sign of detection.

On approaching the watchman's shanty, he paused, sighted out
his path carefully, and then, with the caution of a Sioux, slipped
across the lighted space into the concealing shadow of the building. He continued along the wall where the outer shell of brick
was just high enough to shield his six-foot figure, turned the
corner and picked his path along the whole length of the new
direction to the far end. Here he stopped, lifted his head and
searched anxiously along the top line of the brickwork where the
end of the day's labor had left it, and smiled in great satisfaction.

With the full width of the building separating him from the
watchman and with the near-by street noises to cover the small
sounds of his activity, Aloysius went to work. He set his tools down

between a cement-mixing trough and a pile of sand, tucked the long skirt of his habit up under the knotted cord of his waist, fished a bag of cement from a canvas-covered pile, led out a coiled-up hose that snaked off to a spigot near by, and, with his hoe as a shovel, started measuring out the ingredients for a batch of mortar.

If one has wondered where a humble teaching brother acquired the guile for that sly journey from the back door of the monastery, one would be even more intrigued at this latest bit of the night's performance, because in this Aloysius showed not only a skill that told of long practice but also a good measure of premeditation. It was obvious that he had cased the job. His movements were easy, his hands readily found what they sought—the handle of the water spigot, the ladder, the hods for cement and the brick.

In short order he was seated on the scaffold, with brick and mortar and tools ready for the night's mischief. But there he paused. At the point when the villain would have produced the stick of dynamite, when the honest laborer would have ener- getically started to light his pipe, Aloysius paused, humbly blessed himself, and began to pray.

His pause seemed long, so odd was the tableau, but it was only as long as three Hail Marys before he raised his head and picked up his trowel. Neatly cementing the end and flat of a brick, he began. Brick followed brick, course above course, like the prayers on his beads. Aloysius plied trowel and level and adz with the competence of a journeyman bricklayer until the shadow that had hidden his arrival climbed up the wall and blacked out the light by which he worked. Then only did he stop. For a moment he stretched his big arms and relaxed. With no less caution than he had begun the night, he climbed down from the scaffold, restored the hods, and ladder and hose, gathered up his tools and retreated across the courtyard to the monastery.

The moon set, the sun rose. Workmen arrived and students arrived, and it was on to noon before word of the nocturnal bricklaying crossed the courtyard and garden to the old school, although the violence with which it reached the office of Brother John, the principal, was enough to have carried it clear to Borough Hall. It was carried or rather projected ahead by the bellow of a bantam Irishman whose very bald head glistened with his anger. His arrival seemed to change the shape of the little office. A moment before, the room was tall and quiet and sparse, like the principal; now it bulged and puffed out and squatted to accommodate the round bustle of energy that surrounded the little man. The whole thing stopped seething only long enough to say, "Good morning, Yer Riverince."

"Good morning, Mr. O'Mara. Is there something wrong?"

"Something wrong, Yer Riverince; aye, there is that. I've called me men off the job."

"But why? What is it?" asked the perplexed Brother John.

" 'Tis the dirty capitalist doings of the likes of him," said Mr. O'Mara, pointing a blunt leathery finger past the principal and out the window at a young man running across the yard toward them. "To think that I've worked fur the likes of him." A tremendously aggrieved Mr. O'Mara felt the heavy burden of deception. A great sigh escaped him over his abused trust. His *r*'s rolled wonderfully and his brogue was thickened with his lost faith in man. "Aye, Yer Riverince, man and boy, fur thirty-five years I've worked fur Hollahay's Construction Company. His father was as fine a builder as ever erected a convent or church. But the boy, ha!" snorted O'Mara. " 'Tis the fine schools and the fine clothes and the fine idea fur him!"

With this as an introduction, a panting young man of about twenty-five burst into the office. His suit was undoubtedly more expensive and better cut than Mr. O'Mara's white overalls, and in truth, the only evidence he showed to connect himself with honest toil was an honest face and a little plaster dust on his good-looking tan shoes.

His greeting, however, expressed something of concern. "Good morning, Reverend Brother, have you had any luck—"

"Mr. Hollahay," broke in Brother John, with a slightly aspish edge to his rather pedantic address, "I should be very grateful for even a bare explanation of this dispute."

"Yes, Mr. Hollahay," said Mr. O'Mara, with scorn born of conscious virtue, "tell His Riverince what a connoiving capitalist exploiter the only limb of Patrick Hollahay, Senior, has become."

"Oh, for Pete's sake, O'Mara, stop talking like an editorial in the Daily Worker." Then turning to Brother John, young Hollahay explained, "Tim here claims he found some brickwork on the north wall that his men didn't lay. He has some crazy notion that I'm trying to put on a scab gang at night to speed up the job and pick up the bonus for early delivery. He wanted to knock the brickwork out, and when I refused to let him, he called his men off the job."

"As 'tis me duty, me being the union delegate," said Mr. O'Mara.

"But why undo the work?" asked Brother John of both of them, and with some misgivings about where he would get pinched between the jaws of two belligerent Irishmen.

"Just to make work," Mr. Hollahay spoke bitterly. "We pay the highest scale in the borough."

"Oh, so that's it, is it? With jobs begging all over the city, O'Mara has to make work, does he? Well, 'tis the last day's work I'll do fur the likes of you, Mr. Hollahay."

"Wait, please, Mr. O'Mara," pleaded Brother John. "You mustn't stop work. You know how badly we need the new building. Our old school here is far over its capacity. If you stop, the other trades will stop, too, and the whole thing might be delayed so long that we couldn't open in the fall."

"Indeed I see that, Yer Riverince, and it's not to me liking either. When I get home the missus will give me the back of her hand. She'll call me a black-hearted divil, and she'll give me no more supper than would fill a canary, and say that fasting is good penance fur me sins in stopping the work."

O'Mara finished his speech with an angry look at Hollahay that plainly added this personal grievance to the professional wrong, already laid on the young contractor's doorstep.

"Isn't there some way of keeping your men at work?" persisted Brother John.

"There is that, Yer Riverince. Have Mr. Hollahay tear out his scab brickwork."

"O'Mara," said Hollahay through clenched teeth, "I'll brain you with one of your own ugly hods if you keep on saying that I laid that brick."

"Oh, thin I'm sure it must have been the little people, the fairies!" O'Mara's sarcasm was thick with brogue. "Yes, the little people always come out of a full moon, and they like nothing better than taking a turn at bricklaying, especially fur the Hollahay Construction Company."

Brother John strove to get the business back to an objective point by asking naively, "Can you actually tell your own work, Mr. O'Mara? All bricks look alike to me."

"Well, that they would, Yer Riverince, you having what might be called an eye fur a book, but none fur the fine points of the trade. 'Tis all in the way a man handles his trowel on the mortar, and then we know where a man knocks off and how many bricks he laid that day."

"Yes, and it's about half an honest day's work," broke in Mr. Hollahay derisively.

"Please, Mr. Hollahay. . . . Go on, Mr. O'Mara."

"Well, 'tis as I say. Now, this work last night, 'tis good work." Mr. O'Mara, honest workman that he was, could not let himself belittle even what he thought to be the scab product of a fellow craftsman. "But 'tis different, and then 'tis laid in a queer fashion."

"What do you mean?" asked Brother John.

"Well, 'tis not run straight across the floor level, but only between two columns, like would come of wanting to put a wall in only one room."

"I see. And you both are positive that neither of you had that work done?"

Both denied vigorously. Brother John was perplexed. The room was silent for a moment before he asked, "What room was to be located behind that wall?"

For the first time since O'Mara had entered the office, he was gentle in his speech. "Well, now that you mention it, Yer Riverince, 'tis the chapel."

"The chapel!" Brother John gazed over the heads of the two men at the bare wall behind them, then turned to the window and looked hard at the red-leaded steel columns and solid masonry foundation of the new building across the court. He stared hard and shook his head several times, as though trying to keep himself firmly tied to the present and the concrete. When he faced the two again, he seemed to have got hold of something that tugged him between a hope and a doubt.

He spoke to the younger man first. "What do you know of St. Francis?"

"Well, he founded the religious order to which you belong, Brother John."

"Yes, yes, but I mean more detailed things." Brother John seemed impatient now, as though anxious to have his own thoughts corroborated by another's expression.

"Let me see. Oh, he was once a soldier," continued Mr. Hollahay, obviously becoming embarrassed by how much of the subject he didn't know and groping desperately, like an unprepared schoolboy. "And he liked birds and animals."

"But what did he do, himself, with his own hands?" Brother John was now almost pleading to have the thing he wanted spoken by this young builder.

"At first, I think he fixed up something, a house or a— No, I know . . . a church. That's it; he built the wall of an old chapel."

"Exactly. He built the wall of a chapel." Brother John spoke each word slowly, meditatively.

O'Mara, the real mystic of the three, seemed closest to the heart of the unspoken suggestion, and immediately put it into words. "Now, Yer Riverince, it wouldn't be that yer saying we had a miracle like, here last night."

"No, no, Mr. O'Mara." Brother John disowned the idea, now that it was brought out into the cold light of day, but it was clearly apparent that that was just exactly what he meant.

"Calling such an incident a miracle is only an excitement to the credulous. Crowds gather for less, as you know, Mr. O'Mara, and they attribute supernatural significance to the most fantastic things. I'm afraid your men will noise the thing about."

"Aye, that they will."

"You must prevent a strike, then."

"Well, Yer Riverince, now that you put it in that light, I'll try, but it'll not be before tonight. The union'll have to take a vote on it."

"But, Mr. O'Mara, that will make things worse—having it openly discussed."

"'Twould be little use to try and hush the thing now, Yer Riverince. The Indians would only—"

"Indians, Mr. O'Mara!" Brother John's eyes widened. "Did you say Indians?"

"Aye, three of thim . . . from the Bushwick section. And lately they're the divil's own limbs fur stewing about the rules. 'Tis vote on this and vote on that till every meeting is like a bloomin' powwow."

"But Indians, Mr. O'Mara!" The vision of a feathered redskin scaling his new school with a trowel in one hand and a tomahawk in the other had Brother John floundering.

"Oh, they're good workmen, Yer Rivirince, and good union men too; but someone has got their ear about their tribe coming from Rosshia. ' 'Tis a great journey our ancestors made across Siberia and the Bering Sea,' sez one of them to me. ' 'Tis a journey up that scaffold you better be making,' sez I."

"I can understand then that you might have some difficulty. What will you say to them, Mr. O'Mara?"

"Well, I thought you might do the talking."

"I!"

"Yes, Yer Rivirince. 'Twould be little use of me to tell them that the Hollahay Construction Company has a gang of bricklaying angels on the pay roll. 'Twould seem like the undoing of organized labor and 'twould be the last of O'Mara as a union delegate."

"Yes, I can see that," said Brother John, with a sigh of resignation at the task of explaining how a lot of bricks got themselves set into a wall by no known human agency, and that such things couldn't happen, but that such things, of course, did happen throughout the world every year, and when they did they might be miracles, but that this bit of handiwork wasn't at all a miracle and, of course, no one should mention it to his wife when he got home from the union meeting, because, you see, it's not really anything extraordinary. "Yes, I see," said Brother John. "Very well, I'll be there."

The bell was beginning to ring for the Angelus as the two now pacified Irishmen left the office. Brother John stood a moment in prayer before proceeding to the refectory where the brothers gathered for their silent meals. As usual, the last to enter was Brother Aloysius. As usual, he had been teaching class with no regard for time, and had found himself leading a charge of crusaders across the plains of Damascus when the bell rang to end the period. As usual, his brown habit—and this was his new one —looked less brown from its layer of chalk dust than any of its fellows, so that no one could have detected the sprinkling of cement that it had carried off from the preceding night's labor.

As usual, too, his homely face looked serene and guileless, and if any burden sat on his conscience, his bulging shoulders carried it with ease. Indeed, Aloysius appeared at peace with God and man. But it was a peace about to be rudely shattered, because Brother John wasted no time in preliminaries. Aloysius and his fellows were told that a strike threatened their new school and that the cause was a certain amount of bricklaying, the origin of which mystified the workmen, the construction company and Brother John alike.

At the first words Aloysius tried to speak out, but his tongue just stuck dry. For a moment as he listened he almost began to hope that he was actually not the one about whom Brother John was talking, because the principal, in simple faith that had no difficulty accepting miracles, made the night's feat look indeed superhuman. ". . . and the fence, no entrance except past the watchman. An amount of work equal to what two men accomplish in a day. Yes, my brothers, a very strange affair. I can't— Yes, Brother Aloysius?"

Aloysius had at last found his tongue. "Reverend Brother."
"Yes?"
"I laid the brickwork last night."
The silence that followed was awesome. Poor Aloysius. There he stood at the plain board table that would have held his simple lunch, towering his six-foot bulk over his seated brothers, making

an end to a dream he had nourished from the first moment he had heard of the new school. To emulate in little things so as to be ready for the big thing, the life of the simple Francis, whose footsteps he followed—that was all he ever tried to do. There was scarcely need of any questioning, since each man in the room knew all that was necessary for understanding the reason, but, after that build-up by Brother John, some explanation of the mechanics of this feat was demanded by honest, natural, everyday curiosity, from which brothers are no more exempt than bricklayers.

The questions were asked by the principal in a strangely gentle voice, and Aloysius answered. He was miserable at the disclosure. For the moment, his secret lost all its meaning and appeared almost like a juvenile prank, as he explained how he had studied the blueprint of the building, watched the pace of the work, and on the final night had borrowed the tools from the shed kept by Brother Joseph, the lay brother who mended and patched and did a general handy-man's work about the school.

"But the bricklaying," quizzed Brother John. "Mr. O'Mara says that it's good work. Where did you learn that?"

"Well, you see, Reverend Brother, I learned the trade before I entered the order. I was an apprentice, then a journeyman in Dublin, and after my mother died, God rest her soul, I paid my way through the university by working at it."

"And last night it appears that you did about twice the usual day's work."

"I suppose I expected to get a little better wage than the usual day's pay. Heaven knows, it was small enough when I was at work."

As answer followed answer, Aloysius began to have a feeling that something was wrong with the interrogation. The superior was beginning to be a shade too gentle, too meditative. Brother John was not a calculating man, but he had been through a disturbing morning and, now that they had all returned from the stratosphere to the prosaic level of economics, he found himself facing a distasteful duty of chastising his subordinate's impracticality without censoring the sanctity and childlike faith which inspired it.

"So you are rather well acquainted with the ways of laboring men, my son?" said Brother John blandly.

Aloysius felt uncomfortable, but stood mute. Something was coming; he knew not what.

"Then perhaps," continued his superior, "you can accompany me tonight and explain yourself to Mr. O'Mara's union in a manner that will bring them back to work tomorrow. I think that is all. Shall we have our lunch now?"

Aloysius found little relish in his food or in his classes that followed. The whole business of battles and ballads, of cathedral and castle and cloister that lived in his lectures and made medieval history a bright hour in the shabby lives of the tenement youngsters who comprised his class—all of it was flat. He taught like a good mechanic, not like an inspiring master, for Brother John was right in surmising that Aloysius knew laboring men, and he was worried about the outcome of his evening's mission.

That night Aloysius and his superior found the union meeting assembled in the auditorium of the neighborhood public school. The hall was filled with gnarled-fisted men, each of whom bore the mark of his trade in a face that was filmed with a network of white treads, the ingrained dust of their day's work that no soap and water ever dug out. From the stage where they were standing, Mr. O'Mara and a keen-looking young man came down to meet the two teachers at the door. O'Mara introduced the union secretary, and then, in brief words, Brother John told of the findings that came to light at lunch. Mr. O'Mara, knowing what had been a possible explanation, heaved a gusty breeze of relief.

The old bricklayer had replaced his overalls with a neat blue serge suit and a white starched collar that made him look exactly like a master bricklayer dressed in a neat blue serge suit and a white starched collar. The secretary, on the other hand, wore a comfortably wrinkled tweed suit that would have been appropriate for any smart young man, from a hijacker on his day off to a labor-union secretary on his day on.

He led the party onto the stage and called the meeting to order. With the last rap of his knuckles on the table, a man popped out of a seat in the front row, calling for the floor. He was lined with white like the rest, but on him it stood out in seams against a copper face. He bobbed up and down and jerked about with his hand in the air, signaling to the stage and looking for all the world like a marionette of Boris Karloff.

For some seconds the secretary tried to ignore him, but the gyrations wouldn't be ignored. "All right, Mr. Stalinovsky. What is it?" asked the secretary.

"Comrade Stalinovsky!" corrected the bouncing one in a vigorous voice. "Comrade, not mister! I don't hold with these bourgeois titles! We're all brothers!"

The secretary cut off that speech smoothly by picking up a paper from the table and suggesting, "You wanted to vote on the last minutes?"

"No—no!" danced Stalinovsky. "I want to vote on a strike against the dirty capitalist exploiter, Hollahay Construction Company!"

It sounded as though the union published a list of accepted adjectives to be memorized by members, and always used when referring to the current employer.

"They put this scab labor on last night, and I say—"

"But, that's not so!" burst out Brother Aloysius, as he jumped up from his seat and advanced to the front of the platform. "I laid the bricks! Mr. Hollahay knew nothing about it!"

"You!" exclaimed Stalinovsky. He, in turn, advanced toward

the platform, tilting his head back more and more to look up at
this redheaded apparition in the too tight suit that was obviously
not a workingman, but what was it? The hall began to buzz. Men
in the rear stood on seats to watch.

"You laid the bricks. Who are you?"

"I'm a religious, a teaching brother. Please let me—"

But the comrade would have none of it. "Secretary," he
shouted, "how did he get in here? Don't you know religion is the
opium of the people?"

"'Tis I who asked him," asserted O'Mara, joining the fray
and also advancing to the footlights.

"You! I knew it. We'll never have a dictatorship of the pro-
letariat till we send the foreigners back where they came from."

"Furriners, is it?" bellowed O'Mara. "I'll furriner you—
you—" making a lunge to go over the edge of the stage at his
tormentor.

He was collared in time by Aloysius, and held, sputtering out
his wrath, while the secretary tried to outshout everybody with
cries of "Order! Sit down back there! Shut up, Stalinovsky, or
I'll suspend you!"

When peace returned to the meeting, the contending forces
occupied the same territory as at the onset of the engagement, but
O'Mara and Stalinovsky sat glaring at each other, puffing like the
lids of teakettles just coming to a boil, while Aloysius stood with
tilted head, listening to the sage counsel of the secretary.

"You'd better explain the business right now," he told Aloysius.
"We'll postpone our routine affairs till this is settled. The men
are in no mood for delaying."

"All right," said Aloysius, "but I'm afraid it will sound like a
weak sort of explanation."

"Well, just tell them exactly what happened. They're a little
excitable tonight, but they'll listen."

Will they understand, though? wondered Aloysius as he nodded to the secretary and made his way to the edge of the stage. He had time for only a murmur of a plea to the Blessed Mother before he found himself looking down on the expectant faces, seamed and old and young and hard alike. Then Aloysius began to notice the details—the neatly brushed hair, the meticulous old-fashioned starched collar alongside the clean soft shirt. These were working-men whose horny thumbs would have felt at home in his own handshake. These were his kind of people. And he began to talk, not of mysteries, but about work. He took them to a little Italian town of Assisi, where a special workingman lived seven hundred years ago; and with all the unconscious skill that made his classes inspired, he told them of Francis, not as a saint, but as a work-ingman. They saw Assisi in its true color and life—its guilds and churches and palaces. Not with Aloysius, but with Francis, they were hungry and cold; they embraced a leper and begged for a crust of bread. Then they built. As Aloysius told his story, the ending was inevitable. They would have felt betrayed had they, too, not been asked to creep out that night and with their own hands build that chapel wall, with no touch of bargaining, but just as their own free, unheralded offering.

O'Mara ended the spell. He shattered the hush that filled the hall with a trumpetlike nose blowing. He rubbed his proboscis vigorously and dabbed a bit at his eyes and made a great play of being a very practical, unnonsensical fellow behind a bedsheet-sized red bandanna handkerchief. But Stalinovsky, unrecon-structed rebel to the end, fighting as long as a single shot was left, wasn't to be taken in by a lot of sentimental eyewash. This time he rose quietly and began cunningly. This time he would demol-ish the whole claptrap with one telling blow.

"Does the union have a contract with the Hollahay Construc-tion Company?" he asked the secretary reasonably.

"Yes, of course."

"It calls for a closed shop?"

"It does."

"And any work done on the job must be union work?" said our dialectic materialist.

"Yes," said the secretary, granting a second premise.

"Then the work last night was scab labor because it wasn't done by a union man."

As he nailed down his conclusion, Stalinovsky had the grace merely to raise a quizzical eyebrow. He was a gentleman; he didn't gloat; but his logic left the hall restless. It was embarrassed by this attack. The secretary looked inquiringly at Aloysius, who had begun groping frantically in his pockets. At last he found what he sought, and with a triumphant smile he pulled out a little black notebook. The hall waited in expectancy. Aloysius thumbed through its pages, dropping two dog-eared holy pictures and a tab from a brown scapular before he picked out a card and handed it to the secretary. The latter studied it closely and compared an identification picture it bore with Aloysius' own visage. A whispered conversation between the two followed for a few minutes.

The secretary stood up and, with something of a grin, announced, "Gentlemen, it appears that our visitor is a member in good standing of the Dublin local of the building-trades union in Ireland. We are, of course, allied with them through fraternal bonds."

And then the hall roared. It laughed for ten minutes. This was what they loved.

There was no mood left for routine business. Aloysius now was a hero. Hollahay was a benefactor of mankind. Stalinovsky was routed.

But Stalinovsky had one last gasp. Jumping to the stage, he snatched the card from the secretary and glared at it. Angrily he pointed at the name it bore—"Sean O'Caillaigh." Ha, that was it—a dirty capitalist conniving exploitation. A barefaced forgery.

Had the hall been quiet, he would have hurled the charge broadside. Instead, the frustrated rebel faced Aloysius and the now frankly laughing secretary. He couldn't speak; he could only point. Innocence outraged looked like that.

When enough quiet returned to permit his being understood, Aloysius explained, "It's my name before I entered the order—John O'Kelly, as you would call it. That on the card is the Gaelic spelling."

Stalinovsky still had a gasp left in him. "How can— How do you— What I mean—"

"Perhaps you wonder how is it that I'm a Franciscan and still a trade unionist? Well, the local voted me a life membership when I entered the order. 'Twas a handsome gesture, don't you think?"

Stalinovsky had no reply; he had fired his last shot.

Aloysius saw that the evening held one bit of unfinished business, as he glimpsed O'Mara backstage still sputtering about "furriner" in between bursts of laughter. Holding out a hand to Stalinovsky, Aloysius said, "I hope we'll be friends, Mr.—er—Comrade Stalinovsky."

The comrade tried to ignore the extended palm, but it wouldn't be ignored. To be done with the thing he took it coolly, but then he felt the familiar calluses and the horny thumb of the trade. He looked up.

"You are a workman," he conceded to Aloysius. A smile began to soften his face. "What do you call yourself—brother?"

"Yes. Brother Aloysius."

"That's like 'comrade.' "

"Yes, it is a bit," admitted the newly elected comrade.

"That's a good idea, you belonging to the union," said Stalinovsky judiciously. "Does he belong to a union?" This with a nod at Brother John sitting composed, unmoving, as he had sat all evening.

"Well, you see—" faltered Aloysius. "Well, yes, I'd say he does." Then seeing his opportunity, Aloysius suggested, "Your friend, Mr. O'Mara, now he's a union man, a friend of yours."

"He's a foreigner."

"But yourself," persisted Aloysius, "where were you born?"

"Me!" exclaimed Stalinovsky. "Right here in Brooklyn, on Bushwick Avenue."

"Well, your parents, where do they come from?"

"Brooklyn, Bushwick Avenue."

"But your name?"

"I changed my name, like you; you know. I used to be named Son of Laughing Horse; now I'm Son of Steel."

"Son of Laughing Horse! But that's an Indian name!"

"Sure," smiled Comrade Stalinovsky. "I'm an Indian—a Bushwick Indian. Bushwick Indians always live in Brooklyn."

BARRING THE WEIGHT

W. B. READY

An Atlantic "First," this story introduces us to the lovable Brother John, about whom Mr. Ready has written several other sketches published in the Atlantic. *These stories, with others rich in Catholic atmosphere, are to be published by Bruce, under the title* Barring the Weight.

Mr. W. B. Ready is a Cardiff Irishman who was educated by the Christian Brothers and at the Universities of Wales and Oxford. He married a Canadian girl while in the Service. They have two sons and live in the Twin Cities where Mr. Ready is a member of the History Department at the University of Minnesota. He also teaches creative writing at the College of St. Thomas. He says that most of his energy goes into writing and thinking about Thomas D'Arcy McGhee, a Canadian founding father.

I think that the only deep sorrow that Brother John ever had was that we were a pack of small forwards. There were always God's plenty of big powerful backs, but his forwards never ran to much more than 150-pounders, which was just damned silly in a league where we were up against teams with lumbering heavy packs. We puzzled over it, but there was nothing we could do about it. Dinny Sullivan was a fine heavy man, but he was so lithe and dexterous and cunning that it was a sin not to make a three-quarter out of him, and Eddie Walsh was as wide as a door, but he was such a graceful swerving runner that to put him in the pack was to yoke a thoroughbred with a mule team.

It wasn't just one season; year after year the same thing happened. The forwards were built like the backs, and the backs were big enough to be forwards. I remember Brother John's eyes lighting up when Jack Cotter came to us from one of the North Country colleges. He was a fine figure of a man, well over six feet in height and weighing about 210 pounds. A second-row forward, he was proud and happy in that position. He nearly killed us packing down with him, but at last we were getting the ball in the tight scrums, and the backs were getting a chance to throw it around.

But it didn't last long. Cotter was a good forward, but Brother John saw him fooling around after practice one night, and he saw that the big fellow could really kick and field a ball. He made him into J. Cotter, the great ALL-IRELAND full back, but he still wanted his fine big bustling pack instead of the sharp little terriers he had in the likes of me. After a game, as we would limp off the field, bruised and battered by bigger men, we would wish almost savagely that we were huskier, because a burly pack was all that Brother John needed to win the ALL-IRELAND championship.

He was the greatest coach I have even seen, and he never had to raise his voice. I can see him now, although he's been under the sod these few years, God rest him. He was tall and gray, and stooped. He could only have been a schoolmaster, and even during the holidays there was always a dusting of chalk around him. His face was so Irish that it had a Spanish look, and his thick gray hair grew back from his forehead in the same sort of pompadour as did Jim Corbett's, the fighter. He was vice-principal of the school, and his gentle air fooled nobody. There was iron in the man, and sometimes bitterness would break out of him, so that the Principal and the Provincial and even the Bishop were wary of him. He was a hidden sort of man, and there are plenty of them in Ireland. History was his subject, but Rugby football was his delight. It was far more than a game to him: the strife and the checks, the teamwork and the play, were life as it should be to Brother John.

We'd nearly choke with temper as game after game we would be pushed off the ball by big agricultural louts with no more science than one of these bulldozers they are using now. In the dressing rooms after the game, Brother John would compliment us in his soft Kerry voice: "You played the grand game, Willie. . . . That was a grand tackle of yours, Con. . . . That big fellow never laid a finger on you, Terry. . . ." And all the time we would be glum, drying ourselves silently after the showers. Mick Yewlett, the trainer, would look up from the massage board, where he'd be rubbing one of us: "Ah, Brother, if we had the weight, these boys would beat the world; be God they'd even give Presentation College a run for it!"

But Brother John would never murmur against our flimsiness. "It's the will of God, Michael," was all he would say. But all the days of his life he'd wanted to train the ALL-IRELAND team, and we'd have been a team of champions, barring the weight. I was a member of that team, but I must see a better team before I yield to it. The way we got that ball back from a loose maul I've not seen equaled since. We had the heart, the almost functional perfection of a good machine. We had everything, barring the weight. We'd have gladly changed ourselves into big blond Saxons for the season if it would have brought Brother John the championship.

We were all in our last year in school, and had been playing together for five or six years. We were far out of the class of the average local team, and most of our opponents were University or town teams, but we had to struggle desperately to beat these lesser men, because they had the weight. After twelve games we were still the invincibles, but it was a struggle all the time. For us forwards it was our last season; we'd never make the weight for a University or town team, so that season had all the sweetness of a golden era departing.

Our football field was beside a ruined castle, and in the soft Irish evenings, when the quiet of Christ would be on everything, the thud of boot on ball and the grunts of the tackles would carry clear across to the pavilion where some of us would be sitting around Brother John as he explained some play. The plays he designed were to him not only for the football field, but contained his ideas about everything. He had been brought up on the old nineteenth-century nationalism, and he saw us as a bunch of Cuchulainns, small dark sad men, who would go down in glory before inevitable circumstance. I can see that now, though of course I didn't then.

As the games went on, a faint dim gleam of hope began to flicker. We were the only undefeated team in the country, then in the province. There were good days and bad days, but we always managed to win, sometimes more by the grace of God than by anything else, and then Abertaff asked us for a game! They had beaten the Australian touring team; they had more inter-nationals playing for them than any other team in Wales. Indeed it was almost as much of an honor to play for them as to play for Wales. They had an Irish tour every year, and apparently they had decided that they needed a preliminary loosener before tan-gling up with the tough opposition that led them such a dance every year. So they had picked a school team, and we were the team. We began to train with an intensity that worried Brother John; it was the only chance we would ever have against a first-class side and we knew it. Abertaff would surely beat us, but by God they'd play Rugby to beat us!

2

We played them on the Castle Ground. I remember it was late in February, the second Saturday in Lent. There was a great crowd out to see the game, the biggest crowd any of us had ever played before. The Abertaff pack were big burly men, steel-workers, County Constabulary, dockers, and the like. They were led by the great Lem Jenkins, who had led the Welsh pack for the past two seasons. He was a big bull of a man, and as I left

my father, God rest his soul, to run on the field, he took another
look at Lem and said to me, "Good God! He'll kill you, my son.
I'm glad your mother stayed home."

Lem was my opposite number; he gave me a friendly nod,
which I tried to return nonchalantly, but I had to chew my gum
very hard to get any moisture in my mouth, although the palms
of my hands were wet with sweat. Brother John was away in a
corner of the field shaking. He thought he was sending us to glory,
and it before our time, and we did look a puny pack beside that
solid Welsh forward line. Also their famous red and black jerseys
were clean and new, their ringed stockings matched, and they
were wearing swagger ballooned shorts, so that we looked tawdry
as well as scrawny beside them.

I saw Brother Principal grimacing as he compared us, and I
knew that Brother John was in for another rollicking there, besides
the complaints from our parents, who were already ganging up
on him as they saw the logical result of the clash between Abertaff
and ourselves. They knew that we were out for glory, and that
because we could not bring him the championship we were going
to be his small dark heroes who would solace him by dour struggle
in a hopeless cause.

The whistle blew, and Eddie Walsh kicked off. Before the
Abertaff man could gather it to find touch we were on him, the
whole forward line. We swarmed all over him, and went on with
the ball in a forward rush, only to be recalled for being off side.
That was the game throughout. Abertaff was out for the exercise,
and we were out for Brother John. They held us off good-humor-
edly at first, but gradually our panting silent tenseness communicated itself to them, and they began to play football with all their
national genius.

At half time there was nothing in it, no score in the hardest
game either team had ever played. It wasn't the finest game, only
the hardest, because in a fine game there is often a sort of care-

less rapture, when one time or another the unusual or bizarre play is tried. But nobody was taking any chances in this game. The orthodox passing movements would start cautiously and be smothered by furious tackling. Abertaff got the ball from every set scrum, and we got it from most of the loose mauls. The crowd was so excited that there seemed to be a blurred roar all the time, but I never had time to look at them.

At half time Mick Yewlett ran on the field with his inevitable sponge and bucket of water, and rubbed our faces clear of mud and spittle. Brother John was among us, murmuring, "Boys. . . . Oh, Boys." I remember that we just grinned at him, and didn't say anything. Somehow all of us felt more grown-up than we had ever felt before. It was evident to all of us that his coaching was paying off. Our lightness and speed were useless in the set scrums, so we were giving them to the Welshmen, and we were running them off their feet all over the field.

But in the second half the inevitable began to run us down. Our legs began to weaken. We couldn't push all that Welsh weight around without beginning to feel it. And we were as bruised as we could be without breaking off, yet somehow we still managed to get there in time, until at last their Dai Evans got off on a clear run. Nobody ever caught Dai once he was away; he scored a try, and Gruffydd converted it for them. So they got five points, but no more, and Lem Jenkins was out of the game for weeks with a twisted knee. The final whistle went on two exhausted teams. The crowd was delighted with us, and friends crowded around us. But we pushed our limping way through them and gathered around Brother John. We didn't say a word, and neither did he, but he knew, and we knew, that in our defeat we had won something greater than a championship.

We never were any good for the rest of the season; we played almost as dreamily as Brother John now coached us. The championship receded from our minds; we never really woke up on the field after that second Saturday in Lent. Abertaff never played us again; they explained that we were not quite what they were looking for. Mind you, we never expected to play them again. That once was enough to give us our experience, and to give Brother John the great occasion. We were on our way out, it was our last year in school.

There's a photograph of the team hanging up over there behind the davenport, contiguous to that aquatint of Galway Bay. The wee fellow holding the ball was the pack leader, and that's Brother John sitting beside him. There's myself, I'm heavier now, and alongside me is Tim Coghlan; he was killed, God rest him, at Anzio. All the small fellows are sitting down, and they are all the forwards. The man adjacent to Tim is Con Daly. Do you notice the grin on him? He was always bemoaning his bad luck, and he always ended with ". . . and to cap it all I'll probably marry a fruitful wife!" Our hooker used to ask Con, savagely and blasphemously, to push harder, and back would come Coneen, "Tom, Tom, me navel's scarring the ground." And so it went.

Brother John was retired the next year to the Brothers' House at Waterford, and he died there early in 1940. The team was the right age for the war. Nine of them were killed, including poor Con. God rest them all. My memories of happier days are all tied up with them, and the great team we were, barring the weight.

GINGERBREAD

BETTY WAHL

The old order changeth yielding place to new. And in that change there is an eternal pathos for the old. Its precise flavor is distilled with miraculous economy in one hour with the aged instructor in needlework, Sister Timothy. Between the smart new haste, with its interest in medieval philosophy which is as superficial as its needlework, and the old gingerbread art, with its laborious devotion to detail, there seems little to choose. The value of the story lies in the skill with which three generations of students at a small Midwestern college are projected through the symbols of needlework, and the pin-point accuracy with which the suffering of the human heart emerges as significant. Cutting in many directions, the story exposes layer upon layer of meaning.

Betty Wahl is the wife of J. F. Powers, the author of PRINCE OF DARKNESS. They have two daughters and live in Milwaukee, where Mr. Powers teaches creative writing at Marquette. Besides writing an occasional story for the NEW YORKER, Betty Wahl is working at a novel of which "Gingerbread" is a part.

"I just teach embroidery," Sister Timothy said to the girl standing in the doorway of the needlework room. "If you want a crocheted edge, you'll have to go to Sister Germaine. Hemstitching here, crocheting there."

"Well, which one goes fastest?"

"Fast*er*," said Sister Timothy, who was a bit disdainful of the entrance requirements of St. Bede's.

"Faster," the girl repeated dutifully.

"I'm afraid I don't let anyone hurry here." Sister Timothy, waving her away, turned around just in time to catch another pupil in grievous error. "Rosemary!"

Rosemary, the only girl in the room, quickly clipped twelve inches from her thread.

"That's better. You can't save any time that way, when you

have to spend five minutes getting your thread down to size."

"I forgot, Sister."

"I know. There's a lot more forgetting when my back's turned, I notice. Hurry, hurry, hurry. What for?"

Sister Timothy sat down in her chair by the window, her black habit drinking in the heat of the sun, so that she was almost warm. She looked at the empty chairs, remembering when there had been many more chairs, and none empty. Fifty years ago—the College had been the Female Academy then—there had been three teachers just for needlework. A better school now, it was said, fully accredited and all that, but it seemed to Sister Timothy that everyone had been prouder of it in the old days; the pride of all western Minnesota then, a light to the Dakotas and the outer darkness. A generation of girls, not much younger than Sister Timothy herself then, had come, filled their trunks with the linens they had embroidered, and gone. Then their daughters had come and smocked a thousand georgette blouses and cross-stitched an acre of lunch cloths. And now the granddaughters sat in their dormitories and embroidered "clever little" dish towels "Sunday," "Monday," "Tuesday" . . . *Dish towels*! Nowadays, no one needed Sister Timothy until a few weeks before Christmas, when there was a fast business in luncheon sets. She would unwrap the more elaborate stamped pieces from their blue paper hopefully. "No, not that, Sister. You know, more—more— You know what I mean." Sister Timothy knew what they meant and would open the bottom drawer, where she kept the sets that had only a lazy-daisy design in one corner. For the rest of the year, there were mostly the engaged seniors, who embroidered ring-and-flame symbols on their bridal linens, and a few freshmen, who snagged a profusion of French knots and chain stitches over an occasional dresser scarf.

Sister Timothy looked up as the door opened. It was Mary Shannon—pillowcases, lazy-daisy.

"Hi, Sister," she said.

"How about those pillowcases?" Sister Timothy asked her.

"Golly, Sister, I just don't have the time today. Did I leave my 'Spirit of Medieval Philosophy' here last week?"

Sister Timothy gestured toward the shelf on the radiator.

"Test tomorrow," said Mary. "And I don't know Peter Abélard from William of Champeaux. Hi, Rosie."

Rosemary leaned to one side, so that Mary could see her work.

"Man, are you ever slow!" Mary saw Sister Timothy looking at her. "Well, 'bye, Sister. I'll get to work on those cases first thing next week."

The door swung shut behind her, and the room was quiet again.

"William of Champeaux!" Sister Timothy said. "There's more nonsense going on over there"—she looked out at the new (A.D. 1913) building across the way—"than in all the funny papers put together."

"But, Sister," Rosemary said, "who's going to preserve Western culture if we don't?"

Sister Timothy turned again to the new building, the source of so much foolishness, and said, "And while you're all so busy preserving Western culture, who's going to be preserving your homes for you?"

"All of us aren't going to be just housewives, Sister."

"Then what *are* you going to be—the President of the United States?"

"You know what I mean, Sister."

"The only thing I know is that your stitches are getting too big."

"Yes, Sister."

Sister Timothy settled back in her chair and listened to the sounds next door. She shared the floor with Vestments. It was a bad time, a regular Dark Ages for Needlework, but Vestments, like the Vandals, flourished. Every year, the movable partition of cabinets between the two workrooms edged a little farther her way, so only three windows were left of Needlework's original seven. And yesterday, through the partition, she had overheard Sister Annette say, "I don't know where we're going to put the other embroidery machine when it comes." Sister Timothy, who had heard such innocent speculation in the past, knew where they were going to put it, all right, and so did Vestments. It had been clever of Sister Annette to make her next move known in this way, like Hitler on the radio, with his *Lebensraum.* Sister Timothy was no more than little Luxembourg, and they knew it. She had taught most of them, including Sister Annette, their first outline stitch. And now they couldn't stop until they had pushed her out of the building. Vestments had been respectable once, before they went in for machinery. Now they could put out a cheap fiddleback chasuble along with the worst ecclesiastical-goods dealer. And this morning she'd seen them stitching "SACRED HEART WILDCATS" onto some poor-quality satin jackets—black on orange, at that.

Sister Timothy could hear Sister Annette over there now, showing a visitor the hand-embroidered copes. There was a familiar little rumble as one of the huge semicircular trays fanned out from the cabinet. The copes were stored flat and unfolded in the trays, for even a wrinkle might wear them out in time. Sister Timothy, who had made two of the finest of them, envied Sister Annette her custodianship and rather wished that the chapel sacristy was large enough to hold the case. Then nobody could take credit for them.

She heard Sister Annette say, "How long do you think it would take to make one like this?" and listened for the visitor's answering "I don't know."

"Come on, guess," urged Sister Annette.

"Six months?"

Sister Annette laughed on her side of the partition, and Sister Timothy laughed quietly on her side. "Guess again," said Sister Annette.

A silence, and then the visitor's voice, "A year?"

"Guess again."

"Two years?"

Sister Timothy smiled. Sister Annette said, "No. It would take seven years."

The visitor gasped appropriately, which pleased Sister Timothy, for it was as she had thought; they were looking at *her* white cope, with its twenty angels, so perfect that you could see the moons on their fingernails. "It's forty years old," said Sister Annette. "And look at that silk, still as good as new." Sister Timothy heard the drawer close and another one open. "And this one would take five years," the visitor was informed. That would be the rose cope, Sister Timothy knew—five years' work on something that could be used only for a few minutes on two Sundays of the year. She loved it for that, but the rose cope had no special meaning for Sister Annette.

Now the last tray slid open. Sister Timothy heard Sister Annette turn back the tissue-paper covering and say, "This is the bishop's cope for feast days." That would be old Sister Mary Benjamin's cope, made of the white silk she had brought from Europe when the nuns came to the prairie, nearly a century ago. She had worked at it for thirty-five years, off and on, adding a rose here, a star there, until she died. "That's all solid-gold thread," Sister Annette explained.

Sister Timothy listened for the visitor's reply, but the embroidery machine started to whir. She got up and walked out of the sun, and shivered with the sudden cold. She pulled out her little gold watch, an unnecessary gesture, since she always listened for every quarter-hour chime of the tower clock. She loved the little roses on the watchcase, engraved there when ordinary things had tried to look beautiful.

Rosemary looked up at her. "Closing time, Sister?" she asked.

"Still forty-five minutes," Sister Timothy said. Still time for another girl to come and sew. But no one would come, and she ought to be more thankful to Rosemary. "You're doing fine," she said.

"Yes, Sister. The first couple of days are the hardest, I guess."

Sister Timothy sat down beside the girl, perhaps her last pupil that day, perhaps the last ever, and was moved to talk. "We had a cherry tree at home," she said suddenly. "My father raised it from a seed. It finally grew three cherries. My brother and I couldn't wait for them to get ripe, so we picked all three and then started worrying what my father'd say. So I got out my needle and sewed them back on."

"What happened then?"

"I don't remember. I just know I used green thread, to match the tree."

"Sister?" Rosemary said.

"Yes."

"What was it like in the old days? I mean when *you* came here, I'm just dying to know."

It was an old request—a dodge passed on from one class to the next, the secret of getting along with Sister Timothy, who recognized it as that but today would gladly have taken the bait if the door hadn't opened upon a new girl, wearing a white kerchief machine-stitched with the names of—of movie stars!

Rosemary, for someone just dying to know about the old days, did not seem to mind the interruption. "Ginny's decided to embroider something, too, Sister," she said.

"You mean '*Virginia*,' don't you?" said Sister Timothy. Virginia had been her own name.

"Yes, Sister."

"Then use her right name. Now, Virginia, have you anything you'd particularly like to do?"

"No, Sister. I just want to do something," said the newcomer.

Sister Timothy went to the cabinet and opened the top drawer. "How about a pair of pillowcases?" She put them on the counter. Rosemary came over to watch. "Here's one with a nice scalloped edge. And here's a pair to hemstitch. Or this, with the cluster of flowers here? Maybe you'd rather make a dresser scarf. Lots of girls start with them—easy to handle. How about one with rosebuds on? You could make them pink, or yellow, if you wanted to." She paused. "See anything here?"

Ginny looked and bit her lip. "I don't know. Nothing rings a bell, if you know what I mean."

Sister Timothy nodded. "Well, I do have something extra-special here." She reached far into the drawer for a long package wrapped in blue paper and opened it tenderly. "It's real linen," she said, running the tips of her fingers along the cloth. "Not many of the girls want to undertake a sheet anymore." Not *any*, really. "You see, there'd be a scalloped edge along here, and then these curls and flowers in here, in a satin stitch. I'd suggest white, or a very pale pastel. And then, when you're finished, you turn the hem on this line and sew it down here. That hides the back of your work. Then, see, the blanket goes here, this folds back, and that's how your bed looks." Sister Timothy looked at the folds in her hands and saw it finished and on a bed. She straightened the cloth. "It's very nice."

"It's beautiful, Sister," Ginny admitted. "But, gosh, I got bad eyes. They just never could stand all that fine work."

"No," Sister Timothy said sadly. "It would take good eyes." She folded the blue paper around the sheet and blamed herself again for hoping.

Ginny chose the pillowcases with the hemstitched edge. Sister

Timothy wrote it down in her charge book. "I'll start tomorrow, Sister," Ginny said. Then she and Rosemary left.

Sister Timothy went back to her sunny window for a moment. The outside door slammed. She saw the two girls on the steps beneath her window, pulling on their mittens, and heard their voices—Virginia's, shrill with indignation, saying, "Did you get a load of that sheet she was trying to shove off on me!"

"It'd probably take the rest of your natural life to finish it," Rosemary said.

"And besides it's unbearably baroque."

"Gingerbread!"

Sister Timothy pulled back from the window. Even the sun seemed to give her a chill now. She went to the cupboard and began putting the pillowcases and dresser scarves away in the drawer. She worked carefully, making it last the whole ten minutes until her closing time.

As she walked to the door, Sister Isabel burst in. "Oh, Sister, I was hoping you hadn't gone yet!" she cried.

"No," said Sister Timothy. "I'm still here."

"Sister Jeanette had to have her appendix out in a hurry, and she'll be gone for three weeks."

"That's too bad," said Sister Timothy.

"And now there's no one to give the health lectures to the freshmen, and so I wondered if you could give them a quick course in needlework to keep 'em out of trouble. Three weeks, twice a week? You don't seem to be very busy here."

"I guess I could," said Sister Timothy.

"I prepared this for you—sort of a quick job, but it'll give you the general idea." She handed Sister Timothy a paper and plunged out of the room. She was another to whom time was too precious, an administrator lucky to have a spare minute between her momentous decisions.

Sister Timothy, demonstrating her independence for her own benefit, found a few more things to do before she read the paper. Then she sat down and adjusted her spectacles. It began, impressively, "SHORT COURSE IN NEEDLEWORK—PROJECTED SYLLABUS," which certainly sounded a lot like the college catalogue, with its remarkable references to "advantages" that did not quite exist. Syllabus, indeed! But there, hiding behind the big Roman "I"s and "II"s and little "a"s and "b"s of the outline, were the hard, hard facts: "I. Hosiery Mending— a) holes; b) runners; c) preventive measures." Her eyes skipped like a stone thrown across water from "II. Buttons" to "III. Regular Repair," but at "a) the patch," something in her—her spirit, her dignity, her pride—hit bottom. She let the criminal document slip through her fingers and suffered it to lie unharmed at her feet.

She thought then of old Sister Mary Benjamin, safely dead; she could not have doubted that the New World spun forward to a better day. She had survived the arsonous Sioux, the long nights with rifle on knee, to guide the needles of the daughters of flour kings and lumber barons—girls with gold lockets on black velvet ribbons, solid-silver thimbles, and scissors made in England.

How could Sister Mary Benjamin have doubted? Yet she should have doubted some, for the June grass of the prairies, thick and deep at first, dies before its time, bears no second crop, blows away. And now, beyond the crass new buildings, lay the bones of weeds, the frozen dust. Now the black nonsense on orange satin of poor quality, the clever dish towels. Now the ineffectual voices peeping "Abélard" and "Champeaux" while the needles rusted away. On the other side of the partition, Sister Annette was saying now, "Of course, we could get a little more room if . . ."

PREFECT OF DISCIPLINE

JOSEPH W. CARROLL

It is a joy to know Father Costello. As he describes the five cases of discipline submitted to him for judgment and correction, the fine bouquet and tang of his mellow good humor and intelligence are savored like priceless old wine by the reader.

Joseph Carroll has recently been appointed fiction editor of Collier's. He was born in Chicago and was graduated from a Jesuit high school and Loyola University. After several years as a reporter and publicity writer, he joined the International Division of the National Broadcasting Company in New York as a commentator and announcer. Later he joined the staff of the New York Daily News.

Father Costello looked discontentedly out of the window of his small room on the third floor of the five-story, gray-brick academy building. The room was his office as well as his living quarter, and sparsely furnished as became a priest with a vow of poverty. A scarred old desk with a corrugated roll top was all that made the narrow cubicle an office. For living purposes, it had an iron bed, a wardrobe, a built-in washstand, two chairs, bookshelves and a prie-dieu.

The priest's discontent was not serious enough to be a matter of conscience. Scrupulosity, that subtlest of tortures, never bedeviled Father Costello. He was a goodhearted man, gentle in all his judgments, even of himself.

But the gentleness was beleaguered, both by the memory of recent events in this room and by the view from his window. "Surely," he said, looking down into the wide street, "the ugliest section in all this great, ugly city."

It was a business street of cluttered store fronts and tacky loft buildings. Father Costello did not much care for business, even when it had a comelier mien than the graceless, hand-to-mouth enterprise of the street on which the academy was built. He was grateful that the Order had members who liked conducting its practical affairs, leaving others free for sanctity and scholarship.

"Sanctity and scholarship, my foot!" said Father Costello, reminded suddenly of the occasion of his discontent by a figure in the street below. It was old Brother Morrissey, the church sacristan, in his best street attire: the skimpily cut pants showing unstylish ankles above the laborious polish of the old-fashioned shoes; the black clerical fedora set with severe avoidance of any frivolous tilt. The brother had come out of a side door of the church, which stood next the academy. He walked with stiff agility past the front steps of the church, past the brothers' dormitory building beyond it, and across the intersection at the corner into a shop on the other side of the street.

Father Costello turned away from the window. How unjust it was, he thought, that the sight of Brother Morrissey should have provoked his cynical and mildly profane exclamation about sanctity and scholarship. For the brother in his own person embodied the first quality—and at least he did no violence to the second.

Father Costello chided himself for yielding to this mood of dissatisfaction which had seized him as soon as his working day had ended a few minutes past. The mood held the risk of self-righteousness and uncharity toward others. "I am rebuked," he argued, "by the lively ghost of the saint and scholar for whom this school is named."

The academy was named for a sixteenth-century Spaniard of noble parentage, who had abandoned a promising career as a soldier and founded a religious order dedicated to the education of the young. In his name, both the parish and the academy had been built here years before. But it was old-sake's sake that kept

them going nowadays. The neighborhood had become a slum.
The old-timers had long since moved away. But they still sent
their sons to the academy. And they themselves still came back
on Sundays to hear High Mass in the splendid old church, with
its twin spires towering to the burnished crosses. The church had
been hallowed by the years to the dignity of a shrine. The academy, by the same hallowing, stood as a monument to the reverence for learning, which the old-timers and their priests brought
with them in their flight from an island nation in the rainy
Atlantic.

"But we take a great deal out in reverence," mused Father
Costello. "God forgive me for a snob, is there a true scholar on
the whole faculty—save possibly young Mr. Wagner?" He did
not consciously press his own claims to scholarship. But there had
been a book on the elegiac poets, written soon after his ordination
years ago. It had been respectfully reviewed in the thick-paged
periodicals interested in such things.

Discontent rose, livelier than ever, to the bait of this sudden
memory, bobbing on a cord of ambition, invisible as fine silk and
quite as strong. No doubt of it: he was poorly fitted for his present duties. Perhaps he should discuss it with his superior.

Yet it would be hard to say in words of suitable modesty why
he disliked being Prefect of Discipline. Of all his qualities, he
guessed, a wayward inclination to laughter at odd times made
him an incompetent judge of the peccadillos of schoolboys. He
hoped it was that, more than a priggish yearning for the aloof
and self-sufficient rewards of scholarship.

Through the open transom over his door, Father Costello heard
Mr. Wagner's voice, synchronized with his knock. "May I come
in, Father?"

"Oh, do," said Father Costello cordially.

The scholastic entered and sat down on the kneeling bench of the prie-dieu, hitching his cassock around his knees. It was the kind of thing he did without self-consciousness or fear of criticism. Father Costello liked it in him.

It was interesting that they liked each other, these two. The kinship could not be guessed from their surfaces. Mr. Wagner was an ample young man, who stayed on the pleasant side of corpulence by playing handball every day. He had wild yellow hair, parted in the middle. He smiled most of the time, not merely to show good temper, though he was good-tempered; and not fatuously. It was the smile of a dedicated, comic spirit.

Father Costello, many years older, was lean as a dandy's walking-stick and as elegantly straight. The pallor of his face went well with the intelligence of his eyes and the refinement of his features. He was supposed to resemble Woodrow Wilson, a likeness he did not exploit. For, though he had no politics, he recalled from his early days in the Order that the priests who read the papers believed Wilson's followers with their New Freedom to be obdurately secularist in social philosophy. But Father Costello was not vain of his appearance and did not really care whom he resembled, if anyone. His gray hair was wispy on top and often, as now, wanted cutting toward the neck. The rough black cloth of his cassock was worn at the elbows and seat to an iridescence, like meat when it is turning bad. A big wooden crucifix with a silvered Christus was sheathed in the cord around his middle. He habitually held his right hand on the top of it, as though he were a classic actor clutching a dagger.

"Any more boys due?" Mr. Wagner asked.

"No, indeed," said Father Costello gratefully. "The last two of them left a while since—in halos of utterly insincere repentance."

"Big day?" said Mr. Wagner.

"A full blotter," said Father Costello. "A term used in the

police courts, I believe. Most apt, John, most apt for my duties.
Not that I wish to complain."

"Oh, complain a little," said Mr. Wagner. "I've been correct-
ing English themes. And I'd like to hear what other kinds of
crimes the boys commit."

Father Costello lifted his biretta from the top of the prie-dieu,
twirled it by its pompon as he sat on the window sill. The austere
little room was shadowy, the gradual darkness of a spring evening
falling outside.

"Any difficult cases?" Mr. Wagner asked.

"Nothing that would tax Suarez, John, or call for reference to
the Summa Theologica. Our Order's reputation for subtlety
would suffer, I think, if it were known what kind of disciplinary
cases come up in this school."

"Tell me," said Mr. Wagner. He enjoyed Father Costello's
stately habit of speech, even though it had no quick salve for
curiosity.

"There were five of them this afternoon," the priest said. "Let
us take them in the inverse order of interest and significance. The
first was a first-year boy. He was overheard using an evil or at
least dubious expression by Father Mulcahy—who sent him to
me, enjoined to repeat the whole conversation in which it was
used.

, "The youngster's name is Higgins—a hulk with a bold eye.
Quite respectful outwardly, don't you know, but a suspicion of
the malapert. It is this, I think, which irritates Father Mulcahy,
who does rather stand on his dignity. This is the fifth time Higgins
has been sent to me by Father Mulcahy. The actual charge in
each case was—I thought—trivial."

"What did Higgins say?" Mr. Wagner asked. But Father Costello was not to be hurried into a premature climax, least of all
by an English teacher.

"It was after the 9:30 history period," said Father Costello, in the manner of a conscientious witness dictating a deposition, "which Father Mulcahy teaches and in which Higgins is a less than diligent pupil. The boys were in the corridor outside the classroom, waiting for the bell to ring for the next period. Father Mulcahy, by the bye, misses little that goes on in the corridors, judging by the nature of the complaints he lodges here.

"The shabby little incident was this. A classmate of Higgins— I forget his name—was claiming to have made (isn't that the right verb?) ten baskets in a row from the center of the basketball floor in the gymnasium yesterday afternoon. This feat was accomplished while no one was present to witness it. Father Mulcahy heard Higgins use this objectionable word very loudly. He then ordered Higgins to report to me after classes."

Mr. Wagner listened in ecstatic expectation. This had possibilities for one with Father Costello's gift of indirection.

"The word," said Father Costello, "is a five-letter plural which I have always thought innocuous: the name of a child's toy—the object used in many games. It was easy to guess that Higgins intended to convey—ah—dubiety by the word. He himself made this plain when he told me that his classmate always seems to accomplish remarkable athletic deeds when no one is about. In Higgins' opinion, this boy is incapable of making one basket, even if he were lifted up to the hoop. That was Higgins' illustration," said Father Costello apologetically. He was afraid Mr. Wagner would think him adept at this jargon.

"Father Mulcahy," the priest said, "was not concerned about the discourtesy of doubting a comrade's word. He appeared to know that the expression is in itself an indecent one. He insisted that Higgins explain his use of the word to me—as part of his punishment.

"Higgins is not greatly articulate under the best of circumstances, John. But he muttered it out. You see," said Father Costello naively, "at this point, quite apart from any culpability of the boy or the placating of Father Mulcahy, I was determined to know myself. So awkward for a man in my position not to know these things.

"The word," said Father Costello delicately, "as boys use it, apparently refers—ah—to a private part of the body."

"I know," said Mr. Wagner soberly. He was forever charmed by the lacunae in Father Costello's worldly knowledge. They accounted for his considerable popularity as a confessor. "What did you tell Higgins?"

"I told him that in the first place it is wretched manners to doubt another's word—or to express the doubt. But if he must do it, to use some acceptable term, as 'pshaw' or the expressive Scots 'hoots!' I did think of telling him simply to lift his eyebrows, but he has the pale pink kind that don't show. He said, 'Yes Father.' And I let him go, suggesting that he apologize to Father Mulcahy for using an—ah—improper word in his presence."

"A Daniel come to judgment," said Mr. Wagner.

"I do think, though," said Father Costello, "that Father Mulcahy would save us both a deal of trouble and embarrassment if he would not—eavesdrop."

"Will you tell him so?"

"Well, no. He already regards me as a laxist. But I should like to ask him how he happens to be familiar with the word as Higgins used it."

"Next case," said Mr. Wagner.

Father Costello walked to the big desk; from a pigeonhole he plucked a thin volume bound in blue-gray cloth. "This too," he said, "involves an implication of—ah—lasciviousness."

"Lawks!" said Mr. Wagner. "Gomorrah was a quiet suburb with blue laws and a Sunday curfew, compared with this school. Say on."

Father Costello said on: "Father Scotus is the complainant. He often is. But the case has some interest as a moral question in which intellect and aesthetic emotion both come into play. Far worthier of the reputed—ah—casuistry of the Order than the expletives of the coarse-grained Higgins."

"Oh, boy!" said Mr. Wagner, with simple pleasure. He knew Father Scotus well.

"It is concerned," said Father Costello, "with poetry. Or verse, to use the Aristotelian distinction."

"Either way," said Mr. Wagner, who was not a finicking man.

"Father Scotus, as you know, teaches the mechanics of versification to the third-year boys. He seems to be in a continual embroilment with them. I sometimes wonder if he is perhaps not the best man for that particular assignment.

"The youth he sent up here seemed to me to be one of our better young men. I'm afraid you'll think me harsh, but their faces often appear to me to be—ah—lackluster when matters of intellect are discussed."

"You're telling me," said Mr. Wagner. "Faces like hamfat, the ones in my English classes have."

"As you say," said Father Costello. "This child—I fancy he's about sixteen—has a very bright face. And his conversation I found most engaging. Excellent vocabulary.

"Father Scotus found him shortly before the one o'clock period —that's the versification class—with this book open to this poem."

He took a marker from the book and put on his pince-nez. "The book is by one of the modern poets: a young woman. Her work is not familiar to me. A strenuous life she appears to lead, if the verses can be taken literally. Father Scotus holds that the whole book and the particular poem young Toomey (that's his name) was reading are marked by—ah—lubricity. This quatrain he underscored for me when he sent Toomey up here."

Father Costello read in a noncommittal tone:

Since that which Helen did and ended Troy
Is more than I can do though I be warm,
Have up your buried girls, egregious boy,
And stand with them against the unburied storm." *

"What do you think?" he asked Mr. Wagner, resting the book on his knee.

"There's no mistaking the meaning," Mr. Wagner said. "And yet I'm rather surprised Father Scotus should have got it."

"Toomey says," Father Costello explained, "that Father Scotus has something of an—ah—obsession about such things in poetry. Toomey was a little derisive about the whole affair, I thought. He told me that Father Scotus has warned the class against the moral character of almost every poet in the anthology they use.

"The boy was most correct and courteous. But he pointed out—and I think he enjoyed pointing out—that the anthology was compiled and annotated by our reverend principal, Father Quinlan."

"I rather enjoy it myself," said Mr. Wagner.

"Toomey told me that Father Scotus told the class that only three poets are safe to read—John Bannister Tabb, Abram Ryan . . ."

"They were both priests," said Mr. Wagner.

"I know," said Father Costello.

"Who was the third—Francis Thompson?"

"Mercy, no. He came in for special censure. The third was Joyce Kilmer."

"Yes, I can see the logic there," said Mr. Wagner. "Admitted he was a fool. But what's the matter with poor Thompson? I should have thought 'The Hound of Heaven' . . ."

"Toomey says," said Father Costello, aware that he was using

* From "Fatal Interview," Copyright 1931 by Edna St. Vincent Millay.

the boy's name as though citing an authority, "that Father Scotus finds the imagery in the famous ode inordinately sensuous, in spite of the religious experience described. He takes severe exception to the line, 'Naked I wait Thy Love's uplifted stroke.' "

"Why, in God's name?" asked Mr. Wagner, without blasphemy.

"Presumably," said Father Costello, "Father Scotus thinks it would have been more modest for Francis Thompson to wait for the Deity with something on—at least a . . ."

"A jock strap?" said Mr. Wagner.

"A breechclout, I should have said," said Father Costello. He was not quite sure of Mr. Wagner's term. He was not familiar enough with the locker room and the gymnasium to know whether it was an impropriety, or one of those necessary and unpleasant terms like some in physiology and anatomy. Still, he trusted Mr. Wagner's circumspection. If he used it, it must be all right; though possibly not with Fathers Scotus and Mulcahy.

"A sockdolager," said Mr. Wagner.

"I beg your pardon?"

"Obsolete slang expression," Mr. Wagner explained. "I only mean it's a very interesting case. How did you settle it?"

"I don't know that I did settle it," Father Costello said unhappily. "I questioned Toomey as to what reaction he had to the sonnet. He said he thought it was beautiful. Rather truculent he was at this point. Inclined to make an issue of freedom of the press. I doubt that the verses excited his—ah—concupiscence. He is very young.

"I advised him not to read poetry when Father Scotus is about—except, of course, Father Tabb or Father Ryan or Mr. Kilmer."

"What did he say?"

"Nothing but the usual 'Yes Father.' But bitterly. I fear he thought me something of a trimmer."

"O upright judge," said Mr. Wagner. "What will you tell Father Scotus?"

Father Costello picked up his biretta from the window sill, and put it on his head, as though to make his words more official:

"That one mustn't be too literal about poetry. That the book is not on the Index—and we mustn't be holier than the Church, must we? He teaches Latin too, you know. I wonder what he makes of Catullus?"

"Next case," said Mr. Wagner.

Father Costello put the impassioned book back in one pigeon-hole and from another he brought forth a sheet of lined exercise paper. "There's an exhibit in this one too," he said, holding the paper aloft. "Prima facie, there is no case. But it was interesting."

"Tell me," said Mr. Wagner warmly.

"This also was a complaint of Father Scotus. And really, John, I do think the poor man must be greatly troubled in spirit to quarrel with these boys so. Do you think he is well?"

"It depends on your standards of health," said Mr. Wagner. "I think he would not like to have his particular illness named. I feel rather sorry for the old boy—though I'm just as scared of him as the kids are. I'm sure he regards me as one of those Boccaccio-type religious and doubts that I have a vocation. But come on, let's hear it."

Father Costello studied the scrap of exercise paper. "The only crime I can see is vile Latinity, which is surely out of my present jurisdiction. I'm supposed to bullyrag them for their conduct, not their scholarship.

"The boy's name is Kerwin. A friend of Toomey's, but more of a merry-andrew. They were very thick in the corridor while waiting, and Toomey seemed to find Kerwin entertaining.

"I found him so too," said Father Costello. "Father Scotus evidently did not. He—Father Scotus—confiscated this bit of writing from Kerwin's desk during Latin class—Virgil. Kerwin admitted writing it, but said he did it 'on his own time.' The curious phrase is his."

Father Costello handed Mr. Wagner the paper. The scholastic read aloud in a puzzled voice:

> *Tabernus est in oppido*
> *Cumille sedet quem amo*
> *Et bibit vinum eius laetissime*
> *Et nunquam commemorat me.*
> *Vale, vale, necesse est iri*
> *No oportet tibi flere . . .*

Mr. Wagner looked up. "What gibberish is this?"

Father Costello smiled, as though with an agreeable memory. "Kerwin sang it for me. Very pleasant voice he has, though not quite finished changing. It's a translation. The Latin is, as you well note, ridiculous. The idioms are false and the grammar questionable. And yet, you know, it has charm—like dialect English."

Mr. Wagner construed in gingerly, pony-style language: "An inn is in the walled town . . . where that very one sits whom I love . . . and drinks his own wine (who else's?) most joyously . . . and never recalls me. Good-by, good-by. It is necessary for me to be gone, nor is it opportune or fitting for you to weep. . . "

The scholastic paused. "A song you say?"

"Quite an old one," said Father Costello. "It seems to be having a new vogue. Kerwin says some radio comedian who specializes in reviving old ballads . . ."

Mr. Wagner shouted. "O my bleeding paradigms!" he said. "My withering declensions!" And he sang in a gusty baritone:

> There is a tavern in the town, in the town
> And there my true love sits him down, sits him down
> And drinks his wine as merry as can be

And never never thinks of me.
Fare thee well, for I must leave thee
Do not let this parting grieve thee . . .

Father Costello said: "Kerwin sings it better. It calls for a plaintive. tenor. A rakish type, Kerwin. He wears one of those pullovers, you know, with outlandish colors in zig zag lines—and a pancake hat. Suits the song better, somehow, than a cassock." Mr. Wagner was not offended, though he liked to sing and had a good carrying voice. After all, it was Kerwin's song. "So you dismissed the charge, Father?" said the scholastic.

"Yes," the priest said. "The boy wrote it for his own amusement. I think it's interesting that he should be amused even by bad Latin verse. And the rhyming is rather good." He hummed a little.

"What did you tell Kerwin?"

"That different people are amused by different things, and some people, God help them, are never amused at all. Kerwin said, 'Yes, Father,' the way they all do, winked and left. I overheard him telling Toomey that I said the verses showed an exquisite sense of rhythm. A tarradiddle. I said nothing of the sort."

"What will you tell Father Scotus?" asked Mr. Wagner.

Father Costello sighed. "I wish I could think of something useful to tell him, John. If I suggest that he intensify his instruction in idiomatic Latin, he'll do it—and I shall have more cases from him than ever. I might tell him to be less ready to see malice where none is intended."

"I cannot find it," said Mr. Wagner. " 'Tis not in the bond."

"The next case," said Father Costello, robbing Mr. Wagner of the chance to repeat his whimsy, for he was a little tired of it, "is the only sad one of the day. The saddest of my many months in this wearisome post."

Mr. Wagner responded quickly to a seriousness, an actual sorrow in the priest's voice. He was very fond of Father Costello. "Oh?" said Mr. Wagner. "A bad one, eh?"

"Shabby," Father Costello said. "Painful and sickening. Two offenders for the same offense. First-year boys: cherubs to look at them. Still in knee-pants. Brother Morrissey sent them to me."

Mr. Wagner was surprised. "The church sacristan? I've never known him to turn a boy in before. He's been known to smack them one behind if he ran into any mischief. But it's all out of character for him to report anything."

Father Costello nodded. "This is the one sin, I should think, which Brother Morrissey regards as—ah—crying to academy authority for vengeance. He was very angry."

"Anger's out of character too," said Mr. Wagner.

"Not in this instance, I think you'll find. He's close to eighty, you know. They try to argue him into retirement to the brothers' home every year, but he puts them off. Quite right, too: he does his job better than anyone around here—and he'd hate frowsting all day over devotional works. Not a contemplative, Brother Morrissey."

Well Mr. Wagner knew. "He beat me at handball the other day," he said. "Cheats like anything in the scoring, but I expect he reckons it like a golf handicap, because of his age."

Father Costello continued: "He came in here this noon hour to tell me about the two lads, Fahey and Burke. I sent a note down to the classroom that they were to report to me after hours." He paused, remembering the tremulous indignation of the sacristan, an agile sliver of a man, whose pink scalp showed clean as a baby's through the neat strands of white hair. He recalled the glimpse he had caught of the brother from the window, and his probable errand in the shop on the corner.

Father Costello said: "Brother Morrissey's room in the brothers' dormitory fronts on the cross street down the block. He was looking out of his window yesterday afternoon. He usually does at that time of day, he tells me, while he says a Rosary. He wanted to make it plain that he engages in no espionage on academy boys. It's pleasanter to say his prayers while looking out the window: that's such an active street, always something doing.

"Brother Morrissey's been here for years, you know. Goes all the way back to the old times. He knows everyone in the neighborhood even now. Not just parishioners, but everyone. There aren't many actual parishioners nowadays, anyway. The people who go to Mass and confession at the church are mainly railroadmen from the yards yonder, some of the business people on their way down town, and, of course, some of the old parishioners who come back.

"But Brother Morrissey knows them all, churchgoers or not. Some very special friends of his live right opposite the brothers' building. They own a little candy and tobacco store . . ."

"The Rubins?" said Mr. Wagner. "I know them too. Mr. Rubin's a Spinozist. I buy cigarettes there and we argue about it. Mrs. Rubin thinks I'm some sort of Protestant because I'm called Mister instead of Father."

"Brother Morrissey likes them very much," said Father Costello. "He says they give clothes and things to the St. Vincent de Paul Society. I doubt that he discusses philosophy with them —though he did give them a year's subscription to *The Messenger of the Sacred Heart* for Christmas."

"For Hanukkah, Mrs. Rubin told me," said Mr. Wagner. "She showed me a copy and said she thought the pictures were very pretty."

"Brother Morrissey," Father Costello said, "looked out his window yesterday and saw the two academy boys standing in front of the store. There's a streetcar stop there, so he thought little of it, though the boys were looking up and down the street in a secretive way. But after a while the street was empty. The boys began writing on the Rubins' store window. Some kind of soap they had.

"Brother Morrissey saw Mr. Rubin come out of the store and collar the boys. The brother went out and crossed the street. One boy had written an—ah—exhortation to passers-by not to patronize the store. The other had written one word: an ugly, dirty, insulting word."

Father Costello's face was sadder than Mr. Wagner had ever seen it. "Brother Morrissey took the boys' names," the priest said. "Mr. Rubin said to let it go: they were children only, and didn't know any better. But he thought they should clean the window. Brother Morrissey saw to it that they did."

Father Costello turned to the window. The street lights had just come on, and the front window of the shop at the corner was a patch of yellow in the spring mist. "The brother was still angry when he told me about it today," said the priest. "He said he had never tattled on an academy boy before, but this was the limit. He said we were all shamed in the eyes of the kindest of neighbors. He said he would leave it to my judgment about what to do. But I don't think he really expects anything."

Mr. Wagner waited to hear the judgment.

"They are stupid boys," said Father Costello. "They were afraid of me, but not because of what they had done—only because they think it a terrifying thing to be sent to the Prefect of Discipline.

"I spoke to them about charity—the theological kind, not the almsgiving. I quoted the Second Commandment of the Lord. I asked them where they got such ideas as they wrote on the window. Fahey said his mother told him you could never trust 'those people.' Burke said he always understood 'those people' were against religion. They both spoke in substantives, apparently thinking I would be offended by the proper name of the proud people of an ancient faith."

His voice became scornful. "They said 'Yes, Father,' and 'No, Father,' at what they took to be the right places. And I gave them a routine punishment."

The priest looked at Mr. Wagner with real embarrassment. "It was a failure, John, a grievous failure. They didn't understand a word I said. I had thought the academy might send Mr. Rubin an apology. But one insult is enough, more than enough. You see, the letter would be signed by Father Quinlan, since he is the principal."

"Why not?" said Mr. Wagner.

Father Costello said softly: "I heard Father Quinlan only last week use the same word that Burke wrote on Mr. Rubin's window."

Mr. Wagner rose from the kneeler at the prie-dieu. A bell was ringing in the corridor, which meant it was time to go to the refectory for the evening meal.

"What will you tell Brother Morrissey?" asked Mr. Wagner, moving toward the door.

Father Costello sat motionless on the window sill. "To pray for us, John, all of us. For the ignorant children and those who teach them. I shall ask him to pray for those among us who are second-rate and presumptuous and purblind. Brother Morrissey is an old man of wonderful innocence. But he will understand."

Mr. Wagner had the door opened, and asked from the threshold: "Are you coming to the refectory?"

Father Costello leaned his head against the window pane, his eyes searching the lights and shadows in the street. "John," he said, "this is a wearing post, and I doubt I'm the man for it. Do you think I should ask for a change?"

"I shouldn't," Mr. Wagner said, closing the door.

PROTHALAMION

EDWARD SHEEHY

A man can think he has lost his faith, coasting easily down the incline of sins of omission. But sacrilege is a different matter, as John de Courcy discovered in the confessional, when circumstances make it convenient to pretend to be receiving the sacrament in good faith. As the young priest calls him "son" and speaks earnestly to him, John is shaken to the core of his being: "Where was his cultured agnosticism, his freedom from the superstitions of the vulgar? If it were really true that he didn't believe, he couldn't feel like this." This confession was his preparation for marriage, the morning after it, to a Catholic spinster of exacting temperament! Edward Sheehy is a young writer from Dublin. In "Prothalamion" his astute control of significant substance and psychological insight combined to make a story acceptable to the fastidious editorial standards of Horizon.

John de Courcy was reluctant to leave the comfort of his seat in the warm bus. He waited until all the other passengers had got themselves and their luggage out before he descended to the pavement, where he hurriedly buttoned up the neck of his heavy tweed overcoat against the bitter east wind that was blowing along the quays. Slowly he started to cross the road towards the corner of Westmoreland Street; but hadn't advanced more than a few paces when he hesitated, turned and walked slowly back to the quay-wall, where he stood apparently watching the reflections of the neon signs writhing and twisting on the choppy surface of the river, at the boats pulled by wind and tide straining at their moorings.

No use in trying to think things out in this misery, he decided, as he watched the people hurrying across the bridge, their cold-blotched faces averted from the direction of the wind. He needed a drink, a stiff one, to pull him together. The point was, should

he go over to the Palace, where he'd be bound to run into some
of the boys? The temptation was strong. But no; it would be
simply disastrous to get tied up with a crowd when he had to
have the whole business over in time to get the nine-o'clock back
to Ballyross. Better go somewhere where he wasn't known. Pur-
posefully now he crossed the road and pushed open the door of
O'Mara's.

The outer bar was crowded, mostly workmen and a few clerks.
The warm air was heavy with the odours of beer, tobacco-smoke
and damp clothes. He pressed his way through; the inner bar was
not so full. The drinkers moved respectfully back from the
counter to allow him to order a large gin with a dash of lime. He
liked it less, but at the last moment decided that it wasn't so
noticeable as whiskey. He swallowed it in two draughts before
the curate returned with his change, when he indicated with a
nod that he wanted the same again.

"It's a bad night, sir," an elderly, worn-looking clerk said at
his elbow.

"Wretched, wretched," he answered brusquely, looking away,
shrinking from the proffered contact.

When his second drink arrived he took it to a small table in the
far corner and seated himself with his back to the drinkers at the
counter. As he sipped the gin he relaxed slowly and felt the arms
of the chair comfortingly support his back. He felt better already,
decidedly better, and smiled to think of how Ballyross would be
scandalized to see him, John de Courcy, the highly respected
solicitor, bolting a double gin like that. They'd probably conclude
he was on the verge of bankruptcy, or threatened with an action
for maintenance. A bad job if they guessed the hole he was in.
But they never would, not in a thousand years. As the warmth of
the room and the drink began to steal through him, he threw his
coat open and removed his hat, which he placed on the table
beside him. No, the yokels would never guess, nor Canon

O'Donoghue, nor that craw-thumper Wrigley at the bank. He changed his position slightly to enable himself to see his head reflected in the mirror which advertised Power's whiskey in gilt letters. The result pleased him; it reassured him to look himself fair in the eye, to meet his own glance with confidence and imperturbability. It certainly wasn't the look of a man likely to be the victim of circumstances. No, sir. Vera used to tell him he had a distinguished head. She used to say that he was the only really civilized man she knew: not bad that for a country solicitor considering that she knew half the writers and artists of Dublin. Poor old Vera, he thought, with a sudden access of tenderness; she wasn't so hardboiled as she thought she was with her modern ideas and her bachelor flat. It was the perfect adventure in many ways until she began to get ideas into her head. Poor old Vera. He finished his drink in a sad, valedictory toast.

He turned, caught the curate's eye and indicated his empty glass. The curate ducked under the counter-flap bringing him another gin. He needed it. He decided to take this one more slowly while he thought the matter out. So far he hadn't really faced up to the situation. He couldn't afford to get tight, but the drink would help him to attain the necessary objectivity. That's what he needed, he thought, objectivity. Now this morning he had allowed himself to be panicked, a cardinal error and fatal in dealing with a woman. He should have remembered that from his mother. God, how like his mother Martha had sounded, the same tone, the same angry severity, the same narrow, bigoted. . . . No, you couldn't very well blame the old woman; she had lived through different times. But from Martha, even though she was the Canon's sister, he certainly had never expected anything like that. He went over the conversation he'd had with her in the hallway of Leinster Arms that morning. Had he his certificate of confession? His what? Told him he couldn't be married without it. Completely flabbergasted him. And then going on like a sermon saying what a good thing it was because it prevented people from approaching the sacrament without a proper sense of its sanctity. The same old cant while he stood there like an idiot trying to think of a way out, of how, at least, he could avoid having to go to Confession in Ballyross. He saw his mistake now; he should have brazened it out, told some story or another to the Canon and everything would have been all right. He had let himself be panicked, just as he did when he was a kid and his mother questioned him. His one idea had been to gain time. Told her he had to run up to town to fix up the Collins case which was coming up on Tuesday; didn't want any business worries hanging over him during the honeymoon, he had tried to insinuate. "But barristers don't work on a Saturday," she would think of that. "Oh, this man's been on the circuit all the week. I've arranged to go out to his place in Ailesbury Road." But of course she had to read him a lecture: "And do you really mean to tell me, John, that you wouldn't have gone to Confession anyway? Surely you knew there was to be a nuptial Mass, and that I certainly meant to receive." As if she owned him, body and soul. And worst of it all was that he hadn't an answer except the air of a martyr harried with multitudinous affairs, his business, the decorators in the house and all that. He had to listen to her, to reassure her with his: "Don't worry, old girl, I'll run up to town, see MacFarland, trot over to my little man in Whitefriars Street and be back on the nine-o'clock bus. How'll that do?" But of course she had to have the last word, more in sorrow than in anger: "But you know, John, I really think you ought to give more thought to those matters than you seem to. After all they are more important . . ." and so on and so on, like his mother's "I'd rather see a son of mine dead at my feet than have him, lose the faith." And he was going to spend the rest of his life listening to that kind of thing.

He hurried through his drink in the vain attempt to dislodge the sickly fear that weighed on his stomach. He should have known that gin would have that depressing effect, and wondered if it would be dangerous to change over to whiskey at this stage. Without allowing himself to think he went to the bar and ordered a small whiskey. With a feeling of irritation he noticed that the drinkers were looking at him curiously. He ignored them pointedly while he counted out the exact tenpence so that he wouldn't have to wait at the counter for the change.

The trouble was, of course, that ever since his mother's death he had completely ignored the religious side except for an occasional appearance at late Mass when he happened to be at home for the week-end. It had certainly never entered his head that he'd find in a woman of Martha's education the same narrow bigotry he had come to look on as a peculiar property of Ballyross. For fifteen years he had got away with it. The yokels hadn't an inkling. To them he was the respectable Catholic solicitor. Even the two scandal-mongering terrors, the Misses Kavanagh, had openly canvassed the suitability of his engagement with the Canon's sister. For fifteen years he had pulled it off. They never suspected his weekly trips to Dublin, his evenings with the boys, intellectual little soirées you might call them, mellowed with slow moderate drinking, the discussions, the arguments, the epigrams, the French or Latin tag so exactly right. And Vera, lovely, civilized, cultured Vera. Another world altogether from their stuffy superstitions and eternal prying. *Moi, j'ai été aussi en Arcadie,* he murmured into the collar of his coat. Diplomacy, that's what did it, and the little man in Whitefriars Street. He chuckled audibly to the silent amusement of the drinkers. Splendid little man, Father Sylvester—and entirely his own creation, apart from the fact that the name appeared over one of the confessionals. He loved the little man in Whitefriars Street, his brilliant, tolerant, kindly Carmelite friend whose reported conversations had so often called forth from the Canon the heavy judgment that the Orders had more learning than piety. The whole town knew of Father Sylvester, his great friend, and concluded that his soul was in good hands: a useful state of affairs in a place like Ballyross where a man's soul is considered everyone's legitimate business.

The whiskey was certainly a great improvement on the gin; he ordered another. He prided himself on the fact that drink never obscured or dulled his faculties. On the contrary, a few potations, if anything, gave his mind a certain lucid detachment. Now, up to this morning, his prospective marriage had shown every advantage. Martha wasn't bad looking. She was well educated; had a B.A. degree of Cork in fact. Well connected, and her fortune wasn't anything to be sneezed at. Not that she was getting a bad bargain; she wasn't in the first flower of girlhood, as one might say. The Canon himself had been particularly anxious for the match, active even. A good move putting that income-tax recovery business into his hands and that deed of assignment for the house-property in Listowel. A good deal of the hard-headed Kerry peasant about the Canon, with his: "She'd make you a good sensible wife, John, which is just what you need over in that barracks of yours in the Square. And she won't come empty John, I promise you. That is, of course, if you have a mind for one another." There was no gainsaying the Canon's arguments. Forty was leaving marriage a bit late. As it was he'd be well on the way to seventy before he'd have a son of age to take over the business. And then there was that feeling he'd been having during the past few years, especially coming on to Christmas, of being alone and uncared for.

Of course there hadn't been any extravagant passion: they were both a bit beyond that and, anyway, she wasn't the kind to let her feelings run away with her or encourage any—well—prenuptial familiarity. In a way he respected her for that. When she accepted him he had a vision of the transformation their marriage would bring about in the house in the Square, the clean bed-linen, the well-cooked meals, the little attentions and refinements a man values: a home, in fact. He wasn't sentimental, but he had to admit that 'home' was the only word which expressed exactly what he'd look forward to. This bitterness of hers on the subject of religion was the one fly in the ointment. And it came as a complete shock to him, the knowledge that this woman would consider she had the right to pry into his mind, to question his ideas. And have the whole of Ballyross behind her in the process. He should have foreseen it; that's where he'd made a fool of himself. "By God, John de Courcy," he told himself, "you're in for it now if you don't watch out." Now that he thought of it, she was the kind of woman who'd be still more formidable as a matron, a kind of *arbiter elegantiarum* to the whole of Ballyross; only *elegantiarum* wasn't quite the right word.

He finished his drink and ordered another. He didn't care now that the drinkers at the counter were watching him over their shoulders and glanced at one another with raised eyebrows. Thought he was tight, did they? Yokels! he cowed them deliberately with the contempt of his glance before turning back to his drink and the contemplation of the situation.

He had now considered the worst and was pleasantly amazed at his philosophic detachment. The panic was gone. After a few potations, he considered, the body becomes torpid, and the mind, liberated, is capable of—well—of philosophy. If only he were with a few of the boys to-night, the chosen spirits, how he could talk. The old head was doing its stuff. "Women, gentlemen, have a capacity for hysterical intensity that is proof against any of the intellectual processes. Women are primarily concerned with appearances and not at all with reality." He certainly was in form to-night. It takes the man to get the best out of alcohol. "Drink affects women, as it does stupid men, by making them reckless, not philosophical." Ah, the mood, the epigrammatic mood. He should have been a writer, an artist. But really now he must get down to the business in hand. This Confession now, he taunted himself, let the liberated mind play on that. He smiled at the ease with which he attained the duality of thinker and actor. He took himself to task with frowning severity: "Now, de Courcy, this is all damn silly. We know you haven't been to Confession for donkey's years; we know you don't want to go to Confession. But circumstances, circumstances, old man, over which you have no control make it imperative that you produce tangible evidence of having performed that act before the nine-o'clock bus for Bally-ross leaves Aston's Quay. After all you've only got to make up some harmless story and get it over. It's a mere formality; hasn't the slightest significance for a man of your intelligence. Of course you could play the idiot as you nearly did once when you were a raw undergraduate. You could go back to Ballyross, pitch the Canon and his sister to hell. . . . But I don't think your life after would be any too comfortable. No, old man, you used to profess an admiration for a certain Machiavelli. Now's the time to have the laugh on the whole bloody lot of them. How about bringing the little man in Whitefriars Street to the rescue? No false heroics now; they're in bad taste. After all you can't very well play the martyr for a cultured agnosticism."

A heavy, Italian-looking, white-aproned man carrying a basket stopped by his elbow, muttering sadly: "Fresh shellfish. Oysters fresh." He refused with a shake of the head, and, remembering the cold outside, buttoned up his overcoat.

II

There were few people in the body of the church, but the seats around the confessionals were crowded. He crossed himself with holy water from the font, genuflected and walked slowly towards the high altar, glancing from side to side at the names over the boxes. He was aware of the silence, of the diffused sweetness of the incense. There was something strange and incongruous in the unaffected devotion of a young man telling his rosary. Half-way up he saw the name Father Sylvester over a box to the left. He genuflected again and slipped into a seat. Instinctively he crossed himself again and knelt, bowing his head between his arms. First he had to think out a plausible confession.

Drunkenness, that'd do. And missing Mass on Sunday after a skite the night before. Didn't say his morning prayers. Sounded a bit childish, like disobedience, which was always a standby when he was a kid. He went through the seven deadly sins. Most of them sounded a bit vague. "I was guilty of envy, Father." Too much explanation involved. Or gluttony. If the priest asked: "How do you know?" How did one know, anyway? Immodest thoughts and desires. Yes. And Vera. Good God, surely he wasn't beginning to take the thing seriously. No. Vera's ruled out, he told himself angrily; that's taking the joke too far. Don't be an idiot. You've got to get it over as quickly as possible. First you say: "Bless me, Father, for I have sinned." How long? Say five weeks. And the *Confiteor*: "I confess to Almighty God. . . ." You're supposed to have said it before you go into the box.

After all, why should he have to wait? Those others were just doing their ordinary routine. It'd be hours before he got through that crowd. A penitent came out with bowed head and a man entered. Next came a kindly-looking woman in black. Her sleepy grey eyes wandered without interest, while her pale lips moved in prayer. He approached and bending towards her, whispered:

"I beg your pardon, Madam, I wonder if I could possibly get in quickly. You see I'm to be married in the morning and I've got a bus to catch at nine."

She smiled understandingly, a bit roguishly, and said: "You're welcome, sir."

He knelt on one knee in the aisle while the woman whispered the news to her neighbours. One by one the waiting people looked at him and smiled, pleased to oblige him because he was to be married in the morning and had a bus to catch. The minutes dragged while he listened to the indistinguishable murmur from the interior of the box. At last he recognized the tone of absolution, the sibilant contrition of the penitent. A moment later a sickly-looking youth emerged and John de Courcy slipped into the gloom and isolation of the box.

He knelt upright, facing the shuttered grill. In that position he felt short of breath and his heart began to beat loud and insistently against his ribs. It seemed only yesterday since he had last knelt like this, shuddering with guilt, fearful under the weight of his childish sins, consoling himself with the thought that in a few minutes he would emerge into the light of the church, glad, liberated, free from his load. But now. . . . A horrible sickening nostalgia seized him. He wanted to escape. He wanted to rush from the box. "Don't be an utter idiot," he told himself. "Hold yourself together for God's sake." He tried to distract his thoughts with wondering what Father Sylvester would be like. The little man in Whitefriars Street. But the joke didn't come off. "It's too late now anyway," something in his head kept insisting, "too late. You'd miss your bus. You've got to go through with it." What an age that woman on the other side was. One of those women who tell the neighbours' sins as well as their own ; he reminded himself of the old mission joke. He was stifling. Why did he have to feel so miserable and sick? Perhaps the whiskey on top of the gin.

Again he heard the murmur of the absolution and keyed himself for the moment when the shutter would be drawn back. When it was, he found himself looking into the face of a young man, a boy almost. The priest inclined his head towards the grill without looking at him, and hurriedly John de Courcy explained that he was to be married in the morning and needed a certificate.

"Yes, oh yes," the priest said, "that will be all right. Now your

Confession, my son." He waited through the preliminaries, sighing, weary with the sins of Dublin.

"I was drunk twice, Father," John de Courcy hurried, "I missed Mass one Sunday." He found himself being deliberately simple.

"Drunk, my son?" the priest said.

"Yes, Father."

"Did you become insensible?"

"No, Father."

"Did you lose control of yourself in any way, or do anything you wouldn't have done if you hadn't drink taken? Anything sinful, I mean."

"I might have been a bit unsteady, Father," he said, with pathetic jocularity.

"Being a bit unsteady is hardly a sin," the young priest seemed to be smiling. "I don't think you can have been really drunk, my son. Of course, missing Mass is serious, very serious. Anything else now?"

"No, Father," he forced himself to say. And as he said it a feeling of hopeless wretchedness descended on him which he didn't even attempt to combat. The simple sincerity of the priest's face accused him. He felt he was doing something ineffably mean and loathsome in deceiving him. If only he could make a clean breast of everything, Vera, his lapse from faith, his neglect of the Sacraments. But he couldn't. He couldn't. It was all crazy, insane. He shouldn't feel like this.

The priest sighed and paused. For a moment of panic John de Courcy was convinced that he had seen through the deception, until he said:

"You are to be married in the morning, my son?"

"Yes, Father."

"Well, my son, remember that you are on the threshold of a very serious undertaking. Approach the Sacrament with a pure heart and pure intentions and you will gain **precious** grace from it. You will have children, with the help of God. You will have a duty to them also, to bring them up in the fear and love of God. Your wife you will love, honour and cherish. Together you will do all in your power to make a good Catholic home. The institution of the family has God's especial blessing. . . ."

Slowly and earnestly he talked; but John de Courcy wasn't listening. He knelt there appalled at the weakness in himself in the face of something he had for years refused to contemplate. Where was his cultured agnosticism, his freedom from the superstitions of the vulgar? If it were really true and he didn't believe, he couldn't feel like this. And Martha, with her he'd never escape from it. She wouldn't be fooled by his little man in Whitefriars Street. Anyway his creation was dead; in his place sat this accusing innocent, a good ten years younger than he who called him "my son" without incongruity. He felt himself on the threshold of a galling and endless imprisonment.

"Your penance will be five Our Fathers and five Hail Marys, my son. And now, the act of Contrition." The priest began the absolution.

She'd want to know where he spent his evenings in town. She'd have the run of his books and as likely as not make a bonfire of his Rabelais, his Balzac, his Joyce, any he really cared for. Why hadn't he thought of that? And no way out. He could only get out of it now by taking a boat for the ends of the earth. Good God! he remembered suddenly, MacFarland is on the phone. Supposing Martha wanted something from town at the last moment and rang up to find he hadn't been there. Better ring MacFarland as soon as he got out.

"God bless you, my son," the priest was saying.

He rose wearily, feeling listless and empty.

"Didn't you say that you wanted a certificate?" the priest asked.

"Oh, yes, Father," he said shamefacedly.

"If you wait just a second now while I look for a pen. . . . Your name, my son?"

Perhaps he'd feel differently tomorrow. This had been a bad day, a wretched day. Tomorrow he'd be able to take stock of the situation properly. If he hadn't mixed his drinks he wouldn't have got into this state. That's what made him feel so off-colour. Yes, that was the cause of his breaking down without a doubt.

MISSIS FLINDERS

TESS SLESINGER

This is a great story about birth control. A classic simplicity marks its plan. A man and wife, preferring a career, books, and the "nice" things of life, decide upon an abortion. Unhampered by any religious scruple, they suffer no struggle of conscience.

But they suffer cruelly—shame, a sense of frustration, contempt for each other. That is the story, what happens to two people who have flouted a natural law. But any attempt to summarize what is the quality of their suffering is necessarily futile. For all art eludes summary and paraphrase.

If the plan itself is simple, the psychological development is extraordinarily subtle and brings into play the method of stream-of-consciousness, ironic contrasts (the poor women at the nursing home who have borne many children; the reverent cab driver who thinks Missis Flinders has just gone through the noble ordeal of childbirth), and finally a brilliant use of symbolism. The basket of fruit, a gift from her husband to Missis Flinders during her hospitalization, is like fruit of the dead sea—no one will touch it. They carry it home between them in the car—instead of a living child. "He might have made a woman of her; she might have made a man of him." The story quivers with a sickening revulsion at the enormity of the perversion committed, the refusal of parenthood.

Since there are many members of the Mystical Body who regard Mother Church as a hard dictator in the matter of birth-control, it seems to me that this story makes a remarkable contribution. For it illustrates how God's law is built upon the natural law, and demonstrates from what horrors the law of the Church protects her children, who would so like to take liberties with the natural law.

This story is strong meat. If it were not, it would be less good. Immature and narrow readers are warned to skip it. They will most certainly mistake the physiology for pornography. They will mistake a feeling of shock for temptation. They will mistake a most eloquent sermon on the side of the angels for a disgusting story.

When Story republished its most distinguished stories by way of celebrating a tenth anniversary, "Missis Flinders" was among the very few reprints. The author used it as the last chapter in her novel, The Unpos-

sessed. Tess Slesinger married a moving picture director, has two children, and is a successful citrus rancher. She devotes much of her time to writing for the movies, for which she prepared the script of The Good Earth.

"Home you go!" Miss Kane, nodding, in her white nurse's dress, stood for a moment—she would catch a breath of air—in the hospital door: "and thank you again for the stockings, you needn't have bothered"—drew a sharp breath and, turning, dismissed Missis Flinders from the hospital, smiling, dismissed her forever from her mind.

So Margaret Flinders stood next to her basket of fruit on the hospital steps; both of them waiting, a little shamefaced in the sudden sunshine, and in no hurry to leave the hospital—no hurry at all. It would be nicer to be alone, Margaret thought, glancing at the basket of fruit which stood respectable and a little silly on the stone step (the candy-bright apples were blushing caricatures of Jean; Jean's explanation that he was a good boy: Jean's comfort, not hers). Flowers she could have left behind (for the nurses, in the room across the hall where they made tea at night); books she could have slipped into her suitcase; but fruit—Jean's gift, Jean's guilt, man's tribute to the Missis in the hospital—must be eaten; a half-eaten basket of fruit (she had tried to leave it: Missis Butter won't you . . . Missis Wiggam wouldn't you like. . . . But Missis Butter had aplenty of her own thank you, and Misses Wiggam said she couldn't hold acids after a baby)—a half-eaten basket of fruit, in times like these, cannot be left to rot.

Down the street Jean was running, running, after a taxi. He was going after the taxi for her; it was for her sake he ran; yet this minute that his back was turned he stole for his relief and spent in running away, his buttocks crying guilt. And don't hurry, don't hurry, she said to them; I too am better off alone.

The street stretched in a long white line very finally away from the hospital, the hospital where Margaret Flinders (called there so solemnly Missis) had been lucky enough to spend only three nights. It would be four days before Missis Wiggam would be going home to Mister Wiggam with a baby; and ten possibly— the doctors were uncertain, Miss Kane prevaricated—before Missis Butter would be going home to Mister Butter without one. Zigzagging the street went the children; their cries and the sudden grinding of their skates she had listened to upstairs beside Missis Butter for three days. Some such child had she been—for the styles in children had not changed—a lean child gliding solemnly on skates and grinding them viciously at the nervous feet of grownups. Smile at these children she would not or could not; yet she felt on her face that smile fixed, painful and frozen that she had put there, on waking from ether three days back, to greet Jean. The smile spoke to the retreating buttocks of Jean: I don't need you; the smile spoke formally to life: thanks, I'm not having any. Not so the child putting the heels of his skates together Charlie Chaplin-wise and describing a scornful circle on the widest part of the sidewalk. Not so a certain little girl (twenty years back) skating past the wheels of autos, pursuing life in the form of a ball so red! so gay! better death than to turn one's back and smile over one's shoulder at life!

Upstairs Missis Butter must still be writhing with her poor caked breasts. The bed that had been hers beside Missis Butter's was empty now; Miss Kane would be stripping it and Joe would come in bringing fresh sheets. Whom would they put in beside Missis Butter, to whom would she moan and boast all night about the milk in her breasts that was turning, she said, into cheese?

Now Jean was coming back, jogging sheepishly on the running-board of a taxi, he had run away to the end of his rope and now was returning penitent, his eyes dog-like searching her out where she stood on the hospital steps (did they rest with complacence on the basket of fruit, his gift?), pleading with her, Didn't I get the taxi fast? like an anxious little boy. She stood with that smile on her face that hurt like too much ice-cream. Smile and smile;

for she felt like a fool, she had walked open-eyed smiling into the trap (*Don't wriggle, Missis, I might injure you for life, Miss Kane had said cheerfully*) and felt the spring only when it was too late, when she waked from ether and knew like the thrust of a knife what she had ignored before. *Whatever did you do it for, Missis Flinders, Missis Butter was always saying; if there's nothing the matter with your insides—doesn't your husband . . . and Won't you have some fruit, Missis Butter, her calm reply: meaning, My husband gave me this fruit so what right have you to doubt that my husband. . . .* Her husband who now stumbled up the steps to meet her; his eyes he had sent ahead, but something in him wanted not to come, tripped his foot as he hurried up the steps.

"Take my arm, Margaret," he said. "Walk slowly," he said. The bitter pill of taking help, of feeling weakly grateful stuck in her throat. Jean's face behind his glasses was tense like the face of an amateur actor in the role of a strikeleader. That he was inadequate for the part he seemed to know. And if he felt shame, shame in his own eyes, she could forgive him; but if it was only guilt felt man-like in her presence, a guilt which he could drop off like a damp shirt, if he was putting it all off on her for being a woman! "The fruit, Jean!" she said, "you've forgotten the fruit." "The fruit can wait," he said, magnanimously.

He handed her into the taxi as though she were a package marked glass—something, she thought, not merely troublesomely womanly, but ladylike. "Put your legs up on the seat," he said. "I don't want to, Jean." *Good-bye Missis Butter.* Put your legs up on the seat. I don't want to—*better luck next time Missis Butter* Put your legs *I can't make out our window, Missis Butter* Put your "All right, it will be nice and uncomfortable." (She put her legs up on the seat.) *Good-bye Missis But. . . .* "Nothing I say is right," he said. "It's good with the legs up," she said brightly.

Then he was up the steps agile and sure after the fruit. And down again, the basket swinging with affected carelessness, arming him, till he relinquished it modestly to her outstretched hands. Then he seated himself on the little seat, the better to watch his woman and his woman's fruit; and screwing his head round on his neck said irritably to the man who had been all his life on the wrong side of the glass pane, "Charles Street!"

"Hadn't you better ask him to please drive slowly?" Margaret said.

"I was just going to," he said bitterly.

"And drive slowly," he shouted over his shoulder.

The driver's name was Carl C. Strite. She could see Carl Strite glance cannily back at the hospital; Greenway Maternity Home; pull his lever with extreme delicacy as though he were stroking the neck of a horse. There was a small roar—and the hospital glided backward; its windows ran together like the windows of a moving train; a spurt—watch out for those children on skates!—and the car was fairly started down the street.

Goodbye Missis Butter I hope you get a nice roommate in my place, I hope you won't find that Mister B let the ice-pan flow over again—and give my love to the babies when Miss Kane stops them in the door for you to wave at—goodbye Missis Butter, really goodbye.

Carl Strite (was he thinking maybe of his mother, an immigrant German woman she would have been, come over with a shawl on her head and worked herself to skin and bone so the kids could go to school and turn out good Americans—and what had it come to, here he was a taxi driver, and what taxi drivers didn't know! what in the course of their lackeys' lives they didn't put up with, fall in with! well, there was one decent thing left in Carl Strite, he knew how to carry a woman home from a maternity hospital) drove softly along the curb . . . and the eyes of his honest puzzled gangster's snout photographed as 'Your Driver' looked dimmed as though the glory of woman were too much for them, in a moment the weak cruel baby's mouth might blubber. Awful to lean forward and tell Mr. Strite he was laboring under a mistake. *Missis Wiggam's freckled face when she heard that Missis Butter's roommate . . . maybe Missis Butter's baby had been born dead but anyway she had had a baby . . . whatever did you do it for Missis Flind. . . .*

"Well, patient," Jean began, tentative, jocular (bored? perturbed? behind his glasses?)

"How does it feel, Tidbit?" he said in a new, small voice.

Hurt and hurt this man, a feeling told her. He is a man, he could have made you a woman. "What's a D and C between friends?" she said. "Nobody at the hospital gave a damn about my little illegality."

"Well, but I do," he protested like a short man trying to be tall.

She turned on her smile; the bright silly smile that was eating up her face.

Missis Butter would be alone now with no one to boast to about her pains except Joe who cleaned the corridors and emptied bedpans—and thought Missis Butter was better than an angel because although she had incredible golden hair she could wisecrack like any brunette. Later in the day the eight-day mothers wobbling down the corridors for their pre-nursing constitutional would look in and talk to her; for wasn't Missis Butter their symbol and their pride, the one who had given up her baby that they might have theirs (for a little superstition is inevitable in new mothers, and it was generally felt that there must be one dead baby in a week's batch at any decent hospital) for whom they demanded homage from their visiting husbands? for whose health they asked the nurses each morning second only to asking for their own babies? That roommate of yours was a funny one, Missis Wiggam would say. Missis Wiggam was the woman who said big breasts weren't any good: here she was with a seven-pound baby and not a drop for it (here she would open the negligee Mister Wiggam had

given her not to shame them before the nurses, and poke contemptuously at the floppy parts of herself within) while there was
Missis Butter with no baby but a dead baby and her small breasts
caking because there was so much milk in them for nothing but
a . . . Yes, that Missis Flinders was sure a funny one, Missis
Butter would agree.

"Funny ones," she and Jean, riding home with numb faces and
a basket of fruit between them—past a park, past a museum,
past elevated pillars—intellectuals they were, bastards, changelings
. . . giving up a baby for books they might never write, giving
up a baby for economic freedom which meant that two of them
would work in offices instead of one of them only, giving up a
baby for intellectual freedom which meant that they smoked
their cigarettes bitterly and looked out of the windows of a taxi
onto streets and people and stores and hated them all. "We'd go
soft," Jean had said; "we'd go bourgeois." Yes, with diapers drying on the radiators, bottles wrapped in flannel, the grocery man
getting to know one too well—yes, they would go soft, they might
slump and start liking people, they might weaken and forgive
stupidity, they might yawn and forget to hate. "Funny ones,"
class-straddlers, intellectuals, tight-rope-walking somewhere in
the middle (how long could they hang on without falling to one
side or the other? one more war? one more depression?) ; intellectuals with habits generally from the right and tastes inclined to the
left. Afraid to perpetuate themselves, were they? Afraid of anything that might loom so large in their personal lives as to out-
weigh other considerations? Afraid, maybe, of a personal life?

"Oh give me another cigarette," she said.

And still the taxi, with its burden of intellectuals and their inarticulate fruit-basket, its motherly, gangsterly, inarticulate driver,
its license plates and its photographs all so very official, jogged
on; past Harlem now; past fire escapes loaded with flower pots
and flapping clothes; dingy windows opening to the soot-laden

air blown in by the elevated roaring down its tracks. Past Harlem
and through 125th Street: stores and wisecracks, Painless Den-
tists, cheap florists; Eighth Avenue, boarded and plastered, concealing the subway that was reaching its laborious birth beneath.
But Eighth Avenue was too jouncey for Mr. Strite's precious
burden of womanhood (who was reaching passionately for a cigarette); he cut through the park, and they drove past quiet walks
on which the sun had brought out babies as the fall rains give
birth to worms.

"But ought you to smoke so much, so soon after—so soon?"
Jean said, not liking to say so soon after what. His hand held the
cigarettes out to her, back from her.

"They do say smoking's bad for childbirth," she said calmly,
and with her finger tips drew a cigarette from his reluctant hand.

And tapping down the tobacco on the handle of the fruit-
basket she said, "But we've got the joke on them there, we have,"
(Hurt and hurt this man, her feeling told her; he is a man and
could have made you a woman.)

"Pretty nice girl, you are," Jean said, striking and striking at
the box with his match.

"This damn taxi's shaking you too much," he said suddenly,
bitter and contrite.

But Mr. Strite was driving like an angel. He handled his car
as though it were a baby carriage. Did he think maybe it had
turned out with her the way it had with Missis Butter? I could
have stood it better, Missis Butter said, if they hadn't told me it
was a boy. And me with my fourth little girl, Missis Wiggam had
groaned (but proudly, proudly); why I didn't even want to see
it when they told me. But Missis Butter stood it very well, and so
did Missis Wiggam. They were a couple of good bitches; and
what if Missis Butter had produced nothing but a dead baby this
year, and what if Missis Wiggam would bring nothing to Mister
Wiggam but a fourth little girl this year—why there was next

year and the year after, there was the certain little world from grocery store to kitchen, there were still Mister Butter and Mister Wiggam who were both (Missis Wiggam and Missis Butter vied with each other) just *crazy* about babies. Well, Mister Flinders is different, she had lain there thinking (he cares as much for his unborn books as I for my unborn babies); and wished she could have the firm assurance they had in "husbands," coming as they did year after year away from them for a couple of weeks, just long enough to bear them babies either dead ones or girl ones . . . good bitches they were: there was something lustful besides smug in their pride in being "Missis." Let Missis Flinders so much as let out a groan because a sudden pain grew too big for her groins, let her so much as murmur because the sheets were hot beneath her—and Missis Butter and Missis Wiggam in the security of their maternity-sorority exchanged glances of amusement: SHE don't know what pain is, look at what's talking about PAIN. . . .

"Mr. Strite flatters us," she whispered, her eyes smiling straight and hard into Jean's. (Hurt and hurt. . . .)

"And why does that give you so much pleasure?" He dragged the words as though he were pounding them out with two fingers on the typewriter.

The name without the pain—she thought to say; and did not say. All at once she lost her desire to punish him; she no more wanted to "hurt this man" for he was no more man than she was woman. She would not do him the honor of hurting him. She must reduce him as she felt herself reduced. She must cut out from him what made him a man, as she had let be cut out from her what would have made her a woman. He was no man: he was a dried-up intellectual rabbit; he was sterile; empty and hollow as she was.

Missis Butter lying up on her pillow would count over to Missis Wiggam the fine points of her tragedy: how she had waited

two days to be delivered of a dead baby; how it wouldn't have
been so bad if the doctor hadn't said it was a beautiful baby with
platinum-blond hair exactly like hers (and hers bleached unbe-
lievably, but never mind, Missis Wiggam had come to believe in
it like Joe and Mister Butter, another day and Missis Flinders
herself, intellectual sceptic though she was, might have been convinced); and how they would pay the last instalment on—what a
baby carriage, Missis Wiggam, you'd never believe me!—and sell
it second-hand for half its worth. I know when I was caught with
my first, Missis Wiggam would take up the story her mouth had
been open for. And that Missis Flinders was sure a funny one. . . .

But I am not such a funny one, Margaret wanted, beneath her
bright and silly smile, behind her cloud of cigarette smoke (for
Jean had given in; the whole package sat gloomily on Margaret's
lap) to say to them; even though in my "crowd" the girls keep
the names they were born with, even though we sleep for a little
variety with one another's husbands, even though I forget as often
as Jean—Mister Flinders to you—to empty the pan under the
icebox. Still I too have known my breasts to swell and harden, I
too have been unable to sleep on them for their tenderness to
weight and touch, I too have known what it is to undress slowly
and imagine myself growing night to night. . . . I knew this for
two months, my dear Missis Wiggam; I had this strange joy for
two months, my dear Missis Butter. But there was a night last
week, my good ladies, which Mister Flinders and I spent in talk
—and damn fine talk, if you want to know, talk of which I am
proud, and talk not one word of which you with your grocery-
and-baby minds, could have understood; in a regime like this,
Jean said, it is a terrible thing to have a baby—it means the end
of independent thought and the turning of everything into a
scheme for making money; and there must be institutions such
as there are in Russia, I said, for taking care of the babies and
their mothers; why in a time like this, we both said, to have a baby

would be suicide—good-bye to our plans, good-bye to our working out of schemes for each other and the world—our courage would die, our hopes concentrate on the sordid business of keeping three people alive, one of whom would be a burden and an expense for twenty years. . . . And then we grew drunk for a minute, making up the silliest names that we could call it if we had it—and what a tough little thing it is, I said, look, look, how it hangs on in spite of its loving mother jumping off tables and broiling herself in hot water . . . until Jean, frightened at himself, washed his hands of it: we mustn't waste any more time, the sooner these things are done the better. And I, as though the ether cap had already been clapped to my nose, agreed off-handedly. That night I did not pass my hands contentedly over my hard breasts; that night I gave no thought to the nipples grown suddenly brown and competent; I packed, instead, my suitcase: I filled it with all the white clothes I own. Why are you taking white clothes to the hospital, Jean said to me. I laughed. Why did I? White, for a bride; white, for a corpse; white, for a woman who refuses to be a woman. . . .

"Are you all right, Margaret?" (They were out now, safely out on Fifth Avenue, driving placidly past the Plaza where ancient coachmen dozed on the high seats of the last hansoms left in New York).

"Yes, dear," she said mechanically, and forgot to turn on her smile. Pity for him sitting there in stolid inadequacy filled her. He was a man, and he could have made her a woman. She was a woman, and could have made him a man. He was not a man; she was not a woman. In each of them the life-stream flowed to a dead end.

And all this time that the blood, which Missis Wiggam and Missis Butter stored up preciously in themselves every year to make a baby for their husbands, was flowing freely and wastefully out of Missis Flinders—toward what? would it pile up some day and make a book? would it congeal within her and make a crazy woman?—all this time Mr. Strite, remembering, with his pudgy face, his mother, drove his taxi softly along the curb; no weaving in and out of traffic for Mr. Strite, no spurting at the corners and cheating the side-street traffic, no fine heedless rounding of rival cars for Mr. Strite; he kept his car going at a slow and steady roll, its nose poked blunt ahead, following the straight and narrow—Mr. Strite knew what it was to carry a woman home from the hospital.

But what in their past had warranted this? She could remember a small girl going from dolls to books, from books with colored pictures to books with frequent conversations; from such books to the books at last that one borrowed from libraries, books built up of solemn text from which you took notes; books which were gray to begin with, but which opened out to your eyes subtle layers of gently shaded colors. (And where in these texts did it say that one should turn one's back on life? Had the coolness of the stone library at college made one afraid? Had the ivy nodding in the open dormitory windows taught one too much to curl and squat looking out?) And Jean? What book, what professor, what strange idea, had taught him to hunch his shoulders and stay indoors, had taught him to hide behind his glasses? Whence the fear that made him put, in cold block letters, implacably above his desk the sign announcing him "Not at home" to life?

Missis Flinders, my husband scaled the hospital wall at four o'clock in the morning, frantic I tell you. . . . But I just don't understand you, Missis Flinders (if there's really nothing the matter with your insides), do you understand her, Missis Wiggam, would your husband . . . ? Why goodness, no, Mister Wiggam would sooner . . . ! And there he was, and they asked him, Shall we try an operation, Mister Butter? scaled the wall . . . shall we try an operation? (Well, you see we are both writers, my husband and I . . . well, not exactly *stories*) if there's any risk to Shirley,

M.F   I he said, there mustn't be any risk to Shirley . . . Missis Wiggam's petulant, childish face, with its sly contentment veiled by what she must have thought a grown-up expression: Mister Wiggam bought me this negligee new, surprised me with it, you know— and generally a saving man, Mister Wiggam, not tight, but with three children—four now! Hetty, he says, I'm not going to have you disgracing us at the hospital this year, he says. Why the nurses will all remember that flannel thing you had Mabel and Suzy and Antoinette in, they'll talk about us behind our backs. (It wasn't that I couldn't make the flannel do again, Missis Butter, it wasn't that at all.) But he says, Hetty, you'll just have a new one this year, he says, and maybe it'll bring us luck, he says —you know, he was thinking maybe this time we'd have a boy . . . Well, I just have to laugh at you, Missis Flinders, not *wanting* one, why my sister went to doctors for five years and spent her good money just *trying* to have one. . . . Well, poor Mister Wiggam, so the negligee didn't work, I brought him another little girl—but he didn't say boo to me, though I could see he was disappointed. Hetty, he says, we'll just have another try! Oh I thought I'd die, with Miss Kane standing right there you know (though they do say these nurses . . .); but that's Mister Wiggam all over; he wouldn't stop a joke for a policeman. . . . No, I just can't get over you, Missis Flinders, if Gawd was willing to let you have a baby—and there really isn't anything wrong with your insides?

Jean's basket of fruit standing on the bed table, trying its level inadequate best, poor pathetic inarticulate intellectual basket of fruit, to comfort, to bloom, to take the place of Jean himself who would come in later with Sam Butter for visiting hour. Jean's toobig basket of fruit standing there, embarrassed. Won't you have a peach, Missis Wiggam (I'm sure they have less acid)? Just try an apple, Missis Butter? Weigh Jean's basket of fruit against Mister Wiggam's negligee for luck, against Mister Butter scaling

the wall at four in the morning for the mother of his dead baby.
Please have a pear, Miss Kane; a banana, Joe? How they spat
the seeds from Jean's fruit! How it hurt her when, unknowing,
Missis Butter cut away the brown bruised cheek of Jean's bright-
eyed, weeping apple! Jean! they scorn me, these ladies. They
laugh at me, dear, almost as though I had no "husband," as
though I were a "fallen woman." Jean, would you buy me a new
negligee if I bore you three daughters? Jean, would you scale the
wall if I bore you a dead baby? . . . Jean, I have an inferiority
complex because I am an intellectual. . . . But a peach, Missis
Wiggam! can't I possibly tempt you?

To be driving like this at mid-day through New York; with
Jean bobbing like an empty ghost (for she could see he was unhappy, as miserable as she, he too had had an abortion) on the
side-seat; with a taxi driver, solicitous, respectful to an ideal, in
front; was this the logical end of that little girl she remembered,
of that girl swinging hatless across a campus as though that
campus were the top of the earth? And was this all they could
give birth to, she and Jean, who had closed up their books one
day and kissed each other on the lips and decided to marry?

And now Mr. Strite, with his hand out, was making a gentle
righthand turn. Back to Fifth Avenue they would go, gently rolling, in Mr. Strite's considerate charge. Down Fourteenth Street
they would go, past the stores unlike any stores in the world;
packed to the windows with imitation gold and imitation embroidery, with imitation men and women coming to stand in the
doorways and beckon with imitation smiles; while on the side-
walks streamed the people unlike any other people in the world,
drawn from every country, from every stratum, intellectual and
social—carrying babies (the real thing, with pinched anaemic
faces) and parcels (imitation finery priced low in the glittering
stores). There goes a woman, with a flat fat face, will produce
five others just like herself, to dine off one-fifth the inadequate

quantity her Mister earns today. These are the people not afraid
to perpetuate themselves (forbidden to stop, indeed) and they
will go on and on (humming "The best things in life are free")
until the bottom of the world is filled with them; and suddenly
there will be enough of them to combine their cock-eyed notions
and take over the world to suit themselves. While I, while I and
my Jean, with our good clear heads will one day go spinning out
of the world and leave nothing behind . . . only diplomas
crumbling in the museums. . . .

The mad street ended with Fifth Avenue; was left behind.

They were nearing home. Mr. Strite, who had never seen them
before (who would never again, in all likelihood, for his territory
was far uptown) was seeing them politely to the door. As they
came near home all of Margaret's fear and pain gathered in a
knot in her stomach. There would be nothing new in their house;
there was nothing to expect; yet she wanted to find something
there that she knew she could not find, and surely the house (once
so gay, with copies of old paintings, with books which lined the
walls from floor to ceiling, with papers and cushions and type-
writers) would be suddenly empty and dead, suddenly, for the
first time, a group of rooms unalive as rooms with "For Rent"
still pasted on the windows. And Jean? did he know he was coming home to a place which had suffered no change, but which
would be different forever afterward? Jean had taken off his
glasses; passed his hand tiredly across his eyes; was sucking now
as though he expected relief, some answer, on the tortoise-shell
curve which wound around his ear.

Mr. Strite would not allow his cab to cease motion with a jerk.
Mr. Strite allowed his cab to slow down even at the corner (where
was the delicatessen that sold the only loose ripe olives in the
Village), so they rolled softly past No. 14 (where lived Kilgreen
who wrote plays which would never be produced and dropped in
at breakfast time for a hair of the dog that bit him the night

before); on past the tenement which would eventually be razed to give place to modern three-room apartments with In-a-Dor beds; and then slowly, so slowly that Mr. Strite must surely be an artist as well as a man who had had a mother, drew up and slid to a full stop before No. 20, where two people named Mister and Missis Flinders rented themselves a place to hide from life (both life of the Fifth Avenue variety, and life of the common, or Fourteenth Street, variety: in short, life).

So Jean, with his glasses on his nose once more, descended; held out his hand; Mr. Strite held the door open and his face most modestly averted; and Margaret Flinders painfully and carefully swung her legs down again from the seat and alighted, step by step, with care and confusion. The house was before them; it must be entered. Into the house they must go, say farewell to the streets, to Mr. Strite who had guided them through a tour of the city, to life itself; into the house they must go and hide. It was a fact that Mister Flinders (was he reluctant to come home?) had forgotten his key; that Missis Flinders must delve under the white clothes in her suitcase and find hers; that Mr. Strite, not yet satisfied that his charges were safe, sat watchful and waiting in the front seat of his cab. Then the door gave. Then Jean, bracing it with his foot, held out his hand to Margaret. Then Mr. Strite came rushing up the steps (something had told him his help would be needed again!), rushing up the steps with the basket of fruit hanging on his arm, held out from his body as though what was the likes of him doing holding a woman's basket just home from the hospital. "You've forgot your fruit, Missis!"

Weakly they glared at the fruit come to pursue them; come to follow them up the stairs to their empty rooms; but that was not fair: come, after all, to comfort them. "You must have a peach," Margaret said.

No, Mr. Strite had never cared for peaches; the skin got in his teeth.

"You must have an apple," Margaret said.

Well, no, he must be getting on uptown. A cigarette (he waved it, deprecated the smoke it blew in the lady's face) was good enough for him.

"But a pear, just a pear," Margaret said passionately.

Mr. Strite wavered, standing on one foot. "Maybe he doesn't want any fruit," said Jean harshly.

"Not want any fruit!" cried Margaret gayly, indignantly. Not want any fruit?—ridiculous! Not want the fruit my poor Jean bought for his wife in the hospital? Three days I spent in a Maternity Home, and I produced, with the help of my husband, one basket of fruit (tied with ribbon, pink—for boys). Not want any of our fruit? I couldn't bear it, I couldn't bear it. . . .

Mr. Strite leaned over; put out a hand and gingerly selected a pear—"For luck," he said, managing an excellent American smile. They watched him trot down the steps to his cab, all the time holding his pear as though it were something he would put in a memory book. And still they stayed, because Margaret said foolishly, "Let's see him off"; because she was ashamed, suddenly, before Jean; as though she had cut her hair unbecomingly, as though she had wounded herself in some unsightly way—as though (summing up her thoughts as precisely, as decisively as though it had been done on an adding-machine) she had stripped and revealed herself not as a woman at all, but as a creature who would not be a woman and could not be a man. And then they turned (for there was nothing else to stay for, and on the street and in the sun they were ashamed as though they had been naked)—and went in the door and heard it swing to, pause on its rubbery hinge, and finally click behind them.

I TOOK THEE, CONSTANCE

TED LeBERTHON

Catholics may seek to cut the bonds of the sacrament of matrimony by civil divorce, but by what strange ways the unbreakable troth will manifest itself the reader may discover in this unusual story. Its simple, objective statement opens up avenue upon avenue of reflection, so that the whole pathos of broken human relationships seems to be distilled in the few moments of a drab morning court session.

Several years ago Ted LeBerthon resigned his post as assistant editor of the Catholic Digest *in order to devote more time to creative writing. Born in San Francisco, he received his education, grade and high school, under Catholic auspices in Los Angeles. As general assignment reporter on New York, Brooklyn, Chicago, and Los Angeles newspapers, he developed as a writer through the discipline of journalism. Seeing the white man's injustice to Negroes as one of the gravest national problems, he has used his pen in various ways to help solve the race problem. His efforts in this direction include his work as contributing editor to the* Negro Digest, *his column, 'White Man's Views" for* The Pittsburgh Courier, *the nation's leading Negro weekly newspaper, and his short story* The Racist, *recently published in* The Sign. *He is married and has one daughter.*

The fire department juggernauts thunder up the street this summer night, sirens screaming like banshees. Mrs. Constance Taylor does not hear them, although, embarrassingly enough, the fire is in her bed. The smoldering mattress is sending up sparks and thick smoke. Mrs. Taylor, who passed out following a losing bout with alcohol, dreams she is astride the saw-toothed back of a translucent purple dragon heading starward in the night. Suddenly the tail of the dragon breaks off the body, she is hanging onto the inconsiderate tail, and it is dropping like a charred piece of plane wreckage. She can't stand it, she is going down too fast. She fearfully tells herself that this is death. "Snap out of it," someone whispers close.

Mrs. Taylor opens her eyes. A huge blue woolen form, and a big, sweaty, male moonface swarm above her. And what is that? A snake, thick as a python, is coming through the apartment's one window. She shuts her eyes. It doesn't do to be seeing things. "Still drunk," a man's voice deplores, "and sweating like a stuck pig, and I ask you, has she stunk the place up with liquor!"

"Why do they always fall asleep smoking a cigarette?" complains another man's voice. "Why, I ask you, when these old wooden places are firetraps?"

Mrs. Taylor's eyes now stare in comical surprise from her hard-bitten, alcoholic face, because the snake does not have an ordinary head, but a nozzle, a big nozzle like fire hose have. "This is silly," she titters, and closes her eyes. But a nausea comes over her and she opens them again.

The walls of her room seem in movement and that makes Mrs. Taylor dizzy. Now a light flashes in her sweaty face. Next, night air cools her. She falls back sleepily into something soft, and now she is running up a cow path, up a dusty, weedy hill, to a rock-bound medieval castle. She knocks at a great door, and she is all alone. She knocks and knocks, but no one opens. She turns around and the path is gone, and she stares into windy space.

"Let her sleep," the moon-faced policeman rasps to a police matron in the women's ward of the city jail, with a gesture toward the prone figure of Mrs. Constance Taylor in her lingerie, the gesture of an orchestra conductor quelling a violin section. The matron looks at the matted hair, the open mouth, the clammy legs, and nods.

So Mrs. Taylor sleeps in a lower iron bunk. In other bunks are sleeping forms who will look much the same in coffins. The city is all around, and it's a summer night, and in several hundred thousand homes men and women and children sleep, and many streets are empty, and many houses are dark and blind. Mrs. Taylor stands on an eminence in dream, suspended in nothing,

before a lost door, while her sweaty body is stretched in an iron
bunk in a blowsy jail. Shy, recessive stars crowd the galleries of
the high skies, and stare unseeingly at the dramas of earth. Mrs.
Taylor dreams, just as do other sleepers in the city, and in all the
cities, on farms, on ships, on trains, who slip the body's leash, run
along paths, and knock at old, lost doors. And then it is morning.

Now Mrs. Taylor is eating breakfast, a soggy cereal with
canned milk but no sugar, in a battleship-gray iron room, at a
long pine table. She eats out of a heavy crockery bowl and drinks
weak black coffee from a tin cup. The matron, who carries her
head up like a prancing horse, a heavy-legged horse in white, has
given her a shapeless, slate-gray dress and scuffed bedroom slippers, "—seeing that you came in, *Smallsize,* in your underwear
last night." Mrs. Taylor starts counting; there must be a hundred
women eating.

The women go from the bullpen, malodorous with body sweat
and slept-in clothes, into the courtroom four at a time, and sit on
folded seats against a wall, and the crowded courtroom is noisy
until three sharp raps of a gavel simmer the sounds down to
whispers.

"Mrs. Constance Taylor!" bawls a sturdy, freckled, red-haired
man in khaki wearing a police badge.

"Stand right here, Mrs. Taylor."

She looks up at the judge. Why, he wears a toupee! She knows
a toupee when she sees one, and this is a dirty, feathery, golden-
haired toupee fitting loosely at the neckline. The judge must be a
little man, she thinks. He has a sharp, thin, sour face, and she
fears he will be severe. He stares glumly behind heavily rimmed
spectacles, vaguely appraising her as a middle-aged tart long
soaked in alcohol. He purses his lips, then twangily, and as if
bored with the words, informs her, "You're charged with being
drunk. How do you plead, guilty or not guilty?"

"Guilty."

The word hangs leadenly in a moment's silence, and then Mrs. Taylor knows someone is standing at her right. Even before she glances sidewise, she knows it will be Al, big, tall, prosperous, baldish Al, and now he is making a speech.

"—and although we've been divorced fourteen years, she's not a bad woman, your honor. She's had a good deal of trouble. She lost two children at birth, and we had a little daughter who lived to be five, and then died. She got to drinking—and, well, it's a disease with her. I'm an attorney, and ask to be entered as attorney of record, and in asking you to permit the defendant to be released under a suspended sentence into my custody, I realize it is necessary for the court to understand my interest."

"Do you mean you'll give the little woman a home, and be reconciled, Mister—eh—I didn't get your name, did I?"

"Alfred J. Taylor, 1483 First National Bank Building. No, I can't give her a home very well. I've married again, and my wife's here in the courtroom with me and we have two children home. As the court undoubtedly knows, such arrangements are not practical. Also, the court undoubtedly has my first wife's booking record at hand, and I realize the fact that she has been arrested a number of times for being intoxicated in public places has to be considered. Also, I realize the safety of society always has to be considered, and she has often fallen asleep after getting drunk in a solitary manner in her own apartment, and twice before, in other places she has lived, has set her apartment afire. I've generally paid her fines and tried to get her back to her job, whatever it happened to be, but this time, I'd like to take her to my father's ranch. Fresh eggs, milk, sunshine might help. I might say that the old folks—I refer to my parents—have always liked her."

"Have you ever had her on their ranch before, Mister Taylor?"

"Yes, I induced her, just once, to go."

"Did it help her?"

"She didn't stay long enough. Some little tiff with the folks. But I was never able to find out, from them or her, what it was about. She only stayed a few days. But if a court order obliged her to remain with my mother and dad, for, say, three months or six months as a condition of probation, she'd have to stay."

The judge under the loose-fitting dirty golden toupee turns his attention to the defendant, who stands in a patch of sunlight coming through a window, her chin drawn in and her eyes lowered, looking, in the shapeless gray prison garb, like a sick, blind fowl in a sunny barnyard. Her former husband, smartly dressed, stares at her clinically.

"Why do you drink, Mrs. Taylor?" the judge asks, in a let's-get-to-the-bottom-of-this tone.

"Because I'm lonely, I guess."

"Well, Mrs. Taylor, you don't have to be lonely any more. Your former husband's standing here right now, offering you a home with his folks."

"But I don't want a home with his folks. I didn't ask Mr. Taylor to come here today. I wish he'd just leave me alone."

"Please, Mrs. Taylor! You are embarrassing the court and your husband and his present wife, who must be a very understanding woman. Let's get to the point. You're pretty highhanded, I'd say. You get sottishly drunk, you fall asleep smoking a cigarette, you set your apartment on fire, you endanger the lives of all the tenants, and then you're cheeky enough to show not the slightest gratitude to a man who owes you nothing. When all is said and done, he didn't have to come here and help you. Don't you think you're being a bit unreasonable?"

"No, it's not that, judge; it's that I feel sorry for my husb—I mean, Mr. Taylor, in my heart. I don't want to always be like a weight around his neck. He doesn't understand. He is kind, even if at times he sounds a little pompous. I wish he'd stay away from me. But he won't. I think I know why, and that's why I'll always feel sorry for him, and why I don't like to hear people knock him. That's why I don't want to go to his folks' ranch. They're bitter toward him. They think they're siding with me. They're Catholics —and, of course, so am I, for that matter. But they tell me I'm really his wife, and they tell him that, too. And when they start damning him to me, I resent it. Then they jump me. But what am I, after all? A drunk, judge, and I know it. And I have no intention of putting the blame on Mr. Taylor, or on anyone but myself."

The judge stares hard at Mr. Taylor. "Well, Mr. Taylor, is what the defendant says essentially correct?"

"I guess it is, your honor. My folks were always very fond of her. They scarcely speak to me. They've never spoken to my present wife. I thought Connie would like it with them. I didn't know they'd quarreled about me."

The little sick fowl in shapeless gray in a patch of sun smiles up at him nervously. "Al," she says, "whatever I may be, I never was a stuffed shirt."

The judge literally throws up his hands, looking, for one flashing moment, like a rag monkey. "Mr. Taylor," he expostulates, "this is a courtroom, not a place for a sentimental reunion. We have a heavy calendar this morning. What is the court supposed to do, in the circumstances?"

"I'll gladly pay any fine, your honor."

The sick fowl protests. "Al, you'd better let me go to jail for a while. After that fire, that landlady'll never let me back in that apartment house. I suppose my clothes have all burned up. Can't you see that I'm just going to be a lot of trouble to you? I wish you'd stay away from me, you idiot." And then she burst into tears.

"Please don't cry, Connie."

The judge is upset. "Is the defendant ready for sentence?" he asks disgustedly.

"I am," she weeps.

"It'll be the order and judgment of this court that you spend the next sixty days in the city jail, of which fifty-five days will be suspended, and you will be placed on probation for one year. If you are found guilty, or plead guilty again, within a year, to a charge of drunkenness, you'll have those fifty-five days to do. As for you, Mr. Taylor, the five days your former wife will be serving will give you an opportunity to make some other arrangements for her."

The horsy matron propels Mrs. Constance Taylor toward the jail door.

"Thanks, Al," she says, looking back.

"I'll buy you some clothes, Connie."

And now she is gone, and he feels bitterly sorry for her, and an old hurt is in him, as for a keen, singing moment he remembers how it was with them in the time of first love and their gay wildness. But suddenly a cold hand touches his.

Startled, he finds himself staring into the eyes of his present wife, her strong beauty bulking there in tweeds, her hard confidence making him fear something, as if he were surrounded. "We'd better be going," she says.

THE LITTLE GIRLS

LUCILE HASLEY

Children believe in heaven. They have an absolute logic, which makes grief over the death of a playmate absurd. But such joyous acceptance can burn like acid into the grief-stricken soul of a mother who has lost a little girl. Rich in spiritual implications as well as emotional tension, this situation is developed in The Little Girls *with a freshness and vitality which captures the very spirit of childhood. This story won first prize in the short-story contest sponsored by the Catholic Press Association, 1948. Lucile Hasley is a frequent contributor to Catholic magazines.* Reproachfully Yours, 1949, *is a collection of her sprightly essays on religious subjects published by Sheed and Ward. She is the wife of Louis Hasley, Professor of English at Notre Dame. They have three children.*

It was the little girls that made it so hard. Even though they remembered to whisper (actually, they were as good as gold), they were the ones that made it so hard for the mother. Maybe it was because of their freshly scrubbed faces, trying hard to be solemn but showing only a frank bright interest. Most of them had never seen a dead person before.

There were nine of the little girls and, in their light summer dresses, they looked like a bevy of small white moths as they clustered around her daughter.

"My," whispered one of the little girls, "don't she look *natural?*" She wasn't quite sure what the word meant but she had heard one of the older people say it. "Just as *natural*," she repeated. She reached out and furtively touched the tufted white plush of the casket. It seemed funny to think that this was really Mary Ellen.

In the school plays she had always had the choice roles, the Christmas Spirit, the Snow Queen, the Sugar Plum Princess, because she was easily the prettiest girl in the fourth grade. The other little girls—the ones with freckles, unsuccessful permanents, and big front teeth—simply took this for granted. They even boasted about her. She could act as well as Margaret O'Brien and she was ten times prettier. They hadn't a doubt in the world but what she was going to end up in Hollywood.

She always looked wonderful in the cheesecloth costumes that the nuns concocted, and now the little girls were disappointed to see that Mary Ellen had on her Sunday best dress. The blue rayon one, princess style, with the yarn flowers. They had vaguely expected something different; maybe something white and flowing like the Snow Queen's costume. They also regretted the curls.

Generally Mary Ellen wore her hair in long smooth curls but, during the summer vacation, her mother always braided it because it was cooler. Now it was July and so there were braids.

"Just think," whispered one of the little girls, "she got a stomach ache on Monday and died on Wednesday."

"I know it," said the girl next to her. "I knew about it before *you* did. My mother was the one who called people about the flowers." For the third time, she crossed herself. Carefully and importantly. But she crossed herself because it seemed proper; not to ward off any future stomach aches of her own.

Sudden death did not even seem to brush the little girls. Their fearful mothers had insulated them against fear; their worried mothers, remembering the tears shed over the bullet-torn fawn in *The Yearling,* had talked only about the beautiful happy death.

"See, honey, they operated on Mary Ellen, and she just never woke up again; she kept right on sleeping. Wasn't that a *nice* way to die? And now she's so *happy*."

The mothers need not have worried. The technicolor make-believe death of the yearling was one thing; the death of a classmate another. The little girls didn't get good grades in Christian Doctrine for nothing. They had it reduced to the bone. The saints were the lucky ones. Mary Ellen was in Heaven. You couldn't get into Heaven unless you were a saint. Therefore, lucky.

The odd thing was that Sister Agatha, the one who taught Christian Doctrine, was crying like anything. Her face, generally like smooth marble, was all crumpled up. The little girls nudged each other. Sister Agatha—did you see Sister *Agatha*?

But the little girls themselves, Mary Ellen's closest friends, felt only a lively interest, a certain shared pride in her latest achievement. She had always been two jumps ahead of them, anyway— the prettiest, the quickest, the brightest—and this time *they* shared in the winnings. The parish priest, not slowed down by red tape in Rome, had said that now their new school had a child saint all its own to pray to.

Last year their school had won the Fire Prevention Certificate and the city softball championship. St. Michael's School was doing all right for itself.

The mother stood at one end of the white casket, the father at the other. This had been their only child, a child of their middle years. Somehow they managed to recognize the faces, remember the names of the people that filed along in a steady line: the mothers of the little girls, neighbors, the nuns from the school. They were the grown-ups, and grief flowed through the steady line as from a common wound.

But it was the little girls that made it so hard. The mother could not help being aware of the little girls, brushing against her, whispering importantly. They represented an official body, standing guard as chief mourners. They were all members of the Busy Bee Blue Bird group—fledgling Camp Fire Girls—and Mary Ellen had been their president.

During the year the Busy Bees had sold doughnuts in the Doughnut Drive, gone on nature hikes, learned songs with motions, made pan holders for Mother's Day. Like every stalwart organization, they even had a Way of Life. It was called "The

Blue Bird Wish" and it was pasted on the front page of every good Busy Bee's notebook:

> To have fun
> To learn to make beautiful things
> To remember to finish what I begin
> To want to keep my temper
> To go to interesting places
> To learn about trees, flowers, and birds
> To make friends

There were so many new things to learn; so many interesting places to go. During the past school year their leader had taken them to visit the interesting places: the museum, the bakery, the radio station, the city hall, the dairy. Now, in their bright summer dresses, they were visiting a funeral home.

The last time the mother had seen them they had been wearing bright blue shorts and white blouses. Two weeks ago they had had a picnic at Colfax Park, and Mary Ellen's father and mother had gone along as sponsors. There had been roasted wienies, marshmallows, popsicles, singing, throwing stones in the river. It was almost, said the little girls on the way home, as good as going to camp. Maybe better. They liked to talk big about camp but didn't want it much closer. When you went to camp you didn't get to see your folks for a whole ten days.

All the way home, crammed into the battered old Buick, they had sung their songs. They were too crowded to sing the funny ones with motions, like the one about the eensy weensy spider going up the water spout, but there were plenty of others. Over and over, they had sung the official song of the Blue Bird girls because that was the one you sang at ceremonial meetings:

> Pretty little Blue Bird, why do you go?
> Come back, come back to me;

I go, said the bird as he flew on high,
To see if my color matches the sky.

It was an awfully pretty song except, sometimes, they got it started too high. Then they would end up on a high squeak, and a giggle, like they did with *The Star Spangled Banner*.

* * *

The line had thinned out, and there were only a few more hands for the parents to shake. In one corner of the vestibule a fourth grade mother was busily checking names and donations with other fourth grade mothers. Theirs was the huge spray of lilies and larkspur. They had finally decided on flowers, after a certain amount of confusion as to what was proper. It didn't seem quite right to give Spiritual Bouquets for a little girl who didn't really need them.

The rest of the grown-ups had gone back into the other parlor or drifted out onto the porch to wait for the priest. The July night was warm and still. When the priest came, at eight o'clock, there would be the Rosary.

But the little girls stayed, playing guard at the casket, not giving up their rightful ground. Over their whispering and bobbing heads the parents glanced at each other, sharing the mixed and peculiar pain. The little girls were whispering, all right, but they could hear every word.

"What's her name in Heaven?" one of them was saying. "Is she called Saint Mary?"

Then she frowned, puzzled. "But they're so many Mary's; mightn't they get mixed up?" It was always that way. Even in the classroom there were always too many Marys. She wanted no confusion about the one from St. Michael's.

A newcomer, a late Busy Bee, joined the ranks. She looked warm and breathless, as if she had been running.

"Did you register in the book?" one of them whispered offi-
ciously. The newcomer, still breathless, shook her head dumbly,
and the officious one whisked her off. The mother, her face
swollen with grief, watched them as they darted out into the
vestibule to register proudly another Busy Bee.

They're little, she told herself; they don't realize. The little
girls seemed heartless but her daughter might have acted the
same way. It might have been Mary Ellen darting out into the
vestibule like that. She knew little girls. Maybe it was even unfair
to think they were heartless; they had hearts, all right, but they
were children's hearts. They could believe whatever anyone told
them.

The mother had been told a number of things, too, these past
sixteen hours. The old phrases had dashed against her tired mind
and then fallen away: "Time heals all wounds . . . God's ways
are inscrutable . . . Thy will be done . . . God fits the burden
to the back . . . the Lord giveth, and the Lord taketh
away . . ."

She had grown up with these phrases; heard them all her life.
They were part of her very blood stream. Maybe later, when she
wasn't so tired, the meaning and the sense would creep back into
them.

"How God must have loved you," the priest had said gently,
"to give you so heavy a cross to bear." But her mind was too
heavy, too tired for the paradox. Her mind could only circle back,
again and again, to the simple beginning. It was Monday noon
. . . Mary Ellen had come in from jumping rope to say she
had a stomach ache . . . but kids were always having little
stomach aches . . .

It was a merciful relief when the Rosáry began and the mother
could get down on her knees. She was so tired that she rested one
elbow on the seat of the folding chair next to her. Her feet
throbbed; she had been on them almost constantly since Monday.

But it was funny, since she ached all over, that she should even think of her feet.

The little girls had quit whispering, were kneeling around her, were busily untangling their colored beads. Now there was just the priest leading the prayers: the Hail Mary's tumbling out like water rushing over worn smooth stones. This, too, seemed almost senseless. And yet, between the decades was a strange new line that the mother had never heard before: "May she rejoice with the angels and the saints forever." "May she rejoice . . ."

It was a beautiful death, they said. And tomorrow at the funeral there would be the Mass of the Angels. Oh, she had much to be grateful for . . . they were right, this *was* a beautiful death . . . and there had been mothers far less lucky. The Mass of the Angels. That meant that tomorrow there would be no black in the church because black stood for mourning. The priest would wear white vestments, symbol of innocence and joy, and flowers would be permitted (the fourth grade mothers had sent such a lovely spray) because it was a time to rejoice. Like a feast day.

For a moment, she let bitterness spurt up in her heart unchecked. *They* had their saint but she had no daughter. Let the priest wear his white. Let the little girls wear their bright summer dresses. *She* would wear black, she would wear black forever. . . .

But she could not even hold onto a sustained bitterness. It was alien to her; it wasn't part of her blood stream. Like all the other phrases these, too, dashed against her tired mind and then fell away.

The Rosary was over quickly, as everything else had been going these past sixteen hours. The mother got up from her knees, stiffly and clumsily, but the little girls scrambled to their feet with ease. It was as if they had elastic in their joints. (Even when a child broke a leg or a collar bone, the young bones started mending and healing immediately. Elastic.)

Her eyes followed them as they wandered out into the vestibule to wait for their mothers to join them. For a few more days, she thought dully, the little girls would still talk about the beautiful death.

But one of the little girls seemed to be hanging back, the little girl who had come in late and breathless. She seemed undecided about something and then, with sudden resolution, she walked over to the mother.

"Mama said I shouldn't give it to you," she said with a little rush, "because Mary Ellen didn't need a Spiritual Bouquet but I had already made it and so . . . well, and so here it is." She thrust a folded piece of paper into the mother's hand and, turning, walked swiftly away.

The mother opened the paper. At the top, in heavy black crayola, was a big "J. M. J." Underneath, in uneven printing, it said: "I will say 1,000 Hail Mary's for Mary Ellen Dunlap. Signed, her friend Helen Jo Mackey." Then, this time in purple crayola, was a row of crosses, followed by a P. S. "I will never forget her as long as I live."

The mother folded the paper carefully. It seemed to make even her tonsils ache for she knew all about little girls. She had seen extravagant home-made Spiritual Bouquets before. She knew exactly how much they could mean and yet, somehow, this was the nicest one she had ever seen.

She turned to her husband and handed him the slip of paper without a word. Maybe it would make him feel better, too.

A TABLE BEFORE ME

JILL O'NAN

Literature ordinarily lags behind life. That is why so much Catholic fiction still probes the sterility of religious formalism. Yet the most significant thing in the Church today is the spiritual renascence which is transforming the lives of laymen. Though this new life in Christ is providing a depth of spiritual experience out of which a great fiction can come, it has for the most part been ignored by writers. Jill O'Nan's distinction is that in "A Table Before Me" she has brought Catholic fiction up to date.

Too near the problems of raising a Christian family to view them through the rosy lenses of dishonest idealism, Jill O'Nan highlights one of them in "A Table Before Me": the conflict between Godly parents and worldly children, who are exposed to the daily impact of cinema, television, and the materialistic mores of the adolescent tribe. The mother of four children, Mrs. Fred O'Nan is qualified to present this problem. She has contributed to The Sign, America, Cor, The Marianist, *and other magazines.*

She had come over that Saturday afternoon, she said, for me to trim her hair, because my scissors was sharper and my hand steadier than her mother's. But I knew she really wanted to blow off about something by the way she kept her face blocked against any expression and just answered yes and no to Brian's teasing. Brian is my bachelor brother and I think he sometimes overdoes it. He's Kathie's godfather and she is fond of him in an offhand way, but when she wants to unburden herself to me, she invariably snubs him. Kathie is my godchild, too, and my namesake; she calls me "Aunt Kate" but I'm only a courtesy relation. I've tried not to mother her, though it's often been hard not to. My husband died the first year of our marriage and I lost the only chance I had of a child soon after that. Even if Kathie hadn't had two perfectly good parents of her own, I doubt if I could have replaced

242

one for her. She was always stand-offish, except in rare moments
of impulsive affection, and at fourteen she was too unsure of herself to trust anyone completely. Oh, I took her to dinner once in
a while, to a play or the icecapades or the summer opera afterwards, and we were as good friends as fourteen and forty can be.

"Aunt Kate," she said in her quick, staccato way as I began to
snip her hair, "don't be shocked, but I don't believe in God any
more—hardly."

I went on snipping without a swerve of the scissors. I've eased
enough nieces and nephews through adolescence in my day (I
even remember my own) to know that one often lost one's faith
for a day or two when things were going off keel.

"What's wrong?" I asked, thinking how adolescents are the
true schizophrenics, or scissors-cut personalities, the two blades of
their nature in frantic conflict until the pattern of life is cut, and
then coming to rest in unison one upon the other.

"What's wrong?" she echoed, her voice going shrill. "What do
you think *could* be wrong at our house? You don't think Daddy
got tipsy or Mother said one eensy-teensy bad word, do you?
Nothing interesting like murder or mayhem ever happens to *us*.
Holy, holy, holy, that's all I hear! That's all I *ever* hear! Cut a
little more around in the back, will you? They don't even know
there's anything in the world except God and books."

"Well, that covers a lot of territory," I essayed lightly, feeling
my way.

"You don't know what it's like, living here in this pretty house,
with a car and a television set and a new tile bathroom and everything."

"But—turn your head a little to the left—what's television got
to do with believing in God?"

Kathie suddenly swooped forward and looked directly at me,
that is, at my reflection in the mirror she was facing. There were
tears in her eyes, and though I knew she enjoyed the effect of

having them appear at the appropriate moment, nevertheless I was touched.

"I used to believe in God," she said. "I enjoyed making a novena or saying the Stations once in a while (I always cried a little at the tenth, it's so gruesome), but now *they* are "restoring Christ" all over the house. There's a cross in nearly every room and a holy water font near the front door like a church—I'm so ashamed when someone asks me what it is—and there's special cooking for Feast Days, and Psalms for night prayers. Aunt Kate, it's just plain hell!"

Now here was a moral problem for which the Baltimore catechism had not prepared me. I remembered most of the answers, for I had learned them well and I've tried pretty consistently to apply them as I went along. How did it go? "The duty of a godparent after Baptism is to see that the child is brought up a good Catholic if the parents neglect to do so or die." Clearly that did not apply in *this* case.

Kathie's parents, to my knowledge, had never neglected anything. They are the best friends I have, or ever had, and the only criticism I might make of them would include a certain tendency in myself. We are all too conscientious, having been brought up in a strict and literal code of virtue in which one did one's damnedest to be good. Not that any of us are stuffy. While we are bending over backwards to do our duty, we are laughing at the grotesque figure we're cutting. Johanna (Jo, we call her) has been like a sister to me since the first day of school at old St. Patrick's when she tapped me on the arm and told me earnestly, her little snub nose covered with freckles, her eyes intensely blue, "I'm awfully sorry, but your petticoat is showing." A tomboy in a family of five brothers, I only wore a petticoat under pressure and little did I care how much of it appeared in public. But *she* cared and no other little girl had ever paid any attention to me before. That was how it began and we went through school together. She got

me my first date. I introduced her to Philip Galvin, who was
(and still is) a chemical engineer for our firm. It was a good
match, if I say so myself, who made it. They were more nearly
one than any other couple I've ever known. Maybe that's why I
never married again. I didn't see any sense to a marriage if it
wasn't like that. But now here was Kathie, their first-born, protest-
ing that they were destroying her faith by overdoing it. This was
a problem for theologians and not for a woman like me who tried
to double as a secretary and a housewife, and had not time or
energy left over for spiritual entanglements.

"Look, Kathie," I said in what I hoped was a godmotherly
tone, "have you mentioned this in Confession?"

"Confession!" she hooted. "Why, I only lost my faith today."

"Oh!" was all I could say.

She shook back her hair, murmured "Thanks" and squatted
down on my bed. I cringed to see the dirty saddle oxfords
jammed against my eider-down, but this was no time to get myself labeled as a fuddy-duddy. I didn't blink an eyelash. I even
thought of offering her a cigarette, but I decided Jo would not
appreciate that woman-to-woman touch. The best I could think
of was a coke. When I came back from the kitchen with two
bottles, she was stretched out full-length on the bedspread, her
hands behind her head. She reached for her bottle, gave a deep
sigh and said:

"More calories! *How* do you keep your figure, Aunt Kate?"

"Just lucky," I said, and it was true.

I'm the kind of person who can eat anything any time and
never gain an ounce. I knew Kathie envied her mother and me
our sample size. That was another thing that had drawn us together. We were always paired off in recitals and processions as
the smallest girls in the class. Now pushing forty, I still wear a size
12 dress, and Jo, a trifle more matronly, settles for size 14. Kathie
had inherited her bones from her father, a tall, spare, slightly

stooped man, with graying hair and keen gray eyes which only the wrinkles of kindly humor around them saved from being stern. But Kathie's long frame was well-cushioned and her weight was the bane of her life. She considered herself "fat," but she wasn't; just a big woman in the making, though what comfort is that to a girl entering her teens?

She opened the coke, stuck in a straw, took a long draw and returned to the conversation about her parents, as though I had never left the room, or her mind left off worrying the subject.

"You'll never guess what they've dreamed up now. It's a new high even for them. A Pentecost party! Not exactly a party really; a "prayer meetin' " Daddy said, but that's supposed to be funny —pass me a feather, ha, ha, ha! They call it a vigil, and they serve ale before they begin to pray. That part is all right, lots of people like beer; but what do you think—Daddy is going to *bless* the ale! He has a book with all kinds of blessings in it, even for goats. Imagine! Blessing beer! Did you ever hear of anything so corny?"

I admitted it sounded a little peculiar. Sometimes I got the impression Kathie and I were talking about different people, her idea of her parents was not at all like mine. When I went to see Jo, she usually had a mending basket beside her, but it didn't interfere with our conversation. You could count on her to be sympathetic or amused, whichever you wanted her to be, and always, always sensible. Oh, I allow she was usually up to her ears in some sort of Catholic Action—writing a paper, or making cookies for a committee meeting, or studying with a group some Encyclical or other I'd never even heard of. But Jo and I shared, to an unusual degree, I think, the ability to accept people for what they are. It never entered my head to criticize her for her enthusiasms, or she me because I lacked them. I must be the original of the joke they're telling about the girl who said she was "just a Catholic." Maybe I've been too busy or too lazy to go along with the Galvins in what they called the "Catholic

Renascence," but I can't say it bothered me. I'd been Jo's friend when she discovered poetry and the opera and when she fell in love—she took everything hard, no matter what it was. She was just as tolerant of all those evening courses I'd been taking for twenty years, never even taking the trouble to collect my credits— psychology, Spanish, business English (that was a laugh!), pub- lic speaking, even geology—anything to keep my mind elastic and alive. I went to a Catholic college, too, but somehow we hadn't caught up with the Revival, though we read one of the Encyclicals in an English course once. It was tucked in between *The Hound of Heaven* and *Ah, Wilderness!*

But blessing the ale—well, what of it? I knew Jo went around the house with Easter water and sprinkled it in each room the way my Irish grandmother did, and Phil read some sort of prayer over the Easter lamb and the Resurrection bread which rose so high it hit the top of the oven, but the ale was something else! Still, if Phil wanted to bless ale, or burn it, for that matter, or merely imbibe it, it was all right with me.

"What do you care?" I asked Kathie, trying hard to be casual, "can't you let them have their fun and you have yours?"

She gave me a scornful look.

"Fun! What fun is there in our house? No television or hopes of one, and *they'd* rather listen to a symphony on the radio than a baseball game. When we have company, they never play canasta."

"Your mother used to be a pretty keen bridge player. Can't you teach her to play canasta, or is it too tricky?"

"Oh, it's easy enough. She *could* learn it, I suppose. But she'd rather sit around and talk, or plan an old Pentecost party that's out of this world."

"Look, Kathie," I said, still trying to conciliate her. "You girls have your own radio upstairs and you can listen to whatever you like. Besides, you know you're welcome to watch television here—

Brian and I enjoy having you—Eileen and Sheila too, if they want to come."

"You look, Aunt Kate!" Kathie's eyes pierced me exactly as Phil's do when he's trying to prove a point. "For a business woman you can be awfully slow on the up-take. Don't you understand *anything*?"

"I guess I don't," I said, and waited for her to go on.

She flung herself off the bed and stood at the window, twisting the cord on the Venetian blind.

"I don't give a damn if I never see another television show in my whole life, though I like the baseball games," she amended honestly.

She glanced over her shoulder at me and I nodded to show that I was following her.

"It's not not *owning* one that's so humiliating. It shows everybody what we're really like. Independent, Daddy calls it, but he's just kidding himself. People feel sorry for us; they look down on us. It's like not having a bathroom! Have you got a Kleenex handy?"

I saw that she was really crying this time and I didn't quite know what to do. Demonstrations of affection were not usually well received. I handed her a box of tissues and a powder puff. She used both and then surprisingly grabbed my hand and pressed it to her cheek.

"Gee, Aunt Kate, you're swell! You always know what to say" (I hadn't said a word) "and how to do things right. I wish Mother were like you. My God, she doesn't even use a lip-stick!"

I kissed her lightly on the forehead—I didn't want to overstep my godmotherly rights. I resolved privately to present Jo with a lip-stick and to see that she used it. Aloud I said:

"I've known your mother a lot longer than you have, Kathie. She's not half-bad when you get to know her."

It was a masterpiece of understatement, but what *can* you say to a kid like that?

Kathie was on my conscience all week-end. I went to Confession Saturday evening but it was all too intangible to put into words, especially with a long line waiting outside. Pentecost Sunday I went to Mass in the Chapel of the Holy Spirit on the College campus. It seemed fitting for the Feast, and besides, my psychology professor often said the eight o'clock Mass. We were pretty good friends and he'd often helped me out when something got snarled up at the office. I waited for him after Mass and walked across the campus with him to the refectory. I briefed him on the case as we shared a smoke and soaked up a goodly portion of the Pentecostal dew.

"Converts, I suppose?" he inquired, as I finished.

"Oh no, born that way," I hastened to assure him, "Catholics as far back as St. Patrick, like you and me."

He grinned, took out another cigarette and had a hard time lighting it in the breeze. After a couple of puffs he said:

"Cradle Catholics don't usually shoot the works like that. They take it in their stride."

"Get this straight, Father, before you go on. They're not fanatics. They're nice people—the nicest I know. They have a comfortable home, shabby, I suppose, but rather charming—lots of books and pictures—you know the sort. Any Catholic writer or lecturer who comes to town usually ends up at their house for a little party or a cup of tea. Ye gods, any one of those girls could write her memoirs when she grows up, like Viola Meynell or Maisie Ward, only of course . . ."

"Intellectuals, eh?" he interrupted.

I began to think he was as invincible as Kathie.

"Smile when you say that," I cautioned him. "I don't like your tone. Intellectuals? I suppose you could call them that, but it would never occur to me to do it. They're *real* people, interested in everything—except maybe baseball," I amended, recalling how important that appeared in Kathie's eyes. I'm fond of baseball myself. "Do they sound like freaks?"

"Look here, young lady." (It was nice to be called young, even in fun.) "Are you consulting me as a priest or as a psychologist?"

"A little of each, maybe, and likewise as a friend."

"So be it."

We had reached the Main Hall and he stood with one foot on the lowest step, running his hand through his hair.

"First, as a priest. The kid isn't losing her faith any more than you're losing yours when you criticize the way things are done in your parish church—those lousy sermons and so on. The food is nourishing, but you don't like the way it's being dished up. Got that straight?"

"Quite." I gave him a grateful smile. I'd tried to tell myself words to that effect, but I'm not very convincing when I argue with the stern voice of Duty.

"Now from the psychological angle. The child needs to *interiorize,* introcept, or make part of herself the qualities she experiences in others. It isn't a mere process of imitation as so many parents, and godparents, seem to think. Religious training would be a breeze if good children simply 'took after' good parents. The child has first to *accept* the attitude of her parents and integrate it with her own personality."

I wrinkled my brow. I couldn't think of anything to say.

"Sounds easy enough, doesn't it? Here's the catch." He went up another step and stood a little above me, so that I had the feeling he was literally handing down a decision. "The kid's fourteen. At that age she has a blinding, driving need to conform to those in her own age group. She's smart. She realizes she's being pulled in two directions at once. And she's beating her brains out because she hasn't decided yet which way to go."

"Can any one help her decide, Father?" I asked humbly.

"I'm sorry, Kate, nobody. Neither you nor I. Time and the Holy Ghost are all we can count on. Nice seeing you; come again soon. So long!"

Well, that was that. I waited until the evening of Pentecost Monday and then I dropped in to see the Galvins.

"How was the Pentecost party?" I asked, flopping down in Phil's favorite chair. He was trying out some tune on the piano, and he didn't stop when he answered.

"Great! We had a good crowd for the Vigil—some of them we never saw before. It was very impressive, especially the clap of thunder when we chanted the line: 'He looketh upon the earth and maketh it tremble'."

"*I* was trembling," Jo said, "the kids were making such a racket overhead. There was a thump when the lightning struck—somewhere near, I imagine—and I thought Sheila had fallen out of bed again. I sneaked upstairs—they wouldn't miss *my* voice—and you should have seen them. Kathie was kneeling at the window watching the storm. Eileen in her nightie was sitting on the foot-rail of the bed swinging her legs and chanting: 'This is the gown which my mother hath made; let us rejoice and be glad in it.' Sheila, her eyes half-open, was waving her arms and shrieking: 'Alleluia, alleluia.' When she saw me she said: 'Hi, Mom, I'm the Holy Spirit. May I go back to sleep now, Eileen?' Eileen said, pointing to Kathie: '*She's* an infidel!' How liturgical can you get?"

"See if you can take the bass part of this duet, Jo," Phil said from the piano.

"If it's a long session, Kate," she told me, "go out to the kitchen, and if you can find anything to drink you can have it."

I stayed until midnight. A few people dropped in. One pair had a young man with them who was a leader of the Catholic Youth Movement in Germany; and there was an attractive young Negro couple who were members of an interracial group the Galvins belonged to. I had gone over with a floating intention of saying something about Kathie, about trying to tone down the religious atmosphere, but I never had an opportunity to mention it. Besides, what was there to say?

I tried to get Kathie's reaction to the Pentecost Vigil when I drove her out to the graduation exercises at the Academy. She was only a freshman, of course, but they all had to sing. Her white organza dress was becoming to her apricot-cream coloring and her sleek dark hair. "Wow, but I feel silly in this outfit! Am I really getting any fatter, Aunt Kate?"

I assured her that she wasn't, but she wasn't assured, and I made another attempt to draw her out about the Vigil.

"That German chap at your house the other night said groups of five hundred or more gathered for the Vigil in Germany this year."

"Oh, it's O.K. for foreigners, I guess." Kathie shrugged. "It wouldn't be so bad, if any one I know had ever *heard* of it before." She sighed deeply. "Some of the people who came were keen—not holy-looking, a bit. We kids didn't have to stay very long—Mother ran out of chairs."

"How was the ale? Did she run out of that, too?"

"There was plenty of ale, but I didn't like it much. I was in the kitchen helping Mother pour it out—that part was fun—when a lady brought her glass out for a refill. Mother had never met her before, but she was dying to. Someone brought her along and forgot to introduce them. She was Madge Mellody from Galway, where our folks came from, a rural-lifer who's been lecturing over here. I think they figured it out she was some sort of cousin of ours, 5th or 6th once-removed, or something like that."

She heaved an abysmal sigh. Then she banged her brocade evening bag against the dashboard.

"I can't stand it. I simply can't stand it any longer!"

"What's up?" I asked, as casually as I could, keeping my eyes on the road.

"Oh, you know. Rural Life! They've talked about it before but it always blows over. This time it sounds serious. That Mellody woman talked and talked to them after the others had gone—I admit I love to hear the way she talks—and now they're hellbent on moving to the country."

"Wouldn't it be rather nice in a way, horseback riding and all that?" I suggested weakly. I'm a city gal myself and just the idea gave me goose pimples. She didn't answer me, and after a few blocks she burst out:

"Why must it always happen to *me*? There are half a million people in this city, but *we* have to move to the country. It doesn't make sense."

I tried on the telephone next day to see if it made sense talking to Jo, but she was noncommittal.

"We're trying to work it out. We'd have to be on a bus line for Kathie to get in to school, and near a parish school for the others, and Phil would have to stop going back to work in the evenings. Oh, it sounds too complicated, but we'll get there eventually."

"I don't think Kathie likes the idea, do you?" I inquired mildly. I was surprised by the vehemence of Jo's response:

"Kathie! Is there anything on God's green earth she *does* like?"

" 'Let nothing disturb thee, nothing affright thee; all things are passing,' " I quoted, feeling rather self-conscious and silly.

Jo gave something like a snort.

"It's easy to see St. Theresa didn't have a teen-age daughter!"

I didn't see the Galvins for a week or so after that. Brian was tiling the bathroom and naturally I had to stand around and hand him tiles, his pipe and tobacco, and tools when he needed them.

MCF

He doesn't talk much when he works and it seemed like a long week.

It must have been Friday evening when the last tile went on and Brian telephoned the plumber to come and attach the new fixtures in the morning. I was bone tired and I got into my pajamas and robe and stretched out on the davenport to catch up on my reading. I had skimmed through the papers and was starting on the magazines (it must have been around ten o'clock) when the 'phone rang.

"Kate? Jo. Has Kathie been over there this evening?"

I hated to say she hadn't, hearing the tautness in Jo's voice.

"I wonder where she could be. I've called several of her friends but no one has seen her."

"When did she go out?"

"About eight. I asked her where she was going and she said: 'I don't know and I don't care.' " Jo drew in her breath and paused for a minute, but not for dramatic effect, because that's not her way. " 'I just want to get out of this gruesome place!' "

I began to get scared by that time, too, but I didn't let her know.

"I wouldn't pay any attention to that patter—she enjoys creating a situation. She probably met some pal and went home with her to watch the ball game and forgot about the time."

It sounded plausible but neither of us believed it.

"She hadn't much money with her," Jo went on, "and her bike's here on the porch. I'm not really afraid of an accident. I wish Phil were home."

"I forgot this is the night he's speaking at the Engineers' Club Do you want me to come over?"

"Oh, no. You stay there, in case she turns up at your house. I'll keep waiting. I'm alternating Hail Mary's with cups of coffee. I won't do anything drastic until Phil comes."

The thought of Jo notifying the police sent quivers up and

down my spine. You read in the paper where girls (of good
families, too) run away from home and turn up later in a faraway
city; that is, when they do turn up. But not your own child, or
your godchild. Kathie was too timid, she wouldn't dare—or
would she? I got out my Rosary and began praying furiously.

About 11:10 Kathie tapped on the door. She was wearing a
short-sleeved peasant blouse and she was shivering.

"I'm afraid to go home, Aunt Kate. Will you go with me? I
went to the last show by myself. I wanted to give Mother a good
scare and now I'm scared stiff myself."

She began to cry. I called Jo and told her we were practically
on our way. I had dressed again after her call, and I had asked
Brian to leave the car in the drive when he went to bed—said I
might want to run up to the delicatessen for bread. Galvin's
house was dark, but Jo opened the door for us and began turning
on lamps, as though she wanted to be busy when we came in.

"It was a silly thing to do, I know," Kathie said, before either
of us could say it.

"Could you give us a rough idea of *why* you did it?" Jo asked
in a tight voice.

"Yes, but it would be too rough for *you*. You think this is a
home but it isn't; it's a—a monastery. Why didn't you go to the
convent if you wanted to lead a holy life?"

Jo didn't say anything; just kept staring ahead of her. It was
funny when I thought of it. Every girl in the fourth grade at
St. Patrick's—that's the year we had Sister Paracleta—had
wanted to be a nun except Jo. She'd acquired motherhood with
her first doll, and she'd mothered everybody in sight ever since.
But Kathie broke into my reflection:

"You think if you got me out in the country, I couldn't see my
friends any more, and the girls at school would make fun of me
for being a hick, and I'd never, never have a boy friend, because
nobody would ever drive out in the country just to see *me*."

Still Jo didn't answer her and I realized that they had been over this ground many times before.

"I've been thinking, Jo," I said, though up to this minute I hadn't quite made up my mind. "Couldn't Kathie stay with us during the school year and just go home week-ends?"

Personally I thought this was a *beau geste* which would be hailed by both sides with gratitude and relief. Brian and I were used to a quiet life and it wasn't an easy decision to reach. Godmothering had suddenly acquired a lot of angles. Actually, Jo didn't even hear my offer and Kathie only brushed it aside.

"But I'd still *belong* in the country!" she protested. "What do you think, Mother?"

"I can't think any more." Jo rubbed her hand over her forehead. "If it makes you feel so unhappy and so insecure, it hardly seems worth the effort. I'm the only one who really wants to move, though Phil is willing. It would be pretty hard on him with the long hours he works. Still I didn't think it was selfish to insist." She looked across at me and held my eyes as though appealing to me to understand her. "Somehow it seems a more honest way of life—I don't know how to express it—than this technicolor, double-feature set-up in the city, bounded on one side by Hopalong Cassidy and Arthur Godfrey on the other."

"Oh, Mother, you're hopeless!" Kathie stamped her foot. "I suppose you think in the country they listen to God instead of Godfrey!"

"That was the general idea, Kathie. I was just hoping for a little peace in our day."

" 'I come not to bring peace, but a sword,' " Phil said, coming in from the hall. I wondered how long he had been standing there. He went over to Jo and took one of her hands in his. "Don't you remember how it goes, honey? 'For I come to set a man at variance against his father, and the daughter against her mother . . .' "

"Oh, my God!" Jo burst out, but it was more a prayer than profanity. She broke into sobs—the tears she had been suppressing all evening. Kathie looked as though she might possibly want to comfort her, but Phil said:

"I think your mother's had enough for one evening. Suppose we all clear out. Kathie, go to bed; Kate, come out in the kitchen and split a bottle."

"But Daddy, I can't go to bed yet. I'm practically *starved!*"

We took the prodigal daughter with us to the kitchen, but Jo still sat crying convulsively into her hands. We all kept listening to her and pretending we weren't, and finally we heard her go upstairs. Phil poured the ale (was this the blessed brew, I wondered?) and Kathie set about making herself an elaborate sandwich. Phil blew the foam off his glass and spoke conversationally to Kathie:

"Your mother and I have never forced religion upon you. You're required to do only the most elemental duties—say your prayers, go to Mass and the Sacraments. We never make you go to Holy Hour or Sodality meetings or anything extra-curricular as some parents do. We let you wear shirts and shorts and use cosmetics. We don't censure your friends or curtail your entertainments. What is it you resent so bitterly?"

She took a big bite of the sandwich, washed it down with iced tea, and said helplessly:

"I don't know how to tell you, Daddy. I wouldn't mind if you'd *make* me go to services. It's a different *kind* of religion. When the other girls come home from church, it's all over, but here it just goes on and on. Religion's a part of our whole life!"

Phil got up and patted her gently on the shoulder.

"I think I'd better go up and tell Jo to save her tears. We've not failed you, after all. She'll be glad to know it."

"Poor Jo!" I said.

He turned at the door. "Poor Kathie, you mean."

Kathie held her sandwich in mid-air while she waited for her father to explain his unexpected sympathy.

"She's like a person with a good meal before her who keeps nibbling on peanuts."

"Oh, Daddy, stop talking about *food*! I feel like I'm getting fatter every minute."

Phil shrugged. " 'Thou hast prepared a table before me in the face of my oppressors.' You haven't even begun to *set* the table, Kathie!"

"I always put off everything till the last minute, don't I?"

She went on munching the sandwich.

YUNG MARI LI

BRYAN MacMAHON

When young Bryan MacMahon from Listowel published The Lion Tamer, *his first volume of short stories, in 1949 he was greeted with a rousing fanfare of acclaim.* The Saturday Review of Literature *stated a fact: "Bryan MacMahon takes immediate place in the top echelon of contemporary Ireland's short-story writers. Sean O'Faolain, Frank O'Connor, and Michael McLaverty must move over at once for the man from Kerry . . . His writing rings with the truth of a good bell."*

It is a bell note, however, quivering with overtones of poetry and a strange magic not to be described but to be savored effortlessly by the reader. The story of "Yung Mari Li" communicates it. Father David Neale brings back one of his stray flock by one of the oddest shenanigans ever perpetrated by a shepherd.

By turns poet, folklorist, bookseller, story writer, dramatist, teacher, reviewer, and radio script writer, Bryan MacMahon has recently had a play taken for production by the Abbey Theatre. He is writing a novel.

Father David Neale was parish priest of Aaron (pop. 8104), Montana. When he was returning to Aaron (pop. 8104), Montana, after a six months' holiday spent in his native Tarmoneerla, in County Limerick, he took with him a sod of turf. The task of selecting this sod of turf was, he found, by no means easy. He demanded of his selection that it be a typical sod; but what constitutes the typical has always been an oyster-bed of argument. Father Neale had visualized his typical sod as having an attractive texture and appearance; then it would have to burn well in case an unbeliever in Aaron, Montana, should doubt the authenticity of the souvenir; average size was also desirable; and *nota bene,* it would have to smell well. To smell well, Father Neale repeated —almost aloud. To smell well!

He examined numerous sods from numerous bogs before he

eventually selected one approximating to his definition. He learned
a good deal about turf in the course of his search. Some sods, he
found, are base-bred, gloomy-looking blackguards, and, with
every aperture sealed to gaiety, they sit in peasant stolidity, re-
signing themselves to the advent of the day when they shall be re-
purchased by fire. And then at the last, when they are in the midst
of the conflagration, they have a habit of breaking out into the
laughter of flames and revealing themselves as ill-judged honest
folk. Other sods are nincompoops. They release a granular titter
even at wee provocation, seem to clasp the fire eagerly, and then,
if you please, have the insolence to peter out in a prolonged, slow-
dying sniffle of smoke. Others are perfect in texture, but are huge
awkward louts of fellows in appearance: others are so small that
when you look at them you say: "These were cut by mean men
with mean sleáns on mean mountains!" However, Father David
Neale eventually did find a sod to his entire satisfaction. It was
a good human sod, satisfactory in gloss and weight, its ebon
solidarity fining out to a small combustible tuft at one end.
Father Neale was thoroughly satisfied with his selection and kept
tapping his right nostril to give the world some indication of his
approval.

Returning to one's native place after an absence of twenty-
eight years occasions major adjustments to one's mental machinery. The day of departure is recalled. Heigh ho, after the inevitable
drive in the trap to the station with the two yew trees, you stand
at the window of a carriage and clutch your bright-ribboned
breviary. There over the heads of your lugubrious kinsfolk is a
normal traditional Ireland, all wolfhounds and geometric sun-
bursts and round towers and shamrocks. The train pulls out and
you carry this precious photograph in your heart for close on
thirty years. And then, by golly! you plump back into electric
cookers and a bewildering iron alertness. It's not fair, your poor
mind squeaks, when in dark prank the mahogany stool of tradi-

tional Ireland is pulled from under it. However, there had been compensations. When he did return, the trees were staunch around the new houses, the cool whistle of peace was through it all, he had nephews fit to answer his Mass, aye, and nieces big enough to turn the heel of his stocking.

From the deck of the liner he looked back at Ireland, patted his nose and said, "Good, good, good!" Taking it all-in-all he rather approved of this Ireland that he had not seen for twenty-eight years, so much so that a prompting from nowhere tempted him to revise certain fixed principles of his regarding the use of physical force. Then, with a sigh, he turned from the wisp of Irish shore and looked about for Irish ears into which he could empty his stock-in-trade joke of "Come back to Aaron, Montana, Montana. . . ."

Aaron is an open town within striking distance of Montana's glacier district. Bears walk out on the black highway a few miles from Aaron. Anglers catch prodigious numbers of trout in the mountain streams. The mountains north of the town have generous selvedges of snow, rich long laps of it under the blue tops. Laps and selvedges are greedy for the sunlight seeping through the first slats of day. Whatever about Ireland, *that* had not changed.

Back in harness, Father Neale was at first inclined to view the place with alien eyes. Gradually he eased into the old ways. He cut a few knots of procedure, rebuked three persons in so far as God had built him for rebuke, shied predictably at the deaths of two notable parishioners, and stolidly listened to his curate rendering a desultory parochial account over several meals. Then he made a few adjustments to a typewritten list which he kept in his desk. He struck out the names of twenty-four dead, inserted the names of thirty-three born, added the names of eight new arrivals, subtracted the names of fifteen of his flock departed and computed that the list of his flock now contained 1126 names.

Finally (as a result of the curate's rendering of account) he wrote thoughtful notes, in the space for remarks, after the names of five of his parishioners. He folded the pages sadly and carefully and replaced them in his desk. As he did so his eyes lighted on the sod of turf. His drooping spirits rose. Suddenly he grabbed his hat and went out.

He went along Main Street to the office of *The Aaron Advertiser and Post* and made enquiries about having a poster printed. He was satisfied with the plan the printer sketched out for him. The printer himself irritated him: the man was too workaday, too nonchalant. And besides, the priest fancied he saw a sniffle to the nose under the steel-rimmed spectacles. Still, he found in due course that the man had done his work well. Father Neale liked the type-face used in *A Sod of Turf* and also the fact that that lead was dead in the optical centre of the poster. The border was sturdy and solid; whatever qualms he had had, that solid border squashed them. His own name was, as he had intended, in no way obtrusive. He puckered a little at the word "Lecture," but after a little thought he allowed it to pass as a subterfuge. When he passed the proof he tapped the side of his nose slowly and ponderously and said, "Good, good, good."

At first his parishioners were disposed to be amused, but each one of them retreated two steps into solemnity on finding no responding humour in the priest's face. Without vehemence he succeeded in conveying his absolute earnestness; he did it chiefly by the resolute stare in his eyes and by the set tilt of the jaw. Thus he had always tried to transfer his iron sincerity to his parishioners, mostly Irish, Irish-born and second generation, with a sprinkling of Italians and mid-Europeans. He knew that without this humourless sincerity all his plans would be defeated: all his little conspiracies to prevent the shredding of his community, each new token of which he had noted through the years with troubled eyes —the first zoot-suit on a hobbledehoy named O'Connor, the marriage of Sally Donegan to an Anabaptist salesman, the open rebellion of old Jim Deenihan's son.

He entrusted the task of posting the notices to his curate, but only in the outlying portions of his parish—in Red Springs and Kanahook. The posting in Aaron he reserved for himself. One morning he strode out, the posters fingered to a careful figure of eight lest the fresh ink would kiss and blur. He called first on Charlie Meehan. Charlie became a fanatic at once. Charlie was a person of some consequence in Aaron: He owned twelve chain-stores in the State, and everywhere you went in Aaron you found a sly old lady on the billboards pointing to her bulging reticule and screaming, "Meehan's for Me!" Charlie's main store was on the principal crossing of Aaron, and while the priest was softly explaining the matter to him, Charlie was away ahead of him in fierceness. Charlie had the admirable dexterity of the fat, and while the priest was speaking through well-dressed lips and with round noble gestures, Charlie was proving his marksmanship with accurate movements of his hands and perfectly timed inter-jections such as "Sure! Fine! Fine! Sure!" When Charlie began to speak he did so with such concentrated vehemence that one looked everywhere for the person who was contradicting him. He manipulated his coloured words as if they were snooker balls. In his agony he bit off the end of a cigar, looked at the cigar truculently, then stowed it away quickly as if it had almost tempted him to national apostasy. "Say, Father," he said, "how about lapping the old sod in a white silk scarf and putting it on the centre of my big window? Get one of the School of Art stoo-dents to do a pretty deckle-edged card, say? Stick ribbons and arrows and ticker-tape all around it, see? Make it kind of mys-terious like! Give it the whole darned window, see? On one con-dition, Father. One condition, Father Neale. I gotta see the sod myself, see? And handle it myself, see? You gotta grant me that, eh? You gotta grant me that!" Father Neale said, well, he hadn't figured on showing it to anyone before the night of the lecture—thought it a point of honour like—but seeing that it was Charlie Meehan and that Charlie . . .

By noon the priest had but one poster left. Fingering it nervously he slowed down his pace outside a jeweller's shop in Lime Avenue. The shop was discretion itself. It was painted black, and over the doorway MARY YOUNG was written in gold leaf in a rather elaborate script. The name was flanked by two scrolls bearing the legends JEWELRY: ANTIQUES. But the priest passed the house and then his steps lost momentum. He tapped the side of his nose but he omitted the concomitant "Good." The tappings came slowly and thoughtfully at first, but then they worked up to a crescendo of inner battle and ended with a decisive tap that was tantamount to a blow. He turned and pushed open the glass door of the jeweller's shop. In the act of entering, one of his eyes blinked silver in the left-hand window while the other blinked brass in the right-hand window. The opening door rang a bell above his head. A German shepherd dog lying inside the door raised his jet head from the cream whorls of his chest and tilted his eyes to an angle of intelligence.

Mincing and prinking, the assistant wove among the showcases, and, pouting her lips, sweetly said "Yes?" She had all the awareness and unctuousness of a black pullet. Father Neale raised his hat. "Miss Young, if you please? Yes! Miss Young." The girl bowed and turned towards a brass-studded door behind the glass trays. The door had an oblong inset of hammered glass. The door swooshed out, but the return journey was baffled by its patent-closing and it whispered home with considerable dignity.

The priest was alone with the dog. It was like being alone with a Christian. Softly, very softly indeed, the priest rustled his fingers, but the dog had abandoned him as if saying, "I have no further interest in you; you conform to the standard of respectability this establishment demands." The priest ceased rustling his fingers. He leaned gently against a showcase and raised his head to the ceiling. There he read an old entry in the Baptismal Registry of his church in Aaron. "Mary Young (Yung Mari Li). . . . Father's name, Yung Seng Li . . . Mother's maiden name, Bridget Collins . . . hmm . . . sponsors . . . yes, yes . . . gap of a year and a half between date of child's birth and child's baptism. Mary Young . . . Yung Mari Li." And then the priest thought of the very last name in that typewritten list in his desk; Mary Young; and the blank after her name in the space for remarks.

Bridget Collins, the mother, he had never known. She had died previous to his appointment as parish priest of Aaron. But the father—wryness drew its needle across the priest's lips as he remembered Yung Seng Li and the two skirmishes he had had with him perhaps fifteen years before. Father Neale still carried two tags of Confucius as scars from those little frays. And then he remembered his single encounter with Mary Young after her father's death. The girl was then twenty-five. She had heard him out, not without blandness and gentility, but afterwards there was the poise and the shrugging: "Yes, of course . . . Baptism . . . one's time is so occupied, Father . . . one does never quite get the opportunity . . . you understand how it is. Duty . . . of course . . . duty, but one's conception of duty, even of belief, is so, shall we say personal? . . . arbitrary? Yes, yes . . . if you don't mind, the telephone . . ."

The priest looked over the glass showcases and the silver and the brasses. The intestines of the watches are now in a workshop at the rear, he concluded. A good deal of tone since the old man's time. The old man was a brassworker but he had never quite mated his trade with that of jeweller. His girl had succeeded. There was discretion here, even opulence. He smiled at a pair of brass snakes with tails coiled in an attractive standard

and mouths gaping to receive tall tapers. He looked at the die-
direct edges of the showcases; at the cut glass; at four silver
mannikins. He looked at the sleek dog.

Mary Young came out through the brass-studded black doorway. She bore her Oriental face before her as if it were a shield
of brass embossed with a nose, a brow, and a pair of eye-sockets.
Her dress was the correct black. There were pearls at her throat.
When she joined her defensive, her suspicious fingers, a diamond
ring flashed a low warning at the priest. In the centre-parting of
her black hair the skin of the scalp glowed lime-white. The hair
was gathered to a spinsterish bun at the nape of the neck.
Approaching him she titlted her Eastern head to remote bel-
ligerence and her ten cyclamen nails formed a purely negotiatory
cradle. Without speaking she conveyed: "At the risk of tedious-
ness I must repeat that my attitude towards certain matters is
entirely unaltered." The priest made a quick calculation and
reckoned that her age was thirty-nine.

Smiling, Father Neale raised his hat. Then, replacing it, he
energetically took refuge in his solitary poster. While his head
was bent he resolved to play the part of an old priest whose stock
reaction was benevolence. Then the imp of his temporary embarrassment began to urge him to play his part more fully by
doddering. But behind this absurd play-acting he was trembling
alert. Yet when he raised his head, his face held the incipience
of a counterfeit pastoral palsy. "A whim of mine . . . our
schools, Miss Young . . . repairing. . . . In Ireland. . . . Turf
. . . peat you know. . . . Display it . . . . according as we
grow older . . . primary importance." All the while the alive
eyes were seeking a cranny in her visage of beaten brass.

Mary Young grew amicable. Her eyes said, "Yes . . . yes
. . . is that all? . . . Is that all?" But when she acceded, was
she eager to accede? No, no, he must not betray his eagerness
to recognize her eagerness. He thanked her with a facile sliding

into complete senility and fumbled his way out on to the side-walk.

There he tossed aside the fiddle-face of his weakness. He dismissed the sham saggings of his body by the natural expedient of throwing himself upwards and outwards towards the fullness of his great frame. Now again he was a man with a task before him.

But had it all been a waste of time? How much—if any—of her mother went to her composition? Was there even a tithe of Bridget Collins in Yung Mari Li? Or was she wholly her courteous, inexpugnable Confucian father? He shrugged. He had much more to do, many people to meet, numerous letters to write.

Late that night he brought the sod out to Charlie Meehan's. Charlie had a spacious house on the fringe of the town. The house was ablaze with lights to welcome him. Charlie had allowed his kids up late to see the sod of turf. There they were, whooping in the hallway. Charlie's American wife was as astute as blazes; she had reserved her role until she had observed her husband's face for a while. What she saw in his daft eyes decided her against chaffing. All through the evening she thanked her stars that she had not made the most grievous blunder of her life by falling headlong over the cliff of facetiousness. Charlie handled the sod reverently and thrust it under the nose of his eldest son with, "Get your nose to that, you damn Yankee, and get the smell of home!" The man was roaring; but his sorry bulwark of harshness was as thin as tissue-paper. Yet the next morning the appearance of the wrapped sod with its panoply of streamers and arrows in Meehan's window engendered widespread hilarity. Hilarity and some fierceness. Father Neale was pleased when he heard the rumblings of this fierceness. He tapped the side of his nose and said, "Good, good, good!" By way of superfluous explanation he added to himself, "Fierceness is cement!"

On the night of the lecture the hall was full. Father Neale was at the door shaking hands with the Irish. His curate was busy inside. The Irish had come out of their houses—every man-jack had come. There they were, Jack Mulcahy, Teddy Lysaght, Peter Flynn, Anthony English, Dan and Michael O'Connor, Joe Feehan, Dinny McGinley, with their wives and children, some of them with their children's children. Old Mrs. Sloan (*née* Broderick) drove down from her mansion in the hills. A sprinkling of Italians came. Giuseppe Salvani was there—the richest man in town—and his gargantuan midnight glittering wife with him, waddling up the narrow pathway, circling from leg to leg as a heavy box is trundled by a railway porter. Father Neale pressed Giuseppe to appear on the platform, but the Italian said, "No, the Irish to-night," and after this he telescoped ten no's.

Charlie Meehan, Tim Foley, Anthony English and young Sloan the attorney were on the platform. The wrapped sod of turf was on the table with the carafe of water beside it. Charlie and his fellows were portentous as haystacks. Then, precisely on the stroke of eight, Father Neale appeared on the platform. The people cheered. The priest looked well. He possessed the un-purchasable and wholly natural gift of ceremony.

But though it was clear that he was pleased with the size and zeal of his audience, yet some fraction of him seemed wholly not at peace within himself. Some essential lustre was absent from his lips, and now and again scrawlings came out on his fore-head. His tongue readied his dry lips; he walked forward and looked at the Poles, the Austrians, the Italians—and the Irish. Just then in the pause before he began to speak, Mary Young entered the hall. Sprucely and trimly her body moved forward through the people. The minor ripple of whispering that s-s-s-ed forward and broke upon the priest's boots indicated that the woman's presence at a Catholic meeting was considered abnormal. Father Neale eyed her keenly and nodded to a youngster who immediately vacated his place in the front row. Mary Young graciously thanked the boy and then yielded her face up to the speaking priest.

Now, I cannot tell you with any degree of accuracy what the priest said to his people. My mouth and the priest's mouth are two different mouths. Come, now, be honest with yourself! What would *you* say about a sod of turf in Aaron, Montana? Or in any five other places, pin-pricked at random on a kid's atlas? Emotion is emotion anywhere, even in Aaron, Montana. His end and his beginning was home, and the things of home. Home. Home. Home. Beyond the beloved bits of ceremony he was a baker and his people were dough. He was a potter and his people were clay. He was a sculptor and his people were stone.

When he came to the unwrapping of the sod the Irish, for the most part, were blatantly on the point of tears. Home. Home. Home. God dear! God dear! Home. Over the hills and the steeples and the towers and the salt water. Like the passing of a great wind every single one of them was having daybreak in his chest and a hundred cocks crowing in his heart. These poor drugged Irish were galloping like thunder at the heels of their priest.

The women were crying, and they didn't give two hoots in hell who saw them either. They snuggled against husbands who had grown wondrously fierce, each man's face the hue of a cock's comb. The husbands resented such advances lest they be considered effeminate, and unangrily clucked their womenfolk away. A miner who had come all the way up from Butte took his short pipe out of his mouth and said loudly, "Wisha, Glory on you, Priesht up there!"

And then, when their emotion was at its peak, the priest, by an unpredictable flippancy, smashed the wondrous glass of their mood. This was no error on his part. It was carefully calculated.

He protested his own inadequacy to deal with his subject. If 'twere his brother Dick now or Jim Joe, they could talk on turf till Tibb's Eve. But he! Here he held up his milky-white hands and the people gave back the guffaw he had expected. He reckoned that this breaking would now set them the communal task of gathering the fragments and setting them together again. Ultimate individual fracture, he knew, would have in any case inevitably followed.

He urged them to talk now: Charlie Meehan started off and his naturalness proved infectious. Narrowed down to the intimacy of a family group the men were soon speaking without shyness. They spoke hesitantly thus:

"Would you believe me, Father, when I say I seen turf cut under the red strand of the seashore? In Ballyheigue it was, and 'twas cut out at the low-water mark! Cut in a great hurry, too, and then 'twas saved on the brink of the sandhills. . . ."

"I seen a son a flamin' sleánsman and the father before him as awkward as Euclid. . . ."

"In our place we'd pelt the brúscar on to the top of the rick so that it'd soak the weather. Doin' it of a windy day 'twould blind the two eyes inside your head and . . ."

"Say! Good turf rings even when it's leaving the sleán. It squeaks under the prongs of the pike. The wax in it is sort o' slow to leave go its hoult on anything."

"Good turf darkens on the bank within the hour. Then it glistens, man, like a pony's back. Like a pony's back and her feed thickened with linseed oil."

"Footin' turf is a job you should second to no man. Rogues footin' your turf for you mightn't stir the dead man in the heart of the grogue and then . . ."

"On the mountain in our part we'd pull the single scraw from it. Up t'd walk with the little cubes of solid dark turf dangling off the grass threads. Beggin' your pardon, Father, but 'tis like nothin' on earth more than skulldraggin' a woman down a shtairs . . ."

"Do you know what it is, but the breenshin' man has a proper animal's job, so he has. . . ."

The priest was happy now. The place was crackling about him with vivid yapping. Women were eager that their husbands should be heard. No woman spoke. Instead she pulled at her husband's sleeve to make the vehicle of her contradiction or her addition.

"An odd time the sleán'd strike a gusher. A gusher, man, and then all the water in the wide world'd boil out under your boots. . . ."

"Well, God be with the mornin' I so-hoed a hare in a snug truppal at the butt of our reek of turf. I remember it well. 'Twas a mornin' in June and the mountain was fair drowned in clear blueness . . ."

"I got a trálach in my wrist pikin' turf of a day and I declare to the Man Above if . . ."

"I dare say there's none among ye but found the lovely red bog-sally ten sods deep in the clay. You'd find yourself nursin' it in your hand for the full round of a day. . . ."

The priest handed down the sod to be passed from hand to hand through the hall; he thought it good that each person smelled at it deeply as if to capture even one camera-click of the lost world at home.

And then, when the harvest of words was almost reaped, it happened. Yung Mari Li was on her feet. The Irish was out on her yellow face. Out on her face like a torch. Silence weaved through the groups. The woman's face swung from priest to people, from people to priest. And then she spoke:

"My mother was Bridget Collins from Tobbernagoneen, near Knocknagoshel in the County of Kerry, Ireland. Tobbernagoneen is Gaelic and it means 'The Well of the Rabbits.' Miles on the land-side of Tobbernagoneen is Tournafulla which is a name as strong as a blow of a fist in the mouth, for it means 'The Bleach-field of the Blood.' When my mother was a child growing up she spent all her time out on the bog. She wore a red flannel petticoat you could see two miles away. Tobbernagoneen is a townland with nothing in it but bog. My grandfather Joseph Collins had the grass of three hungry cows on the cutaway but he had up to sixty acres of bog. He used to let it to the farmers around at five shillings a bank for the year. I remember, too, my mother saying that a sleán of turf is what three men would cut in the run of a day, one man cutting, one man breenching, one man spreading. A sleán of turf worked out about thirteen rails. My grandmother Maria Collins used to make pillows out of the canavawn that grows on the bog. I recall my mother saying that a noted fiddler named Kevin Regan was drowned in a bog-hole on my father's turbary. My mother said that he used be heard playing 'The Job of Journeywork' there afterwards and that she and her sisters were mortally afraid to stir out after dark for fear of Kevin Regan's ghost. . . ."

Invisibly the arms of the women were out, groping about to embrace the Chinawoman. Their arms stopped short of her, re-pelled by the foreignness in her face. Then again the poor bewil-dered women sent up their arms to clutch at the garments of their priest, to pluck at him, to hook him, to ask him, "What? Why? Who? Why? Why?" And the priest was tensed and re-laxed and meticulously sensitive to their pitiable queries, and hinging his face over them he chided them silently (even dan-gerously, lest even their clumsy breaths should knock over his lovely house of cards) and they interpreted his eyes and mouth as saying: "This is utterly normal; utterly normal, remember! I tell you that a good deal depends on it that you should believe that this is utterly normal." Then, after the small negation, the wave of their perplexity ebbed and they were at peace. The priest approved of their acceptance and lidded up his eyes till he looked like an old hen. He began to stroke his face in thanksgiving; he put the pads of thumb and forefinger on the lids of his eyes, stroked briskly out over the cheekbones, ran them up the lip corners and vouchsafed the finger-tips a minor osculation in the middle of the lips.

Afterwards the people went home through the dark.

The priest allowed five agonizing days to elapse before he called on Mary Young. As he expected, he found that she was eager to receive him. Even then, he spent five minutes lipping the tittle-tattle of the town. He skilfully avoided the topic that was a mutual urgency in them both. And then the guard of her grandeur was down. . . .

"An exclamation of my mother's," she said: "Reenan-angel! What does it mean?"

"King of Angels," the priest said.

"King of Angels?"

"Yes! King of Angels!"

Then they both said "King of Angels" together.

After that she was nothing but an unsure groping woman. She indicated the studded door with its rectangle of hammered glass. "If I'm not taking up too much of your time, Father?" Then, "Miriam!" she said, clicking the girl to her station. She put her carmine fingers on the studded door and the door shrank open. The dog saw the priest's grey head pass in, high and mighty amid the splendour of the brasses.

UNHOLY LIVING AND HALF DYING

SEAN O'FAOLAIN

It is the gentleman roomer who does the unholy living and his landlady who has a habit of half-dying, so that fear of death keeps Jacky Cardew uncomfortably on the edge of repentance. Insight, humor, a disciplined art which makes room for irony as well as warmth, have given Sean O'Faolain a place among the best short-story writers of our day. Born in Cork in 1900, he earned his first M.A. degree in Dublin, and his second at Harvard, where he taught Gaelic. Besides several volumes of short stories, he has written biography, novels, essays, and currently The Irish, *a candid character study of his fellow countrymen.*

Jacky Cardew is one of those club bachelors who are so well-groomed, well-preserved, pomaded, medicated, and self-cossetted that they seem ageless—the sort of fixture about whom his pals will say when he comes unstuck around the age of eighty, "Well, well, didn't poor old Jacky Cardew go off very fast in the end?"

For thirty years or so he has lived in what are called Private Hotels; last winter he said to his friends, "These bloody kips are neither private nor hotels, I'm going to take a flat." What he got in the end was the sort of makeshift thing that goes by the name of a flat in Irish cities—two rooms (that is, one room cut in two), with the W.C. on the ground floor and the bathroom on the top floor; and in the bathroom an unpleasant, greasy-looking gas-stove such as Prince Albert might have unveiled at the Great Crystal Palace Exhibition of 1851. But Jacky was delighted. At least he now had privacy. Nobody lived in the house but himself and his old landlady; for a tinsmith had the ground floor (rather noisy and smelling of solder), there were solicitors' offices on the

274

second floor, the old lady lived under the slates, above Jacky's flat, and he hardly ever saw her except when he paid his rent.

About two o'clock one bad February morning just as Jacky and a few friends were settling down for the fourth time to their last game of solo they gradually became aware that a dog was beating his tail on the floor above. There was no other sound for a while but the flick of the cards and the rain spitting on the window and the slight exclamations of the players. Then they heard the rapping again.

"Better go easy, boys," somebody said, playing a card, "we're keeping the old lady upstairs awake."

They played on intently. Again they heard the rapping, this time insistent and loud. Jacky glanced around at the lifted eyebrows, at his wrist watch, at the dying fire, at the drops sparkling on the pane in the arclight of the Square below, and went out with the sort of frown he would have turned on a junior in the Bank who had not been soapy enough. Striking matches he climbed the stairs. The nail-heads shone. Hearing him stumble and curse she called his name, and he made his way towards the voice, stooping under the great rafters of the attics, elbowing aside the damp washing that she had hung there to dry, feeling the cold within a few inches of his poll. He found her room, a bare attic. He was affronted by its poverty, its cold stuffiness, its sloping attic-window that wept in the ripples with the lights of the city.

In the matchlight he saw her pale eyes staring up at him in terror from the pillow; he saw her hollowed cheeks; the white beard on her chin; her two pigtails tied with bits of red wool. The match burned his fingers. Through the dark he heard her whisper:

"Mr. Cardew, I'm dying."

He was so frightened that he immediately lit another match.

He was even more frightened by what she replied when he asked
her if he could call in one of her friends.

"God help us," she panted. "Friends how are ye? I haven't
a friend to wet me lips. Not a friend. In the world."

He raced down the stairs. One of his pals was a doctor; he
went up and examined her, soothed her, came down and said
there was nothing much wrong with her except old age and perhaps a touch of indigestion, and ordered two aspirins and a hotwater bottle on her stomach. They made her comfortable for the
night and the party went home, heads down to the rain, shouting
commiserations all around.

Jacky came back to his dishevelled room and sat by the cold
fireplace. He heard every quarter-hour strike from the City Hall,
sometimes bold and clear, sometimes faint and sad, according to
the mood of the wintry wind. He suddenly remembered that his
own mother had gone on a night like this. He wondered who
would attend to the old woman if she died, and for the first time
he took notice of the family photographs hung around the walls,
mainly young men and women, and vacant-looking babies with
their mouths open. There was a big black enlargement of a man
with a gray mustache and a bald head. He reminded him of old
Cassidy, his last Manager, who now dined regularly every Tuesday of the year with another retired banker called Enright. As
Jacky poked the dead cinders, it came to him that Cassidy probably had no other friend in the world, and, begod, anyway, once
you turn fifty what is it but a gallop down the bloody straight?

At half-past three he went up to have another look at her.
She was asleep, breathing heavily. He tried to feel her pulse but
could not remember what a normal beat is and felt hers was
as slow as a hearse. He returned to his cold room. It was still
raining. The Square below shone. He felt a dull pain in his
groin and wondered could it be appendicitis. He thought that

he should have called in the priest to her and he counted the years since he last went to Confession. At half-past four he had another look at her and found her breathing easily and decided she was all right. As he pulled up his pajamas he gave his paunch a dirty look.

He was awakened at his usual hour by the old lady herself, bringing him his usual hot cup of tea and buttered toast. She had a prayer book under one arm and was dressed for the street.

"Good Heavens," he gulped, "I thought you were. . . ."

Her tall lean body swayed over like a reed with the gusts of laughter.

"Mr. Cardew, 'tis well known you can't kill a bad thing. My little hot seat in Purgatory isn't ready for me yet. Ah, I knew I'd pay for that load of bacon and cabbage I ate yesterday." An inelegant gesture from her stomach to her throat made him hastily lay down the buttered toast. "I was all swelled up with it the day long."

Jacky dressed, blaspheming. On his way out he decided to have a serious word with the woman. She had returned from chapel and was sitting in her kitchen sucking up a big basin of soup.

"Look here, Mrs. Canty," he said severely, "is it an actual fact that you have no friends what-so-ever?"

"I have plenty friends, Mr. Cardew," she smiled happily. "The best friends any woman ever had."

She laid her bony hands on a pile of prayer books—there must have been about twelve of them, a pile a foot-high, all in shiny black cloth coverings.

"And haven't I the souls suffering in Purgatory? I have Saint Anthony." Her glance directed his to a big brown-and-cream statue on the dresser. "And haven't I the Sacred Heart?" He eyed the red-and-gold statue over the sink with the withered palms of last Easter crossed before it. "And look at the Little Flower smiling at me. And what about Saint Joseph and Saint Monica?"

Jacky's head was going around like a weather-cock.

"And amn't I only after coming in from praying to the Left Shoulder? Friends, Mr. Cardew?"

She smiled pityingly at him. He strode out, to prevent himself from saying, "Then why the hell didn't you call on them last night instead of rapping me up to you?" Instead he took it out of his secretary at the bank. "Pure damn superstition, that's what I call it. Crawthumpin' by day and bellyachin' by night. The usual Irish *miserere*. All based on fear and terror of hellfire and damnation. It would turn anybody into an atheist." The girl talked up to him; they almost quarrelled; she told him he should be ashamed of himself; she even told him his "day would come"; she drove him beside himself by telling him she "would pray for him." At lunch he got into a violent argument about religion during which he kept using the word, "Benighted! Benighted!" He was still at it that night in the club, but he had to go easy there as most of the members were Knights of Columbanus and business is business. He took the middle line of:

"Mind you, I have a great regard for what I call real religion. And, mind you, I'm no saint. I'm honest about that. Though I suppose I'm no worse than the general run. Aye, and maybe a bit better if the truth were told? And I'll say this for it, religion is a great consolation for old age. But if religion doesn't go with character—character first and before all—then it crumbles away into formalism and superstition."

They all considered it safe to agree with that. He surveyed his cards contentedly. "I think it's your lead, Maguire?"

He found himself strolling homeward with Maguire. It was a gentle night after all the rain, and there was a delicate spring touch in the air.

"We won't know where we are now," said Maguire, "until Easter is on us." And he gave an uncomfortable little laugh.

"What's the joke?"

"Wisha, I was just thinking there tonight when you were gassing about religion that . . . begod, do you know, 'tis a year since I was at Confession. With Easter coming on I suppose we'll have to get the ould skillet cleaned again. Easter Duty, you know. Where do you go? I always pop up to Rathfarnham to the S.J.'s. Men of the world. Nobody like 'em."

"I usually go there too," lied Jacky. "You can talk to those fellows."

And he began to wonder would he or would he not make a dash for it this year.

On the Thursday of Holy Week, just after midnight, as Jacky and the boys were in the middle of a hot game of Nap, a faint knocking percolated through the ceiling. He went on with his deal.

"No bloody fear," he grunted. "Once bitten twice shy. More cod-acting."

They gathered up their hands and began to play. Through the slap of the cards the rapping came again, this time more faintly.

"That one now," said Jacky. "Your play, Jim. That one . . . God, have you nothing but the Ace? That one is a typical example of the modern Irish crawthumper. Behind all this piety, believe you me . . . Who said I reneged? What are you talking about, didn't I put the seven on Redmond's deuce? Behind all this so-called piety there's nothing but a child's fear of the dark."

Maguire laughed at him.

"Now, Jacky, there's no earthly use your beefing about religion. The stamp of the Church is on you. 'Tis on all of us. 'Tis on you since the day you were born and sooner or later they'll get you and you may as well give in and be done with it.

Mark my words, I'll live to see the day you'll have holy pictures all around your bloody bedroom! The stamp is on you, the stamp is on you."

Jacky flared. Here was a fellow who barely confessed once a year and he was talking as if he were a blooming saint.

"Stop wagging your finger at me, please. And, anyway, with all your guff when were you at Confession last, I'd like to know?"

Maguire laughed smugly.

"I don't in the least mind telling you. I was there three days ago." He clicked his fingers and looked around him at the group. "A grand old priest. He let me off like that. I think if I'd told him I'd committed murder all he'd say would be, 'Any other little thing troubling you, my child?' " They laughed approvingly.

"Ah, there's nothing like an S.J. Listen, did ye ever hear the one about the fellow that went to Confession the time of the Troubles here and said 'Father, I shot a Black and Tan.' Do you know what the priest said? 'My child,' says he, 'you may omit your venial sins.' Honest to God, I believe 'tis a fact."

They all laughed again although they had heard the yarn many times before: it was the sort of story every hardy sinner likes to hear. Through their laughter the knocking came once more.

"I'm afraid, Jacky," said another of them, a commercial named Sullivan, "you'll have to have a look at the ould geezer."

With a curse Jacky flung down his cards. He climbed to the attic. He struck a match and gave one look at her and at once he knew that she was bad. Her forehead was beaded. Her chest rose and fell rapidly.

"Mr. Cardew. I'm finished. Get me the priest. For God's sake."

"Certainly. Certainly. Right away. And I'll get the doctor."

He bolted down the stairs and burst in on them.

"God, lads, 'tis no joke this time. She's for it. I can tell it.

I can see it. Maguire, run out for the priest like a good man, Sullivan, there's a telephone down by the kiosk, call the doctor, get Cantillon, Hanley, Casey, any of 'em. Hurry, man, hurry."

He brought her up a stiff whisky but she was too weak to sip it. When the priest came, a young man with the sad eyes and bent head of a Saint Francis, the gamblers huddled outside under the rafters, looking through the skylight at the wide Easter moon. They were all middle-aged men, younger than Jacky, but replicas in every other way.

"Oh," whispered Maguire. " 'Tis true. Just as the priest told me. Like a thief in the night. We never know the day or the hour."

" 'Twas a terrible winter," whispered Sullivan. "I never saw so many people popping off. I see where old Sir John Philpott went off yesterday."

"Ah, God, no?" begged Jacky, shocked at the news. "You don't mean Philpott of Potter and Philpott's? I was talking to him in the club only three days ago." He said it as if he were affronted at Sir John's giving him no previous warning of the event. "He was a comparatively young man. Was he sixty-two itself?"

"Heart," whispered Wilson. "He went off very fast in the end."

"Here today," sighed Maguire. "Gone tomorrow."

"The best way to go," murmured Sullivan. "No trouble to anybody."

"That is," whispered Maguire, "provided our ticket's been punched for—" And he pointed respectfully upwards. "I heard a preacher say one time that he knew a man who came into his confession-box after being twenty years away. He said he had just lifted his finger and said the *Absolvo te*," and Maguire lifted his two first fingers, "when the man dropped dead in the box! There was a close shave for you!"

Jacky moved uneasily on his feet; he knew the story was just a preacher's yarn, but he had not the spirit to say it.

"The best death of all," murmured Sullivan, "is the soldier's. I believe, just before a battle, a priest can give a whole regiment a General Absolution and if a man is killed he goes straight up to heaven. That's what makes Irishmen such good soldiers. Straight up to heaven!"

"Grand in attack," said Jacky judiciously, "not so good in defense."

"And that's why," said Sullivan. "And, what's more, I wouldn't be surprised if that isn't why the English are better on the defensive than in the charge. Sure any man would fight like a divil if he knew what was coming after. Death has no terrors for a man in a situation like that."

They fell silent. A cloudlet dimmed the moon; then all their faces were lit again. The city's roofs were blanched and shone. The priest's voice murmured softly.

"He's taking a long time," said Jacky. "And it isn't," he whispered, trying to make a little joke, "as if she had so much to tell. An old woman like her can have nothing to tell. She's all right anyway."

They all sighed deeply. The priest came out, stooping under the beams, removing his stole and kissing it. Maguire asked him, "Will she last, Father?" The priest sighed, "A saint, a saint," as if he were sighing for all the sinners of the world. Jacky showed him out, and as he walked away the doctor came down. Jacky shut him into his car and shoved in his head anxiously.

"Is she bad, doctor?"

"Anno Domini. We can't live for ever. The works give out, just like an old motorcar. All we can do at that age is wait for the summons." He beckoned with one finger. Jacky drew back hastily. The headlamps whirled and the car purred away across the empty Square as if its red tail-light were running away with somebody.

Jacky was left alone in his room. He sank into an armchair by the open window. The spring night was gentle; the blood of youth was pulsing through everything. He was looking again over the shining roofs and the blank chimney-pots, and as if a shutter flicked he felt for one moment the intense vacancy and loneliness of life; and he saw it, as the years went by, becoming more and more lonely and empty. And when he was gone that moon, the old trees would still be there, still throbbing. A little wind scurried furtively in the dust of the Square. He looked at the decanter. Low tide. His own life. He'd be able to rest tomorrow anyway. He paused before the mirror. Good Friday morning. One more day to Easter. A veined, red face with a blue nose, thin ruffled hair, bags under the eyes, was grimacing at him out of the mirror as he licked his lips and got a horrible taste in his mouth and felt an uneven thumping in his heart.

He sat down heavily by the open window, under the moon's indifferent beauty. He began to go back over the years. There were a couple of things it wasn't going to be too easy to . . . "Not, mind you," he assured the empty Square, with bravado, "that I'm going to hand myself over to some bogtrot from the County Meath. Pick the right man and . . . Well, Father—" he rehearsed, flicking a grain of ash from his pants and pulling his ear, "I'm afraid, er, I've got more than a few little peccadilloes to tell you. I'm only human, Father. Child of Adam, and all to that and so on." That was the ticket. Frank and open. Two men of the world. "Of course, there's been a spot of liquor, Father. And, er . . . Well, er . . . I mean, er . . ." Jacky coughed and ran his finger around inside his collar. It was going to take a bit of doing, all right. He closed his eyes and began to think of all those nights that had seemed such grand nights, at the time.

When he opened his eyes again the sun was warm on his face, the Square was gay with sunlight, somebody was shaking his shoulder. It was his landlady smilingly handing him his tea and buttered toast.

"Well, Mr. Cardew," she cackled, "since I didn't go last night I'll live to be a hundred."

As Jacky looked blearily down at the three plane trees, all the misery of the night flooded on him. He gave her one maddened look, banged down the cup, and started up to tell her just what he thought of her. An unholy gripe pierced a redhot needle through the small of his back.

"Oh, Mr. Cardew, what on earth made you sit by the open window?"

The pain ran across the back of his neck. With a hand to his back and a hand to his neck all he could do was to crawl moaning to his bed.

As he lay there through the holidays he found himself being petted and cossetted as he had never been in his life before. She rubbed his neck and she rubbed his chest and she brought him hot punch and fed him with Easter delicacies until, gradually, if sourly, he decided that he would be a fool to change his landlady. At the same time, and especially on Easter Sunday morning as he lay with the sun slanting warmly across his chest, his hands behind his head, smoking his after-breakfast cigarette, his Sunday paper on his lap, listening to the silvery bells of all the churches of the city, he was aware of a certain feeling of discomfort: nothing much, just a coiled shadow at the back of his mind, the merest hint of apprehension. Cautiously he turned his stiff shoulders to look at the mantelpiece where she had placed a little spray of Holy Palm in a glass vase, and beside it a little glass bowl of Holy Water. He grunted as he considered them. He'd get rid of those things all right when he got on his feet again. But just then he remembered Maguire, and all that about the stamp being on you. He smiled uncomfortably. Oh, well! He flicked his ash on the carpet. Some day, no doubt. Some day. He took up the paper and began to study Form.

How lovely the sun was. It was nice to hear all the footsteps across the Square below, going to Mass. Their shadowy reflections passed softly on the ceiling. All over the city the silvery bells went on calling everybody to be happy because Christ was risen.

K

THE JILTING
OF GRANNY WEATHERALL

KATHERINE ANNE PORTER

Second to none among contemporary short story writers is Katherine Anne Porter, who has published many of her best stories in three volumes: Flowering Judas, *1930;* Hacienda, *1934;* Pale Horse, Pale Rider, *1939.*

Her psychological insight and extraordinary gift for characterization are well illustrated in The Jilting of Granny Weatherall. *In the broken colored chips of Ellen Weatherall's consciousness as she lies dying are pieced together the whole of her amazing personality. In this age, when fictional characters are often spiritual pygmies or unhealthy borderline cases, it is a joy to meet one of Granny's stature. The sheer spunk of the old lady is as bracing as wind on a March morning. But Granny is dying, and the bitterness of death brings back with staggering clarity the intolerable pain of her jilting as a young woman, while over and above the whirl of memories is the prayer of the parish priest administering Extreme Unction.*

Had Granny really forgiven the wrong done her? Is she damned or saved? In the artistic projection of her character the reader is permitted to watch the mystery of human individuality, strongly marked, as it asserts itself in its final hour and in that ultimate moment is only the summation of what it has always been.

She flicked her wrist neatly out of Doctor Harry's pudgy careful fingers and pulled the sheet up to her chin. The brat ought to be in knee breeches. Doctoring around the country with spectacles on his nose! "Get along now, take your schoolbooks and go. There's nothing wrong with me."

Doctor Harry spread a warm paw like a cushion on her forehead where the forked green vein danced and made her eyelids twitch. "Now, now, be a good girl, and we'll have you up in no time."

"That's no way to speak to a woman nearly eighty years old

just because she's down. I'd have you respect your elders, young man."

"Well, Missy, excuse me." Doctor Harry patted her cheek. "But I've got to warn you, haven't I? You're a marvel, but you must be careful or you're going to be good and sorry."

"Don't tell me what I'm going to be. I'm on my feet now, morally speaking. It's Cornelia. I had to go to bed to get rid of her."

Her bones felt loose, and floated around in her skin, and Doctor Harry floated like a balloon around the foot of the bed. He floated and pulled down his waistcoat and swung his glasses on a cord. "Well, stay where you are, it certainly can't hurt you."

"Get along and doctor your sick," said Granny Weatherall. "Leave a well woman alone. I'll call for you when I want you. . . . Where were you forty years ago when I pulled through milk-leg and double pneumonia? You weren't even born. Don't let Cornelia lead you on," she shouted, because Doctor Harry appeared to float up to the ceiling and out. "I pay my own bills, and I don't throw my money away on nonsense!"

She meant to wave good-by, but it was too much trouble. Her eyes closed of themselves, it was like a dark curtain drawn around the bed. The pillow rose and floated under her, pleasant as a hammock in a light wind. She listened to the leaves rustling outside the window. No, somebody was swishing newspapers: no, Cornelia and Doctor Harry were whispering together. She leaped broad awake, thinking they whispered in her ear.

"She was never like this, *never* like this!" "Well, what can we expect?" "Yes, eighty years old. . . ."

Well, and what if she was? She still had ears. It was like Cornelia to whisper around doors. She always kept things secret in such a public way. She was always being tactful and kind. Cornelia was dutiful; that was the trouble with her. Dutiful and good: "So good and dutiful," said Granny, "that I'd like to

spank her." She saw herself spanking Cornelia and making a
fine job of it.

"What'd you say, Mother?"

Granny felt her face tying up in hard knots.

"Can't a body think, I'd like to know?"

"I thought you might want something."

"I do. I want a lot of things. First off, go away and don't
whisper."

She lay and drowsed, hoping in her sleep that the children
would keep out and let her rest a minute. It had been a long day.
Not that she was tired. It was always pleasant to snatch a minute
now and then. There was always so much to be done, let me see:
tomorrow.

Tomorrow was far away and there was nothing to trouble
about. Things were finished somehow when the time came; thank
God there was always a little margin over for peace: then a person could spread out the plan of life and tuck in the edges
orderly. It was good to have everything clean and folded away,
with the hair brushes and tonic bottles sitting straight on the
white embroidered linen: the day started without fuss and the
pantry shelves laid out with rows of jelly glasses and brown jugs
and white stone-china jars with blue whirligigs and words painted
on them: coffee, tea, sugar, ginger, cinnamon, allspice: and the
bronze clock with the lion on top nicely dusted off. The dust
that lion could collect in twenty-four hours! The box in the
attic with all those letters tied up, well, she'd have to go through
that tomorrow. All those letters—George's letters and John's
letters and her letters to them both—lying around for the children to find afterwards made her uneasy. Yes, that would be tomorrow's business. No use to let them know how silly she had
been once.

While she was rummaging around she found death in her
mind and it felt clammy and unfamiliar. She had spent so much

KATHERINE ANNE PORTER 289

time preparing for death there was no need for bringing it up again. Let it take care of itself now. When she was sixty she had felt very old, finished, and went around making farewell trips to see her children and grandchildren, with a secret in her mind: This is the very last of your mother, children! Then she made her will and came down with a long fever. That was all just a notion like a lot of other things, but it was lucky too, for she had once for all got over the idea of dying for a long time. Now she couldn't be worried. She hoped she had better sense now. Her father had lived to be one hundred and two years old and had drunk a noggin of strong hot toddy on his last birthday. He told the reporters it was his daily habit, and he owed his long life to that. He had made quite a scandal and was very pleased about it. She believed she'd just plague Cornelia a little.

"Cornelia! Cornelia!" No footsteps, but a sudden hand on her cheek. "Bless you, where have you been?"

"Here, mother."

"Well, Cornelia, I want a noggin of hot toddy."

"Are you cold, darling?"

"I'm chilly, Cornelia. Lying in bed stops the circulation. I must have told you that a thousand times."

Well, she could just hear Cornelia telling her husband that Mother was getting a little childish and they'd have to humor her. The thing that most annoyed her was that Cornelia thought she was deaf, dumb, and blind. Little hasty glances and tiny gestures tossed around her and over her head saying, "Don't cross her, let her have her way, she's eighty years old," and she sitting there as if she lived in a thin glass cage. Sometimes Granny almost made up her mind to pack up and move back to her own house where nobody could remind her every minute that she was old. Wait, wait, Cornelia, till your own children whisper behind your back!

In her day she had kept a better house and had got more work done. She wasn't too old yet for Lydia to be driving eighty miles for advice when one of the children jumped the track, and Jimmy still dropped in and talked things over: "Now, Mammy, you've a good business head, I want to know what you think of this? . . ." Old. Cornelia couldn't change the furniture around without asking. Little things, little things! They had been so sweet when they were little. Granny wished the old days were back again with the children young and everything to be done over. It had been a hard pull, but not too much for her. When she thought of all the food she had cooked, and all the clothes she had cut and sewed, and all the gardens she had made—well, the children showed it. There they were, made out of her, and they couldn't get away from that. Sometimes she wanted to see John again and point to them and say, Well, I didn't do so badly, did I? But that would have to wait. That was for tomorrow. She used to think of him as a man, but now all the children were older than their father, and he would be a child beside her if she saw him now. It seemed strange and there was something wrong in the idea. Why, he couldn't possibly recognize her. She had fenced in a hundred acres once, digging the post holes herself and clamping the wires with just a negro boy to help. That changed a woman. John would be looking for a young woman with the peaked Spanish comb in her hair and the painted fan. Digging post holes changed a woman. Riding country roads in the winter when women had their babies was another thing: sitting up nights with sick horses and sick negroes and sick children and hardly ever losing one. John, I hardly ever lost one of them! John would see that in a minute, that would be something he could understand, she wouldn't have to explain anything!

It made her feel like rolling up her sleeves and putting the whole place to rights again. No matter if Cornelia was determined to be everywhere at once, there were a great many things left undone on this place. She would start tomorrow and do them. It was good to be strong enough for everything, even if all you made melted and changed and slipped under your hands, so that by the time you finished you almost forgot what you were working for. What was it I set out to do? she asked herself intently, but she could not remember. A fog rose over the valley, she saw it marching across the creek swallowing the trees and moving up the hill like an army of ghosts. Soon it would be at the near edge of the orchard, and then it was time to go in and light the lamps. Come in, children, don't stay out in the night air.

Lighting the lamps had been beautiful. The children huddled up to her and breathed like little calves waiting at the bars in the twilight. Their eyes followed the match and watched the flame rise and settle in a blue curve, then they moved away from her. The lamp was lit, they didn't have to be scared and hang on to mother any more. Never, never, never, more. God, for all my life I thank Thee. Without Thee, my God, I could never have done it. Hail, Mary, full of grace.

I want you to pick all the fruit this year and see that nothing is wasted. There's always someone who can use it. Don't let good things rot for want of using. You waste life when you waste good food. Don't let things get lost. It's bitter to lose things. Now, don't let me get to thinking, not when I am tired and taking a little nap before supper. . . .

The pillow rose about her shoulders and pressed against her heart and the memory was being squeezed out of it: oh, push down the pillow, somebody: it would smother her if she tried to hold it. Such a fresh breeze blowing and such a green day with no threats in it. But he had not come, just the same. What does a woman do when she has put on the white veil and set out the white cake for a man and he doesn't come? She tried to remember. No, I swear he never harmed me but in that. He never harmed me but in that . . . and what if he did? There was the day, the day, but a whirl of dark smoke rose and covered it, crept up and over into the bright field where everything was planted so carefully in orderly rows. That was hell, she knew hell when she saw it. For sixty years she had prayed against remembering him and against losing her soul in the deep pit of hell, and now the two things were mingled in one and the thought of him was a smoky cloud from hell that moved and crept in her head when she had just got rid of Doctor Harry and was trying to rest a minute. Wounded vanity, Ellen, said a sharp voice in the top of her mind. Don't let your wounded vanity get the upper hand of you. Plenty of girls get jilted. You were jilted, weren't you? Then stand up to it. Her eyelids wavered and let in streamers of blue-gray light like tissue paper over her eyes. She must get up and pull the shades down or she'd never sleep. She was in bed again and the shades were not down. How could that happen? Better turn over, hide from the light, sleeping in the light gave you nightmares. "Mother, how do you feel now?" and a stinging wetness on her forehead. But I don't like having my face washed in cold water!

Hapsy? George? Lydia? Jimmy? No, Cornelia, and her features were swollen and full of little puddles. "They're coming, darling, they'll all be here soon." Go wash your face, child, you look funny.

Instead of obeying, Cornelia knelt down and put her head on the pillow. She seemed to be talking but there was no sound. "Well, are you tongue-tied? Whose birthday is it? Are you going to give a party?"

Cornelia's mouth moved urgently in strange shapes. "Don't do that, you bother me, daughter."

"Oh, no, Mother. Oh, no. . . ."

Nonsense. It was strange about children. They disputed your every word. "No what, Cornelia?"

"Here's Doctor Harry."

"I won't see that boy again. He just left five minutes ago."

"That was this morning, Mother. It's night now. Here's the nurse."

"This is Doctor Harry, Mrs. Weatherall. I never saw you look so young and happy!"

"Ah, I'll never be young again—but I'd be happy if they'd let me lie in peace and get rested."

She thought she spoke up loudly, but no one answered. A warm weight on her forehead, a warm bracelet on her wrist, and a breeze went on whispering, trying to tell her something. A shuffle of leaves in the everlasting hand of God, He blew on them and they danced and rattled. "Mother, don't mind, we're going to give you a little hypodermic." "Look here, daughter, how do ants get in this bed? I saw sugar ants yesterday." Did you send for Hapsy too?

It was Hapsy she really wanted. She had to go a long way back through a great many rooms to find Hapsy standing with a baby on her arm. She seemed to herself to be Hapsy also, and the baby on Hapsy's arm was Hapsy and himself and herself, all at once, and there was no surprise in the meeting. Then Hapsy melted from within and turned flimsy as gray gauze and the baby was a gauzy shadow, and Hapsy came up close and said, "I thought you'd never come," and looked at her very searchingly and said, "You haven't changed a bit!" They leaned forward to kiss, when Cornelia began whispering from a long way off, "Oh, is there anything you want to tell me? Is there anything I can do for you?"

Yes, she had changed her mind after sixty years and she would like to see George. I want you to find George. Find him and be sure to tell him I forgot him. I want him to know I had my husband just the same and my children and my house like any other woman. A good house too and a good husband that I loved and fine children out of him. Better than I hoped for even. Tell him I was given back everything he took away and more. Oh, no, oh, God, no there was something else besides the house and the man and the children. Oh, surely they were not all? What was it? Something not given back. . . . Her breath crowded down under her ribs and grew into a monstrous frightening shape with cutting edges; it bored up into her head, and the agony was unbelievable: Yes, John, get the Doctor now, no more talk, my time has come.

When this one was born it should be the last. The last. It should have been born first, for it was the one she had truly wanted. Everything came in good time. Nothing left out, left over. She was strong, in three days she would be as well as ever. Better. A woman needed milk in her to have her full health.

"Mother, do you hear me?"

"I've been telling you—"

"Mother, Father Connolly's here."

"I went to Holy Communion only last week. Tell him I'm not so sinful as all that."

"Father just wants to speak to you."

He could speak as much as he pleased. It was like him to drop in and inquire about her soul as if it were a teething baby, and then stay on for a cup of tea and a round of cards and gossip. He always had a funny story of some sort, usually about an Irishman who made his little mistakes and confessed them, and the point lay in some absurd thing he would blurt out in the confessional showing his struggles between native piety and original sin. Granny felt easy about her soul. Cornelia, where are your manners? Give Father Connolly a chair. She had her secret comfortable understanding with a few favorite saints who cleared a straight road to God for her. All as surely signed and sealed as the papers for the new Forty Acres. Forever . . . heirs and assigns forever. Since the day the wedding cake was not cut, but thrown out and wasted. The whole bottom dropped out of the world, and there she was blind and sweating with nothing under her feet and the walls falling away. His hand had caught her under the breast, she had not fallen, there was the freshly polished floor with the green rug on it, just as before. He had cursed like a sailor's parrot and said, "I'll kill him for you." Don't lay a hand on him, for my sake leave something to God. "Now, Ellen, you must believe what I tell you. . . ."

So there was nothing, nothing to worry about any more, except sometimes in the night one of the children screamed in a nightmare, and they both hustled out shaking and hunting for the matches and calling, "There, wait a minute, here we are!" John, get the doctor, now, Hapsy's time has come. But there was Hapsy standing by the bed in a white cap. "Cornelia, tell Hapsy to take off her cap. I can't see her plain."

Her eyes opened very wide and the room stood out like a picture she had seen somewhere. Dark colors with the shadows rising towards the ceiling in long angles. The tall black dresser gleamed with nothing on it but John's picture, enlarged from a little one, with John's eyes very black when they should have been blue. You never saw him, so how do you know how he looked? But the man insisted the copy was perfect, it was very rich and handsome. For a picture, yes, but it's not my husband. The table by the bed had a linen cover and a candle and a crucifix. The light was blue from Cornelia's silk lampshades. No sort of light at all, just frippery. You had to live forty years with kerosene lamps to appreciate honest electricity. She felt very strong and she saw Doctor Harry with a rosy nimbus around him.

"You look like a saint, Doctor Harry, and I vow that's as near as you'll ever come to it."

"She's saying something."

"I heard you, Cornelia. What's all this carrying-on?"

"Father Connolly's saying—"

Cornelia's voice staggered and bumped like a cart in a bad

road. It rounded corners and turned back again and arrived nowhere. Granny stepped up in the cart very lightly and reached for the reins, but a man sat beside her and she knew him by his hands, driving the cart. She did not look in his face, for she knew without seeing, but looked instead down the road where the trees leaned over and bowed to each other and a thousand birds were singing a Mass. She felt like singing too, but she put her hand in the bosom of her dress and pulled out a rosary, and Father Connolly murmured Latin in a very solemn voice and tickled her feet. My God, will you stop that nonsense? I'm a married woman. What if he did run away and leave me to face the priest by myself? I found another a whole world better. I wouldn't have exchanged my husband for anybody except St. Michael himself, and you may tell him that for me with a thank you in the bargain.

Light flashed on her closed eyelids, and a deep roaring shook her. Cornelia, is that lightning? I hear thunder. There's going to be a storm. Close all the windows. Call the children in. . . . "Mother, here we are, all of us." "Is that you, Hapsy?" "Oh, no, I'm Lydia. We drove as fast as we could." Their faces drifted above her, drifted away. The rosary fell out of her hands and Lydia put it back. Jimmy tried to help, their hands fumbled together, and Granny closed two fingers around Jimmy's thumb. Beads wouldn't do it, it must be something alive. She was so amazed her thoughts ran round and round. So, my dear Lord, this is my death and I wasn't even thinking about it. My children have come to see me die. But I can't, it's not time. Oh, I always hated surprises. I wanted to give Cornelia the amethyst set— Cornelia, you're to have the amethyst set, but Hapsy's to wear it when she wants, and, Doctor Harry, do shut up. Nobody sent for you. Oh, my dear Lord, do wait a minute. I meant to do something about the Forty Acres, Jimmy doesn't need it and Lydia will later on, with that worthless husband of hers. I meant to finish the altar cloth and send six bottles of wine to Sister Borgia for her dyspepsia. I want to send six bottles of wine to Sister Borgia. Father Connolly, now don't let me forget.

Cornelia's voice made short turns and tilted over and crashed. "Oh, Mother, oh, Mother, oh, Mother. . . ."

"I'm not going, Cornelia. I'm taken by surprise. I can't go."

You'll see Hapsy again. What about her? "I thought you'd never come." Granny made a long journey outward, looking for Hapsy. What if I don't find her? What then? Her heart sank down and down, there was no bottom to death, she couldn't come to the end of it. The blue light from Cornelia's lampshade drew into a tiny point in the center of her brain, it flickered and winked like an eye, quietly it fluttered and dwindled. Granny lay curled down within herself, amazed and watchful, staring at the point of light that was herself; her body was now only a deeper mass of shadow in an endless darkness and this darkness would curl around the light and swallow it up. God, give a sign!

For the second time there was no sign. Again no bridegroom and the priest in the house. She could not remember any other sorrow because this grief wiped them all away. Oh, no, there's nothing more cruel than this—I'll never forgive it. She stretched herself with a deep breath and blew out the light.

BROTHER BONIFACE

MARY LAVIN

The reasons why men enter religion are indeed various. Brother Boniface entered the monastery because he wanted time to stand and stare at the stars, to lay his soul open to the loveliness of flower and grass ana bird-song. Any person who lives under the swiftly-paced discipline of monastic rule understands immediately the ironic implications of Boniface's motivation.

But Mary Lavin understands not only this irony, which is touched off with striking artistic finesse in the final incident of the story, but also the spiritual depth of the discovery made by Boniface. He came to find God in looking at the stars; he discovered that he could not pray unless his eyes were closed. And a thousand menial tasks, the likes of which he despised in the world, drained him utterly of self. The story is written in a flawless style, which is never less than poetry yet never inappropriate to prose.

Born in America in 1912, Mary Lavin returned with her parents to Ireland at the age of ten. She has lived in Ireland ever since and is one of the many Catholic writers of Ireland who are giving us distinguished short stories. Her collections of short stories include Tales from Bective Bridge *and* At Sallygap and Other Stories.

Brother Boniface sat in the sun. The sun shone full on the monastery wall, and brightened the gold coins of its ancient lichen. It fell full on the rough stone seat where Brother Boniface sat smiling. It fell through the leaves of the elm trees and littered the grass with its yellow petals. It splattered the green and white palings that shut off the kitchen garden from the blazing flower beds on the lawn.

There was no one to be seen out under the hot midday sun but Brother Boniface and the monastery cats. There were five cats. There was a great yellow fellow, stretching his long paws up the bark of an elm. He had green eyes. There was an old white cat sitting in the grass. He kept his eyes shut tight against the piercing sun rays. There were two fat cats abask on the stone seat, one each side of Brother Boniface. And there would have been a great peace over the sunny place had it not been for the fifth cat. The fifth cat was very young. She was pretty and slender and she ran among the grasses. Her fur was gray with markings of gold. Her eyes were amber-yellow. She ran at the waving grasses. She ran at the falling leaves. She caught at the flies in the air. She ran at the splatters of sunlight and pinned them against the palings with her paw. Brother Boniface watched her for a little while, but when he saw the other cats with their great eyes closing every few minutes, blinking and narrowing and closing, his own eyelids began to grow heavy and he fell into a little sleep.

Brother Boniface was sleeping lightly, with his chin in his cowl, when a cinnamon-colored butterfly, with black and brown spots on its wing, flew unsteadily into the sunlight and went towards the blazing flowers. At once the young gray cat sprang after it, leaping lightly through the grass and springing after the butterfly into the very center of the laden flower bed. Under the weight the flower stems snapped and broke. The fat cats opened their eyes. The white cat sat up. Brother Boniface jerked his head upwards and looked from right to left. When he saw the bent stems of the lovely blossoms he rose up unsteadily to his feet and clapped his hands together, and shuffled the gravel with his sandaled feet and called out to the cat:

"Pussy! Pussy! Pussy! Come out of that at once!"

He waved his arms in distress.

"Pussy! Pussy! Pussy! Come out of that at once!"

The young cat started up with a pretty fright. She laid her ears back against her sleek gray head and she arched her back fantastically. She looked at Brother Boniface and forgot the cinnamon butterfly, who fluttered away through the grass. She

looked at him while he waved his arms, and soon she slackened
the arch of her body and pricked up her ears once more, and
then she leaped out of the flower plot and ran after a splatter of
sun petals—capricious, giddy, but full of grace.

Brother Boniface stood in the sun for a while and watched
her as she went away, scrambling from shadow to shadow as
the trees moved lightly in the breeze. His warm brown habit fell
in heavy folds about him and seemed to tug at him with their
weight. When he was a young monk he used to think that the
folds of his sleeves and the folds of his cowl gave him an added
speed as he strode the corridors, in the way that the sails of a
ship speed it on before the wind, but at eighty he felt a weariness
in the weight of the brown wool, although, in places, it was worn
thin enough to be little more than a network of woolen threads.
When the young cat disappeared around the bole of the tree,
Brother Boniface went over and bent down to examine the
broken flowers. He picked up three that were severed from their
stems and he laid them gently on the grass border. There would
be three flowers less before the great marble altar on the feast of
Corpus Christi, and Brother Boniface was saddened at the
thought. He was looking forward to the great feast day, when
there would be a thousand candles blazing before the Host and
a thousand flowers as well. Even three blossoms were a loss. He
went back to his stone seat, moving slowly over the smooth
pebbles that made the pathway from rectory to the chapel.

The pebbles on this path were all very smooth and round.
They were smoothed over by the soles of a thousand sandaled
feet, and every day they were carefully raked by Brother Gardener. Brother Gardener had come to join the order exactly ten
years after Brother Boniface, and so Brother Boniface always
looked upon him as a very young man although Brother Gardener had been now fifty years in the garb of the order.

The day that Brother Gardener came up the driveway with a

red carpetbag in his hand, Brother Boniface was clipping the ivy on the chapel wall and the air was scented with the bitter green sap from its stem. The young man asked to see the Father Abbot, and Brother Boniface got down from the ladder and went around with him to the door of the Abbot's reception room. While they stood waiting for the Father Abbot to come out, they began to talk.

"You shouldn't cut ivy at this time of the year," said the young man, who had been a gardener in the world before he got the idea of entering a monastery.

Just as Brother Boniface was going to answer him the old Abbot, Brother Anselm—God be good to his soul—opened the door, and joined in the conversation as if he had known the young man all his life.

"Will it grow again?" he asked.

"Nothing will stop ivy from growing, once it has started," said the young man, "but it looks better if it's clipped before the new growth has started for the year."

"I'm glad to know that," said the Abbot. "Still we can't leave it the way it is now." He looked at the wall where there was a great gray patch of clipped twigs, and another great patch of hanging leaves that fluttered in the wind. He turned back to the young man and glanced at his red carpetbag, and looked him straight in the eye for a minute, and then he spoke again.

"Leave your bag in the hall, young man," he said, "and finish clipping that ivy. See that you cut it at the right time next year," he paused, "and the year after, and every year," he said, and he took the shears out of Brother Boniface's hand and gave them to the new man.

"You can help Brother Sacristan to clean the brasses," he said to Boniface. That was the kind of man he was, Brother Anselm, God be good to his soul. And Brother Boniface was very fond of him.

The new young man was given the name of Jennifer but it wasn't very long till he was known as Brother Gardener, in the same way that Brother Boas was called Brother Sacristan, and Brother Lambert was called Brother Vintner. But Brother Boniface always kept his own name because he never did anything well enough to be left at it for long. He was changed from one task to another. He cleaned the brasses and snuffed the candles. He sharpened the knives and he fed the chickens. He waxed the oak *prie-dieus* and he chopped pine logs for the fire. He peeled apples and turned the churn and in October every year he went out with a basket and picked the purple elderberries. Later he took the scum off the vats. He had a thousand tasks to do, and he loved doing them all. He helped with everything, and one day Father Abbot said that he should have been called Brother Jack, because he was Jack-of-all-trades.

But Father Abbot sent for Brother Boniface when he felt that his end had come, and although all the monks clustered round him, he wouldn't let anyone minister to him but Brother Boniface. It was Brother Boniface who wet his lips. It was Brother Boniface who held the crucifix up for him to kiss, and it was he who held the candle firm in the old man's hand when he finally freed his soul to God. And when the soul of the Abbot had fled its clay, the hands of the corpse and the hands of Brother Boniface were bound together by a twisted rope of wax that had knotted its way downward, drop by drop, from the candlewick to their clasped hands.

Every year when the ivy was cut, and its bitter scent freed upon the air, Brother Boniface thought of the past and he prayed for the old Abbot. There was very little time for thinking about the past, but it was still very vivid in Brother Boniface's mind. Memories stay greener where memories are few.

And as the old monk sat in the sun, basking in its warmth with the lovely indolent cats, he had the first hours of leisure that he ever had in his life and he thought about the years that had fled. They had gone by swiftly one after another till it seemed now as if they had been but the flight of swallows coming out one after another from under the eaves of the barn.

The earliest thing that Brother Boniface could remember was standing between his father's knees in a big wagonette with yellow leather cushions as it rolled along a road in the middle of the night. He had been on a picnic with his father and his mother, but he could only remember the ride home in the dark.

The brake was rolling along the roads, under the rustling poplar trees. The songs of the picnic party volleyed through the valley. The horse-hooves rang on the road. He, Barney, had never been out so late before. His mother hadn't wanted to bring him. She thought it would be bad for him to stay up so late. But his father had insisted on taking him. He said that he could sleep in the brake coming home.

But the brake, going home, had been the real enchantment for Barney and was the only part of the picnic that he remembered clearly. The rest of the day was only a broken memory of sun and trestle tables and people laughing and swaying from side to side on the benches. He remembered a tall man pouring out lemonade from foaming bottles, and he remembered a lady with a green feather in her hat who kept telling him to "run away and play like a normal child." But he could remember every moment of the drive home, along the darkening roads through the valleys. He remembered looking down over the sides at the traveling road, and he remembered his mother pulling him by the sleeve.

"Look up, Barney Boy," she said. "It will make you sick to lean down over the sides like that." So he looked up, and when he did the wonder of the world came upon him for the first time. As his head jerked up he saw a shower of brilliant sparks riding down through the skies, riding straight towards them; it seemed he screamed with fear and excitement, and everyone in the party glanced their way.

"Oh, look! Look, Father," he shouted, as the gilt stars rode downwards towards him.

"Where?" said his father, looking up in fright. "What do you see?"

"Look," shouted Barney, and he pointed at the stars.

"Is it the stars you mean?" said his father, laughing, and looking around at the rest of the party.

"Is that what you call them?" said Barney. "Why are they up in the sky?"

"They're always up in the sky," said his father. "You often saw them before." He looked around uneasily, hoping that no one was listening.

"Were they there last night?"

"I suppose they were."

"Why didn't I see them?"

"You were in bed."

"Were they there Sunday night?"

"They were. Now that's enough about them," said his father.

"When will I see them again?" said Barney, and his father slapped his hand on his knee.

"It will be many a long day before you see them again, if I have my way," he said, turning around and laughing with the lady who wore the green feather in her hat; and after that everyone began to laugh and they laughed for a long time, while the brake rolled along the road under the rustling poplar trees, and Barney stared upwards until his head began to reel.

After that every night he asked to be let stay up until the stars came out. But long before they rode out into the sky Barney was in bed, and although he tried hard to remain awake he was always asleep before the first of them rode forth. And so, in time, he forgot them. And when he went to school he learned, among other things, that it was silly to get excited about common things like stars and rainbows and whirls of wind, flowers and rain and drifts of snow. They were natural phenomena, the teacher said. And she spent two days teaching Barney how to spell the word "phenomena," because Barney was backward at his books.

All the way along his school career, Barney was slow and it took him all his time to avoid being made the butt of the master's jokes. And only for one poor lad that was simple, he would have been always at the foot of his class. Of course, if he had had more time to look over his lessons he might have made more progress, but his father was a man who could not believe that any real work could be done sitting in a chair, and so Barney was more often helping in the shop than he was reading his books. His father kept him always on the move.

At nine o'clock he opened the shop, although no one ever came into it till long after ten. But between the time of taking down the lice-eaten shutters, and the entry of the first customer, there were a hundred things to be done. He had to sprinkle the floor with tea leaves to keep down the dust while he swept the floor. And often before he swept the floor he had to undo the twig of bound faggots and fasten them up tighter with a thong of leather.

One morning when he was sweeping out the dust into the gutter his father came out and saw that he had sprinkled tea leaves on the pavement as well. His father gave him a clout on the ear.

"Waste not, want not," his father said, and after that Barney had been careful.

Then sometimes there were large packing cases to be splintered open with a gimlet, and cups and saucers and statues and lamp globes to be taken out and counted, one by one, and the sticky tissue paper that wrapped them to be peeled off with a penknife. Then they had to be arranged on the shelves, and after that the sawdust had to be swept up, and the shavings picked out by hand from the cracks in the boards, and carried in to the kitchen fire without letting any fall. There was something to be done every minute and on a Fair Day there was so much to be done that he had to stay at home from school.

On the morning of a Fair Day Barney had to be up at four o'clock, and out in front of the shop with a big ash plant in his hand to beat off the beasts that came too near the windows. The night before a Fair Day there were beer barrels rolled out to the front of the shop windows and boards were nailed across them to make a barrier, and to protect the plate glass; but all the same Barney had to be there, because sometimes a beast was strong enough to break through the barrier and buck at the glass with his horns.

One terrible morning, when Barney stood with his stick in the dawn, a great red heifer gave a buck to the barrels and before Barney could raise his stick she had butted against the barrels with such force that the nails of the boards were lifted out and the boards rose up and crashed through the glass. That was the worst day in Barney's life. He stood in the gray street while his father roared at him and the drovers all came up and gaped at the hole in the window. The cattle themselves were excited and they butted one another, backward and forward, some of them slipping on the dirty street and falling, while the men yelled at them and kicked their rumps and caused such confusion that Barney couldn't even hear the curses that were hurled at him.

But later in the morning when his mother stroked his head, and begged him to stop crying and promised to ask his father to forgive him, Barney began to remember some of the things that had been shouted at him, and it seemed to him that, more than anything else his father had said, the thing that was the most terrible was the question he kept shouting: "Where are your eyes? Where are your eyes? Why weren't you looking at what you were doing? Where were your eyes? Why didn't you see the beast?"

And Barney was frightened because he couldn't remember looking at anything but the big red-chalked barrels, and the dry dusty boards, and the great steaming nostrils of the cattle. He had been looking at them all the time, and if he looked away it could only have been for a minute when a wisp of scarlet cloud floated out between the chimney of the barrack and the spire of the church. The cloud had only floated there for a moment, before it was blown out of sight, but it was such a strange and beautiful color that Barney had stared at it. And when he cried with his head in his mother's lap it was not because he had been beaten but because he began to feel faintly that there was something odd about himself, and that ordinary successful people, people who were respected in the town, like his own father, would never be foolish enough to stand with their hands down by them, doing nothing, as he longed to do, for hours and hours, just staring at the trees or the grasses or the stars or the rains.

But if Barney himself was beginning to notice his difference from other young men of his age, his father was beginning to notice it too, and if it bewildered Barney, it had a more positive effect on his father. One night the merchant was coming back from the station late at night, where he had been lading crates of china, and he came upon Barney, who was leaning against the yard gates staring up into the sky. There was nothing in the sky but the usual display of gaudy stars and the tinsel moon, and Barney's father was filled with rage against the stupidity of his only son.

"Are you getting soft in the head, I wonder?" he said as he pushed past him and went into the yard, and Barney could hear his voice through the kitchen window, as he told Barney's mother: "That son of ours is abroad at the gate," he said, "leaning up against the piers with his hands in his pockets and staring

up into the sky like a half-wit. Can he never find anything to do
for himself without being driven?"

"Leave him alone," said his mother. "You drive him too much
as it is. You're always yelling at him, and sending him here and
sending him there. He never gets a moment to rest his poor feet."

"He's not resting his feet out there, gaping up at the sky," said
his father, and then Barney heard his heavy steps on the stairs,
and he knew that his mother was alone. He looked around him
once more at the strange splendor of the heavens and he looked
around at the dark town where every window was shuttered and
curtained and he shivered suddenly, partly because of the cold
night air and partly because of the great loneliness that he felt
in his heart when he thought of his difference from other men.
Even from his own warm-hearted mother he felt a difference
that made him dread going in to the lighted kitchen where she
would be waiting for him. But he opened the door and went
inside.

"Are you cold? Sit over here by the fire," his mother said,
looking at him sharply, and pulling a hard chair across the tiles
with a clattering sound that jarred his nerves.

"What were you doing out there in the dark by yourself?"
she said.

"Nothing," said Barney, and he felt her glance upon him
although he was staring into the flames.

"People will think you're daft if you stand about like that
gaping at the stars," she said, and he felt that there was a questioning tone in her voice, and that she was asking for an explanation rather than giving advice. He knew that the slightest
explanation would have won her over to be his champion, but
the feelings that drove him out into the starlight were too vague
to be expressed even in thought, much less in speech. They
remained mere feelings, drawing him out of doors, drawing him
into silent places, drawing him away from his fellows.

His mother put her hands on her hips. She felt rebuffed.

"It's true for your father," she said. "You must be getting soft in the head. I don't know what kind of a person you are at all. But I know one thing! The devil makes work for idle hands to do! That's an old saying and it's a true one." She picked up a candle and went out into the hall with her head held high and her lips pursed together with annoyance, but as she went upstairs she leaned down over the banisters and watched him for a few minutes where he sat by the fire. He knew she was watching him, and his perplexity deepened and darkened his soul. He wanted to please his parents, but every hour that passed was bringing him a surer knowledge that their way of life was small and mean and that there must be a way of life that would leave time for glorying in the loveliness of field and flower and in the blazonry of stars.

After the night that his father found him gazing into vacancy, Barney was given more to do than ever he had been given before, and even at evening time, when the shopboys were gone off to the ball-alley to play handball, or off with their girls to walk on the old town ramparts, Barney was often sent out into the country on his bicycle to deliver some parcel that might easily have been delivered the next day. They were determined to keep him from idling. They were determined to keep him moving.

But although for a long time there seems to be something vague and indecisive about our destiny, after a certain point has been reached it is often clear not only that there is a continuous progress, but that events which seemed at first to impede it later seem to have facilitated it. So, riding along the country roads on messages that were intended to keep him from strange dreaming, at every new delight of nature along the way he was forced to wonder more and more how it was that all the men he knew spent their leisure hours as drearily as their working hours, and only exchanged the stuffiness of the storehouse for the stuffiness of the billiard room.

At first when he went into the country lanes Barney was little better than a city man, exclaiming at the blatant beauties that paraded more brazenly in the hedgerows, the dowried hawthorn and the rambling honeysuckle. But after a time he grew in knowledge of the secrets and subtleties of nature, and he passed by the blossoming trees almost heedlessly and went into the deeps of the fields to seek out the secret scents that are released from the grass when the heavy cattle tread it down. And it was in the very depths of a pasture at evening, with the heavy cattle standing idle beside him in the clover, that he vowed to evade the way of life that had been destined for him by his father and his mother.

At first his pale rebellious dreams merely freed him from the dread of spending his life behind the dusty counters of the shop; but he soon realized that he must choose an alternative way of earning his bread, and he set out to choose the one that would allow him to appreciate the qualities of the earth. From then on he began to wander around the town and take an interest, for the first time, in the rest of the townspeople. He spent many stolen hours walking around the town, in such apparent search for something that people came out into the road, after he had turned the corner, and furtively shuffled a foot in the gutter in the hope of some anonymous gain. But Barney was only looking for an idea. He stood at the great dark doorway of the smithy and watched the sparks threading up the flue. He stood at the door of the livery stable in the east side of the town and watched the horses with their trembling withers, while they were groomed and soothed by the stableboys. There were strange dappled roans, strawberry and gray, and there were bays and chestnuts that were dappled with their own sweat. He watched the farmers bringing home the goodlihead of golden grain. He watched at the doors of shops that were bigger than his father's, and the only

real difference that he could see between them was that the big
shops were noisier than his father's and had more spits on
the floor.

One evening, just before the last of the light went out of the
sky, Barney saw a man sowing seeds in the last few furrows of
his field. The picture that he made against the darkening skies
of the evening was one that startled Barney and made him think
for a moment that he had found the beautiful life at last. But
as he came nearer he saw that although the tall man made a picture of great grandeur as he stood out against the skies with his
raised arm flinging the unseen seed, he himself was unaware of
the grandeur of the scene, because he never lifted his eyes higher
than the hand he swung in the air, tossing the grain, before he
groped in his bag for another fistful. And realizing this, Barney
stepped back from the top of the ditch where he had been standing in a trance, and went away in sadness.

His sadness deepened as he walked along the road; for it
seemed to him that whether you cobbled or whether you hammered, whether you measured up rice in a scales or whether you
led a young colt round and round and round and round in a
training ring, or whether you opened or closed your hand to let
fall a shower of seeds, you had to keep your eyes upon what you
were doing, and soon you forgot that there was a sky over you
and grass under your feet, and that flowers blew for your delight
and birds sang in the bushes all day long.

At last Barney settled down to follow the life his father had
planned for him, and he let his mother buy him a yellow canvas
coat to keep his trousers clean when he would be weighing out
whiting or weed killer that might put dust on his clothes. And
everyone said that he was shaping out much better than they
would have expected. The canvas coat kept the dust from getting
on Barney's trousers; but there was dust getting into his mind,
and soon he would have been using half a sheet of paper instead

of a whole sheet, and weighing the whiting in the bag to make weight, and it is probable that in no time at all he would have been taking down the shutters from the windows five minutes before eight in the hope of catching another penny. Just before he had relinquished the last shreds of his dream, however, a message came down from the Abbot of the monastery outside the town, to know if the monks could be supplied with a gallon of colza oil three times a week.

"There's no need for you to go with it, Barney," said his father, "I'll send one of the boys"—because he was anxious not to impose too much on Barney at the moment when he was beginning to show some taste for money-making.

"I think I should go myself," said Barney. "I might arrange to supply them with candles as well."

His father took the yellow coat out of his hand.

"I'll hang that up for you, my boy," he said, and he saved Barney two or three steps across the shop, calling back as he hung up the coat on a nail behind the door, "Take your tea before you go. It's a long push on a bicycle out to that monastery, and as well as I remember there's a rise on the road most of the way."

There was a rise on the road, and Barney was so tired by the time he reached the monastery gate that he left the bicycle at the gate lodge and began to walk up the avenue. The night was coming down gently between the dark yews and cypress trees and a scent of flowers rose from some hidden place behind the walls. But Barney's mind was filled with thoughts of the interview with the monks and he was planning what he would say to the monk who would open the door.

It was an old monk who came to the door, and he seemed to be deaf. He took the can from Barney and he looked out past him through the open door and then pointed to a hard oak seat in the hall, and told him to wait for the can. He went away

down a corridor and left Barney sitting all alone in the bare hallway with the yellow waxed floor, and he felt very young all of
a sudden. He began to look around him. There were high pointed
windows and through them he saw the high pointed stars, and
they reminded him of something far away and indistinct in his
childhood but he could not know what it was exactly. It was
something sad and beautiful and it was something that he had
lost a long time ago. And he began to wonder why it was that
the memory came back to him now; and then he noticed that the
windows were without any curtains, and his thoughts raced away
on another speculation; and it seemed to him suddenly that of all
the silly things in the world the silliest was hanging heavy curtains across the windows to blot out the glory of the night with
its sky and its moon and its welter of stars.

The old man came back with the empty oilcan. Barney took it
silently and went out into the dark. There was no sound but the
closing of the door and he thought of all the foolish words that
another man would have wasted upon the simple transaction.
He is a wise old man, Barney thought, and he wondered about
him as he went down the driveway.

Halfway down the avenue there was a great sycamore tree,
and when Barney had nearly passed by it he saw that under its
great shade of leaves there was a young monk standing; and there
was such a strange stillness in his standing figure that Barney
turned around when he had gone a few paces farther and looked
back at him. His face was turned upwards to the stars and his
hands were lifted in adoration of their Creator. Barney tilted up
his head too, and it was all that he could do to keep himself from
falling upon his knees.

All that night and all the next day he thought about the
young man with his face tilted to the stars, and at the end of the
second night he knew that his own eyes had been blinded forever
to the gross of tawdry coins and the gaudy pattern of bank notes.

The only change that others could see in him was that his yellow overall was getting a bit short in the sleeves.

One night soon afterwards Barney's father was wakened in the night, and he thought that he heard rats down below him in the shop. He came down in his nightshirt with a spluttering candle stuck in a bottleneck. The counters were piled with carefully weighed bags of whiting and weed killer, red lead, tacks, and grass seed. There was enough weighed out to last all winter, and when his father asked Barney why he had weighed out so much he was almost relieved at hearing the answer, because he had thought, when he first looked around at the laden counters, that his son's sudden interest in business had sent him out of his mind.

Next evening Barney took an old fiber suitcase belonging to his mother, put a few things in it, and tied it to the back of the bicycle.

"I'll send one of the boys up to bring back the bicycle."

"You can take back the case too," said Barney. "I won't need it after today."

His mother wiped her eyes on the corner of the tea cloth that she held in her hand.

"Are you sure you'll be contented, Barney, inside those big walls?"

"Remember there's only seven acres, all told, timber and pasture, inside those walls," said his father. "It's a small place to pass the whole of your days."

But Barney had a vision before his mind of the great starry expanse of sky over the walled garden, and he thought of the shivering elms, and the deep grasses where the wind raced; and it seemed that the monastery garden was as wide and spacious as the world because there men had time to meditate and dwell on the beauties the Lord had laid open to their eyes.

The evening that he arrived he found out that the monastery itself was as big as a city and that it took five or ten minutes to

go from one end of it to another, and that three lengths of the
corridor were equal to half a mile. He was shown over the whole
place by a young lay brother recently joined himself, and when
they came back to the place where they had started out from, the
arches of his instep were aching and he could hardly believe that
it was nine o'clock.

Nine o'clock would have seemed a ridiculous hour to retire at,
but Barney was so tired, and his feet ached so much, he was glad
to lie down. He meant to get up later in the evening and look out
of the thin pointed windows of his cell, at the dark garden where
the birds defied the silence with their song.

In the middle of the night Barney sat up in bed when there was
a knocking on the door, and he sprang to the floor when he saw
the light of a licking flame through the great windy cracks in
the door. He dashed to the door and he opened it wide, to rush
out; but a dash of holy water, chill and sudden, cooled his fright,
and he saw that the flame was from a candle in the lay brother's
hand.

Dominus vobiscum . . .

The young Brother Boniface joined the thronging feet that
went down the stone steps to the chapel; and the knocking of the
wooden rosary beads, and the sliding of the sandals from step to
step, and the jostling movement of the heavy worsted habits
made him forget that it was night and gave every appearance
of daytime.

When the real daytime came at last, and the birds began to
fly out from under the chapel eaves, Brother Boniface was set
the task that always fell to the latest member of the order, and
that was peeling potatoes. It took a lot of potatoes to feed sev-
enty-two monks, specially when they didn't eat meat with them.
But it didn't take long to eat them. Brother Boniface was used
to eating quickly and so he would have been finished as soon as
anyone, but he was so interested in the gospel story that the

Brother Lector was reading during the meal that he had to hurry at the end in order not to be last.

There was community prayer after the midday meal, and after that there was recreation, but on that particular day there was an important visitor coming to see the monastery and the Abbot wanted all the community to be present in the hall to receive her. She didn't arrive at the time she had arranged. In fact she came so late that they had only seventeen minutes for supper; and they had a great rush to make up the time, and clear away the meal and lay table for breakfast, before the great bell rang out the hour of evening prayers. And that night an old monk died. He had lingered longer than anyone could have imagined, and even at the end his soul lingered among the candle flames and candle shadows while the monks knelt around him in prayer. Boniface had never seen anyone dying before. Death made a great impression on him. That night he had a few minutes of freedom and he went out into the cool garden that was dampened with rain, but afterwards when he tried to remember whether the stars had come out or not, and whether the birds had been singing or not, he could not remember anything about the time he had been in the garden. He had been thinking of death, and the shadows it cast upon life.

There was a very wet week after that, and during wet weather there were a great many things to be done indoors. Corridors were waxed and passageways were distempered, and the benches and *prie-dieus* were carefully examined to see if they were free from wood-lice. But on the seventh day there was a bright starry sky and Brother Boniface went out for a few minutes. He walked away to the right a few paces and then he saw that he was getting near the sycamore tree that stood near the gate. He remembered the young monk that he had seen standing under it with his head tilted to the stars that pricked the dark greenery with their thin light. The monk was there. Brother Boniface had not yet made his acquaintance. He stepped into the damp grass and went across to the tree. But as he drew near he saw that the young monk's eyes were closed and that his lips were moving. And Boniface knew that he was saying his office, and not looking at the stars at all. And he remembered that he himself had not said his office yet, and he raised his eyes to heaven and began to say it, where he stood, under the sycamore tree, in the damp evening grasses, with the stars blazing brightly above all. But he soon found that he could not pray with open eyes. The stars distracted him too much. He closed his eyes, and when he opened them again the curfew bell was ringing and the sky was overcast.

The year went flashing by, and Boniface did not feel it passing. When his father came up the avenue to see him he was often hoeing in a field and did not think of stopping, so intent was he on his work. And when his father called out his name—"Barney! Barney!"—the other monks had to pluck him by the sleeve and tell him that someone was calling him, because Brother Boniface had almost forgotten that he had once answered to the name of Barney.

Life went flashing by the monastery, leaves and petals were blown past the uncurtained windows, trees tossed in the wind, and the webs of rain were spun across the glass. The skies shook out the gay confetti of the stars. Brother Boniface stepped into his sandals some twenty thousand mornings, and the days slipped by so fast that one fine morning he was eighty years old.

On the morning that Brother Boniface was eighty he was coming out of the bakehouse with a trough of dough that he had kneaded for Brother Breadmaker, and he met the monastery doctor in the middle of the courtyard.

"Good morning, Brother Boniface. You get younger every day," said the young doctor, looking at him closely and watching after him when he went on his way. The doctor turned his feet and went back to the Abbot's room.

MCF

L

"I met Brother Boniface in the yard," he said, to the young monk who was Abbot, and who was a personal friend of his, "and I didn't like the way the veins on his forehead were swollen. He was carrying a heavy tray of dough. He does too much work for a man of his age."

"He loves work," said the Abbot.

"That is the kind of person who needs rest most. He must be forced to take life easier."

"I will see that he is released from some of his duties," said the Abbot.

"That is not enough," said the doctor. "He must be freed from all of his duties. He must sit out there in the sun, and remain as quiet as possible."

"Poor Boniface," said the young men, both together, as they stood at the low casement window of the Abbot's room and looked out at Brother Boniface, who was going across the grass with a saucer of milk, followed by five cats who ran in front of him and circled around him and lifted themselves up on their hind legs to caress him with the back of their necks.

"You can't call that hard work?" said the Abbot.

"Any work that never ceases is hard work," said the doctor.

"I'll send him out tomorrow morning to sit in the sun and I won't let him inside the door till nighttime, except for his meals and prayers."

Brother Boniface took the sun like the monastery cats. He sat on the sunny seat, and smoothed down the folds of his warm brown habit. He smiled and he followed the ballet of the butterflies. The cats sometimes slit open their lazy eyes and gazed into the grass, where glossy jet insects ran up the green blades and bent them with their weight.

Brother Boniface sat in the sun and thanked the Lord that he had been led into the shade of life so safely. And he began to wonder how he had merited such happy anchorage. He tried to remember what it was that had first turned his mind to the cloister. He remembered the shop where he scattered tea leaves to keep down the dust. He remembered that he wore a yellow coat and that it got too short in the sleeves. He remembered stealing into the centers of the fields and breathing the fragrance of the trodden grass. He remembered riding in a black and yellow brake, under rustling poplar trees, while voices volleyed in the valley and the stars showered down through the sky. But for a long time he could not remember why he had left his home and come to the cloister. Then suddenly he slapped his hand on his knee and he laughed so loud the cats sprang up and arched their backs. When they saw they had nothing to fear they relaxed again, but they walked away to a more quiet place with disdainful hips and fastidious paws.

Brother Boniface continued to laugh in short indolent chuckles. He realized that he had entered the monastery in order to have more time to meditate upon the glories of the earth, and that his life had circled round, from matin to lauds, from daylight to starlight, with greater speed than it could possibly have sped out in the world. It had gone by so fast that he could hardly tell what color the trees were and whether the stars were blue or green. And he looked up and kept looking up till his eyes ached from the brilliance of the blue sky, because he was filled with joy to think that now, at the end of his days, having earned his leisure honestly, he would at last be able to spend long hours in appreciation. He stared upwards again. The leaves of the elms spread out wide over him till he fancied the sky was green. Just then there was the sound of a snapping stem and Brother Boniface looked down. The gray cat sprang out of the flower bed when she saw him move, but a great yellow dahlia lay broken on the grass. Brother Boniface clapped his hands at the cat and went over to the flowers, but at the same time there was a light step on the gravel and the young Abbot came down the path with an agile gait and flowing sleeves and a cowl that filled up with wind as he walked and gave him the weighty appearance of an elderly man, although he was the youngest Abbot that had ever been chosen.

"Good morning, Brother Boniface," he said, as he stooped and lifted up the broken dahlia. "What will we do with those cats? The feast of Corpus Christi is only a few days away and we must have every single flower we can get. I wish we could dispense with the cats, but there are unfortunately too many mice for that. Did you hear them behind the wainscoting in the chapel this morning?" He bent and examined the stems of one or two blossoms that seemed a little lopsided.

"What will we do?" he said, and he straightened up and looked around the garden thoughtfully. Then he snapped his fingers. "I know what we'll do," he said, and he ran across the grass to the low casement window of the refectory, and he brushed aside the strands of ivy and opened the window.

"Brother Almoner!" he called out, in a clear gay voice. "Hand me out a paper bag."

Brother Almoner could be heard shuffling around on the tiles, and pulling out drawers and opening cupboards, and then he came to the window and handed out a stiff tinfoil tea-bag, open at the mouth.

The young Abbot came striding back across the grass and when he reached the gravel path where the stone seat was set he bent down and gathered up a handful of pebbles. He threw them into the tinfoil tea-bag and nimbly bent to gather up another handful, and another. Then, when the bag was filled to the top with smooth gray pebbles, he set it down on the rough stone seat beside Brother Boniface. "Here is a little job for you, Brother," he said. "You can do it without standing up, without moving an inch. Every time you see the cats going near the flowers, all you have to do is take up a little pebble and throw

it at them to frighten them away. We must have a gorgeous blaze
of flowers at the altar for Corpus Christi. Isn't that right?"

Brother Boniface took up the tea-bag full of stones.

"I'll keep it in my lap," he said.

"I'm delighted that we have you out here," said the Abbot.
"Now I need not worry about the flowers. I know I can depend
on you, Brother Boniface," said the Abbot, and he strode
away again.

Brother Boniface sat in the sun. The Abbot's footsteps died
away. There was no sound in Brother Boniface's ears but the
bells of silence ringing. A brilliant red insect crawled up a blade
of grass. The blade bent. Boniface watched him. The blade was
weighted down till the insect was almost on a level with the
ground. He put out a feeler and caught at another blade of
grass that was short and stiff and seemed to stab the air, it went
up so straight. The insect began to crawl upwards. The blade
began to bend. Boniface leaned out closer. He wondered where
the insect was heading for that he took such a dangerous and
devious path. And he felt the full luxury of indolence in realizing
the triviality of his occupation. He was excited. He clasped his
hands and bent closer to the grass.

Just then there was a sound of dry stems snapping, and
Brother Boniface looked up in dismay. The young gray cat was
in among the blossoms. The blossoms were breaking and falling
to the ground. Three white butterflies flew among the leaves
and the young cat sprang at each of them in turn.

"Pussy! Pussy! Pussy!" shouted Brother Boniface.

"Pussy! Pussy! Pussy! Come out of that at once" And he
groped for a pebble in his tinfoil bag, and stamped his feet at
the gray and gold cat.

"Pussy! Pussy! Pussy! Come out of that at once!"

And years and years after, when Brother Boniface was laid
away in the close and secretive clay, the young monks who

entered the monastery were told about his industry. They were told that he was never, never idle for a moment. They were very impressed and they strove to follow his example. And they in turn told younger men when they themselves were old. And the part of the story that the old monks liked best to tell, and the young monks liked best to hear, was about the last days of Brother Boniface, when he was so old he couldn't even hear the bells of silence in his ears. Because then he was busiest of all. Day long, and day long, his voice could be heard, as he guarded the flowers for the feast of Corpus Christi by keeping the cats from breaking their stems.

"Pussy! Pussy! Pussy! Come out of that at once!"

THE HINT OF AN EXPLANATION

GRAHAM GREENE

Evil in this world has always been a scandal to souls who find its existence incompatible with the idea of a good God. Greene here fabricates a story which adumbrates the problem of evil and also gives the hint of an explanation—namely, that God brings good out of evil. All of Paradise Lost *was written to prove the same thesis. This answer is a commonplace in Christian thought. But always with the qualifying statement that the full justification for the evil which stems from man's free will remains a partial mystery. Not so Greene. Personifying evil in the terrible Blacker, and then abstracting the idea under the title "this Thing," Greene says:*

> . . . this Thing, whatever it is, that
> seizes every possible weapon against
> God, is always, everywhere, disap-
> pointed at the moment of success.

But the story itself does only what fiction permits: it gives one example of the defeat of evil. It is a memorable example. The Power and the Glory *as well as* The Heart of the Matter *seem to illustrate the same thesis—with Mr. Greene's penchant for letting evil get away with as much as possible before the strange and unpredictable triumph of good.*

The publication of the two above-mentioned novels placed Greene among the top-ranking contemporary English novelists. Other long fiction, significant under the guise of the detective story, he chooses to name "Entertainment." It includes such books as Brighton Rock, The Confidential Agent, *and* The Ministry of Fear. Nineteen Stories *contains his best short stories.*

A long train journey on a late December evening, in this new version of peace, is a dreary experience. I suppose that my fellow traveller and I could consider ourselves lucky to have a compartment to ourselves, even though the heating apparatus was not working, even though the lights went out entirely in the frequent Pennine tunnels and were too dim anyway for us to read our

323

books without straining our eyes, and though there was no restaurant car to give at least a change of scene. It was when we were trying simultaneously to chew the same kind of dry bun bought at the same station buffet that my companion and I came together. Before that we had sat at opposite ends of the carriage, both muffled to the chin in overcoats, both bent low over type we could barely make out, but as I threw the remains of my cake under the seat our eyes met, and he laid his book down.

By the time we were half-way to Bedwell Junction we had found an enormous range of subjects for discussion; starting with buns and the weather, we had gone on to politics, the government, foreign affairs, the atom bomb, and, by an inevitable progression, God. We had not, however, become either shrill or acid. My companion, who now sat opposite me, leaning a little forward, so that our knees nearly touched, gave such an impression of serenity that it would have been impossible to quarrel with him, however much our views differed, and differ they did profoundly.

I had soon realized I was speaking to a Catholic, to someone who believed—how do they put it?—in an omnipotent and omniscient Deity, while I was what is loosely called an Agnostic. I have a certain intuition (which I do not trust, founded as it may well be on childish experiences and needs) that a God exists, and I am surprised occasionally into belief by the extraordinary coincidences that beset our path like the traps set for leopards in the jungle, but intellectually I am revolted at the whole notion of such a God who can so abandon his creatures to enormities of Free Will. I found myself expressing this view to my companion, who listened quietly and with respect. He made no attempt to interrupt: he showed none of the impatience or the intellectual arrogance I have grown to expect from Catholics; when the lights of a wayside station flashed across his face that had escaped hitherto the rays of the one globe working in the compartment, I caught a glimpse suddenly of—what? I stopped speaking, so strong was the impression. I was carried back ten years, to the other side of the great useless conflict, to a small town, Gisors in Normandy. I was again, for a moment, walking on the ancient battlements and looking down across the gray roofs, until my eyes for some reason lit on one gray stony "back" out of the many, where the face of a middle-aged man was pressed against a windowpane (I suppose that face has ceased to exist now, just as I believe the whole town with its medieval memories has been reduced to rubble). I remembered saying to myself with astonishment, "That man is happy—completely happy." I looked across the compartment at my fellow traveller, but his face was already again in shadow. I said weakly, "When you think what God—if there is a God—allows. It's not merely the physical agonies, but think of the corruption, even of children. . . ."

He said, "Our view is so limited," and I was disappointed at the conventionality of his reply. He must have been aware of my disappointment (it was as though our thoughts were huddled as closely as ourselves for warmth), for he went on, "Of course there is no answer here. We catch hints . . ." and then the train roared into another tunnel and the lights again went out. It was the longest tunnel yet; we went rocking down it, and the cold seemed to become more intense with the darkness like an icy fog (perhaps when one sense—of sight—is robbed of sensation, the others grow more sensitive). When we emerged into the mere grey of night and the globe lit up once more, I could see that my companion was leaning back on his seat.

I repeated his last words as a question, "Hints?"

"Oh, they mean very little in cold print—or cold speech," he said, shivering in his overcoat. "And they mean nothing at all to a human being other than the man who catches them. They are not scientific evidence—or evidence at all for that matter. Events that don't, somehow, turn out as they were intended—by the human actors I mean, or by the thing behind the human actors."

"The thing?"

"The word Satan is so anthropomorphic."

I had to lean forward now: I wanted to hear what he had to say. I am—I really am, God knows—open to conviction.

He said, "One's words are so crude, but I sometimes feel pity for that thing. It is so continually finding the right weapon to use against its Enemy and the weapon breaks in its own breast. It sometimes seems to me so—powerless. You said something just now about the corruption of children. It reminded me of something in my own childhood. You are the first person—except for one—that I have thought of telling it to, perhaps because you are anonymous. It's not a very long story, and in a way it's relevant."

I said, "I'd like to hear it."

"You mustn't expect too much meaning. But to me there seems to be a hint. That's all. A hint."

He went slowly on, turning his face to the pane, though he could have seen nothing real in the whirling world outside except an occasional signal lamp, a light in a window, a small country station torn backwards by our rush, picking his words with precision. He said, "When I was a child they taught me to serve at Mass. The church was a small one, for there were very few Catholics where I lived. It was a market town in East Anglia, surrounded by flat, chalky fields and ditches—so many ditches. I don't suppose there were fifty Catholics all told, and for some reason there was a tradition of hostility to us. Perhaps it went back to the burning of a Protestant martyr in the sixteenth century—there was a stone marking the place near where the meat stalls stood on Wednesdays. I was only half aware of the enmity, though I knew that my school nickname of Popey Martin had something to do with my religion, and I had heard that my father was nearly excluded from the Constitutional Club when he first came to the town.

"Every Sunday I had to dress up in my surplice and serve Mass. I hated it—I have always hated dressing up in any way (which is funny when you come to think of it), and I never ceased to be afraid of losing my place in the service and doing something which would put me to ridicule. Our services were at a different hour from the Anglican, and as our small, far-from-select band trudged out of the hideous chapel the whole of the townsfolk seemed to be on the way past to the proper church—I always thought of it as the proper church. We had to pass the parade of their eyes, indifferent, supercilious, mocking; you can't imagine how seriously religion can be taken in a small town, if only for social reasons.

"There was one man in particular; he was one of the two bakers in the town, the one my family did not patronize. I don't think any of the Catholics patronized him because he was called a free-thinker—an odd title, for, poor man, no one's thoughts were less free than his. He was hemmed in by his hatred—his hatred of us. He was very ugly to look at, with one wall-eye and a head the shape of a turnip, with the hair gone on the crown, and he was unmarried. He had no interests, apparently, but his baking and his hatred, though now that I am older I begin to see other sides to his nature—it did contain, perhaps, a certain furtive love. One would come across him suddenly sometimes on a country walk, especially if one were alone and it was Sunday. It was as if he rose from the ditches, and the smear of chalk on his clothes reminded one of the flour on his working overalls. He would have a stick in his hand and stab at the hedges, and if his mood were very black he would call out after one strange abrupt words like a foreign tongue—I know the meaning of those words, of course, now. Once the police went to his house because of what a boy said he'd seen, but nothing came of it except that the hate shackled him closer. His name was Blacker and he terrified me.

"I think he had a particular hatred of my father—I don't know why. My father was manager of the Midland Bank, and it's possible that at some time Blacker may have had unsatisfactory dealings with the bank; my father was a very cautious man who suffered all his life from anxiety about money—his own and other people's. If I try and picture Blacker now I see him walking along a narrowing path between high windowless walls, and at the end of the path stands a small boy of ten—me. I don't know whether it's a symbolic picture or the memory of one of our encounters—our encounters somehow got more and more frequent. You talked just now about the corruption of children. That poor man was preparing to revenge himself on everything he hated—my father, the Catholics, the God whom people persisted in crediting—and that by corrupting me. He had evolved a horrible and ingenious plan.

"I remember the first time I had a friendly word from him. I was passing his shop as rapidly as I could when I heard his voice call out with a kind of sly subservience as though he were an under servant. 'Master David,' he called, 'Master David,' and I hurried on. But the next time I passed that way he was at his door (he must have seen me coming) with one of those curly cakes in his hand that we called Chelsea buns. I didn't want to take it, but he made me, and then I couldn't be other than polite when he asked me to come into his parlour behind the shop and see something very special.

"It was a small electric railway—a rare sight in those days, and he insisted on showing me how it worked. He made me turn the switches and stop and start it, and he told me that I could come in any morning and have a game with it. He used the word 'game' as though it were something secret, and it's true that I never told my family of this invitation and of how, perhaps twice a week those holidays, the desire to control that little railway became overpowering, and looking up and down the street to see if I were observed, I would dive into the shop."

Our larger, dirtier, adult train drove into a tunnel and the light went out. We sat in darkness and silence, with the noise of the train blocking our ears like wax. When we were through we didn't speak at once and I had to prick him into continuing. "An elaborate seduction," I said.

"Don't think his plans were as simple as that," my companion said, "or as crude. There was much more hate than love, poor man, in his make-up. Can you hate something you don't believe in? And yet he called himself a free-thinker. What an impossible paradox, to be free and to be so obsessed. Day by day all through those holidays his obsession must have grown, but he kept a grip; he bided his time. Perhaps that thing I spoke of gave him the strength and the wisdom. It was only a week from the end of the holidays that he spoke to me on what concerned him so deeply.

"I heard him behind me as I knelt on the floor, coupling two coaches. He said, 'You won't be able to do this, Master David, when school starts.' It wasn't a sentence that needed any comment from me any more than the one that followed. 'You ought to have it for your own, you ought,' but how skilfully and unemphatically he had sowed the longing, the idea of a possibility. . . . I was coming to his parlour every day now; you see, I had to cram every opportunity in before the hated term started again, and I suppose I was becoming accustomed to Blacker, to that wall-eye, that turnip head, that nauseating subservience. The Pope, you know, describes himself as 'the servant of the servants of God,' and Blacker—I sometimes think that Blacker was 'the servant of the servants of . . . ,' well, let it be.

"The very next day, standing in the doorway watching me play, he began to talk to me about religion. He said, with what untruth even I recognized, how much he admired the Catholics; he wished he could believe like that, but how could a baker believe? He accented 'a baker' as one might say a biologist, and the tiny train spun round the gauge O track. He said, 'I can bake the things you eat just as well as any Catholic can,' and disappeared into his shop. I hadn't the faintest idea what he meant. Presently he emerged again, holding in his hand a little wafer. 'Here,' he said, 'eat that and tell me. . . .' When I put it in my mouth I could tell that it was made in the same way as our wafers for communion—he had got the shape a little wrong, that was all—and I felt guilty and irrationally scared. 'Tell me,' he said, 'what's the difference?'

" 'Difference?' I asked.

" 'Isn't that just the same as you eat in church?'

"I said smugly, 'It hasn't been consecrated.'

"He said, 'Do you think, if I put the two of them under a microscope, you could tell the difference?'

"But even at ten I had the answer to that question. 'No,' I said, 'the—accidents don't change,' stumbling a little on the word 'accidents' which had suddenly conveyed to me the idea of death and wounds.

"Blacker said with sudden intensity, 'How I'd like to get one of your ones in my mouth—just to see. . . .'

"It may seem odd to you, but this was the first time that the idea of transsubstantiation really lodged in my mind. I had learned it all by rote; I had grown up with the idea. The Mass was as lifeless to me as the sentences in DE BELLO GALLICO; communion a routine like drill in the school-yard, but here suddenly I was in the presence of a man who took it seriously, as seriously as the priest whom naturally one didn't count—it was his job. I felt more scared than ever.

"He said, 'It's all nonsense, but I'd just like to have it in my mouth.'

" 'You could if you were a Catholic,' I said naively.

"He gazed at me with his one good eye, like a Cyclops. He said, 'You serve at Mass, don't you? It would be easy for you to get at one of those things. I tell you what I'd do—I'd swap this electric train for one of your wafers—consecrated, mind. It's got to be consecrated.'

" 'I could get you one out of the box,' I said, I think I still imagined that his interest was a baker's interest—to see how they were made.

" 'Oh, no,' he said, "I want to see what your God tastes like.'

" 'I couldn't do that.'

" 'Not for a whole electric train, just for yourself? You wouldn't have any trouble at home. I'd pack it up and put a label inside that your dad could see: "For my bank manager's little boy from a grateful client." He'd be pleased as punch with that.'

"Now that we are grown men it seems a trivial temptation, doesn't it? But try to think back to your own childhood. There was a whole circuit of rails there on the floor at our feet, straight rails and curved, and a little station with porters and passengers, a tunnel, a footbridge, a level crossing, two signals, buffers, of course—and, above all, a turntable. The tears of longing came into my eyes when I looked at the turntable. It was my favorite piece—it looked so ugly and practical and true. I said weakly, 'I wouldn't know how.'

"How carefully he had been studying the ground! He must have slipped several times into Mass at the back of the church. It would have been no good, you understand, in a little town like that, presenting himself for communion. Everybody there knew him for what he was. He said to me, 'When you've been given communion you could just put it under your tongue a moment.

He serves you and the other boy first, and I saw you once go out behind the curtain straight afterwards. You'd forgotten one of those little bottles.'

" 'The cruet,' I said.

" 'Pepper and salt.' He grinned at me jovially, and I—well, I looked at the little railway which I could no longer come and play with when term started. I said, 'You'd just swallow it, wouldn't you?'

" 'Oh, yes,' he said. 'I'd just swallow it.'

"Somehow I didn't want to play with the train any more that day. I got up and made for the door, but he detained me, gripping my lapel. He said, 'This will be a secret between you and me. Tomorrow's Sunday. You come along here in the afternoon. Put it in an envelope and post it me. Monday morning the train will be delivered bright and early.'"

" 'Not tomorrow,' I implored him.

" 'I'm not interested in any other Sunday,' he said. 'It's your only chance.' He shook me gently backwards and forwards. 'It will always have to be a secret between you and me,' he said. 'Why, if anyone knew they'd take away the train and there'd be me to reckon with. I'd bleed you something awful. You know how I'm always about on Sunday walks. You can't avoid a man like me. I crop up. You wouldn't ever be safe in your own house. I know ways to get into houses when people are asleep.' He pulled me into the shop after him and opened a drawer. In the drawer was an odd looking key and a cut-throat razor. He said, 'That's a master key that opens all locks and that—that's what I bleed people with.' Then he patted my cheek with his plump floury fingers and said, 'Forget it. You and me are friends.'

"That Sunday Mass stays in my head, every detail of it, as though it had happened only a week ago. From the moment of the Confession to the moment of Consecration it had a terrible importance; only one other Mass has ever been so important to me—perhaps not even one, for this was a solitary Mass which would never happen again. It seemed as final as the last Sacrament when the priest bent down and put the wafer in my mouth where I knelt before the altar with my fellow server.

"I suppose I had made up my mind to commit this awful act —for, you know, to us it must always seem an awful act—from the moment when I saw Blacker watching from the back of the church. He had put on his best black Sunday clothes and, as though he could never quite escape the smear of his profession, he had a dab of dried talcum on his cheek, which he had presumably applied after using that cut-throat of his. He was watching me closely all the time, and I think it was fear—fear of that terrible undefined thing called bleeding—as much as covetousness that drove me to carry out my instructions.

"My fellow server got briskly up and, taking the paten, preceded Father Carey to the altar rail where the other communicants knelt. I had the Host lodged under my tongue; it felt like a blister. I got up and made for the curtain to get the cruet that I had purposely left in the sacristy. When I was there I looked quickly round for a hiding place and saw an old copy of the UNIVERSE lying on a chair. I took the Host from my mouth and inserted it between two sheets—a little damp mess of pulp. Then I thought: perhaps Father Carey has put out the paper for a particular purpose and he will find the Host before I have time to remove it, and the enormity of my act began to come home to me when I tried to imagine what punishment I should incur. Murder is sufficiently trivial to have its appropriate punishment, but for this act the mind boggled at the thought of any retribution at all. I tried to remove the Host, but it stuck clammily between the pages, and in desperation I tore out a piece of the newspaper and, screwing the whole thing up, stuck it in my trousers pocket. When I came back through the curtain carrying the cruet my eyes met Blacker's. He gave me a grin of encouragement and unhappiness—yes, I am sure, unhappiness. Was it perhaps that the poor man was all the time seeking something incorruptible?

"I can remember little more of that day. I think my mind was shocked and stunned, and I was caught up too in the family bustle of Sunday. Sunday in a provincial town is the day for relations. All the family are at home, and unfamiliar cousins and uncles are apt to arrive, packed in the back seats of other people's cars. I remember that some crowd of the kind descended on us and pushed Blacker temporarily out of the foreground of my mind. There was somebody called Aunt Lucy, with a loud hollow laugh that filled the house with mechanical merriment like the sound of recorded laughter from inside a hall of mirrors, and I had no opportunity to go out alone even if I had wished to. When six o'clock came and Aunt Lucy and the cousins departed and peace returned, it was too late to go to Blacker's, and at eight it was my own bed-time.

"I think I had half forgotten what I had in my pocket. As I emptied my pocket the little screw of newspaper brought quickly back the Mass, the priest bending over me, Blacker's grin. I laid the packet on the chair of my bed and tried to go to sleep, but I was haunted by the shadows on the wall where the curtains blew, the squeak of furniture, the rustle in the chimney, haunted by the presence of God there on the chair. The Host had always been to me—well, the Host. I knew theoretically, as I have said, what I had to believe, but suddenly, as someone whistled in the road outside, whistled secretively, knowingly, to me, I knew that this which I had beside my bed was something of infinite value— something a man would pay for with his whole peace of mind, something that was so hated one could love it as one loves an outcast or a bullied child. These are adult words, and it was a child of ten who lay scared in bed, listening to the whistle from the road, Blacker's whistle, but I think he felt fairly clearly what I am describing now. That is what I meant when I said this Thing, whatever it is, that seizes every possible weapon against God, is always, everywhere, disappointed at the moment of success. It must have felt as certain of me as Blacker did. It must have felt certain too of Blacker. But I wonder, if one knew what happened later to that poor man, whether one would not find again that the weapon had been turned against its own breast.

"At last I couldn't bear that whistle any more and got out of bed. I opened the curtains a little way, and there right under my window, the moonlight on his face, was Blacker. If I had stretched my hand down, his fingers reaching up could almost have touched mine. He looked up at me, flashing the one good eye, with hunger—I realize now that near-success must have developed his obsession almost to the point of madness. Desperation had driven him to the house. He whispered up at me. 'David, where is it?'

"I jerked my head back at the room. 'Give it me,' he said. 'Quick. You shall have the train in the morning.'

"I shook my head. He said, 'I've got the bleeder here, and the key. You'd better toss it down.'

" 'Go away,' I said, but I could hardly speak for fear.

" 'I'll bleed you first and then I'll have it just the same.'

" 'Oh, no, you won't,' I said. I went to the chair and picked it—Him—up. There was only one place where He was safe. I couldn't separate the Host from the paper, so I swallowed both. The newsprint stuck like a prune skin to the back of my throat, but I rinsed it down with water from the ewer. Then I went back to the window and looked down at Blacker. He began to wheedle me. 'What have you done with it, David? What's the fuss? It's only a bit of bread,' looking so longingly and pleadingly up at me that even as a child I wondered whether he could really think that, and yet desire it so much.

" 'I swallowed it,' I said.

" 'Swallowed it?'

" 'Yes,' I said, 'Go away.'

"Then something happened which seems to me now more terrible than his desire to corrupt or my thoughtless act: he began to weep—the tears ran lopsidedly out of the one good eye and his shoulders shook. I only saw his face for a moment before he bent his head and strode off, the bald turnip head shaking, into the dark. When I think of it now, it's almost as if I had seen that Thing weeping for its inevitable defeat. It had tried to use me as a weapon, and now I had broken in its hands and it wept its hopeless tears through one of Blacker's eyes."

The black furnaces of Bedwell Junction gathered around the line. The points switched and we were tossed from one set of rails to another. A spray of sparks, a signal light changing to red, tall chimneys jetting into the grey night sky, the fumes of steam from stationary engines—half the cold journey was over, and now remained the long wait for the slow cross-country train. I said, "It's an interesting story. I think I should have given Blacker what he wanted. I wonder what he would have done with it."

"I really believe," my companion said, "that he would first of all have put it under his microscope—before he did all the other things I expect he had planned."

"And the hints," I said, "I don't quite see what you mean by that."

"Oh, well," he said vaguely, "you know for me it was an odd beginning, that affair, when you come to think of it," but I never should have known what he meant had not his coat, when he rose to take his bag from the rack, come open and disclosed the collar of a priest.

I said, "I suppose you think you owe a lot to Blacker."

"Yes," he said, "you see, I am a very happy man."

NIHIL OBSTAT:
  Philip J. Donnelly, S.J.
            Censor Deputatus

IMPRIMATUR:
  ✠ *Richard J. Cushing*
            Archbishop of Boston

Boston, October 3, 1950